Skyrmion

Book One of The Sweetland Quartet

Duane Poncy

First Edition, 2022
Rainy Nights Press
an imprint of Duane Poncy & Patricia J McLean
ISBN: 979-8-9861523-1-8 (print)
979-8-9861523-0-1 (ebook)

Prologue

The thing's breath, hot and foul, touches the back of her neck. Muscles tense as adrenalin kicks in. The predator's shadow, crouched and waiting, hangs just off to the right. She attempts to judge the distance, but its other, fainter, shadow, a little further out and behind, complicates the calculation. What have they taught her? *Triangulate.* She senses the vircat tense, its movement imperceptible. Perspiration rolls down her forehead. *Time to decide. Now.* She jumps, whirls around, swinging her long knife point forward toward the vircat. *Miscalculation.* The creature's huge claw rips into her shoulder with a terrible tearing sound, and Gretel deVoid falls hard under the full weight of the cat.

The vircat disappears, and she scrambles back to her feet. "Damn, I don't think I'll ever get this right."

"You're doing just fine, Gretel." Toxine's voice comes from nowhere and everywhere. "You need to speed up your calculations. Practice. Shall we try again?"

"I can't. Homework tonight." Homework has never decided her life in the past. But it's different now. This homework *means* something.

"Very well," says Toxine, as the nighttime forest with its two moons fade, and the classroom at *Universidad Simón Bolívar* resolves around them. Toxine looks at Gretel with pride. "You are a brave girl, you know, leaving for an unknown world, forging into the wilderness."

Gretel scans the floor, self-conscious.

"How are things progressing with your dad?" Toxine asks.

Toxine's not unexpected question produces a heavy sigh. She'd hoped to avoid this subject, which brings up all her doubts and fears. Her eyes continue to lock on the floor for a moment before she looks up to meet Toxine.

"I haven't told him yet. I still can't figure out how to get through that stubborn wall of his."

"That will come in time. Just don't let it slide. Now off to your homework, eh?"

"Thanks, Toxine."

Jessie Larivee, aka Gretel deVoid, zoned from the Grid and sighed. A silence had grown between herself and her father. She'd let it go too long. Now, when she played the scenario in her head, she heard his voice saying, "It's impossible, Jessie, you can't get to another planet on the Grid," or "You're only fourteen. You're too young to make these kinds of decisions on your own," or maybe he'd stand slack-jawed and silent before sending her off to her room. How could she possibly convince Joe Larivee, the proud luddite, that yes, you can go to another world, I've talked to people who have been there, and no, I'm not too young, and yes, I would like you to go too, Dad, but whatever you decide, it won't deter me.

A conversation with Jolene would be so much easier.

She'd neither seen nor heard from her mother in nearly six years—why would the woman care one way or another? But Toxine urged her to speak with both of them. "You know," she said, "you may leave them forever. You need to have closure."

Toxine was at Masters Level. She had taken Jessie on as protégé, helping her through the tough exam preparation. The Sweetland sim was as close to the real thing as possible. With the new citspecs mods, you could smell the odors and feel the ground beneath your feet as though it was some solid thing. Amazing! Even the claws of the vircat ripping through her shoulder had left a lingering discomfort; not pain, exactly, but more like the scratchy stinging that comes when you reached barehanded through a blackberry bramble. Most sims had yet to be programmed for the new mods. But it was only a matter of time before every sim on the Grid would be hyper-sensed. Except, of course, she reminded herself, there'd be no time for that now. The world she knew would soon be ending.

Pox Americano, Toxine's younger brother, claimed to have worked on some of the sim, but Jessie didn't know whether to believe him. He was a bit of a braggart. "You should try the glitch sex script I wrote for the Sweetland sim, cherie," he had said earlier in the day in his cute Quebecois accent, and she laughed at him.

"I suppose you want to try it out with me?"

"As the designer, I could show you how to get the most out of it."

"A product demonstration. How romantic," she said. "Well, it so happens that I plan to stay a virgin. Forever, likely, if all boys are like you."

"You are a virgin?" He pretended astonishment. "What a pity."

Jessie shook herself out of a developing fantasy. Dinner. Homework. She had a bunch of homework for her immigration classes. Tomorrow morning she had to make that call to her mother. And then Dad.

What is she going to do about Dad?

Part One

Drowning

"Our drowning cities have brought on a new kind of flood, as refugees by the millions compete with those fleeing the dust bowls of the midwest for safer ground. Riots have broken out in Chicago, Los Angeles, New York, and elsewhere, as new arrivals discover that there is nowhere left to go. The army has removed tens of thousands of squatters from private property into hastily-constructed reservations."
—*Newshour, September 20, 2035*

"The weeping child could not be heard,
    The weeping parents wept in vain."
—*William Blake*

The ancient TriMet bus lurched forward without warning, throwing Joe Larivee into the passenger standing behind him, upending Joe's bag and spilling its contents. "Sorry," he managed, as he watched his sandwich skid down the aisle toward the back of the bus. A skinny bare arm, red and pocked with oozing sores, reached out and snatched it.

Shit, no lunch today. He should have left it in the fridge at work. Payday was late again this month. The Agency was out of funds, and he was out of food stamps. And out of creds with the burrito man on Division, not that Arturo had any edible tortillas anymore.

Joe squatted to retrieve his belongings from the floor. As he rose, the bus pitched, and he braced himself on the back of the nearest seat. The SmartSpots above the bus windows flashed in red, white, and blue. *Make her happy tonight. Guaranteed.* The hackers had struck again.

"One-hundred-twenty-second and Stark," announced the prerecorded voice on the com. "This stop sponsored by Tommy Tonkin Bicycles by Toyota."

An old woman rose with difficulty from the seat next to him and hobbled from the bus. Joe sat in her place. A large gaping wound in the plastic seat pinched and poked his buttocks each time the bus encountered a pothole. The young man beside him gripped a ragged backpack against his chest. He looked frantic, his eyes darting between the window and the front of the bus, as though searching for an escape. Joe's heart skipped. Thoughts came unbidden. What's in the backpack? Why is this boy so scared? That was what he was, just a boy with a few scraggly hairs jutting from his chin. Settle down, Joe told himself. There's a thousand reasons this guy might be scared. Too much like a jackrabbit to be a 'cider.

In front of him, a woman wearing buds jerked her head to some fast-paced music. Tweaking. She was likely younger than him, but her teeth were gone, her face scarred with the pockmarks of an old-fashioned meth addict. *Trash-tweaker.* Not so many of those anymore, with all the new designer drugs. Plenty of his customers were recovered tweakers or had moved on to a drug more subtle in its ravages.

Next to the tweaker a young woman with wrap-around sunglasses, her head turned toward the aisle, moved her lips almost imperceptibly, her throat pulsing. He had a vague idea about the wraparounds: popular new hardware that tapped into the simulated worlds of the Grid. Just another way for the advertisers to get into your head and sell you crap.

He sighed and pulled a worn file folder from his bag, "Connie Velasques" written in pencil on the tab. Beneath the name, the ghosts of Mary Snider, Tomas Sylvan, Letitia Jackson; erased just enough so that a stranger would not recognize them. But Joe did. And he knew their children, and their ex-spouses and lovers, their job history, their drug habits, and their pain.

"You've got to remove yourself from all that." Susan Miller's voice echoed from some cubicle of memory. "You've got to mind your boundaries, Joe. You're not responsible for the mess these people's lives are in. If you hold on to all this suffering, you'll drown in it."

That was five years ago, his first week on the job. Whatever became of Susie? One day she just didn't show. It was a recurring script. Many new caseworkers didn't last six months, but even old-timers like Susie disappeared without notice, worn out, unable to heed their own advice.

He opened Connie's folder. A routine check-in today to

find out how Connie was managing at her new job, how the children were faring, if she was keeping clean. Connie had just kicked a seven-year heroin habit when his supervisors assigned her to Joe in January. She had done well over the past nine months. School had started last week, so daycare would be less of a money sink while Connie looked for work or performed the occasional temp job. He had high hopes for her.

But Joe's heart sank when the bus pulled up in front of the apartment building—the ambulance, the blue and red flashing lights of police cars, a knot of officers standing around an open door. The door to Connie's apartment.

Another one of those fucking days.

Joe tucked Connie's folder back into his bag and stepped off the bus. He hated talking to the cops. Uncle Louis had been a cop, and Joe knew a little too much of what went on in the back rooms. He didn't like most of the young uniforms, just back from war, with their arrogance and their disgust for these poor people trying to survive on the broken streets—as if this wasn't a battlefield, too. But here the land mines were everywhere, not just underfoot.

At least he was in popo territory and didn't have to deal with the clean-n-safes. He held another level of disdain altogether for the private security firms hired by Portland's wealthier business associations as a local solution to social and economic breakdown. The poor, less-organized East County businesses couldn't afford to hire their own private police force. There would be anarchy here when full Privatization hit, and the PPD auctioned off to the highest bidder.

Across the street, a blackwater stood sentry at the westbound MAX stop, clutching a semiautomatic. Even from a block and a half away, Joe saw the nervousness in his youthful face and the uncertainty of his footing. Waiting commuters eyed him with skittish diffidence.

Joe approached the popos with caution, flashing his identity badge to show them he worked for the Agency.

"You got business here?" said the officer at Connie's door.

"I'm her caseworker." Joe looked askance through the window. Inside, Connie slumped on a couch, a rubber tourniquet wrapped around her arm, the hypodermic needle still dangling from her flesh; on the coffee table, the lighter, the spoon.

"You *were* her caseworker," said the cop. "Your docket just got cleared of one problem. This one's gone to Sweetland."

"She's got kids at school," Joe said, adding *asshole* under his breath.

"Well, I guess you get a paycheck then, after all."

Joe swallowed his anger and nodded.

"You should go take care of them kids, now," said the young cop, dismissing him.

Don't argue. Arguing just gets you in jail. Or disappeared.

"I'll do that. Thanks, officer."

He retreated to the bus stop across the street, weaving his way carefully through the bicycle traffic. Out of nowhere, a group of young boys dashed past. A bottle flew, landing at the feet of the blackwater, who raised his gun, threatening. Adrenalin rushed through Joe's body as he ran the remaining distance across the bus lane. His heart raced as he waited for the oncoming bus to pull up to the stop. He stepped into the vehicle, and two of the young trouble-makers broke from the pack, boarding behind him, taking the seat across the aisle.

Joe clenched his jaw and wiped the perspiration from his forehead with the back of his hand.

"Did you see that blackwater's face?" one kid said.

"Yeah, chuck," replied the other. "He was friggin' ready to piss his pants."

"You boys should be a little more cautious," admonished the sixtyish woman behind them.

"Whatever, Grandma," said the first, but they became silent and left the bus after two more stops.

Joe exhaled.

The General Dynamics Church of Christ building housed the Agency in its basement. They had converted the chapel to corporate offices, but a few die-hard church members still met in an attic room. After losing their tax exemption, the Church had succumbed to the realities of Privatization. Soon the Agency would follow. In two more years, there would be no public sector, just the so-called Free Market; police, libraries, schools, churches, social services, all under the dictates of private profit. Even the spontaneous co-ops and workers' collectives which had sprouted up like spring weeds wouldn't be sustainable against the determined kleptocracy. There was nothing Joe could do about the havoc being wreaked by the Free Market gods. Nothing anyone could do. It was a done deal.

A deep despair consumed him as he entered the basement and walked along the dim, shabby hall, its light green paint peeling and scuffed by the shoes of hundreds of weary people resting their feet against the wall as they waited for assistance—help that often never came and wasn't enough when it did. He slunk past Christi, the receptionist, signed in, and bee-lined to his cubicle to verify that Children's Services Corp employees were picking up Connie's kids. Then he discon'd and put in his buds, surfing to his favorite Gridcast channel to zone out on some soothing music.

No one would know or care.

SHE HADN'T PLACED THE TAP YET. BUT SOMEONE OR something was already pinging her, searching for a chink where they could inject a tracer. She tried to not let it bother her as she waited for Maxi to scan the server code for a hook of her own.

"We're in," said Maxi. "Here comes the flood, hon."

Data flashed across her VR overlay. Intermediate level code. She'd have to get Stan to scrutinize it, but even with her untrained eyes she picked up some important references: Grid nodes; likely top security government and corporate pipes; pipes which controlled the utilities and other infrastructure; and references to something called Sweetland; more references to skyrmion. Code words?

"Tracer," said Maxi with urgency.

Shit. She'd waited too long. She shut down the tap, and a tingle of electricity shot up her spine, a vague shock that ended at the base of her skull. Her head about to burst, pixels scattered into a rainbow of static. Without warning, she was sitting on her virtual office floor, her real-life head throbbing.

"What the fuck was that?"

"Something trig'd your mods, hon," said Maxi in her syrupy Appalachian drawl. "Tried to boot you right out the back door, so I pulled you."

The gorgeous, middle-aged brunette with a no-nonsense demeanor stood in the doorway behind Claire Deluna's desk. Claire's personal assistant, Maxine Magnolia, custom-programmed by KT Willow, one of the best hackers on the planet, more sophisticated than your typical out-of-the-box PA, coded for the PI biz, a package with access to several corporate, law enforcement, and DHS databases. If anyone could protect her butt, it was Maxi.

"How deep did they go?"

"Might have compromised your alias."

"Shit. Any origin data?"

"Negative, darlin'."

"But we captured code?"

"Couple hundred megs."

"Okay, Maxi. I need you to trace those pipes. Find out everything you can about Mitologias and Futures, LLC in relationship with this Sweetland thing. Do a level six matrix search. Any relationship at all to our investigation, I want to know what we're looking at here."

"I'll get right on it, darlin'. You know Maxi never sleeps." Maxi winked and disappeared through her door.

It was supposed to be a quickie, a simple in and out, a parent corporation checking up on its kids; that's what Bigshot told her, that's what Claire knew how to do best. But she feared the job had transformed into something else, something more difficult and dangerous. The damn pipes passing through the Bolivarian firewalls had trig'd some phantom feelers before she was even close. Not by a mile.

The Mitologias SA backend connected to a complex maze of pipes carrying data between a number of discreet servers. Some or most of those servers were behind the so-called Jalapeño Firewall, a tricky gate to crash. She'd copied the node information for Maxi to google and decided on a faucet capture. The faucet—the point where the quantum encrypted data translated into readable code—was the only option, unless you discovered a leaky joint to exploit. These guys would have impeccable plumbing. They would discover her presence the instant she intercepted the quantum encryption key and rerouted the datastream. That was a given. But how did they get that tracer on her so damned fast? It was as though they had been waiting for her. And how the hell did they trig her mods to send that shockwave through her body?

She hadn't seen that coming.

When she started out in the biz seven years ago, a mere girl, she had expected backend snooping to be like the glamorous depictions in those cyberpunk sci-fi movies from the Turn, but it happened there were no whirling data streams or fancy eye candy taking up precious bandwidth here, no complex avatars slowing down the code; that was gamer fantasy, and this was the work world. Most of it involved looking at long strings of boring alphanumeric code. She was no code expert, but she had a special skill, an intuitive edge that helped her to access the gateways, recognize patterns, and find the data she needed.

There was an adrenalin factor, too, that helped keep her going. The excitement of waiting in the shadows, watching, slipping in undetected to ferret out secrets, knowing they might catch you in a dangerous place, that made the game fun.

Now she was no longer so sure of herself. She had been in hard places before, but her targets had been minor players, not transnational corporations and foreign powers.

She needed to rest, recharge her batteries, somehow. More than a nap. A vacation, maybe. But she had no idea what that would be. She didn't have an actual life.

She made her way to her old, battered forties couch, with virtual stuffing spilling from the tear in the cushion. She had spent hours getting every detail of her office just right, including stains, paper-strewn desk, overflowing ashtray, half-empty whiskey bottle. Her clients, those few who actually came to *her*, always got a friendly laugh from the decor.

Reclined on the couch, she tried to immerse herself in *Red Harvest*, a Dashiell Hammett novel she had recently begun. But concentration seemed impossible. She needed to make an escape from all of this. But where? How? She came to New Life to get away from the real world. Now she felt trapped in some kind of closed loop.

AFTER MAKING CERTAIN DAD WAS ON HIS WAY TO WORK and not likely to spot her, Jessie slipped from François' Coffeeshop, next door, where she'd grabbed a few sample pastries for breakfast. François was always generous with his samples. Then she biked across the Morrison Bridge toward the downtown library, stopping at the top to survey the barren landscape. It was one of her rituals, paying homage to her childhood memories, to the city that once existed.

She recalled the vast urban forest that once populated Portland, when everything greened in early spring, the dogwoods, and cherry trees blooming, Dad walking her to school along sidewalks covered in a magic carpet of pink and white petals; and later, as summer approached, the bumblebees emerging from their earthen hives to swarm the lavender and rosemary Grandma Amy had planted in the front yard, everything smelling so wonderful.

This time of year, mid-October, the leaves would drop, and there had been so many leaves that the city sent out trucks to help residents clear the streets so that the drains wouldn't clog and cause flooding when the rains came. Mountains of leaves by the curbs, smelling of sweet decay.

The first die-off came when she was seven. Dutch elm disease, spread by elm bark beetles, left dying trees throughout the city. A few years later, most of the city's old black walnut trees died, destroyed by a twig beetle which carried the spores of a deadly fungus. By that time, the bees vanished. And the cherry trees. The die-offs continued throughout her young life, the horse chestnuts, and oaks and more exotic, imported trees first, then the evergreens.

Now there were only patches of trees left on the West Hills and some higher elevations, like the Alameda ridge and Mount Tabor. Drought and fire had decimated forest Park. The path of destruction left a massive scar where the huge blaze had traveled up through the hills, turning posh houses and everything else in its path into cinders.

The West Hills were greening again from invasive ivy, at war with thickets of immigrated kudzu, choking life from dozens of indigenous species. Only the native willows and dogwoods survived in abundance, springing up in the alleys and along the river, like weeds. If anything will survive, she thinks, it will be the grasses and the dogwoods.

Public libraries, like the trees, would also soon be extinct, so she visited the Central Library as often as she could. She loved the smell of the old books, and the feel of them in her hand. She sought a quiet corner to study and to call her mother. She might have phoned Jolene at home, but the thought of calling her with Dad in the apartment made her feel like a traitor somehow. So she put on her citspecs, set the visuals to transparent, and opened a comlink to her mother.

"Hello?" said a strange voice. Jessie panicked, considered shutting down the connection. The voice repeated, "Hello?"

"Mom?" Jessie's voice a tentative whisper.

"You must have the wrong party," the woman said.

"Mom," Jessie repeated a little louder. "It's Jessie."

"Jessie? Jessie? How did you find my number?" Was this all her mom had to say after so many years?

"I'm sorry," Jessie said, "I think I made a mistake."

She was about to cut the link, when Jolene said, "Jessie, are you okay?"

"Yeah, I'm okay. I just want to say goodbye."

"Jessie, what are you talking about?" Her mother's voice had an edge of panic. She needed to explain. A little, anyway.

"Mom, I'm not going to off myself or something. I'm leaving, and I thought you should know because you won't be able to reach me again." *Ever. In case you're interested.* Jessie felt six years of anger and confusion bubbling to the surface.

"Jessie, what do you mean? You aren't making any sense."

"Mom." She raised her voice, almost hysterical. "Six years. *Six fucking years.* I cried the first two, every single night. And then, I got pissed. And now I just want to frigging say good bye." I will not cry, she told herself. I will not cry.

"Well, I can see your father taught you how to swear just like him." Jolene was cold. "So, where are you going?"

"You won't understand," Jessie snapped.

She remembered her surroundings; looks of disapproval penetrated the thick air, and she glared back in defiance. Go ahead, get the gestapo.

"Try me," challenged Jolene.

"I'm going to Sweetland."

Through a long silence, Jessie could hear her mother breathing on the other end. "What did you say?"

"I said Sweetland, Mom. I'm going to Sweetland. And I told you that you wouldn't understand. I just had to hear your voice before I left."

"Sweetland? What is that?"

Jolene's tone had changed, softened, became the sound of a mother interested in her daughter's life. How was she going to explain Sweetland?

"It's a place—there's a community in the forest," she said, leaving out the part about the two moons. "It's a kind of environmental community. There's no Grid or any way to stay in contact with—" She almost said the Earth, before catching herself. "—with you."

"Is this your dad's idea?" Jolene said.

"Not exactly. I learned about it in New Life."

"You have a New Life account?"

"Of course," she said. "All the kids have one."

"Why don't we do lunch or breakfast or something, inworld, and you can tell me more."

Sweetness and concern. "After six years, just like that, you want to have lunch?" *Not even a real lunch,* she thought, *but a virtual one.*

"Isn't that why you called? To say goodbye."

"Sure, I guess. I'm Gretel deVoid. You can message me inworld."

"Okay, I'll do that. My handle is SUATO2." She spelled it out. "That's numeral 2. Thanks for calling, sweetheart. Talk to you soon."

Silence. Jolene had discon'd.

JOLENE CHENG DISENGAGED FROM THE GRID AND CRIED. After one minute and twenty-three seconds, she determined an appropriate amount of time had passed, and ceased. Not that she watched the clock, or anything so crass as that. She had feelings, after all. It was because she had feelings she had maintained a complete distance from her daughter. Her responsibilities were too great. The second-in-command at SUATO was far too important to become distracted by sentimentality.

Jolene went to the kitchen and poured the morning's third cup of coffee. She didn't need this. She really didn't. But the kid said she was going to Sweetland. This could be important. It didn't surprise her to find her daughter involved in this Bolivarian shit. She was Amy and Frank Larivee's grandchild, after all. And Joe, the spineless bastard, was no different, deep down beneath that quivering surface. He was weak, was all.

But her ex be damned.

What Jolene wanted to know—what the Anti-Terrorism Office wanted to know—just what the hell is Sweetland?

For the past several months a cloud of lies and disinformation had descended on the Grid, on New Life, in the undernets–a cloud so thick, it reeked of black ops. It didn't help that the corporate world had already moved in and co-opted it, adding another layer of obfuscation with their own Sweetland crap. Something was up. Something big. It could be theirs, it could be ours, but it was big. Her job was to understand it. And she would.

She just didn't need this emotional garbage screwing up her investigation.

"Today," said the news announcer, *"the war in sub-Saharan Africa has taken a new turn. Nigerian federal troops, advancing on rebel camps, met no resistance. The camps were empty, claimed commanders. They reportedly found no insurgents, yet inside the tents, arms, and ammunition waited, along with some meager food supplies and a handful of field computers. One British observer reported that, 'it appeared the mothership came along and beamed them up. Very eerie…' Meanwhile, in New York, to no one's surprise, Governor Chelsea Clinton announced she would run for President in the coming election. At a news conference announcing her candidacy, she stressed the need to combat domestic disorder…"*

Joe pulled out the buds, put his head between his hands. All the children—and the missing rebels were children, because it's the children who fight the wars, who go missing like the children of his clients—never heard from again.

"To hell with this," he said, almost silently. "To hell with it all," once more, shouting this time, not caring who might hear. He picked up a broken cup he used as a pencil container and threw it across his cubicle with a violence that startled him.

"I'm going home," he announced to the office, making sure that everyone could hear. "Fuck this!"

Joe coasted to the curb and dismounted, pressed his bike through the vendors, hawkers, and hustlers who daily set up shop on the inner city sidewalks, up to his apartment building bicycle corral. The Buckman Cooperative Defense Committee, which patrolled the neighborhood streets, tolerated the sale of wares on the sidewalk, technically illegal, according to the impotent city government. The self-organized neighborhood committees held the actual power in Portland, and most did their best to keep people safe. Even though it often irritated the fuck out of him, how else were people going to earn enough to eat if they couldn't sell what they made? The soup kitchens were never enough.

From Jessie's window emanated the faint but unmistakable blue glow of her VJ screen. He remembered clearly going into her room after she left this morning to make sure she shut everything off. It was routine because Jessie inevitably left something on. She had been like that since she was a little girl. Her Grandma Amy used to tease her, "You'd forget your head if it weren't screwed on."

So what was Jessie doing home on a school day?

Inside the apartment, all was quiet, except for the murmured voice emerging from Jessie's room. He put down his bag and crossed to her bedroom door, nudging it open. His daughter sat at her desk, leaning back in her chair, involved in some fantasy world, talking to the air, wearing a pair of those wrap-around sunglasses like the ones worn by the woman on the bus.

"Jessie." No answer.

"Jessie," a little louder.

No acknowledgement. Joe walked up behind her and removed the glasses. Jessie jumped and wheeled around in her chair.

"God, Dad. You scared the pee wadding out of me. What are you doing home so early?"

"The question is, Jessie, what are *you* doing home so early?"

He saw the look, the evasive movement of her eyes; his daughter was about to lie. Instead of stopping her, he would let her spin her story. He would gently challenge her until she became caught up in her own web. It never failed; the fourteen-year-old was a terrible liar.

"I wasn't feeling good."

"So why aren't you laying down?"

"Well, I wasn't feeling *that* bad."

"Who are you talking to?"

"Just some friends." The Look again.

"And what friends would these be?"

"Pox and Cedar," she said. Names he'd not heard before.

"So, why aren't Pox and Cedar at school? Are they sick, too?"

"I think maybe they're in a different time-zone or something."

"Jessie," Joe lit into her, "how often have I told you that people you meet online are not your friends? You don't know them. You know nothing about them. They might not be kids at all. They might be rapists or terrorists or human traffickers. You have no idea who or what these people are. Don't you get that?"

She looked as if she were ready to cry or scream at him,

Joe couldn't tell which. It could go either way these days, but to his surprise she did neither. "I'm sorry, Dad. The kids told me about this sim on New Life. It's really glitch. Everyone's doing it."

"So, where did you get the hardware?" He held up the glasses.

"They're citspecs, Dad," she said, rolling her eyes. "I've had them for a couple of months now."

"What do they do?" Of course, he knew what they were. But he had no idea what he should ask her.

"God, Dad. You are so living in the past. They're the latest Mixed Reality glasses. They were selling them in the mall at SimWorld. I've been saving my allowance all summer. They only cost $20."

He wanted to object about the cost, but he reminded himself that twenty dollars was equivalent to five or less when he was her age. "You've got to be kidding. How can they sell these sit-specks thingies for so little?"

"I think the idea is to get people into the sims so they shop and buy stuff on New Life. But I don't buy stuff. It's stupid when we can't afford to eat."

He had heard of New Life. How could he not, the ads were everywhere? It was the latest generation of life sims on the Grid, not so much a game as a simulated world. For a couple of years now it had been the buzz among the Agency's customers and some of his coworkers. Joe examined the glasses more closely and found they were thicker than normal sunglasses, with a tiny reset switch and two removable modules on the inside of the frame. They had bone conduction earpieces attached. Otherwise they appeared quite ordinary. He grunted and put them down on her desk. Escapism. But no worse than some of the Grid games kids played, or those stupid reality shows. Perhaps he was being too harsh with her.

"Jessie," he said, "I just want you to be safe. You know that, right? Just keep your actual identity safe, okay? Be careful. And promise me you won't skip any more school for this nonsense."

"I won't, Dad," she said. "I promise." Joe looked her in the eyes for an extended moment, frowning, not entirely trusting, before he shut the door and retreated to the kitchen where he pulled a beer from the fridge. He intended to zone out on the couch for the rest of the afternoon, and not think about work, or Connie Velasques, or Jessie, or the state of the world. He just wanted to close his eyes and sleep.

Claire awoke to see Maxi lounging in the client chair, eyeing her. Maxi took a long sensual drag on her cigarette, releasing the smoke slowly, allowing it to billow out around her face. The image of her sophisticated assistant laying back in the comfortable overstuffed chair, a cigarette between her full red lips, gave her an almost sexual pleasure. A hundred years of advertising and popular culture had done its work.

"Hey, hon," said Maxi, exhaling a geyser of smoke toward the ceiling. "I have that research you asked for."

"Thanks, Maxi. Go on."

"Two of those nodes are data servers based in the Alliance of Bolivarian States. Two other pipes terminate on a sim farm called New Patagonia. Lots of typical tourist stuff there; it's a bit of a New Life showcase for the Bolivarians. One node belongs to the *Universidad Simón Bolívar, School of Science.*"

"A research conduit?"

"Could be, hon. The other one is called the Temple of New Life. Its sim address is 54 Calle Tierradulce, New Patagonia. Data flow analysis suggests a pipe may connect this node to its own agricultural complex, bigger than the New Patagonia server farm itself."

"Where does the final pipe go?"

"The origin node belongs to D-Brane Technologies."

That made sense. DBT was a Mitologias sister company, and the two had been the object of the months-long bidding war between her client's company, Futures, LLC, and the New America Corporation.

"What about Sweetland?"

"The term Sweetland came up several times."

"Context?"

"All over the map, darlin'. The term has been in popular use over the past year, possibly the result of a guerrilla marketing campaign. There's speculation that it's a new sim technology or some sort of nanotech breakthrough. But the bulk of the Sweetland buzz seems to be around this Temple of New Life."

"What is this Temple thing? An RPG? Or an actual religious organization?"

"Maybe both—the religious element is definitely there." Maxi examined her cuticles, then eyeballed Claire. "I found something else interesting. There seems to be an unusual correlation between the Temple of New Life and missing persons in the FBI database. The undernets are full of speculation that the Temple might be a cult of some kind."

"No shit?" This was a complication she didn't particularly care to hear.

Maxi batted her big eyelashes. "And I got very unusual hits on some of these Temple of New Life names, darlin'."

"Yes?"

"We have clusters of recently missing or deceased. Over a thousand altogether, out of some ten thousand names. That's a lot, hon; way outside statistical probability. Most of them are young—under thirty. You have about two dozen from Phoenix. Most of them reported missing or at the morgue. You have nearly an equal number of missing in both Denver and Portland, but no correlations at all to reported deaths. That's why I say clusters. And here's the really interesting thing—I found this article in *The Albuquerque Journal.* I quote: 'Police found seven bodies today in an abandoned storage facility. All the youths, between fourteen and twenty-one years of age, were wearing cyber immersion technology devices called citspecs. They appeared to have died of starvation and dehydration. Authorities are investigating a possible suicide cult.' Hon—"

Maxi hesitated, and the feeling returned—the sinking fear that she might be onto something bigger than she could handle.

"Yeah, Maxi?"

"Hon, five of the seven correlated with that Temple list and all were wearing D-Brane Technology mods, according to FBI memos."

"I don't like this, Max. Make an appointment with Andy Stephens, would you? After my date with Mickey Nines. And after my visit with Seguda. Maybe Wednesday morning. Have we heard from Mitologias, yet?"

"They're playing hard to get. But Seguda agreed to see you for a few minutes at ten tomorrow morning."

Bigshot had hired her in part to audit Mitologias, but

they were being very resistant to her probing. She wondered why.

"Thanks, Maxi. Now, I'm out of here."

BRIDGE WHITEDEER TRANSLUCED HER OCS AND SIGHED. Some cautionary tic in her neural pathways nagged at her—you're in way over your head, girl. Sheer exhaustion quashed the nascent protest. It had been a hard day, and it was time to put Claire Deluna to bed.

She always regretted leaving her VR persona behind–that life for this. For this… what?

She gazed out her window over the darkening waters of what had once been the south edge of downtown Seattle. Most of the newer waterfront high rises south of Pioneer Square remained standing, and during high tide, rose like drowned ghosts from the sea. A few people still lived inside these doomed towers. At high tide, they exited through windows just above the waterline and rode one of the taxi dinghies or homemade rafts created from plastic bottles and other floating garbage. When the tide dropped low, some donned waders and slogged their way through the mud to higher ground. At night, you could see their dim lights flickering in the windows. Other buildings leaned and twisted, undermined by the rising water which had flooded the Seattle underground, eroding their footing. Many older brick structures were crumbling, subverted by the invisible seawater eating away at the sinking infill upon which they'd built much of old Seattle. The city engineers had declared that Smith Tower would likely go within the next few years. The skyscrapers further north remained, for now, untouched by the advancing shoreline. Federal aid to build new seawalls never came. The government was both bankrupt and broken, and had been since the first pandemic-caused crash, and the waves of constantly mutating disease which killed over thirty million North Americans by the mid twenties.

Protected by the Sound and the Olympic Peninsula from the worst effects of the rising ocean, Seattle had fared better than other cities, such as San Francisco, where the strong tides pushed constantly at the western hillsides, pulling the old structures, and the hills themselves, into the sea. A sea which had already begun its unstoppable journey into California's central valley.

Bridge hunched her thin shoulders and pushed her short black hair back from her eyes with knobby fingers. She considered her reflection in the window, absentmindedly teasing the mods embedded like tiny jewels behind her right ear. She looked nothing like her alter ego, Claire Deluna. Claire was attractive—glamorous even—with her cute red hair and breasts you could actually see. A girl with moxie and flair, unlike her real life puppet master.

More suitable as a private eye, Bridge imagined.

She couldn't envision herself as an investigator in the real life world. She was barely twenty-five, and who would take a scrawny NDN kid like her seriously, anyway? And yet, Claire Deluna was the best. Even someone like Mr Bigshot knew that.

She continued to gaze out the window for a time, watching the lights and listening. The drumming had begun, its tribal rhythm calling out from the homeless enclaves and the drowned buildings, as it had every night since summer began. It became even more insistent now as the weather grew wet and inhospitable. There was something indescribably comforting in it.

Finally, Bridge crossed the floor to her tiny refrigerator,

grabbed a half-eaten sandwich. She sat at her little kitchen table and took a bite. Then she put her head down on the table and fell asleep.

☼

"Jessie," Dad called from the living room, "please take out the recycling."

"In a minute." Jessie shut down the Grid and waited for his objection. It came like lightning.

"*Now.*"

"Recycling on the Titanic," she mumbled under her breath. When you're drowning, why the hell are you bothering to sort the garbage?

Her futile resistance was an old habit from childhood when occasionally she escaped some dreary task or another. No more. And yet she couldn't help displaying her defiance. Everything seemed so pointless.

"You have a stubborn gene," Grandma Amy used to say. "Got it from your Grandpa."

Jessie sighed and with heavy feet marched to the kitchen nook where the recycling containers spilled over onto the floor. She rounded up stray cartons and bottles and fit them into the bins as best she could, leaving a scattered few behind. Then she carried the bins down the hall to the back door of the apartment. Steel plates reinforced the grimy exit to the alley stairway, and the lock disengaged with a heavy *thunk* as she pulled down on the lever. She dragged the bins out onto the landing.

The mist that had been falling earlier in the day had subsided, and the gray Portland sky showed signs of clearing. The alley was wet and standing pools of rainwater filled the depressions in the aging pavement. From the shadows came a voice she recognized, the words muddled and incoherent. A rustling sound arose from the garbage dumpster. If not for the familiar mumbling cadence, Jessie might have thought rats were scuttling through the bins. She stopped at the top of the stairs so she wouldn't frighten him.

"Alan," she called, "are you hungry?"

"Jessie," came the pleading reply, "I'm looking for something to eat. You got something for me to eat?"

She still couldn't see him, but the edge of his cart protruded from behind the fence that shielded the dumpster from the street. She set the recycling bins down at the foot of the steps. "If you'll put these bins out for me, I'll go get something for you."

Without waiting for a reply, she returned to the apartment and tiptoed into the kitchen. Dad was on the couch, oblivious, as usual. Nearly every evening, he came home and fell asleep on the couch or at his computer, exhausted by his impossible job. He might as well be a Gridhead. At least on the Grid, he could learn a few new things and interact with other people.

Jessie opened the fridge quietly. She couldn't let Dad know about Alan. She promised. Alan was one of Joe's old school buddies. She met him for the first time when she was about eight, shortly before he'd joined the army and gone to fight in Africa. He had visited several times that year, and to a little girl he had seemed a kind, easy-going, witty young man. He always stayed late in those days, talking into the night with Joe, Frank and Amy. Jolene always disappeared when Alan came over, finding something to take her away from the house. The four of them would argue about capitalism and the wars and whether it was better to work inside the system or out, whether joining the military was morally defensible. Amy attempted to dissuade Alan from signing up, arguing that war is seldom ethically justified, but Alan pointed out his limited options.

"What am I going to do if I don't join up. I got no work. I got no skills or education. The army will pay for college."

"It's a chimera, Alan," Amy said prophetically. "I've seen those kids coming back, too damaged to go to school or hold down a job."

In the end, Amy lost the argument and Alan shipped out to Azania. Then about six months ago he had shown up again at their new apartment door while Joe was away at work. Alan had lost all of his quick-witted charm and had become dull and confused. "I been out of work," he had mumbled. "I thought maybe Joe could help me—I think I made a mistake. Don't let Joe see me like this. Please don't tell him, Jess. I should never have come here. Promise me."

Jessie had promised. It was easy at the time, because she had secrets of her own. She'd been skipping school, and it was a lot easier to just forget the whole thing than face the possibility of getting caught. Then less than a month later she saw Alan again in the alley, rummaging through the dumpster, and she offered him some food. She suspected Alan was schizophrenic or something, but he seemed harmless enough. He began coming around on recycle days, and Jessie had taken to feeding him leftovers, when they had them, heating them in the fred. Sometimes she would take him a new carton of beans or a peanut butter sandwich. Then they would sit on the bottom step and talk while he ate.

Jessie discovered yesterday's leftovers in the fridge and she heated the sautéed veggies with tofu on brown rice, careful to remove it before the fred's alarm sounded and alerted Dad. It was some disgusting pre-packaged dinner, therefore uneaten. She was well aware of the irony—that the world was starving, that her friend Alan was malnourished, that there were days at the end of every month when she and her dad also went without. Yet here she stood, spoiled and picky.

"Got a nice hot dinner for you tonight, Alan," she said as she descended the stairs. The recycling was still at the bottom of the steps where she'd left it. She needed to remind him.

"Alan." No answer. Had he moved on down the alley?

"Just put it on the step, Jessie." The delayed voice came from behind the dumpster. "I'll get it in a minute."

Something was wrong. Alan didn't just come around to eat. His loneliness was as acute as his hunger. If he hadn't told her as much, she could see it in his face, hear it in his attempts to hold her attention. Many nights she awkwardly interrupted him, saying, "Goodnight, Alan. Dad's going to come looking for me if I don't go in."

She put the dinner on the step and picked up one bin, carrying it around to the pickup area. Alan stood in the shadows, unmoving, except for his hand, which he quickly raised to cover his face. But not before she caught sight of the split eyelid and swollen, mangled lip. One side of his face bore a huge purple contusion.

"Alan, what happened to you?"

"I don't want you to see me like this, Jessie. I don't want to scare you."

"What happened to you, Alan?" she repeated.

"Some fucking gestapos beat me up. They kicked me in the face. They said I was sleeping in their place. But I been sleeping there, Jessie. I been sleeping there since summer, fucking bastards." Alan punched a fist in the air above his head, staring wildly at some phantom opponent, his voice an intense whisper. "Who had a fucking election and elected you fucking assholes dictator of the fucking planet? I didn't have no chance. The bastards come down on me like a fucking blitzkrieg from the USA fucking air force. Like I was some fucking peasant in fucking Afghanistan or something. Jesus Christ, take me to Sweetland. Jesus Christ."

Jessie stepped back. She had never seen him so angry before. "Take it easy, Alan," she croaked. He wrapped his arms around his torso and said, "Jesus Christ, Jesus Christ," over and over, rocking on his heels until the rhythm of his mantra seemed to calm him.

Finally, Jessie extended her hand. "Come. Dinner's getting cold."

He refused to take her hand, but he followed her to the back steps. She brushed away the flies and pushed the plate at him. He grabbed it and began shoveling the now-cold food into his mouth, wincing at the pain from his injured face. She made a few attempts at conversation, but he just stared down the alley, his eyes glazed.

Then he vomited. The dinner he'd just eaten spewed over the apartment stairs, mixed with blood and reeking of alcohol. "God, Alan, you need to get some medical help."

"No, no. Leeches won't help me. They use leeches. Suck your blood dry. That's what they do. They suck you until you're dead. Fucking hospitals. Fucking doctors. Just wanna go to Sweetland. Can you help me go to Sweetland, Jessie?" A rheumy film glassed over his eyes.

"Alan, let me talk to Dad—you need help."

"No, Jessie. Don't tell Joe I been here. You promised. Remember."

Jessie's stomach knotted and she's became nauseous

from the stench. Think. What can you do? Her own eyes were tearing now. Take some time to think this out.

"Wait here, Alan," she said. "I won't tell Dad. I promise. Wait while I go get a mop to clean up this mess. I'll figure out something." She ran up the stairs to the building's custodial closet on the second floor and grabbed a bucket and mop. As she filled the bucket, her mind raced. How can I convince Alan to find help? Is that co-op clinic in Old Town still there?

She dragged the bucket back down the hall to the rear door and pushed it open. Alan was nowhere in sight. She left the bucket and bound down the stairs. "Alan," she called. She looked into the dumpster cage, then rushed down the alley to the street, searching for his cart, calling out his name. He'd vanished.

JESSIE ATE HER OWN DINNER IN HER ROOM, PICKING AT HER food, Alan foremost on her mind. Dad would know what to do, but she'd promised Alan. Don't be ashamed of mental illness, she wanted to tell him. But it would do no good. It sounded too much like one of Dad's liberal platitudes.

Just behind Alan in her thoughts were the goodbyes to come over the next couple of weeks: Mel and maybe Dad, too, if she couldn't get through to him.

Pushing her food aside, she lay face down on her bed, clutching her pillow to her chest. The sound of a drum circle drifting in from St Francis Park seeped through her cracked window, comforting her. She tried to remember the first time she heard the drums—maybe last year, maybe before. At some point the rhythm became a nightly event. Whenever the drumming faded, other drums in the distance called back, seemingly saying, "You aren't alone. We're here with you."

Her thoughts took her to school, actual pit school, where she hadn't been since early September. It felt like going to a foreign country, but she had to say goodbye to Mel. Melissa Monroe had been her best friend since sixth grade. Over the summer Mel lived off-Grid in Eugene with her dad, while Jessie roamed New Life and discovered Sweetland. She'd abandoned Mel. Something about the whole Sweetland thing had made her withdraw from her old friends, even Mel—the decision had been too monumental, too life-changing, too sudden and unexplainable. Now she carried around a pack full of guilt.

If school seemed like a major distance, how could she measure the journey she was about to undertake? The enormity of her decision once again overwhelmed her until she could no longer think about the life she was leaving behind —about the possibility that she might lose her father forever.

Instead, she closed her eyes and lulled herself with the drumming, until she drifted off to sleep.

It was nearly eight when Joe woke, his back stiff from sleeping on the couch. Jessie had covered him with one of Amy's frayed old quilts from the closet. She could be a sweet and thoughtful girl. He needed to give her more slack.

Joe stood and stretched, a faint headache lingering. He closed his eyes momentarily and rubbed his temples. He folded the quilt with care, laying it across the back of the sofa, then he washed, shaved, and changed his clothes. This morning he would prepare a real family breakfast. Maybe a couple of those rare and precious eggs he had saved in the fridge and some toast made from what passed for bread these days.

He took out the eggs and placed them on the counter. Then he pulled out the little infrared cooker stashed away at the back of the counter, an appliance Jessie called the 'fred.' He seldom used it anymore, except to reheat leftovers; most of their meals came in self-heating cartons these days. He set the table before knocking on Jessie's door. "Hey, little girl, breakfast is cooking."

No sound came from the room, so he pushed the door open. Jessie sprawled on top of her bed, sound asleep. He watched her for a long moment with something that felt a little like sadness. A pretty young woman with her mother's eyes and cropped dark hair. She was growing up too fast. In a few years, he would be alone, and what would that be like? He didn't want to think about it just now. He surveyed her room, still in transition from a little girl's. Teddy bears and childhood games mingled with posters of pop stars and the paraphernalia of teenagers. On her desk, the screen of her virtual journal glowed. He walked over to turn the VJ off, and he picked up her gamer glasses. What did she call them? Sit-specks? He pronounced it slowly in his mind. Then, with a brief twinge of voyeuristic guilt, he attempted to peer into her world, but he saw only a dark screen.

When he placed the glasses gently back on her desk, he noticed a slip of scratch paper there, "Old Paris" and "Malafreña" written on it in Jessie's scrawl. It looked like some RPG. Wasn't Malafreña a reference to some old classic Ursula Le Guin book Jessie liked? He smiled with nostalgia, trying to remember being a teenager, engulfed in sci-fi and online role-playing games in the middle of the night. Things really hadn't changed that much.

He turned off the VJ and roused Jessie from bed. She seemed more groggy than usual.

"Up too late playing on the Grid again," he complained.

"Oh, Dad, do I have to get up?"

"I've fixed breakfast, believe it or not."

She buried her head beneath her pillow, pulling the quilt over her. "I choose not to believe," came the muffled reply.

"I have a riddle for you," he said. "What has five bare toes and is connected to a silly bone?"

Jessie giggled and pulled her exposed foot under the covers. "Don't you dare, Dad! I'm not a kid anymore!"

"Okay, sweetie. There'll be no feet tickling today. But come have breakfast with the old man."

"You know, civilized people consider tickling a form of barbaric torture."

"Just preparing you for life," he quipped. He regretted the words the moment they left his lips, but he couldn't stop them. They sounded cruel and cynical and whining.

Jessie must have sensed his despair, because she sat up in bed and took his hand.

"Better times are coming, Daddy," she said. "Don't you always say that?"

"Yeah, sweetie," he said, "better times will come."

But Joe couldn't see how that was possible. For himself or his daughter. Maybe in another life.

☼

Kick-Ass Claire dropped into an alley in Chi-Town, 1920s Chicago as it had never been, where for a price you could buy exotic highs at underground speakeasies, experience mind-blowing sex with hot little flapper girls or gangster boys with Gatling gun penises, complete with police raids and, if you liked, a little S/M in handcuffs on the jailhouse floor. She emerged from the alley onto a street teeming with streetwalkers, little boy hustlers, trannies, chicks with dicks sporting hardware-studded cunts between their mammoth tits, bartering, hawking their sex scripts, detachable organs, dope patches; any type of thrill the human mind could imagine. She pushed back the bangs blocking her camera eyes, smoothed down her short, jet-black hair, sculpted in a sport car swoop, a tiny braid dangling down the left side of her face in the style of the working girls, porn rockers, and neo-punk molls on the SinWorld circuit.

Kick-Ass was a rougher and ruddier persona than Respectable Claire or Sexy Claire or the beautiful noir redhead, her everyday Claire, Claire Deluna's other skins, her dolls she wore to suit the occasion. Her tight little dress revealed one bare breast to just below the nipple, her left breast to signify she wasn't cruising for a date, not that it would stop the propositions rolling in from any number of lowlife creeps. Layers of dark paint, black and brown and blue gave her a ravaged look, as if her pimp had just beaten the crap out of her or she had crawled out of a street brawl. Her digital snarl said, unmistakably, "Don't fuck with me."

Finding Mickey Nines was never difficult. It could be boiled down to three or four locations, unless he'd changed his routine, which wasn't damned likely. Mickey was a creature of habit, bad habits, mostly, and the high stakes card games in Chi-Town's back rooms—that would be his major vice. Mickey believed he owed Claire Deluna big time, and Claire didn't dissuade him of that notion. She had helped him out of a tight spot with an oil syndicate a few years back; to Claire it had been nothing, just a little investigative work in the backend of another mob's server farm, but it saved Uncle Mick's skin, and he had professed that he would do anything for her. Well, almost anything.

Mickey had been a Wall Street trader at The Turn until they caught him in a sweep of insiders and scam artists after the crash of 2024. Mickey now offered his intimate knowledge of the corporate world to another class of criminals, to the cops, or to whoever could pay his price. He kept his finger on the pulse of international business, and if anyone could give her the dope on Futures, it would be Mickey Nines.

She stopped at a nondescript door with a single card, a queen of clubs, pinned just above her eye level. She knocked. A panel slid away and a grizzled face peered out at her. "Wachawan?" it growled.

"I'm a friend of Mickey Nines," she said.

"Whoshoodeyesay?"

"Tell him Claire wants to talk to him."

"Beeryeback." He scowled and the little window slammed shut.

A few minutes later the door opened and Mickey Nines himself stood before her in his dapper blue suit and fedora, chewing on a toothpick.

"Claire, darling. It's so nice to see you." He leaned over, kissed her cheek. "Gorgeous as usual."

"It's been a long time, Mickey," said Claire. "You got a few minutes to chat, or you got a game waiting?"

"I always have time for you, lady. I'm finished with these losers, anyway."

"Not going so well, huh?"

He sighed. "Down twenty grand. Let's go get some coffee, catch me up on the PI biz."

Claire laced her arm through Mickey Nines', and he led her down the street to Danito's, a little hole in the wall in a more upscale, hustler-free zone. At least, the hustlers here didn't harass you on the street. Funny, Claire thought, how the syndicates in the undernets ran their sims just like the respectable, commercial sims. The same laws and zoning and committees and hearing boards you could grease with a little extra cash. Just like the real world, as a matter of fact. They sat at a booth by the window, and when the server sauntered over with the coffee pot, Mickey insisted on some male prerogative of buying. A rather old-fashioned world view. But Mickey Nines was old-fashioned. She figured he must be some old guy, too, on the other side of the digital divide.

"So, my love," he said, sipping his coffee, "tell Uncle Mick what you're up to these days."

"Working for a new client," said Claire, "Futures, LLC."

She studied his face for a reaction. Mickey let out a low whistle. "Hanging out with the big boys, are we now?"

"Yeah, Mick," she said. "Futures just bought a couple of subsidiaries, and they need a third party to check them out. That's me. What's the word on the street about Mitologias? Anything you can tell me?"

Mickey Nines shook his head. "You're playing with dangerous stuff, lady. Shit, Claire—excuse the French—you ain't the only one interested in what Mitologias is up to."

"Yeah?"

"Well, the feds to start with. And there are a couple of the syndicates. I don't know this for certain, but supposedly, Futures, itself, might be under control of the Silicon mob. If the syndicate doesn't own a piece of Futures, they have their tentacles way up its ass. And there's the Bolivarians. You better watch your back, Claire. You'll get yourself crushed if these guys start butting heads."

"What can you tell me about the Bolivarians?"

"Mitologias is a private company, but the Bols have some financial interest in it. Not sure how far it goes, but far enough for veto power."

"What about corporate espionage?"

"With these guys, it's a given. The reactionary klepto-crats and the mob types have wormed their way into nearly everything down there." *Just like up here*, Claire thought. "Information is for sale. For that matter, the Bols have an extensive network in this country too; especially up and down the west coast. You can't trust them because there are agents and double agents and triple agents; gangsters, drug traffickers, you name it. Who's working for whom? Your guess is as good as mine."

"What do you know about the New America Corp? I understand they made rival bids for Mitologias and D-Brane Technologies."

"Mining, resource extraction. Typical Midwest corpo-rate cowboys. Recently got into the blackwater biz. No syndicate connection I've heard about, which doesn't mean a damn thing. Word is they put in the winning bid for Mitologias, but the Bolivarians turned them down flat. Wanted nothing to do with them."

"Hmmm. Any idea what Mitologias is developing that would cause so much interest?"

"No idea, but it must be a game changer, considering who's trying to get their hands in it. There's a lot of talk about taking the sim tech to the next level, new sophisticated mods from DBT, nanotech, and all of that."

"*Sweetland* mean anything to you?"

"The word floats by now and then. But it's like the latest hipster buzzword or something. Everybody's jumping on the Sweetland bandwagon, and I don't know if it means anything or not. Could be a sim they're working on, or just some PR bull."

Claire stood. "Thanks, Mickey, you're a dear. Wish I could stay longer, but I gotta go."

"So soon?" Disappointment crossed his face. "Well, anything for you, Claire. Come back and see me now— sometime before the next decade."

"Sure, Mickey. Soon." She waved melodramatically and zoned to her next appointment on Fitzgerald's Pipe.

THE YOUNG WOMAN LAY CURLED ON THE SIDEWALK AT THE base of the apartment steps, just inside the bike corral, covered by a shredded sleeping bag. Oily knots of matted hair escaped from the stained blue bandana wrapped around her head. Over her eyes, she wore MR glasses like Jessie's. Joe stepped gingerly over her and unlocked his bicycle. It was a rare day when no one claimed this spot to bed for the night. He had an urge to leave his card on the sidewalk next to her, but it would be a futile gesture. A young woman with no children wouldn't get through the door at the Agency. There was no room for the likes of her.

Morning commute dragged, and bicycle traffic came to an abrupt halt at 122nd, barricaded for a military convoy heading south from the Edgefield Compound. Edgefield made him think about Frank and Amy. An outing for a summer concert when he and Jolene were still in college and struggling. In those days, the former poor farm comprised an inn, several restaurants, and an outdoor concert venue. The only thing he could remember about the band was that they were very good. Frank always had impeccable taste in music.

The military had taken Edgefield over in '31 and turned it into a barracks and training ground, one year after the oligarchy had cemented its grip on the nation. They had all seen it coming: the Republican electoral coup of 2016; the formation of the Democratic Free Market Party in '24; the military counter-coup and its violent aftermath in '29. People still deceiving themselves and believing they lived under a democracy, rather than the fascistic oligarchy America had become.

The convoys took over the avenue two or three times a week recently. Something in the wind, but he had no idea what it might be. There was so little news you could trust these days. They might be simply exercises, or they might be preparing to move against the rebel enclaves scattered along the I-5 corridor from Ashland to British Columbia. Or maybe it was all just bluster. He would like to believe that the separatist rebels had a chance in hell. But their Free Cascadia was a pipe dream.

JOE WOVE A PENCIL IN AND OUT BETWEEN HIS FINGERS, waiting impatiently for Windows 2020 to load. Some computers in his section were fifteen or more years old, with software created in aught-nine. Or so it seemed. The Agency had been too god-damned cheap to purchase new ones, though the poorest transient on the street now had some portable device with ten times the power of these dinosaurs. It was a miracle that any of them could actually function on the Grid.

He was keenly aware of the way his coworkers avoided his eyes this morning, but so far Chandra, his supervisor, hadn't spoken with him. He viewed this as a good sign. The closest thing to an acknowledgment of yesterday's misbehavior was the smirk on Roger Howard's face as he passed Roger's cubicle on the way to the copier. Roger, of course, had meant him to see it. Roger didn't like Joe, and the feeling was mutual.

Joe looked up to see Anya Dorena Kerenskaya leaning over his cubicle wall, a solemn look on her pretty face. Anya eyed Joe for a moment and gave him a little sad smile. Sometimes he thought a mutual attraction existed between them, but he put it away next to his paranoia. He wasn't sure that he wanted to become involved with anyone just now, especially someone from work.

"Another one missing, Joe," said Anya. "Third one in two weeks. What the hell is happening here?"

"I wish I knew, Anya. I still think it's the military. Recruitment, you know?" As usual, Anya rolled her eyes at his paranoid theory. "Have the police said anything, yet?"

"They're still being all hush-hush. Damn Joe, I care about these kids. I think we should do something, but I don't know what."

"It would be better if we just let the police handle it, Anya. Our hands are full enough." Joe uncomfortably spouted the company line. But the police would do nothing —could do nothing—in all probability.

Anya looked resigned. "Yeah, I suppose you're right. Say, I heard about Connie Velasques, Joe. I'm sorry. That's so tough when a customer dies on you."

"Yeah, I guess I made a fool of myself yesterday, flipping out like that."

"Don't worry about it, Joe. Everyone understands. I talked to Chandra this morning. She is worried about you. You are too valuable to the Agency. There aren't many of us left who really give a damn, you know." She gave him a sympathetic smile. "Say, are you eating in the break room today?"

"Since they deposited paychecks this morning, I thought I'd go for a taco at La Cocina."

"Mind if I join you?"

"No. Please do."

She flashed him another smile. "See you then."

MOST OF THE MULTIS KEPT THEIR OFFICES ON PROSPERITY, a mainstream high-security sim, but Mitologias maintained its presence on a small EU-based sim called Fitzgerald's Pipe, a land of dark castles and faerie woods, populated by mythical creatures from European lore. Claire's hacker friend, KT Willow, lived here also, in a little cottage in the woods. Run on a network of powerful and highly secure servers catering to high-end techies, Fitzgerald's Pipe was rather old school in appearance. Claire appreciated the change of pace from the ubiquitous realism of New Life and the over-amped grit of the undernets.

Maxi had identified three administrative employees of the Special Projects Division—Dr Nina Vogt of Mar del Plata, Argentina, Dr Neal Olson, Los Angeles, California, and the principal software engineer, Carlos Seguda, of

Caracas. Only Vogt had a traceable personal history, which involved various leftist political affiliations and some high-profile causes connected to the scientific community.

She would have preferred meeting with all three of them, had authorization to interview them all, in fact, but Maxi had only secured an appointment with Seguda. They were stonewalling her. She could have used her clout with *el jefe*—Mr Bigshot—but Seguda was the one who most interested her. There was no point in playing that card just yet.

Seguda's profile seemed sketchy, and her instinct instantly told her not to trust him. Arriving at the laboratory just as an assistant left, she slipped in before the door fully closed. Always best to catch them by surprise. Carlos Seguda, the avatar, had an unimposing profile, a standard-issue laboratory geek persona, complete with pocket protector. In the V of his white coat hung a curious medallion like an old-fashioned clock at ten til three, the only non-generic item in his wardrobe.

As soon as he noticed her presence, Seguda shut down his code with a smooth sweep. He held up a hand, palm out. "Excuse me Ms, you're not allowed in this space."

"On the contrary. I'm here on behalf of the boss." She loved saying that. She sent Seguda the credentials provided by the corporate office, which essentially gave her carte blanche.

He accepted them and smiled wanly. "You're here a little early, aren't you, Ms Deluna? I wasn't expecting you for another ten minutes."

She nodded and returned the smile without answering his question. "What are we working on, here, Dr Seguda?"

"We call the project Sweetland."

"And what is Sweetland?"

The lengthy pause suggested he was calculating how much she knew.

"It's a new sim technology," he said at last. "It's going to wipe New Life off the map. Streamlined code. Super fast, increased realism, that sort of thing." He had carefully chosen his words, leaving them intentionally vague.

New Life was the popular name for virtual reality, but it also was the moniker of the biggest player in the game. What they called a genericized trademark.

She made a gesture encompassing the hyper-realistic laboratory. "I don't know how you can get more realistic than all of this."

"Well, this is all *visually* lifelike, but what if you could use controlled nano-devices to manipulate the human brain and nervous system, so that you could simulate tactile pressure and heat, as well as trigger specific taste and smell sensations? One might take it for reality. One might argue, in fact, that it *is* reality, of a sort."

"Aren't you and some of your competitors already doing something like that with these new mods?"

"Not like this new code will, Ms Deluna. Our little fellows go deeper into the cerebral cortex, tap into the mind in a new way, one never attempted before. In a sense you may *become* your in-world self."

It sounded farfetched to her.

"Yes, that would be pretty amazing, Dr Seguda. So tell me what skyrmion is about?"

There was a long pause. Had that been a brief look of surprise in his shifting eyes? Maybe he hadn't expected her to know about skyrmion.

"Skyrmion. Yes. It's a counter-espionage smokescreen designed to protect our product from competitors. Top secret." The lie was obvious on its face. But what was it covering up?

He fumbled for something more to say, but she cut him off. "I need some of your code, Dr Seguda. A few megs from your sim program. Nothing proprietary, just a snippet for comparative analysis."

"May I ask what code you will compare it with? None of our development code has been outside of this laboratory."

"That's for me to know, Dr Seguda." He already suspected, but she wasn't about to admit her capture of the skyrmion code. "I will also need a list of your coders on this project and an annotated sample from each so we can compare coding styles."

"I'll have my PA forward a list and sample code to you."

"Now, if I could have that Sweetland code."

He shrugged and after a few brief seconds transferred a chunk of code to her. It would most likely be useless to her investigation. But this new piece might help verify the source of the code she had snatched yesterday with her tap.

His interesting reaction to her use of the term 'skyrmion' made her little visit worthwhile. Now to find out what skyrmion was all about.

Jessie grabbed her backpack and left the apartment earlier than usual, tossing her dad a perfunctory, "Bye Dad, see you tonight," as she slipped out the door without looking at him or meeting his eyes. She made her way to François' Café, nearly stumbling over a woman sleeping on the side-walk at the bottom of the stairs. She ordered her usual vanilla latté, which contained neither vanilla nor milk. Not to mention the total absence of coffee. But it contained a lot of sugar, and its artificial caffeine perked up her mood. The daily routine took all of her piddling weekly allowance, but she had nothing else to spend it on, anyway. She enjoyed chatting with François, who always had some interesting take on the English language, even if it was often in the telling of some morose tale. And occasionally, like this morning, he'd have free samples of his delectable French pastries. François must have Connections. Unlike most other bakeries around, he always had pastry flour. People with Connections got what they needed.

On normal school days, conversation and pastry were side benefits of hanging out at François'. The actual purpose was to wait for Dad to leave for work, so she could slip back into the apartment and onto the Grid. It seemed her father never had time or inclination to stop in for a coffee before cycling to work.

Today, of course, she was actually going to school.

She nibbled at a piece of cheese brioche, savoring the delicate flavor. "I'm gonna miss this great baking when we're gone, François."

"You going away, Jessie?"

"We'll be moving soon."

"Out of town, may I ask?"

"Yes, out of the country."

"That's quite an undertaking. I wish you well. When I left Quebec for America, it took several years for me to adjust, you know. Though I knew many Americans and spoke English well, I did not understand how different life here would be. So many things to learn."

"I've been taking classes to prepare," Jessie said.

"Well, good for you. I am glad you could obtain an exit

visa. If I could get one, I think I might go back to Canada, although I can't say for sure. It is nearly as bad there, my family tells me."

"Yes, and it will probably get worse."

"What do you mean?"

"When Canada tires of pumping all its water down here and we invade."

"Oh that," laughed François, "that's just politics. They spread those old stories to sow mistrust between America and Canada, you know. Canada has an endless supply of fresh water. They can afford to share it."

"It's not true, François," said Jessie. "They started having shortages of fresh water years ago. You should go to New Life and talk to some Canadians."

"I receive all the information I need from my family in Quebec."

Jessie could see François was getting uncomfortable, and she felt obliged to snipe. "They censor those letters you get, you know."

"Jessie, you are wrong. I recognize my sister's writing. It is unmistakable. Everything is intact, nothing is blacked out, or missing."

"It's called cut and paste. It's done digitally, so you can't tell."

François glared, his face beet-red. "Don't you have to be in school?" he said. "Damned left-wing propaganda you bring in here."

Jessie smiled sweetly at him. "*Je t'aime, aussi*, François," she chirped. "See you on Monday."

François shook his head, muttering something about "damned disrespectful kids." Jessie slung her backpack over her shoulder and blithely bumped a chair so that it scraped as she strode toward the door.

· · ·

ON THE STREET A MAN PEDALED BY ON A BIKE CART CALLING out, "… pirogies, latkes, soybasa. Get a genuine Polish breakfast here." The rich aroma of food wafted by, and Jessie tried to imagine what type of synthetic garbage they substituted for expensive potatoes and sausage. There was a Somali food cart near the park, where she ate when she had a few dollars, but she could seldom afford to buy food from the vendors, and the quality sucked most of the time.

The workday bicycle traffic had picked up by the time she ambled down Belmont Street to Twelfth and turned north toward school. Passing the little park at St Francis Church, she scoured the clumps of homeless people, hoping to spot Alan. A bicyclist nearly collided with her as she crosses the street for a closer look.

"Goddamn it, kid, watch where you're going."

A big woman sitting on the sidewalk howled with laughter. "Better watch out, Missie," she said, panting between the guffaws, "them fuckers'll run you over."

Jessie approached the big woman, who sat flat on the walk with her legs sprawled out before her.

"Say, do you know a guy named Alan?"

"Well, I know a couple of Alans, I suppose. Which one you looking for?" She looked Jessie over. "You're not ho-ing, are you, child?"

"He's about forty," Jessie said, ignoring the insinuation. "A vet. Talks kind of slow, and talks to himself a lot. I'm worried about him. Some people beat him up."

"Oh that Alan," said the woman. "Ain't seen him for over a week. Heard them nazis smashed him up pretty good. Friend of yours?"

"Just a guy who comes around sometimes and talks to

me. If you see him, could you tell him that Jessie is worried about him?"

"Big Martha'll do that, hon," the woman said as Jessie turned back toward school. "You take care of yourself, now."

"Thanks," she called back over her shoulder. "I'll do that."

A VERY SOFT RAIN FELL AS JOE AND ANYA WALKED IN SILENCE along the chain-link fence separating the sidewalk from a former car lot, an empty, weed encroached expanse of asphalt, recently filled with makeshift tents constructed of cardboard and ragged plastic tarps. Trash gathered against the fence, bits of paper, syringes, soft-drink cups, a pair of jeans, and one worn out sneaker.

"Wonder where they're from?" Anya asked.

Joe shrugged. "It's hard to say. Nobody seems to keep track anymore, do they?"

There was not quite enough rain to warrant an umbrella on such a short stroll, but Joe pulled his jacket collar up tight around his neck. As they neared the little taqueria, Anya said, "ABW offered me a job, Joe. I wanted you to know, because... well... I think you should consider pursuing employment with them. It's going to be hard finding another job out there."

The news stunned Joe. He realized how unprepared he was for full Privatization. Anya was his sole confidante at work. Not that he didn't feel a need for a social life, but his reserved nature didn't make it easy for others to get close.

And as a single parent, he had an insignificant life outside work. He listed the reasons in his mind, but none of them washed. The truth was, when he socialized with his colleagues he felt an acute sense of alienation, not from anyone specifically, but from comfortable humanity in general.

"I think you'll have to move soon," Anya continued, "They won't take all of us. How can they?."

"I know, Anya." And he did know, had known for a long time, and yet he couldn't prompt himself to act. "I'm not sure I have what it takes to do this work anymore. I feel like such a coward—I just don't know where I could get another job."

"Joe, one thing you are not is a coward. You have more moral fiber than everyone else in that office put together. You go out on a limb for someone every single day."

If only you knew about Frank and Amy and what I did to them, he thought, you'd know I'm no hero.

"Well, I guess I have little choice," he said. "I'll miss our conversations when you move on."

"We don't have to lose touch, you know."

"I suppose you're right." He had doubts. They would call each other for a while, have lunch once or twice, then drift apart. It always happened that way, didn't it?

The young woman behind the counter informed them that there were no flour tortillas or soy burger today. They ordered bean tacos, which Joe preferred anyway, and chatted about office trivia until the food came. It relieved him that Anya didn't bring up ABW again.

He studied her face as they talked, trying to read some personal meaning into it. She was strikingly pretty, in an offbeat way. She wore no makeup, but her cheeks and her lips had a deep rosy color when flushed from the chilly wind.

She had a high-bridged Adriatic nose, unlike the other Ukrainians he knew. Perhaps some southern European genes. Her small mouth had a permanent downturn at the edges, which gave her a serious appearance, even when she was being lighthearted. She played this feature to superb effect, exhibiting a droll sense of humor. She was lovely, really.

"Look, Joe," said Anya, biting into a taco, "these kids… what I said at the office… I didn't want to talk about it there but—"

"—Anya—"

"—Just hear me out, Joe. I've done the research. I connected most of these kids through the Grid."

"The kids are all plugged into the damned Grid these days, aren't they?"

"It's not just the Grid; they run together in the same social networks—rebellious, angry teens—and many are ending up dead?"

"That's what often happens to rebellious, angry teens, Anya."

"I don't know, Joe. No violence, no obvious cause—just dead. Gridheads."

"What can we do, Anya? What can *I* do?" Joe's heart ached, but he felt impotent.

Anya shook her head. "I don't know—maybe just be aware, look for signs."

"Sure, Anya," he said, feeling the insincerity in his voice. "I'll let you know if I hear anything."

"Something else, Joe. I have a client family I'd like to refer to you. She has some special problems with her teenage son and school, and I know you have some resources to help her deal with that."

"Sure, send them over." His schedule was full, but an

extra family consultation would only add a little more paperwork.

"Their name is Watkins," she said. "You have time this week?"

He touched his mobe calendar. "How about three tomorrow?"

"Thanks so much, Joe. You're a sweetheart." Anya paused before continuing, "Say, Joe… could I ask you about something more personal?"

"Sure, Anya, anything at all."

"Well… there's a new band playing Friday night, and…" Anya paused. Was she trying to ask him out on a date? Joe felt his heart quicken. Was he ready for this? "… I have this friend, Allison, and…" Joe's heart sank—*a blind date*, "… she hasn't been out on a date for a long time. She's very nice, Joe. And personable. And pretty. And I was planning to go with my girlfriend, Sam, and I thought, if you wouldn't mind, we could make it a kind of double date. I just thought maybe…"

Anya was trying to fix him up with a date, and she was in a relationship with another woman, and how could he have been so wrong about her attraction to him? It felt like charity, and his self-confidence took a sharp dive. He hoped it didn't show.

"I don't know, Anya. I haven't… how do people date these days? I haven't been on a date since before Jessie was born."

"It would be good for you to have a life outside work. You know, get out and meet people. Meet some nice women."

"I hate to be so crass, but doesn't a live show cost about a week's salary these days?"

"It's at the New Life Emporium. It's not real world live.

Allison got us a special deal. It's the latest hipster thing. It will be fun, I promise."

Joe didn't want to say no to Anya. Although his small hope had just been crushed, she was still his only friend. "Okay," he said. "I'll do it for you, Anya."

"Great." He could hear genuine enthusiasm in her voice. "I'll email the details. Oh, and you'll need to bring your citspecs."

Citspecs? He couldn't tell her he didn't own a pair. A vague feeling of panic played in his mind, and he nervously tapped his fingers. Don't obsess with this, he told himself, she's just a friend of Anya's. You haven't even met her yet. You'll be just fine.

"So, how is Jessie doing?" asked Anya, changing the subject.

Jessie. He chewed until his mouthful became manage-able. "She's been missing a lot of school. Doesn't talk to me much. I don't know what's going on with her."

"It's probably just that age," said Anya. "It's tough for girls. I was a horrible little brat at fourteen."

"I've gone home during the school day twice now to find her in her room on the damned Grid. You see what I mean about the Grid? Twice, Anya. In five years I've left work early exactly twice, and both times I've found her home, skipping school. So, how often does this happen? And her school has no idea, as far as I know. Do they even take roll anymore?"

"Well, Joe, if it's any consolation, I dropped out of school at fifteen, got my GED, went to community college. It's not the end of the world. She's a bright girl. I'm not saying you shouldn't try to find out what's wrong and be a supportive father and all that. I'm just saying... you know."

"Thanks, Anya. I know she has to live her own life. It's just hard is all."

Anya reached out, took his hand in hers, and smiled. "Yeah Joe, I know."

A DARKNESS DESCENDED AS JESSIE ENTERED THE HALLS OF Benson Polytechnic High School, where only a dim light illuminated the filthy, peeling paint on graffiti-covered walls. The floors contained more potholes than Burnside Street, large pits in the broken tile deep enough to break an ankle. Everything about it depressed her.

She looked around for a friendly face and, seeing no one she recognized, panicked. Why had she come here? She turned and started for the exit, when a voice behind her called out, "Jessie Larivee."

She swung around to face Jennifer Mosley, her first period biology teacher, who was striding toward her. "Ms Mosley."

"We haven't seen you for a few weeks, Jessie," said Ms Mosley. "Have you been all right?"

Jessie smiled. "Just getting ready for the big move. I came by to say goodbye to a few friends."

"Are you moving? I didn't know. We were just getting to know you." Ms Mosley sounded disappointed.

"Well, opportunities come up. My dad's not one to pass up a shot at the old American Dream, you know."

"Good for him. What does your dad do?"

"Oh, he works for the government. You know, the one they sold to the oligarchy. I think he waterboards terrorists, stuff like that." She looked at Ms Mosley with a straight face and shrugged.

Ms Mosley wrinkled her brow, giving Jessie the Concerned Elder Look. "You know that type of talk is dangerous, Jessie. You would do well to be more circumspect."

"If by circumspect, you mean mindful, then I'm good with that. But, if you mean keeping my mouth shut out of fear… well, you can see where that's gotten us."

Ms Mosley frowned. "You not only put yourself in danger, but you risk others around you. Well, anyway, come on to class, and say goodbye to your friends."

Jessie followed Ms Mosley down the hall to the biology lab. Biology was her favorite subject, especially ecology. She could probably come to like Ms Mosley, who was young and easy going and enthusiastic about her subject. All the older teachers were just biding their time, resigned to keeping the brats in line.

JESSIE MADE HER WAY TO THE BACK OF THE CLASSROOM, sidling up next to her pal Mel, a tall black girl with a sweet face and a wry, cutting sense of humor to match Jessie's own, a trait that had brought them together back in middle school.

"Hey, Jess," whispered Mel, "where the hell have you been?"

"It's a long story. I'm getting ready to leave. If you want to skip second period, I'll tell you all about it."

Mel looked at her hard, considering the proposition. "You're leaving, Jess?"

Jessie nodded.

"Okay, we can sneak over to the mall or something."

Jessie gave a thumbs-up and when the bell rang, the girls slipped out a side exit and headed north up Twelfth Avenue. The sun filtered down through a break in the clouds, and Jessie felt her spirit lift again. They chatted about boys and school, and Mel filled her in on the past few weeks of high school drama.

As they crossed the bridge over the old Banfield freeway, the girl's conversation stopped as they took in the homeless encampments which had grown up along the former freeway over the past several years, tents and homemade shanties as far as they could see. Some of the more able had built or obtained tiny houses which somehow they'd located on the old freeway, a neighborhood where they grew pothole gardens and hung clothes out to dry on makeshift clothes-lines. At the far end of the bridge, the bored guard ignored the girl's ID cards and waved them through the Lloyd-Broadway checkpoint. Jessie said, "Let's go to that park—the little one over on this side of the Max. They have covered benches that won't be wet."

"Sure," said Mel. "So, where're you moving, Jess?"

"You know about Sweetland, right?" Her voice was a whisper.

"Yeah, of course, but it's not real."

"It is, Mel. It's real, and I'm going."

"Oh, Jess. You're not getting sucked into that cult stuff, are you?"

"It's not a cult, chuck."

Mel glowered. "How do you know it's real?"

"Because I've talked to people who have crossed over. I just finished classes at a real university. And Monday we start the actual emigration process."

"A legit university?" Mel gave her a concerned frown. "Anyone can put together a fake university on the Grid."

"I checked it out, Mel. It's a real, legit university."

"So, tell me."

"It's *Universidad Simón Bolívar.* I've been studying survival and ecology since August. I'm so psyched, Mel. I wanted so bad to tell Ms Mosley, but I don't think that would be such a good idea."

"So, what does your dad say?" asked Mel.

"I don't know. I haven't talked to him about it yet. I just can't figure out how to tell him. To convince him. And I want him to go, too."

Mel looked astonished. "But Jessie, you're such a Daddy's girl. I mean, sometimes I feel like he's my dad, Sister."

"I know, Mel. I'm so glad I can talk to you about this, 'cause it's really hard. I think I can convince him. But if I can't, you know, I have to live my own life. There's only another month at the most before the Grand Rupture."

"Grand Rupture? What's that?"

"They're afraid the corpos will figure out the tech, or something, so they're shutting all the gates down, I guess. The entire Grid is going down. Everybody who wants to has to leave by then."

"You're sure, Jess? That sounds crazy. You're sure this is all real?"

"Yeah, Mel, I'm sure. You know there's a war coming, don't you? There's going to be a bloodbath."

"Everybody can see that," said Mel, lowering her voice to a whisper. "It scares the hell out of me."

"Not everybody," Jessie said, thinking of her father. "Way too many people are still sleeping. Like Dad."

Mel's intense gaze penetrated her. "Can I go, Jess? To Sweetland? Would they let me go?"

Jessie stammered, "I... I don't know, Mel. I don't know

why not? You have to do some orientation at the Temple of New Life."

"Is this some kind of religious thing?" asked Mel.

"Not really. It's like a big RPG you gotta play to get in. Like a screening or something. And you need new specs, ones with the new DBT mods."

"Can't I just swap mods, so I don't have to re-reg?"

"You can wipe your citspecs and get the mods swapped at SimWorld, I think. Then you won't need to re-reg I s'pose. But we have to hurry. Orientation starts Monday."

"Oh, Jess, I really want to do this. I want to be with my bestest."

Jessie turned and looked her friend in the eye. "You sure you don't want to talk some more about this first, Mel? You know, before you wipe your citspecs and everything? I had to think this over all summer."

"Member, Jess, how all through eighth grade we talked about going to Bolivia or someplace? How we vowed to escape together? I've been thinking about it forever. Before Dad left, all he talked about was moving to some eco community. And he did it, Jess. Mom doesn't give a fuck. Now I have a chance to leave with my best bud. 'Sides, I'm only getting some mods swapped. It's not like we're going tomorrow, right? I can still back out if I get chickenshit, right?"

"Right." Everything Mel said was true. They'd have a few weeks to talk it over.

"Good," said Mel, "it's settled. Got a pin, or something?" Jessie reached into her pack and found an old-style metal paper clip. She watched while Mel straightened it out and used it to push the tiny reset button on the inside of the citspecs. "There. Done. Let's go get those mods."

☼

THE WATKINS' ARRIVED A FEW MINUTES EARLY, AS JOE finished up his weekly reports for the county. Aleesha Watkins was a thin woman who appeared to be in her early thirties. She had a very unhealthy look about her, although the files Anya had sent over didn't indicate any medical issues. Thirteen-year-old Gameliel already stood a head taller than his mother and had his hair cut very short in the popular 'blackwater' style.

"Anya tells me that Gameliel is having trouble with school," said Joe.

"Yes," said Aleesha Watkins, "ever since his brother Micah up and ran away a couple of months ago he's been getting into fights, and now he refuses to go to school at all. I just don't know what's got into this kid. And now the land-lord's all over my ass, saying Gameliel's been bothering the neighbors while I'm at work."

"He ain't run away," snapped Gameliel. "I keep telling you that."

Joe turned to the boy. "Where is your brother, Gameliel?"

"He's gone to Sweetland."

"You talk like that's someplace," reprimanded Aleesha. "That's not a place." She looked at Joe with a what-do-you-do with-them smile. "That's just something kids say, like 'I got that cool new song by so-and-so and now I'm in Sweetland.'"

Gameliel harumphed.

"You miss your brother, Gameliel?" Joe asked.

"I'd go with him 'cept they won't let me in 'cause I'm a kid. Ain't right."

"Who won't let you go?" asked Joe.

"You know," said Gameliel. "They won't let you sign up for New Life and stuff until you're fourteen. And I can't wait for another year."

"What the hell are you talking about, son?" demanded Aleesha. "You got those city spectacle things or whatever they're called, and I told you I would sign you up for Kid's Life. That New Life, that's dangerous for kids." She was looking at Joe, expecting confirmation. Joe shrugged.

"I told you, I don't want Kid's Life. I want to be with Micah."

Aleesha turned back to Joe. "They got porn, and gambling, and every kind of garbage that's no good for kids on that thing. That's what the news man says. No good for adults either, you ask me."

"Okay, Aleesha," said Joe, "I'll talk to your landlord and try to smooth things out. Let's see if we can get Gameliel back in school." He turned to the boy. "Gameliel, I know it's hard without your brother, and it's hard not being allowed to do what the older kids are doing, but the counselor Anya recommended is a cool guy, and I think you'll be able to talk to him and work out some of your frustration. Okay?"

"Whatever," said Gameliel. He was clearly going to be a hard sell.

He handed Aleesha Watkins a card with the counselor's information on it. She gave Joe an apologetic look and thanked him.

"I wish I could do more," said Joe, meaning it. The world was such a mess. What could he do? Aleesha Watkins smiled, but the smile had a weariness about it, maybe a little sardonic.

And then they left.

JOE LOGGED HIS TIME AND TURNED TO HIS EMAIL. ANYA'S directions for Friday night awaited halfway down the list. They were to meet at The New Life Emporium at 8 tomorrow night. The address was not too far from Joe's apartment.

The last time he had been on a date, about seventeen years ago, he owned a car, with a clear expectation that he would pick up his date and take her… where? Where had he taken Jolene that evening? He recalled the little middle eastern restaurant in Montavilla. And then they had gone to a movie at the old Laurelhurst. What had they seen? Some old film from the nineties, if he remembered correctly.

Things had changed since those days; the times called for a whole new etiquette and Joe felt quite lost. Now he had to find some citspecs and learn how to use them. He wondered if getting a life could be worth all the trouble.

☼

AFTER PURCHASING MEL'S DBT MODULES, THE GIRLS stopped for a soda before making their way past the rows of empty stores to a little nook of filthy disintegrating couches at the east end of the mall. The area was empty, like the mall itself, and the two of them stretched out their legs and chatted about New Life and Jessie's classes at the University. Mel's eyes lit up when Jessie told her about the Forest Survival Simulation. "I'm pissed at you, Jess. Why didn't you tell me about these glitch classes?"

"Sorry, Mel." Jessie sucked up the last bit of soda, which gurgled in the bottom of her cup. "But you were off Grid all summer with your dad, doing his hippie thing."

Mel chewed on a mouthful of ice. "Yeah, I guess we're glitch, but I'm still pissed."

"Well, you don't need the classes to go. Just gotta go through the Temple screening. And you're the thing, Mel. They'll love you."

After hours of conversation, Jessie dragged Mel up from the couch and toward the south doors. Outside, the sun hung on the western horizon, and a cool, dry breeze pushed the day to a close. They strolled together down 12th Avenue in the growing twilight, and Jessie felt a glow of satisfaction. They were going to see unknown lands together. The two of them. Just like they once dreamed.

"So," Jessie asked, "what's your avi name?"

"You'd know, if you hadn't abandoned me."

Jessie felt another twinge of guilt. She had spent little time with Mel since they were old enough for New Life. But the complaining was getting a little tiring.

"Sorry, Mel, but we've been through that." She hoped her response wasn't too sharp.

"Anyway, it's BensonGirl." Mel cringed. "But you can call me Benson. I know it's kind of old school and all, but I don't do much except hang out with some people from school. Gossip and stuff. New Life is so boring, unless you like to shop and shit. But who's got money, anyway."

"Well, it's not all New Life, you know. There're the universities and there are the undernets. And New Patagonia, which is *almost* like the undernets, but less creepy. I can show you some stuff that isn't so boring."

"You mean that forest sim you were talking about?"

"Yeah. Lots of stuff like that. There's Old Paris, which is

maintained by the students at the Sorbonne, which like no longer exists in the actual world, but it's all inworld now, like the *Universidad.* How about we meet tomorrow night after dinner? I'll send you an invitation to Gretel deVoid's place on *Malafreña?*"

Mel beamed. "That would be glitch."

THE DARKNESS HAD SETTLED IN BY THE TIME THEY REACHED St Francis Park, and it looked like a hundred people were waiting in line for evening soup. Many of their faces had that sunk inward look from missing teeth. Some of them glared at the girls, others smiled. Jessie examined the lined and weathered faces of the men and women, some with kids in tow. Alan was not among them. Emptiness opened up inside her. She hadn't really expected to find him, but she had allowed herself to hope.

At the edge of the soup line, about a dozen young men and women, dressed in a rag-tag assortment of clothing scavenged from who-knows-where, sat on the ground with small drums made from wood, metal, ceramic, plastic buckets, aluminum pans, tapping tentatively, trying to get into a rhythm they could all follow. Someone had hung a home-made, green and blue Free Cascadia flag from a tree branch overhead. The girls watched the drummers as more people straggled in from all directions. The drumming grew louder, taking on a hypnotic quality. A young woman offered Jessie a plastic bucket. A part of her wanted to stay and drum with them, but she could sense Mel's wariness.

"Oh, Jessie, it makes me so sad," Mel said as they walked away toward her apartment. "All these people; I want to take care of them all, but you can't take care of them all, can you?"

Jessie didn't answer. At Mel's door, she said goodnight to her friend and headed home alone in the dark. Her dad was going to light into her about the dangers of being alone at night and he was right, of course. She hurried along, keeping to the curb, as far away from the buildings as possible. Despite her wariness, an indescribable mixture of sadness and joy distracted her. She wiped at the sudden tears filling her eyes.

Part Two

New Life

"Throw your dreams into space like a kite, and you do not know what it will bring back, a new life, a new friend, a new love, a new country."
—*Anaïs Nin*

He sits in the living room of Frank and Amy's Montavilla home. Jessie is on the floor playing with the rag doll. His mother sews a quilt, quietly humming an unrecognizable tune, which sometimes sounds like "Amazing Grace," and at other times like the refrain to "There is Power in a Union." Amy's quilt is a puzzle, Frank explains, and each piece tells us something about the future. She picks up a new patch, and the design is a black, leafless tree against a deep, red background. There is overwhelming sense of hopelessness as Frank cries out, "No, Amy."

Amy replies, with her sad smile, "But, Frank, it's too late. This is the last piece. I can't change the design now."

TAP TAP TAP. EYES CLOSED, HEART RACING, JOE AWOKE WITH a lingering sadness from his dream. *Tap tap tap.* His eyes popped open. Jessie stood at the kitchen counter banging on a self-heating carton with a heavy wooden spoon, trying to force the last few hot morsels onto a plate.

"Hi, sweetheart," he mumbled. "You're fixing dinner?"

"Hi, dad. We're having your favorite veggie chili and cottage cheese—we're out of veggies. I hope that's okay."

"Wonderful." He realized he actually meant it—not for what it was, but because Jessie was actually preparing it. "How was school today?"

"Oh, it was okay. You know, same old stuff."

Jessie looked sullen. Joe wanted to talk to her about school, but pressing her would lead to a fight. Whenever he brought up school, she reacted as though he was prying into her private life where he had no business; it left Joe hurt and confused. He always had such good advice for his clients about their kids, but he could never figure out what to do for his own family.

"Dad?"

Jessie took the cottage cheese from their mini fridge.

"Yes, dear?"

"If we could move somewhere… somewhere like the wilderness, say."

"Jessie, even if there were any wilderness left, how would you live in such a place? And why would we want to go there?"

"Just hear me out, Dad. This is a hypothetical. Say it was the days of the Oregon Trail or something, when the West was being settled, and you had a chance to move somewhere and start all over again… would you do that?"

"Is this a school project or something?"

"Yeah."

"Well, I don't know. I guess it would depend on a few things."

"What if a bunch of people were going, and you had a way to make a living when you got there, and a place to live? A community." She opened the cottage cheese.

Would he leave this misery behind? What did he have to stay for? "It's sounding better. Pretty good, actually."

Jessie's face lit up, and he suddenly wondered if this was something more than a school project.

"What if I decided I was going, regardless?" She studied him as she dished the food onto plates. Joe analyzed the conversation. What was this all about?

"Jessie—"

"Remember, dad, it's a hypothetical." She handed him a plate of beans and cottage cheese.

"Well, darling, hypothetically, it wouldn't thrill me. I mean, I would prefer a more mutual decision. But, yes, I would seriously consider it. Probably I would come. Hypothetically. I think I would. If it was real."

Jessie smiled and plopped on the couch next to him. It

was the first time he had seen her smile for weeks. For a moment, the old bond between the two of them returned. He ached to reach out and hold her to him, but he feared she would push him away again, and so he just soaked in the feeling from a distance.

As he basked in his contentment, his thoughts turned to Anya and his coming date. "Jess, where did you say you bought those citspecs?"

"I got them down at the mall. SimWorld," she mumbled, chewing on a mouthful of food. "Are you going to join the 21st century, Dad?"

"I'm thinking about it."

"Dad. What's going on?" She beamed, pleased at this news.

"Some people are going out to New Life Emporium to hear a band, and I was thinking about joining them."

"Some people? Dad, you're not going on a date, are you?"

"Sort of," he admitted. "A blind date."

Without warning, the sullenness returned to Jessie's face.

"What's wrong, Jessie?" he prompted. "I thought you would be happy that I'm going out and meeting people."

She didn't reply. She took her plate and disappeared into her room.

JESSIE SULKED FOR MOST OF THE WEEK UNTIL BY WEDNESDAY evening Joe couldn't stand any more. "Look, kiddo, I don't know what's been eating at you, but if it's my date tomorrow night, I think you need to back off. I'm permitted to have a life outside of this house."

"Oh, Dad," said Jessie, "It's not you. It's just me, but…."

"But what?"

"I'm just not used to you… you know… you dating and stuff."

"I know, sweetie. I'm only doing this for a friend. It's nothing. I don't even know this woman."

"Well, don't go too fast, okay?"

"Sweetheart, you're still number one in my life. If I meet someone I like, I promise to take it slow."

"Okay. Thanks, Dad."

Jessie sounded half-hearted—some heavy weight still lingered. He could see it in her eyes.

"Jess, what else is bothering you?"

He watched her closely as she tried to formulate a statement, half expecting her to give up in exasperation and retreat to her room. Instead she said, "Dad, you remember a guy named Alan who used to come round when I was about eight or nine? He was an old school friend of yours or something?"

The question was entirely unexpected. "Alan? Alan Tolliver? What made you think of Alan?"

"I ran into him the other day. He was really sick, and I tried to get him to find some help. But he's paranoid about doctors, so I told him to come and talk to you. He went freaky and said he didn't want you to see what had become of him. He made me promise not to tell you I saw him. I didn't know what to do. I promised him."

"You did the right thing, sweetheart. But I don't know what we can do for him if he doesn't want to be helped."

"Can't you find him and talk to him?"

"Did he tell you where he's staying?"

"He's homeless, Dad. He's living under a bridge somewhere, or in a camp."

"I'll go out this weekend and ask around. But don't get your hopes up. There are a hundred and sixty thousand homeless people in this county, last census." And they counted less than half of them, he didn't say.

"I know. Thanks, Dad." Jessie gave him a kiss on the cheek and returned to her room, still looking as though she bore the weight of the world.

Dr Andrew Stephens was the chaplain of Whitehall University, a small inworld college run by the Methodists. He was also one of the world's foremost authorities on cults and religious fringe movements. Claire Deluna had consulted him early in her career, when a case led her to an extremist cult. She'd needed to know the group's mindset, and Dr Stephens' insight had been invaluable.

The secretary directed her to the lecture hall, where Claire peered timidly in on Dr Stephens' class. There was something about schools and classrooms that brought out feelings of inadequacy in her; maybe it was having dropped out of high school in tenth grade. She dealt with street toughs, and hustlers, and other assorted business people, and yet, when she entered the halls of education, she always dissolved back into a stammering fifteen-year-old.

"As the authority of the Roman Church waned," Dr Stephens was explaining, "the cults proliferated. There had always been this idea among some Christians—and this is true of nearly every religion, not just Christianity—that the individual can experience God privately, without a Pope or Rabbi or Mullah or shaman interpreting the experience, without a church or temple as a proper setting, that it was something inherent in the human condition, this ability to experience God. The body is the temple. This is the basis of religious mysticism. So, when the early Anabaptists and Protestants questioned the supremacy of the Church, a new mysticism also bloomed, led by charismatic leaders. Many of these new cults mouthed the heresy that every person was a god unto himself. Sometimes, this new belief in individual godhead led to such extremes as ritualized rape and even mass murder, as the strictures of the all-seeing, punishing God fell away."

Spying Claire in the doorway, Dr Stephens paused and flashed her a brief smile. "Class, I would like you to think about this and compare it within the context of the contemporary cults of the past several decades, which we examined last week. Friday, we will discuss some of the ancient cults in more depth. Now, if you will excuse me, I believe I have a visitor."

Dr Stephens shuffled the papers on his podium while the class streamed out the door past Claire, who waited for the room to empty.

"Claire Deluna," he said, beckoning her inside. "What brings you to the dreaded halls of academia?"

Hesitating for a moment, Claire entered the classroom, her hand extended. "Good to see you, Dr Stephens."

He shook her hand. "I do wish that you would call me Andy, Claire. Those moldy old titles are so last century."

"I... Andy... I have a case which might involve some type of cult, and I would like to pick your brain, if you don't mind. In particular, do you know anything about the Temple of New Life?"

Dr Stephens' eyebrows raised. "Yes, I have a graduate seminar studying that very phenomenon. Please come to my office, won't you?"

He led her out of the lecture room and down the

hallway to a small alcove with office doors around the perimeter. His office was in one corner of the alcove. Books overflowed the bookcases, scattered helter-skelter in piles along with papers held in place by various sorts of paper-weights. She recalled her own office and smiled, thinking she understood. Dr Stephens, like her, preferred working in this atmosphere of old-fashioned clutter, when it was possible to have a single book or reading device with all these titles inside.

"So, Claire," he said, shutting the door, "tell me about your case."

"Doctor… uh… Andy, I'm investigating a company which seems to have some connection to this Temple thing… and I'm… I'm trying to get to the bottom of it. I thought perhaps you could give me some ideas… uhm… you know… what might be going on." Claire felt stupid and inarticulate, and it didn't help that Dr Stephens—Andy—was looking at her as though she was a lost child.

She tried to explain. "It's just that… people might be dying. I have evidence of that… and, well… none of this detective stuff has ever spilled over—"

"—into the actual world." He sighed, finishing her sentence. "Claire, throughout history, the middle classes have always lived in virtual reality."

"What do you mean? I don't get that."

"What I mean is that we always build a level of abstraction, a simulated bubble of denial around ourselves to protect us from the consequences of our decisions. How does that Brecht verse go?

"What keeps Mankind alive?
"The fact that millions are daily tortured
"Stifled, punished, silenced and oppressed.
"Mankind can keep alive thanks to its brilliance

"In keeping its humanity repressed
"And for once you must try not to shrink from the facts
"Mankind is kept alive by bestial acts."

Claire was more puzzled than before.

"What I mean to say, dear girl," said Andy, "is that, just because we may hide from an ugly old world here on New Life, it doesn't mean that brutal world does not exist. And our decisions, every single one of them, no matter how slight, have consequences out there in that world. All right, enough lecture. Where should I begin?"

"What do you know about the Temple? About its origins and how it works, that sort of thing."

"Just over a year ago the Bolivarian governments began distributing free citspecs in the barrios of all their major cities, as well as many smaller towns and villages. A few months later, in New Patagonia, Amazonia, Havana, Old Paris, and other Bolivarian sims, the cults of *El Templo de la Vida Nueva* began to appear."

"You say cults? Plural?"

"Yes. They take many forms, which is what first interested some of my grad students. The cults multiplied phenomenally, so we started a monitoring program. My students come from all over the planet, you understand. We estimate that within three months these cults had upward of ten million followers worldwide, from every religious and secular segment. Ten million. Can you believe that?"

"Wow," said Claire, "so what's the common thread among these cults?"

"Sweetland," said Andy.

"Sweetland?"

"Heaven, The Golden City, Nirvana, Valhalla,

Erewhon, Utopia. The exact nature of Sweetland depends upon whom you ask, but that's the gist of it. It seems like there is a Sweetland for every taste. One of the larger cults believes that it's actually another planet, where colonists are setting up some type of utopian eco-community."

"Anything else in common among these groups?"

"Many appear to be... let's say... apocalyptic. They believe in an event called the *Gran Rupture*. Coming soon to a sim near you."

"Rupture... like a rupture in the Grid?"

"Exactly. They call those *Petit Rupture*. The *Gran Rupture* will cripple the entire Grid and destroy civilization as we know it. Or so the narrative goes."

"So, let's see if I have this right... er... correct. They equate a major disruption of the Grid with the end of the world?"

"I don't grade on grammar, you know." Andy smiled at her, and she felt her face flush with embarrassment. "Actually, it's not as clear as all that. Some cults clearly believe *Gran Rupture* is the end of the world, but others seem to take it metaphorically."

"Is there a date when this *Gran Rupture* happens?"

"Soon, Claire. Very soon. No precise, agreed upon date, but within weeks."

"Do you know anything about the people behind these cults?"

"Just that many of them seem to be gnostics of some sort."

"What's that?"

"The gnostics follow an ancient belief system. They believe in the co-divinity of the female and the male, and that the secrets of the universe are ultimately knowable. To their way of thinking, the material world corrupts the true nature of things, and we all live beneath a veil of illusion. Those who know the mysteries and sacred formulas can discover the genuine nature of the pleroma—the true universe beyond the veil. These modern day gnostics, however, have shed much of the ancient mythology and fancy themselves a cult of science."

"Then, why all the religious stuff?"

"Politics and power struggles within the elite may account for some of it—a competition to sway new followers. Or, they are perhaps following the Roman Catholic model of absorbing other religions by adopting their most important rites and turning them toward the new religion. Another possibility—they are weaving a veil of their own to obscure some secret agenda. And, of course, some of these cults are imitative and have no connection to the dominant groups at all."

"Are any of these cults… uhm… suicide cults?"

"Suicide cults? I don't know. I'm unaware of anything like that."

Claire told the professor about her research and the bodies found in Albuquerque and elsewhere.

"This is news to me," he said. "I'll have my grad students look into it. Disturbing, actually—this is very disturbing."

"If I wanted to check out a typical cult, where could I begin? Any ideas?"

"Check out 54 Calle Tierradulce, on New Patagonia," he said. "That seems to be some type of nexus for several of these things."

Isn't that the address Maxi had given her? The node connecting to Mitologias?

"Thanks, Professor. I appreciate it. Let me know if your

grad students come up with anything interesting, would you?"

"I'll do that, Claire. You take care of yourself, now."

GRETEL DEVOID LEANED BACK IN GRANDMA AMY'S ROCKING chair and waited for Benson to arrive. Her creation was as close to Grandma Amy's chair as her memory allowed her to make it. Now and then, she'd recall another minor detail, which she'd incorporate into the design, such as the initials her dad had carved on the inside of the runners when he was a child. Amy had laughed when Jessie first asked about them. "I don't think we ever told him we witnessed him carve them. Frank saw your dad sneaking around with his Swiss army knife and watched quietly from the kitchen. He called me over when your dad started carving, holding his finger to his lips to keep me from giving us away. Joe thought he was doing something that would get him in trouble. But it's just a chair, for crying out loud. As long as he wasn't sawing the legs off. Frank might have let him do that, too. But, they would have caught hell from me—Joe and Frank both."

That's what she remembered and loved about Amy and Frank, how easygoing and accepting they were. How, when you wanted to stretch your wings, they didn't stop you or slow you down, and yet you knew they were watching over you. Dad wasn't like that at all. He was fretful and over-protective.

When the doorbell rang, Gretel called out, "Door's open, Benson. Come on in."

The avi that walked through the door surprised her. A sexy, sienna-skinned girl with a short skirt and cleavage-revealing blouse tied around the waist, hair floating down in big strands of curl in front of her eyes, gave her a coy look. This is a side of her friend she didn't know.

"Is that you, Benson?"

Benson looked at her, defensive. "Yeah, I know, I know. It's just that—"

Gretel cut her off. "No need to explain, Benson. Damn, it's hard to call someone you know in the pit by an inworld name." It was hard sometimes, but necessary for privacy. Inworld protocol, at least on most sims, frowned upon a public breach of anonymity. Some would kick you out for it. But for the rebels she called friends, it was mandatory at all times.

"You get used to it pretty fast. It's kind of funny, you know. I only hang out with kids from school, and you only hang out with strangers."

"They're not strangers. And I don't have much in common with kids from school. Except you, of course."

"Are you sure about that, Gretel? I've always been a feminist and I feel like such a sell-out in front of you."

Gretel huffed. Mel was still embarrassed about her glamor girl persona. A recent wave of feminist thought had returned to criticizing objectification and what it called "lookism," and Mel was always more rigid about those things than Jessie had ever been.

"The only thing I might get on your shit about is if you use one of those slave-bots… concierges, or personal assistants, or whatever they're called."

"No way, chuck. None of the kids I know uses those, or I'd be on their ass about it. Even if they're just programs, they're so bourgeois. Please bring around the Bentley,

Chahles. Some of those bigots even have like mammies and racist shit like that."

"Well, anyway," says Gretel, "there's nothing wrong with wanting to look sexy. Some of my friends here are total sluts, chuck. And they're as feminist as anything. It's just you—I never knew this about *you*."

"We haven't hung out together since last spring. I'm different. Things change, you know. Anyway, you'd know if you hadn't abandoned me."

Is she never going to let up on this?

"I'm sorry, Benson. I hope you're going to forgive me someday."

"You know I have, Gretel. But that doesn't mean I won't rub it in while I can."

"Okay, if you swear you've really forgiven me."

"I swear. I really swear."

"Okay, then, that's settled. Shall we go to New Patagonia first, or Old Paris?"

"New Patagonia is where the forest sim is, right? That's where I want to go."

"Okay. Afterwards we'll look up Pox and Cedar."

A DARK MOOD CAME ON AS HE RODE HOME FROM WORK. JOE pedaled past his apartment toward the mall. He wasn't prepared to face his solitude just yet. Or Jessie's sulking. A busy mall might give him some vague sense of comfort. He had waited until the last minute to buy his citspecs, spending these last days obsessing about this step into the artificial world of the Grid.

Jessie thought he was a technophobe, and maybe he had become one, but it wasn't always so. He had once been a committed member of the internet generation, a so-called Millennial. He'd grown up on multi-player video games and the "social net," back in the day when there was still a free internet, before the quashed youth revolutions, and before the governments of the world decided the people's internet was too dangerous. Shutting it off like the tin-pan dictators was too crude, and too difficult. The corporate-subsidized politicians turned to that effective and time-honored tradition used when dealing with popular media. They offered key pieces of the infrastructure to the highest bidders. Gave them the freedom to price the rebellious youth out of the marketplace. Then they threw the masses a sop—let's call it New Life, a tightly controlled shopping channel, a virtual mirror of real life, where the poorest soul can live like a king. At least a virtual king. The beauty of it is, if you want to shop, the bandwidth is free or cheap. But if you have a message, if you're a troublemaker, if you want to preach to more than a very few people at a time, the bandwidth costs an absurd amount. The price of bandwidth was the cord used to strangle the youthful rebels. And, oh, how effective it had been.

We could have built anything imaginable in virtual reality, anything at all, and, instead, we created a banal mirror-image of our real-world, dysfunctional selves. He despised the media, he despised the whole idea of New Life, yet he couldn't continue to cut himself off from the world. Jessie had somehow kept her idealism intact while plugged-in, so it could be done.

He focused on his daughter as he pedaled through the twilight. What was going on in her mind? She was trying to figure something out, but what? Was she insecure about him? Maybe it was just teenage angst. All he could do was reassure her. Let her know he was there for her.

The ominous drumming had begun from the city parks and Swan Island, casting its call and answer across the city. It reminded him of the crows which gathered by the dozens in the trees, awakening him in the morning with their loud, riotous conversation echoing through the crisp air. The drums frightened him, they signified anarchy, a change of the guard. Wasn't the new guard always worse than the old?

The bicycle traffic was heavy for Wednesday evening, and several buses lined up in both directions at Twelfth and Burnside. The Eastside Business Association OLED display came to life.

"This intersection brought to you by The Tollgate Group," said the voice of a suave man in a business suit, "bringing you tomorrow's reality today." The picture cross-faded to a young man and woman, holding hands, laying in a grassy meadow with citspecs over their eyes. "I'm in Sweetland," the pretty young woman cooed. The screen dissolved to white, and the familiar logo of New Life appeared briefly, before fading.

"The light has turned green," said the smooth male voice. "You may proceed. The light has turned green."

Half way across the intersection, a loud explosion shook the ground beneath him, startling him so that he nearly collided with another bicycle. The *pop pop pop* of gunshots followed the blast. Far down Burnside, at the edge of his vision, a clean-n-safe in his fluorescent green vest lay in the middle of the street, his body draped over the top of his mangled bicycle. Several dark figures scattered down the side streets.

Shit, now the security assholes will sweep the streets. And when the mercenaries go hunting, more people will die. You can count on it. Joe put his head down and pushed forward as quickly as he could pedal until he had safely entered the Lloyd-Broadway Consortium Protective District. He passed through the Transit Authority checkpoint with no problem, and secured his bike at the Lloyd Center bike corral.

A scruffy young man wearing layers of ragged clothing stood near the mall entrance holding a sign that read, *Don't Let Them Put You to Sleep*. Joe stared until their eyes met, wondering how he had slipped through the shopping district checkpoint.

"Hear the drums?" The young man spoke in a conspiratorial whisper. "Do you know what they're saying?"

There wasn't much Joe could do for him other than give him one of the referral cards he always carried and encourage him to go to St Francis and get a free shower, some food, a set of clean rags. Joe was reaching for his wallet when a pair of rent-a-cops appeared from around the corner, their truncheons drawn. One glared at him as if to say, Don't get involved in this, Buddy. The man in rags stood his ground, making no attempt to flee. They would drag him away soon… but to where?

Joe didn't want to know the answer to that question.

GRETEL TOOK THE HAND OF BENSON GIRL AND TOGETHER they zoned to the *Universidad Simón Bolívar*. It didn't surprise her to find Toxine at the lab, studying. Toxine practically lived there.

"Hey, Toxine," she said in greeting.

"Hey, Gretel, *mon amie.* What brings you here on such a late night?"

"I'm on the west coast, remember, Toxine, it's not so late here. Anyway, I would like you to meet my friend, Benson. She's the one I told you about. Benson is *mon amie dans le vrai monde.* Did I say that right?"

"Close enough." Toxine smiled. "In Montreal Grid-speak, we might say *my vrai monde buddy.* More likely it would be, *my pitter buddy.*"

"Oh." Gretel smiled sheepishly and changed the subject. "Toxine, can I show Benson the forest sim? You know, without the vircats and stuff. Benson thought she wanted to go to Sweetland with us, and I promised to show her around here."

"Sure, I don't see why not." Toxine smiled warmly at Benson. "We have duplicated the environment of Sweetland fairly well, I think. It's based upon an amalgamation of descriptions which the messengers have provided us. But the vircat and other predators are merely 'what ifs.' That's what the programmers call them, *watifs.* No one has discovered any actual large predators yet, which doesn't mean that they don't exist. They have only explored a tiny portion of the southern continent."

"Who are the messengers?" Benson asked, looking confused.

"Those are the returnees," says Toxine. "When you travel to Sweetland for the first time, you will stay only about four hours, then yanked back. You must make an ultimate commitment within four days. We call it the four-four rule. Physics and all of that. We debrief the messengers upon return. Some take advantage of the First Crossing to observe the finest details of the physical environment, while others are more interested in connecting people to their loved ones—that sort of thing. Others are too bewildered to be of much use. But it's all good, whatever one can do."

"Okay," said Benson, "I can't wait."

Toxine laughed. "Very well, then. I will begin the forest sim."

"Great," said Gretel. "Thanks, Toxine."

Gretel led Benson to one of several doors along the wall of the lab. "Each of these doors leads to a different kind of simulation environment classroom."

"It's all so weird," said Benson. "We are already in a sim, and we have to go through a simulated door to get to the other sim? Don't you think that it's weird?"

"It's like the story inside a story." Gretel shrugged. She ushered Benson into the sim. Once inside, the door vanished, and they stood in the midst of a forest at twilight. The two moons hung overhead, spreading their reddish light down on the unfamiliar foliage, casting odd, dual shadows on the landscape. The trees were sparse, but Gretel had seen other areas where they were too dense to view the moons at all. Tonight, Pia was overhead, and Little Brother in front of her about ten degrees. Gretel explained that the two moons orbited the planet in a complex pattern, and were never more than nineteen degrees apart. "At times they look nearly the same size, but Pia is actually much larger. It's all actual time. They have it set to mirror what's happening near the actual Sweetland Colony."

"Colony? I thought we're supposed to be anti-colonialists."

"Think bee colony, Benson. We're not exploiters. And besides, there are no people there to colonize."

"How do you know that? Toxine just told me that they've explored only a tiny bit. What if there are people, or other intelligent beings? What if we end up being the new imperialists, Gretel?"

"Oh, Benson, you are too much of a pessimist. We go with good hearts and a sensitivity to the environment. How can that be bad?"

"Well, I don't know, Gretel. I'm just saying."

JOE DUCKED INTO THE MALL. A BRIEF ADRENAL RUSH OF FEAR gave way to the familiar clench of apprehension that always gripped him in these consumer oceans of light and mirror and flashing video monitors, singing their sirens' songs at him from every direction. How long has it been since he'd been in a mall? Seven years? Eight years? He'd forgotten what it was like to be at sea in this world of slow-motion, his senses at once foggy and heightened, everything a confusing kaleidoscopic jumble.

The Stones were singing, *because I'm free to do what I want, any old time.* The overhead lights flickered and buzzed in the background. Do OLEDs hum like mercury vapor lights? Or is it another effect? "Virgin Mobile here." The voice sudden, sexy. As he turned toward it, a pretty brown-skinned young woman twinkled at him from a vid monitor. From another direction, a suave man in an expensive suit smiled a knowing smile. *Buy her a genuine, sustainable SynDiamond. It's the contemporary way to say, I love you.* Joe turned away in retreat from the kiosks, and nearly collided with another sharply dressed man behind him.

"Hello," said the man, who looks vaguely like someone he's seen in a vid.

"Hi," Joe replied.

"My name is Michael Comstock, and I would like to make you an offer…"

Joe shook his head, walked through the holovert. Where are the *actual* people? None of the kiosks seemed staffed. Finally he saw a couple walk by, blank looks on their faces, pausing for a moment at a SmartSpot 3D product demo before wandering off to the next. He took in the closed and gated shops, some containing unsold goods heavy with dust, never fully vacated. Yet in every direction the advertisements flashed their messages. *Buy me. Buy me.*

But no one has any money, he was thinking.

"May I help you?" a short, balding young man asked the moment he walked through the door. He always hated that hard-sell come on, the way they pounced on you the instant you entered a store. But today he needed the help.

"Yeah, I want some… uh… citspecs?"

"Well," said the man, "we sell those. We have your standard plug and play mods for work and school. Of course, those will soon be obsolete. Over here we have the new stand-alone, holo display models… may I ask how you will use them?"

Joe forgot again why he came. "Sims. I need something for the sims."

"Yes, that's what they are for." The sales attendant had an annoying, patronizing tone. "You're new to this, I take it?"

"Yeah. I played at sims and role-playing games when I

was young; you know, WoW, Second Life, that sort of thing."

"Well, this is different." The attendant picked up a sleek pair of glasses like Jessie's. "Citspecs: Cyber Immersion Technology Spectacles. Instead of looking at your simulated world on a flat screen, it completely immerses you in the world. Fifteen or twenty years ago, those worlds were cartoon-like and slow to load. Technology has advanced since those times. Like I said, we have the newer holographic models. You will find yourself in a world nearly indistinguishable from the real one. They come with a variety of control devices."

"I want something maybe I could stash in a drawer at work." He gave the clerk a wink, not willing to admit that he wanted them for a date like some teenager. It just felt way too weird.

"Oh, yeah," the man said. "Not to worry. These are pretty much the standard now."

He handed Joe the citspecs.

"Where is the CPU?" Joe asked.

The man tapped the glasses in Joe's hand. "That's it. Beautiful, isn't it? The latest. High speed CPU, GPU, holographic viewer, headset, all in one gorgeous little set of sunglasses. Until you become proficient, you can control movement through the optional paw." He held up a glove that looked to Joe like one half of a pair of ordinary bicycle gloves. "But they're for training."

"Training?"

"Once the citspecs sync your nerve impulses, you use your mind and eye movement. You can ride the train, or sit on a park bench, or..." The man leaned close to Joe and dropped his voice to a whisper, "... sit in your office. With these set to transparent, no one will know you're logged into

New Life or whatever. And you need only subvocalize. The nanos read the vocal nerve synapses, translate the information into speech." He moved away and raised his voice to a normal speaking level. "The only thing more sophisticated than these babies are the ocs that the Virtuals use, the contact lens models, but they're real pricey. We don't even carry those. So, what do you think?"

"How much?" Joe asked.

"This model is three hundred and fifty bucks." Joe sighed and shook his head. He wouldn't be able to pay the rent if he spent that much.

"I can give you a subsidized model for ninety, if you don't mind a little advertising."

Joe shook his head again. No way did he want to listen to adverts. He wanted to turn and run; instead he said, "My daughter claimed she got hers for twenty bucks."

"She had one of those special coupons they've been passing out to the kids. Promo from some new Colorado simtech company."

"Sorry to waste your time." Joe reached the door, when the little man called out to him, "Tell you what, pal, I have a refurb in the back here… complete with DBT mods preinstalled, yours for just a hundred smackaroos. It's a steal. Shit, I'll go out of business if I keep doing this, but I can see you want it bad, my friend."

Joe glared at the guy. "I'm not your friend—save the show for someone who cares. I'll give you eighty."

"Sure." The man was unfazed. "You got yourself a deal."

The clerk ran his hand over his bare head as he disappeared into a back room, a gesture meant to convey that Joe had somehow gotten the best of him. He should have offered less. The clerk re-emerged with a set of citspecs and a paw identical to the ones he had just shown him.

After the iScan read Joe's info and debited his account, the clerk explained how to connect to the virtual plane and move through the overlay menus.

"It's all in the hand-eye coordination. It takes the slightest movement," he said. "These lovelies auto-detect your eye position, focus, all of that. They are MR devices. ARO and VRO menus are voice driven. ARO stands for augmented reality overlay; VRO means virtual reality overlay. ARO tells you about things in the real world, like where to find restaurants, their ratings, and so on. VRO allows you to do things like teleport and, of course, you can see others' stats, just like in AR mode."

"How do I talk? I suppose it reads my mind, too." The man smiled at Joe's sarcasm.

"Subvocalize. Standard vopro commands. Play around with them, then adjust the settings to suit yourself. Any problems, just come back in and I'll give you some pointers. Oh, and you might get a little disoriented the first time in. It's not like looking at a screen—or even like the old-style immersives. The graphics surround you, lifelike, like you're actually there inside. Can almost make you forget who and where you are. And then there's the special nanotech."

"Special nanotech?" asked Joe.

"Yeah," the clerk said, "these new mods… they suppress bodily needs like pissing. And it kind of numbs you. Physically, that is, so you get the illusion you're not in your own body. Like some drugs do, you know. And a few programmers are adding things like smell and taste and so on. Spooks out a lot of virgins. That's why I'm warning you."

Joe walked out of the store feeling uneasy, half-certain that he had done something stupid. Too much money for fun and games. Yet he'd probably do it again. He was tired of being the only adult with whom he ever spent any personal time.

But he hadn't counted on this nanotech bonus. All we needed was one more thing to numb us to the world.

AN URBAN SLUM RES'D AROUND CLAIRE DELUNA, VIRTUAL trash in the gutters, digital weeds breaking through the asphalt, no toilet or dressing room here to make your entrance—perhaps that was a statement in itself. An eight-foot wooden wall proclaimed "Viva la Revolución," in huge graffiti-style letters. A mural on the stucco building depicted peasants in a field at the edge of a huge, green forest. On the building's window, hand-painted, *"El Templo de la Vida Nueva"* and the address, *54 Calle Tierradulce.*

Some sort of bookstore, from the look of it. If a person didn't know the staggering bandwidth behind this sim, it might not impress them. But the art was good. Very good, even. Looking in the window, it just seemed so simple. Inside, an avatar—human or bot, she couldn't tell—sat behind a small desk in the corner, appearing to read a book. In the center of the room, rows of bookshelves, about chest high, held a wide variety of titles.

She stepped inside, the door triggering the sound of an old-fashioned bell. She wandered over to the shelves and browsed, attempting to be nonchalant. Next to religious texts stood classics and books about economics and left-wing political movements. Most were in English or Spanish, but she also recognized Portuguese, French, Italian, and

German. She saw a Quaker guide to consensus decision-making, books about simple living, organic agriculture, and appropriate technology. The few books dealing with religion were all over the map.

She approached the desk where a young female persona emerged over the top of her book, serious and unsmiling.

"*Hola,*" the persona said. "*Puedo ayudarle?*"

"*Inglés, por favor?*"

"Yes? May I help you?" The accent originated somewhere in New York, so she guessed an actual person, although not necessarily.

"Do you have any information on Sweetland?"

"Sorry. Normally, we would send people into the Temple to answer your questions. But I'm afraid the sims are all down today." Was that the standard script for snooping outsiders?

"Do you have any books about Sweetland?"

"Sorry. Nothing remaining on Sweetland, per se. Just what you see there."

"Is anyone here who can talk to me about it?"

"I haven't been, myself. I'm staying behind. But Brother Dave is available for an appointment, if you like."

"Yes, please."

Could it be as easy as that? This made little sense—there had to be higher wall to climb than simply asking for an appointment. Wouldn't there? Was this all a wild goose chase?

The woman remained silent for a moment, scrutinizing Claire, before she said, "Brother Dave can see you next Monday at eleven."

She handed Claire a virtual address. "Be prepared to make First Crossing soon, if that's your intent. There's only a few more weeks."

The woman made a chopping motion with her hand. Claire nodded, although she hadn't a clue what that gesture signified. The *Gran Rupture*, perhaps?

"I'm jealous," Maxi said with a wink upon her return to the office. "You were just probed big time, darling. Pretty sophisticated dildo, too. I'm afraid they might know a bit more about you than you wanted to reveal."

"Shit. The Bols, you think?"

"Might be, hon. The tech is deeper than anything we've encountered before."

"Damages?"

"They may know your ID isn't legit. They may not trust you now."

"Hell, Maxi. What kind of shit have I gotten myself into?"

"Don't know, darlin', but I suggest caution."

"Okay, Max. I'm calling it a day."

Her first thought was to zone back to the pit, as if that might be a safe place to run. Not from the Bols or whoever, but from herself. She was making too many fucking mistakes. But the thought of her trashed out apartment depressed her.

Jasper, on the other hand, was always good for a laugh.

Eastside JavaWorld had a dark, calm ambiance. The java wasn't as good as François's, but it felt safer here, somehow less conspicuous. They didn't carry real coffee here, but Joe couldn't afford that, anyway. Most of the customers were talking on some device or another. Near the door, a handsome couple sat across the table from one another, each talking to someone else, somewhere else. A young man in the corner wore citspecs, like those Joe just purchased. He wouldn't be conspicuous here. He felt as though he were an old man, or someone caught in a time warp, not a thirty-eight-year-old living in the twenty-first century. "Technology will do that to you," he remembered his dad saying, completely serious. "It turns the world upside-down at a constantly increasing rate until it makes you crazy. A person can't keep up with this pace for an entire lifetime." He had laughed at his dad for being a fogey back then.

Joe ordered decaf java and sat as far as possible from another human. He put on the citspecs and touched the tiny button on the inside of the frame and waited while the glasses scanned his iris and adjusted to his eyes. The initial sensation was a bit like the first time he had been under a strobe light, a visual stuttering, a queasy feeling in his gut. Then a slow, creeping loss of sensation beginning in his extremities and moving toward his torso, like a massive shot of Novocain. A trip to the dentist, complete with nitrous oxide. He had just been transported to another world, and if it weren't for the disconnect between the intellectual awareness of his sitting body and this vague formless place where he stood, he might have believed it. He envisioned hundreds of nanobots running around in his brain with their white smocks and pocket protectors, flipping switches, engineering the desired responses.

In a moment, the formlessness became a room, very plain, with a door in one wall and a window, complete with a beautiful mountain view, and decorated with a simple table and a few chairs. A woman–or avatar–stood before him, a dark-haired beauty with silky black hair, wearing a sari.

"Welcome to your WorldsVision home. I am Kali, your concierge." Her sultry voice revealed a slight Indian accent. "I am here to serve you. I can perform many functions, such as teleport you to your choice of destination, or help you with your settings and view modes. I can also answer questions about your current sim. My programmers have named me Kali, but you may choose a name, voice, and personality to your liking. You may also change my appearance. We have several pre-designed concierge packages. I can model them if you like."

"Kali, you will be fine."

"Thank you. What is your name, please?"

"Joe," he said. "Don't you know that already—from my iris scan?"

"Oh, no, that information is not available to me. Your privacy is protected that way."

Joe laughed. Privacy? He had privacy? In what universe? Then, it occurred to him she wanted an inworld handle, not his actual name.

"What is your last name, please?"

Joe froze. What name should he use? Was a last name required? "Just Joe," he said at last.

"All right," said Kali. "Your name is Joe Justjoe. Is this correct?"

Joe chuckled. "No… uh… yeah. Correct." Why not?

"Good, Joe Justjoe. Would you like me to call you Joe Justjoe, or just Joe?"

He laughed. "Joe, Joe Justjoe, I don't care."

He pulled the citspecs down on his nose and peered over the top. He must sound like a crazy man, alone, laughing with an invisible friend. But no one was paying the slightest attention to him. He pushed them back into place.

"All right, Joe Justjoe," said Kali. "Your WorldsVision citspecs are now digitally locked to your iris scan. No one else can use them and compromise your security. Remember, when away from your WorldsVision home, use standard Vopro to communicate, just as though you were speaking to a pitter device."

"Pitter?" Joe asked.

"A pitter is one who lives and works in the pit, Joe."

"The pit?"

"The real world, Joe. In Gridspeak we call it the pit."

"So I have to learn a whole new language, now?"

"There are certain common phrases; you'll learn them quickly. Now, before exploring the sims, I would suggest that you may wish to sign up for an avatar, and get a decent body on you. It is the polite thing to do."

For the first time Joe noticed his digital hands and realized they were a featureless, monochrome gray. "Do I need to sign up or something?"

"Your device ID has been recorded in the government data base and tied to your iris scan. Everyone who is important knows who you are, Joe. One more thing, Joe: protocol. There are restrooms and privy closets everywhere. I strongly recommend you change and zone to other locations in private, so as not to interrupt the aesthetic. ITA, as we call it, is a no-no here. We socially frown upon the destruction of another's illusion of reality.

"Now, shall I introduce you to New Life, Joe?"

☼

GRETEL AND BENSON MET UP WITH CEDAR AND POX AT THE *Fontaine St Michel* in Old Paris. After Gretel made introductions, the four of them walked toward Boulevard Sainte-Germaine, urged on by Pox. "Let's go down toward the *Pont-de-Sully,*" he said. "The water in the Seine could use some finessing. I'd like to check it out."

Gretel laughed. "I hope you're not going to fix it now."

Pox snorted. "Of course not. I don't have access to the code, although I suppose it's all open source. I might work on it later when I have a few minutes. Maybe tonight."

"Pox, you're hopeless," said Cedar. "There's no time for that, anyway. We'll be on Sweetland in a few weeks. And this sim will be gone."

"Yeah, forgot about that." Pox grinned.

Old Paris was one of several Grid recreations of the city before the fascist dirty-bomb attack in destroyed its cultural center in '25. The following year, a massive storm flooded the Metro and left much of the city under water for weeks. All that remained in the real world was an unrecognizable ruin, and a city too socially, environmentally and economically dysfunctional to heal itself.

This simulation of Old Paris went back to the historical times of The Paris Commune. "Drowned Cities of the World" was one of many projects taken on by the International Federation of Digital Artists, or IFDA, and lovingly remade on the Grid. It was an act of generosity, taking thousands of donated hours by hundreds of volunteers. Most of the IFDA sims were on servers in Bolivarian South America, removed from the world of the transnational corporations. They had become increasingly popular with millions who had grown weary of the inescapable commercial messages beamed from every street corner in New Life.

The sim bustled with activity. As they danced along the boulevard, they met others dancing and singing and engaged in deep conversation. It felt like the beginning of a celebration. Everyone, it seemed, had turned up on the Boulevard today. From a window came the tune of an old song of the Italian Partisans and the popular English lyrics from The Turn:

> The world is waking outside my window,
> Bella ciao, bella ciao, bella ciao ciao ciao,
> Drags my senses into the sunlight
> For there are things that I must do

The Gran Rupture would soon shake the real world. The entire system was going down, and Gretel almost regretted that it would take place without her. But she couldn't possibly be present. First Crossing was coming, and then they'd all be in Sweetland.

The idea of it frightened her a bit. When Final Crossing came, the work would be difficult and physically hard—harder than she'd ever worked before. Everything would have to be done by hand: planting and harvesting, making clothing. She could see how difficult it will be. An entire society had to be built. People would die in the harsh climate of a new planet with few cities and no infrastructure. But she would have Mel and her other friends; they'd keep each other strong. And maybe her dad would see the light before it was too late.

The brave ones, she told herself, were these staying behind to fight so that their comrades could begin the New World.

The four of them danced down the street singing, at the top of their voices,

> Next time you see me I may be smiling
> Bella ciao, bella ciao, bella ciao ciao ciao
> I'll be in prison or on your tv
> I'll say, the sunlight dragged me here!

Gretel grabbed Benson by the hand and swung her pinwheeling down the cobbled avenue until she was giddy with laughter and almost collided with two jugglers performing in front of a fountain. The two friends stopped there to chat while waiting for Pox and Cedar to catch up. Nearby, a young man pontificated about the sins of consumerism, with the typical sardonic humor of the Sorbonne students. The Sorbonne and *Universidad Simón Bolívar* had a tradition of amiable competition, but the Sorbonne possessed a *joie de vivre* lacking elsewhere. But they would, wouldn't they? Paris was a tradition you'd just have to live up to, even if it had never been real. And like Pox always said, "Who's to say, really?"

GARISHLY LIT WITH ORGANICS, THE NEW LIFE EMPORIUM appeared to be an old-time saloon. The technological advances in organic light-emitting diodes—OLEDs—had allowed the city to become brighter for a fraction of the electricity it once consumed. But it took oil shortages and an economic collapse to get the politicians to force the switch to organics. Now every dying business district had the look of the Las Vegas strip. Inside the smoky, dimly lit club, young people filled the cafe tables, most wearing citspecs. It reminded Joe of an old black-and-white photo from the

1950s he had seen once in a magazine—rows of movie-goers with 3D glasses. A young hostess greeted him and asked if he would like to be seated.

"I'm looking for some friends," he said. "Kerenskaya."

"Yes, the Kerenskaya party is in the Moroccan Room. Follow me."

She led him through the maze of tables and he realized that the smokiness was an illusion, some sort of fog device, while any actual smoke was being vented out somewhere. She held aside a curtain, and they passed through a dark entryway. Once inside, he could make out a series of stalls in the shadows. Instead of cafe booths, Persian rugs and pillows covered the floor; in the center of each nook a hookah gave the place the ambiance of an Arabian hashish parlor.

The hostess led him to a stall near the back of the room where he saw Anya sitting with two other women. Joe thanked the hostess as Anya rose to her feet and gave him a hug. "Hi, Joe. It's so good to see you outside of work."

"Yeah, Anya," he said. "Guess it's about time."

"Joe, I want you to meet Sam and Allison." His eyes had adjusted now to the darkness, and Joe could make out the two women now standing next to Anya. A beautiful, dark-skinned woman put her arm around Anya. The other woman was pretty, with long, black hair, dressed in turn-of-the-century retro, complete with the nerd glasses. Her smile was engaging. But something about it, maybe the hipster smirk leaking out the edges, put Joe on alert.

"Joe Larivee," said Anya, squeezing her partner, "this is Samantha Roberge."

Samantha smiled. "Nice to meet you, Joe."

"You too, Samantha."

"And this," Anya said, nodding toward the other woman, "is Allison Marquam."

Allison stepped forward and hugged him. "Nice to meet you, Joe."

"You too, Allison." She moved back and flashed him a sardonic smile.

They all took their places around the hookah, Anya and Samantha on one side, holding hands, Joe opposite Anya, and Allison curled up next to him, close enough that he could smell the faint scent from her hair.

"What's in the hookah?" he asked.

"That's right," said Anya. "Joe hasn't been here before. Joe, this is the smoke of the gods. You must try it."

Joe hesitated. He hadn't been stoned since before Jessie was born. Back when smoking pot was risky and employers tested your piss or hair to find out if you had been naughty. Joe normally abstained from intoxicating substances other than an occasional beer, clinging to a vague fear that he might lose the little control he had over his life. But as he watched the lovers across from him and listened to the quiet, seductive conversation drifting over from a group in the next stall, temptation overcame him—let the night take him where it would. He grabbed one of the mouth pieces and sucked the sweet hashish smoke into his lungs, feeling a sense of peace as the world slowed down around him.

"Allison is a Creative Marketing Specialist," said Anya. "She works for The Tollgate Group. We've been friends since college."

"Creative Marketing Specialist?" Joe echoed.

"That's a fancy name for an advertising flunky." Allison laughed.

"Actually," said Anya, "Allison is being modest. She's on the design team for Tollgate's New Life account."

"Oh." Joe felt out of his league. "So, you help make those ads, like the ones on the intersection billboards?"

"My team creates those ads," said Allison, "but most of my work is online, keeping the brand name out front. New Life is what we call a 'Love Brand.'" The words came out of her lips with a sexual overtone, and the way she smiled at Joe, and looked into his eyes when she said it, left him flushed. "Those are brands consumers fall in love with, that connect with them on some deep subconscious level. Love brands sell themselves, because people will advertise them for free, talk their friends into purchasing them. They are brands you must have to be glitch. You know, cool. New Life is a love brand in the fullest sense."

"I'm afraid I'm a bit of a noob at New Life," Joe admitted.

Allison smiled. "A pitter, huh? Don't worry, Joe. I'm the very best guide you could have." Her hand moved, for just an instant, to rest on Joe's thigh. "The performance is about to begin at the Amphitheater on Prosperity. What's your inworld name, Joe?"

"Joe Justjoe," he said.

She laughed. "I love it. I'm known as Lindsay Lane. I'll send you a teleport invitation online. Now, we should all don our citspecs, brave ones, and go forth into the unknown."

JOE FOUND HIMSELF STANDING AT A URINAL. HAD HE LANDED in the wrong place? Then someone appeared beside him and Joe followed him out of the restroom into a large arena.

The first thing he noticed was the dust, the way it billowed up around his feet when he walked. The stonework of the Amphitheater held amazing detail, not just a series of tiled images as he had expected, but each stone individual, with dozens of facets, each meticulously and uniquely textured. If he touched them, would they be cold and hard and real? Not just an image, but a solid thing? The night sky was clear and filled with stars, and the pampas grass near him moved ever so slightly in a non-existent breeze. The eerie realism left him feeling anxious. How was it that a world which could no longer afford to feed and shelter people could construct an illusion like this?

Boisterous and festive, the tightly packed crowd chattered and laughed. How would he find his friends? Nearby, a pretty blond looked him over, assessing him. Her appearance reminded him of the images of women in the popular magazines, the latest romantic styles, with a pinch of the girl-next-door, a dash of the edgy artiste, a subtle concoction. He smiled at her.

"Joe Justjoe." She performed a dramatic curtsy. "Lindsay Lane."

"Nice to meet you, Lindsay Lane." He smiled at her. "Where are our companions?"

"I think they decided to sit separately. We'll hook up again, afterwards."

"Oh," he said. Did that sound like a complaint?

"Do I hear hesitation?" A soft hand touched his knee. He looked down and saw nothing, of course, because the touching was happening somewhere else, in another plane of existence.

"No, no. Just unexpected is all."

She took his hand and led him through the crowd. How did she do that? He made a note to ask her about it later. Finally they arrived at a quiet little nook, a private viewing area.

"Sit," she commanded.

"Don't we have to pay, or something?" he asked as he lowered himself into a seat.

"Complimentary tickets. My team organized this little event."

"I'm impressed." It relieved him that he didn't have to pay for what had looked like a very expensive night out. The cost of the citspecs was already more that he could afford. "So, how did you recognize me?"

"I had my concierge identify you. Learn to use your concierge. They can do amazing things. VR isn't as transparent as it used to be in the old days. The sim worlds have become more realistic. The old floating menus detract from the aesthetic. And the world is a little more exciting with some anonymity, anyway. So go into private mode and ask your concierge if you need to find out about things."

The band tuned up their instruments, and Joe leaned back and peered at the stars.

"Aren't they beautiful?" asked Lindsay.

"Not as beautiful as the real thing." He recalled summer trips to Central Oregon as a child. "In the desert, the stars seem to go on forever, and they have a depth you just can't recreate. You can smell the sage and feel the cool air on your skin. It's magic, really."

He felt her hand slide up his thigh. He reached toward her, in that other plane where he was Joe Larivee, but Joe Justjoe went flying and landed on his face. Lindsay laughed. "I'm sorry," she said, after catching her breath. "Let me teach you how to use those things."

Joe was embarrassed and had a sudden urge to flight. "I'm pretty clumsy."

"It's okay. It's always awkward at first." He could feel her body move against his. "Have your concierge put Joe in pose mode and take off your paw."

He followed her directions and found that he now had freedom to move his hands. He put his arm around her.

"There, that's better," she said. "This will all be much easier and way more pleasant when they program more of the sims for the DBT mods. Coming soon to a venue near you."

☼

CLAIRE DELUNA FOUND HERSELF SITTING ON A SQUEAKY barstool at The Downbeat, fiddling with the straw in her vodka cran. In the background, an acoustic blues band played a slow, dreamy number. Jasper eyed her. "You ready for another one of those, sweet cakes?"

Claire giggled. She couldn't help herself. She always giggled like a girl whenever the make-believe bartender asked if she wanted a make-believe drink.

"What's so funny, Ms Deluna?" he asked. He always asked it in exactly the same way.

"All of it, Jasper. The whole damned ridiculous idea of it. You know what I mean? Grown-up people playing dolls for a living. Jesus Christ, it's funny."

"Yeah, it's pretty funny all right." Jasper gave a brief, reserved laugh as he turned to serve a customer at the far end of the bar. Claire admired the neat rows of vintage liquor bottles artfully lined up on the shelf as she watched Jasper go through his routines, dutifully wiping down the counter with a bar rag and chatting up customers. All perfect, all so disney.

A typical weeknight crowd had been filling up the place until the steady drone of conversation morphed into something more boisterous. Claire leaned back on her barstool, eyeing a boisterous new group of patrons. They were definitely not her type. The males were too male, the females too girlie for her taste.

Claire looked longingly around the dark room. The type of guys she liked rarely hung out in places like this—at least, not alone. She wasn't sure what that type of man looked like, but he wasn't a cartoon football player; just a plain guy, maybe a little geeky, the type of guy you might meet at an art gallery or the library. Someone you could actually talk to about things that mattered. Now that was *sexy*.

"So, Jasper," she said, turning back to the bar, "you mind if I query your database?"

"That's what I'm here for, sweet cakes," said Jasper.

"Do you know anything about religions?" she asked.

"You mean, can I quote a passage out of the Qur'an?" he said, "Or do I believe in the hereafter? Something like that?"

"No," Claire laughed, "nothing like that. What do you know about a group called the Temple of New Life?"

"Oh, I had someone in here once, was really into that stuff. She thought I was an actual person, I think, because she wanted to convert me, lead me to salvation. It seems they believe that Paradise is somewhere in New Life. Crazy, huh?"

"Yeah, that's pretty crazy, all right."

"Not much different from any other religion. Not as far as I can see. But, there was one thing… she said that she had actually been there. She said that her earthly body would die when she returned to Sweetland."

There it was again. Sweetland. "Do you have any idea what this Sweetland could be, if it's not Heaven or something?"

"You know, there was once speculation about mapping human consciousness, digitizing it, uploading human minds to some kind of storage device on the Grid."

"I find it hard to get my head around that concept, Jasper. Another planet seems more likely."

"Maybe it's a sim where they fool actual people into leaving their corporeal bodies behind."

"A suicide cult, you think?" whispered Claire.

"I wouldn't know about that kind of thing," said Jasper.

"Thanks, Jasp."

She recalled Jasper's story and the information Maxi had dug up. It was horribly disturbing, but what did this have to do with Futures? And how was she going to figure out what was relevant in this Sweetland business? She thought about this until her exhausted mind drifted back to the couples who had walked in earlier. She eyed them curiously, loneliness seizing her. She turned back to the bar to see Jasper gazing at her. "See the dude at the table by the jukebox?" He nodded toward the opposite wall.

Reading her mind again. She had already checked the guy out. "Looks gay. And who hired you as my pimp?"

Jasper laughed. "Well, he hasn't been looking at the boys in the band all evening."

"Are you sure you're just an AI, Jasper? I swear there's intelligence behind those pixels."

"AI means Artificial *Intelligence*, sweet cakes."

"Maybe they forgot to tell you, Jasper," said Claire, "but you're just a program."

"Pretty damned sophisticated program, if I may say so myself."

Claire laughed. "Got me there, Jasp." She glanced back toward the man by the juke. "So, send my gay friend one on me."

. . .

TWO HOURS LATER, CLAIRE ROLLED OUT OF BED, LANDING on the floor. Damn, she said under her breath. Going smoothly from horizontal to vertical was one thing she hadn't yet mastered after seven years in VR. She noted the opulence of his bedroom with indifference. Satin and mirrors and walnut tables. Sex toys lined up on an intricately carved, oak shelf. A self-styled playboy's mansion. With a touch, she put her clothes back on and gazed at the avi laying on the bed. How natural his skin looked. The color of his arm, so much like the color of light, reflected off an actual man's arm. He almost looked like a real man, stretched across the sheets, but she could tell by the vacant stare that his master had checked out, gone to wash up or something. She had already forgotten his name. No need to say goodbye. That was the agreed etiquette. Some people had a ritual with these things, down to make-believe post-coital cigarettes. But, it was just mutual masturbation, after all, with someone who might be on the other side of the planet for all she knew.

Bridge Whitedeer ran her hand along the inside of her thigh, a little quiver of pleasure from one last long caress before she zoned and transluced. She picked up a cup of tea she had placed on the little wood table next to her Murphy bed before leaving The Downbeat and took a sip. It was cold. Cyber sex might be better than the real thing, she thought. At least, while you are having it. You don't have to worry about disease, or awkward goodbyes, or clumsy men who can't find the right spot. It was just the other side of it. The coming down; feeling how fucking alone you are in your tiny studio apartment; lying with your own shadow in the dark.

☼

THE BAND BEGAN, AND JOE FELT ODDLY AT EASE WITH Allison curled up in his arms. The music had an ethereal quality, and it accentuated an odd duality that was playing in his mind: this thing going on under the covers and this thing on the surface, this concert where Joe Justjoe, the actor, sat next to the beautiful woman, Lindsay Lane; and the Moroccan Room at The New Life Emporium, where a party of friends reclined around a hookah, wearing black glasses. He noticed the inverted reality. It was like those touchy-feely games teenagers played behind blindfolds. He felt a lot like a teenager at the moment. And was he supposed to pretend afterwards that it was nothing? Just a little anonymous petting?

Joe examined the exquisite creation beside him. Lindsay Lane was glamorous, the sort of woman, if she had been an actual woman, who wouldn't give someone like him a second glance in actual life. He didn't think that he was Allison Marquam's type either. Why would a successful marketing professional want to hook up with a lowly social worker? It mystified him. He wondered if he wasn't perhaps a customer research specimen, when Lindsay turned to him and met his eyes. Her gaze lingered there for a moment before she leaned over and kissed him. In perfect synchronization, Allison's moist lips touched his, and her warm tongue slipped into his mouth. He responded by letting go of his inhibitions, attacking her mouth like a starving man. With his free hand, he ran his fingers over her breasts, and down the length of her body.

He gasped as they came up for air. "How did you do that?"

"Like this." She repeated the kiss, and when it was over, they caressed one another until his heart rate slowed back to something like normal. "It's Geo-positioning," she said. "It only works with the kisses, so far, not the hands. I told my concierge to sync Lindsay to Joe, so when I move my citspecs toward you, and turn my head like this...." She demonstrated by kissing him again, a little less intensely this time. "... then Lindsay moves in tandem. You see?"

"Not quite. Show me one more time."

THROUGH THE REST OF THE CONCERT, JOE AND ALLISON reposed on their pillows, entwined, kissing occasionally. By some unspoken mutual agreement, they kept the heat down and the kisses became less passionate. The band finished its last song to a standing ovation that turned into a stomping demand for an encore. The audience chanted, "Sweetland. Sweetland. Sweetland." After a long pause the band returned to the stage, and the stage lights came back up, revealing a giant backdrop: "Sweetland. Why not?"

"Thank you. Thank you. My name is Leder Baat, and we are Sweetland, playing for you tonight at New Life Stadium." The audience stood in rousing applause, and the tall, imposing Baat took a deep bow.

As the cheers died down, there was a sudden motion on the catwalks above. The audience looked up as two figures dropped a banner in front of the backdrop. *Resist the Police State.* Gasps. Someone shouted, "Right on," and a small cheer went up, but most of the audience was nervous. Just as suddenly as they had appeared, the banner and the two figures vanished. Leder Baat grabbed the mike from the stand and yelled into it, "They won't ruin our fun, will they?" About half the audience roared back, shoving their fists in the air. The rest were eerily silent. "That's so rude. Am I right? Let's all get along tonight. How about it?" A small, half-hearted cheer arose. "Now, the boys and I are going to close with a song that's become a sort of anthem for us. This'll help to balance things out, remind us why we're here. One, two, three, four…"

Guitar power chords blasted out an explosion of sound. Silence. Then, the song began with quiet phrases, building into an anthemic chorus:

> Sweet land of promise
> Where hope, like a river
> Flows through my dreams
> Sweet land of my dreams.

The audience went wild. Joe couldn't tell what the fuss was about. As far as he could see, they were pretty ordinary musicians. Competent, but bland and commercial.

Somewhere near the end of the performance, Allison disengaged. "You've been a great audience," the lead singer said, "we hope we've taken you to Sweetland tonight."

Lindsay smiled at Joe as the last squeal of guitar feedback faded. "Enjoy the concert?"

"It was fun, but I still feel awkward with all of this."

Lindsay laughed. "You'll get the hang of it, Joe. It's called sync dating. This is how it's done, now. It's time to rejoin Anya and Sam, don't you think?"

JOE REMOVED HIS CITSPECS. ANYA AND SAM HAD ALREADY discon'd, and Allison was sitting beside him, her nerd glasses back on, just as she had been when they started their journey. The women were all looking at him expectantly.

"Wow, that's some good smoke."

"What did you think of the band?" said Anya.

"They were okay. A little too slick for my taste."

"Yeah," said Samantha. "Pretty ordinary, really."

Allison laughed. "Yeah, but they're hot. And they're rising on the charts. That's what counts."

Joe couldn't tell if she was serious or being sarcastic. The women all laughed, and Joe felt as though he was on the outside of some inside joke.

"What was that banner thing at the end?" Joe said. "That was pretty gutsy."

"Oh, nothing to get excited about," said Allison. Did she wink when she said that? "Just some malcontents. Disruptors. Happens all the time." Anya and Samantha looked at each other with a slight smile on their faces.

Anya leaned over the hookah toward Joe. "That was Sam and I."

"But, Anya, it's dangerous."

Anya put her finger to her lips, signing silence, and grinned at at Joe.

"So, Allison," said Anya, changing the subject, "tell us all about your work with New Life. What are you up to these days?"

Allison pushed her glasses up on her nose with her forefinger, and looked at Anya. "Well, you know, Anya, I can't talk about the confidential stuff. But I can give you a general idea. You know what I said earlier about Love Brands? There's another aspect of New Life as a brand that's problematic. We call it The Coke Syndrome. It's what happens when your brand becomes the generic name for all similar products. Like Coke. Fifty years ago, 'Let's go get a Coke' came to mean, 'Let's get a soft drink.' In an environment like that, the name Coke loses meaning, and an opening occurs for competitors to exploit. Along comes The Pepsi Generation, and your market share slips. So you have to remind consumers that your product is 'The Real Thing.' You create Coke Classic to recall the mythical good old days.

"That's where New Life is right now. It's losing its identity, its cachet. When people say 'New Life,' they mean the Grid. But the Grid is like the generic 'soft drink.' It is a vast, worldwide network of interconnected–and competing–entities. Stepping across the border is effortless. Competing against New Life are dozens of up-and-comers, some of which are poised to conquer the market. My job is to prevent that."

"And how do you do that?" asked Joe.

"Sweetland," said Allison.

"Sweetland? What is it?"

"A year ago," said Allison, her voice lowered to just above a whisper, "no one had ever heard of Sweetland. Now, everyone is using it. One of our cool-hunters picked the term up in Rio. Tierra Dulce. Everybody down there was using it. It's like Nirvana, a mythical place, a synonym for paradise and coolness and getting high. It's dying and going to heaven. And it's tied to the New Life brand. We own the copyright and trademark. I'm a proud soldier in the ultimate guerrilla marketing campaign."

"Some kids talk as though it's an actual place."

"That's the beauty of it. People believe it's real, because they want it to be real. Just like people believe in the afterlife."

"Don't you think that could be harmful? Like false hope."

"Is there any other kind?" said Allison.

"There is no such thing as a free lunch."
— *Barry Commoner*

JOLENE CHENG, AKA SUATO2, BURIED HERSELF IN A BOOK as she waited for her daughter to arrive for lunch. She had mastered the art of waiting. In five years, she had risen from a mere clerical to number two in the unit. Her secret was patience. And she knew when to make her move. She wouldn't be in the Department at all if she hadn't jumped and left her loser of a husband when she did, and this girl he had wrapped around his finger. She never missed an opportunity. You miss the limo, you get left on the street, it's as simple as that. She learned it as a kid fighting for scraps at a table with too many hungry siblings.

Patience and allies. After she and her sisters turned the tables on their big brother, Dwight, she learned the value of allies and finely tuned rage. She was only seven, and he was already bullying her on the way to school. "I think it's about time you started sharing your sandwich with me, Jo." He grabbed her lunch from her hands, and she flew at him in a rage. "Give me my lunch, Dwight. I'm going to tell." Dwight just laughed and pushed her into the mud. Her mother's reaction was to tell them both to stop bickering. So, that's how it is, she learned, the biggest cat gets the meat.

Until the girls got desperate. It wasn't going hungry at

school that pulled them together. It was what happened in the dark. After all these years, Jolene still felt a thrill of power when she thought about how they put a stop to him. Together. They had fixed Dwight good, she and her sisters. Society was another unruly house, full of brawling children clawing each other over bullshit. Jolene knew how to apply discipline and that required knowing who you were dealing with.

She read her book intently, a Spanish-language primer on class dynamics in post-industrial society. She believed in the adage, 'know your enemy.' This was one of the best books available on current Bolivarian thinking. The DHS upper brass had a tendency to see everything as some sort of international chess match, relying on the tech boys to keep them on the cutting edge. But the tech had failed them so far; it hadn't been capable of outwitting the defenses of the homegrown lefty bastions, let alone enemy nations. The agency needed another approach. They had paid too little attention to the thought process of the bad guys and other subtleties which nuanced the game. They had failed to understand their opponents, who had no homogenous ideology, but a complex mixture of socialist, Zapatista-anarcho and indigenous philosophies, with a common, misguided vision of communal democracy. Misguided, she thought, because all socialist ideologies failed to consider the selfish nature of humanity. Selfishness encouraged the industrious to rise to the top when given the freedom to do so. The price of socialism was stifled greatness.

She looked up from her book to see the girl arrive. SUATO2 studied Gretel deVoid with interest, noting the cropped black hair with a streak of glowing blue and old-fashioned goth makeup. The avi looked like the generic, standard issue. Of course, the fourteen-year-old daughter of a social worker wouldn't be able to afford anything more sophisticated. Gretel wore layers of disparate clothing styles that reminded her of her own youth. In fact, she looked like an odd mixture of subcultures from The Turn. The change of the millennium had taken on a kind of mythical quality among various groups of youth, some of whom looked upon it as the awakening of society to its desperate situation, and by others as a type of mystical dawning of a new age.

"Mom," said Gretel, "sorry I'm late. I was skating with friends and lost track of time."

"No problem," said SUATO2. "I had something to read."

Gretel looked at the book cover. "Morales. I read that for one of my classes."

"They're teaching this stuff in high school, now?"

"I'm going to *Universidad Simón Bolívar*."

"Oh my, you're a college girl."

"Well, not exactly. I've just been taking a few classes inworld. In preparation."

"For Sweetland?"

"Yeah," said Gretel. "They want us kids to have a basic understanding of science and philosophy. It's a kind of scholarship. I'll enroll in classes full time once I'm there."

"I'm impressed," said Su. "You know, of course, that the Bolivarian States are our country's enemy?"

"We're not at war with them, now," said Gretel, "that's the past."

"True, but our current government doesn't see things that way."

"The current government is a bunch of fascist pigs," shot Gretel. Su could hear the nasty edge of anger in her daughter's voice. Time to back off.

"So, tell me about Sweetland. Does it have anything to do with all of this advertising I see?"

"No, I don't think so. That's corporate bullshit."

Su regarded her daughter thoughtfully. "So, Sweetland is a community somewhere, you said?"

"Yes, it's in South America somewhere."

"And your dad is going, too?"

"Yeah."

"So, how long before you leave?"

"Three weeks."

"So soon?" She put her hand over Gretel's. "Can we do this again in a week, sweetheart? I have to leave now for an important meeting."

"I just got here," Gretel snapped.

"This is Monday. It's a workday. If you hadn't been late, we would have had more time." Su heard the scolding mother in her voice and changed tones. "Look, this is all new and tough on both of us, so let's take it slow, okay?"

Gretel's angry stare softened to a mild scowl. "Same place?"

"Same place," Su replied.

BRIDGE STARED OUT HER WINDOW, DEPRESSED, YET UNABLE, unwilling to jack back into her hardware dopamine fix. New Life was no longer an escape from the sadness of the world. Her profession had always been a game, but now the game spilled over into the real lives of innocent everyday people, and Bridge didn't know if she was ready to face what she knew was true but could never acknowledge, that there were actual human beings behind most of those avies, made of flesh and blood and bones. It's hard when the ones you do business with day after day are criminals; the corporate criminals and the syndicate criminals, the Mr Bigshots and the Mickey Nines. Now fourteen-year-olds were dying in Albuquerque warehouses, and something tied it to this game of New Life.

Her brain could burst into a million tiny fragments at any moment. She folded her skinny legs beneath her body in a full lotus and attempted to center herself by chanting a mantra she had learned from Vandi, her Hindu friend from the Self-Help Center, one of the few places in the pit she frequented. She sang the hypnotic syllables, repeating them over and over until the tension eased and her body relaxed. Allowing the mantra to fade, she began the visualization. She recalled the forest, remembering the green luscious undergrowth, a deer trail winding around the slope of a hill, a small brook nearby, singing its water song, like a lullaby from her childhood.

Dad and Mom are walking with her. Johnny Whitedeer carrying a red and white blanket and a large thermos bottle, leading the way. His wife Molly following with the picnic basket. Bridge chattering, like eight-year-olds do.

"Hush." Dad puts his finger to his lips in a shushing motion. He kneels on the path and crooks his finger at her. He raises his forefinger to his lips again and shows her the track on the trail. "Big game." Bridge can see her father made the impression from the knuckles of his hand. But the fun is in the pretending.

"We must be very quiet, so we don't scare it away. I'll go ahead and see if I can scout it. If I'm not back by the time you count to thirty, then come after me." Dad winks and hands her the blanket and thermos. Mom rolls her eyes. She has a grin on her face.

Of course, Dad would hide somewhere on the trail and Bridge would go after him. She knows this game by heart. He will hide or try to circle around behind her. But today she's determined to get him. She silently counts to thirty. Then she sets the thermos down on the path and hands the blanket to Mom.

"Dad must be in trouble," she announces. "Be right back."

As soon as she is out of her mother's sight, she veers off the trail toward the shallow creek. She skips across on the rocks and makes her way along the stream, keeping her eye on the trail above. But when a beautiful gold and black butterfly flits in front of her, she forgets and follows it, instead, transfixed by its hypnotic flight. She has lost track of the time when she hears Dad call out. "Bridge!"

She looks up, and there in the water, not fifty feet from her, stands a black bear on all fours, looking at her with curiosity. "Oh my god," she says under her breath, and backs away, ever so slowly, her heart pounding in her chest. Terror and awe at this wild creature, at least ten times her size, paralyzes her for a moment. "Hello, Mr... Mr Bear." She whimpers as she stumbles backwards, tripping over a large rock. She looks up to see the bear, startled, bounding off away from her.

A thin line of blood oozes from a long scrape on her leg. The wound stings, and she can feel the tears running down her cheek.

"Bridge." The voice of Dad from above on the trail. Then, "Bridge," again. This time Mom. She runs up the hill, crying, and the next thing she knows, Mom has her arms around her. "Did you fall, sweetie?" Bridge nods her head, wiping the tears from her eyes. "But I saw it," she reports.

"Saw what?" asks Dad.

"Saw the bear. Down on the creek. It ran away."

Mom laughs. "My big-game hunters." She elbows Dad.

Dad joins Mom's laughter. "Looks like our daughter is a real sleuth." He winks. "Must be that Indian blood in her."

When she was older, she learned her parents had never believed in her bear. Dad knew nothing about tracking animals and very little about his Salish traditions. He was a city Indian. He tried with his jokes and games to conjure a connection to the lost world of his people and identify himself somewhere within it. There was a wild emptiness inside him and it tore apart his family. The lives of Johnny and Molly Whitedeer ended in a horrible, fiery, alcoholic rage behind the wheel of his Chevy pickup truck. Bridge avoided memories of those later years. She hated that they reduced her family to a stereotype. She wanted to remember the happier times, walks in the forest, quiet picnic lunches, overnight camping trips, a world of magic before all the tragedy.

The dull, heavy sadness she always felt in the pit world overcame her. This life tired her, and she didn't want to be in the business anymore. She wanted a world that no longer existed. All left of the wilderness, all not logged off or burned or eaten by insects, were tiny patches reserved for the elites. Those with enough money to travel and to pay the huge fees meant to keep out riffraff like her.

That too would die soon, because now the world was dying. Bridge knew it in her bones.

☼

Part Three

Beneath the Surface

"Those who go beneath the surface, do so at their peril."
—Oscar Wilde, *The Picture of Dorian Gray*

"Can all you lost children hear me out there today above the jammers and security state static? The weather report is for rain 24-seven for the next few weeks—they're working OT to close us down before the really big storm blows in. So, travelers say your goodbyes, big mama is riding in from the north on blackwater. Next broadcast fourteen o'clock. You know where, now you know when. Out."
—Raven Tree Radio

Z oning back to the real world, Jolene Cheng grabbed a decorative paperweight from the end table and hurled it across her living room. It landed with a loud thud, leaving a deep impression on the surface of the drywall. Damn that girl. Why do I let her get under my skin like that?

She recalled the photo an FBI cohort in Portland had shown her. He'd taken it, along with dozens of others, while surveilling a Mayday march in the spring. "This your daughter?" he had asked her, and she hadn't been sure. The girl in the photo was a stranger, a pretty child with that mixture of innocence and defiance so common among the more intelligent youth. Jolene hadn't liked how that picture had disturbed her, and she didn't like how the meeting with Jessie today was pulling her mind away from her work.

Perhaps she needed new tactics. How had this Sweetland meme burrowed into the public psyche? It wasn't just kids like Jessie who bought into it. Whatever 'it' was. Even the Bols and other committed Politicos remained under its thrall. It wasn't just another social media meme, like those she remembered from her youth. New Life had given memes a whole new breadth. But this one felt as though it were being transmitted by the air.

Her mind wandered back to her surroundings. Beside her on the end table lay a letter, half out of the envelope, half read. A job offer from some outfit called The New America Corporation. The thick, decadent paper was a pronouncement of power. The offer attracted her, and not just because of its audacity. She needed to think about the future. With privatization coming, the world didn't require a bunch of unemployed spooks.

She leaned back in her comfortable living room chair, running her hand over the warm, supple leather, reminding herself how much she deserved the comforts she had gained. It wasn't as though she were rich, but she had a few perks of the job, certain access to confiscated property as a reward for her diligence and service to her country. She put her feet up on the ottoman. She picked up the letter and read it again. They were offering her a job as chief of security. The position promised exceptional pay, without a precise figure, but certainly much more than she made now. It included a round trip fare to St Louis for a two-week orientation and a formal offer. She tried to imagine why they might want to do that, when it could all be done inworld. The cost of flying her to St Louis would be astronomical. And the mere thought of flying made her sick to her stomach. In fact, the whole thought of spending several days in the RW gave her chills, made her think of all of those long boring days in the office after her training, meeting contacts face-to-face in their pitter bodies.

But maybe she needed to get used to that again. Maybe that was the way forward. She had vacation time, and her FBI chums in Portland could help her follow-up on this Sweetland business and monitor Jessie's involvement. She could do it inworld as easily from her own ATO office, but there was no point in alerting DHS to a family connection. It would be best to let her allies in Portland handle it—no more emotional shit mucking things up.

She didn't need to decide about the position New America Corporation was offering until the session in St Louis was over. It would be a pleasant break. Yes, that's what she'd do. She would attend their orientation and get away from this place for a while.

Now she had to call Joe. Find out what he had to say about this Sweetland business with Jessie. The idea of contacting him was repugnant. He was going to whine around and want answers. And what could she tell him that would mean anything? She had moved on from all of that, had put Joe and Jessie so far from her mind they might as well be part of someone else's past.

JOLENE SPOKE THE VOPRO COMMANDS AND WAITED FOR JOE to pick up, her thoughts focused on staying calm. Joe would push her buttons, he always did, although he didn't seem to have a clue about it. It was just the way Joe was—oblivious.

"Larivee," said the voice in her auds.

"Hello, Joe." Why did it take so much effort? The mere sound of his voice stirred up an impulse in her to scream.

"Jolene?"

"I'm calling to find out about Jessie, Joe. What's going on with her?"

"Jessie?" Joe sounded confused. "I don't understand. You've been talking to her?"

"She just blew up on me. On New Life. It was partially my fault, I admit. But what is this Sweetland thing she's talking about?"

"So, how long have you two been in touch?"

"I didn't call to chitchat, Joe. Just tell me what's going on with Jessie."

"What has she told you?"

"She said you two are going off to live in some fucking commune or something in South America?"

"Oh shit. I don't know where that idea came from, Jolene. Honestly. She's going through a lot of changes lately and acting up, but I'm sure it's all just teenage drama."

Jolene doubted it.

"You may be right, but you'd do well to see what she's up to on the Grid. Her handle is Gretel deVoid if you're ever interested in checking up on her."

"I don't really do New Life," he said. Why didn't this surprise her?

"Maybe you should think about going inworld. Try to keep up, Joe. Look, I'm leaving for St Louis, two weeks from Friday. I'm going to be out of town for a few weeks until the seventh. I'll be unreachable, but you can leave a message if you have to." She hoped she had put enough emphasis on "if you have to."

"Yeah. Thanks, Jolene."

"Goodbye, Joe."

JOE DISCON'D HIS MOBE AND STARED AT THE BLANK WALL OF his cubicle, feeling numb. Jolene was the last person on Earth he had expected to call him at work. Funny how a kid in trouble can bring the bitterest exes back together. Funny how those exes bring memories you want to forget. Memories that led down old paths of betrayal and guilt—that last day he'd seen Jolene, trying to figure out what had gone wrong, and, as always, coming back to the hard knot at the center of his being—his parents…

… APRIL EIGHTEEN, TWO THOUSAND THIRTY-ONE. MONDAY morning. Jessie is nine and in the third grade. It is seven a.m. so she is dressing for school. They are living with Frank and Amy in a much-too-small house in Montavilla. He and Jolene and Jessie. It is like an image burned into a screen for so many years that it has become as vivid as the original.

Joe and Jolene are dressing for work. He is working part

time as a clerk in a mini-mart and taking social service classes at PCC. Jolene works for the County, an administrative assistant. Frank Larivee is a free-lance programmer and hasn't had a contract for several months. Frank's wife, Amy, an accountant for most of her life, is retired. They aren't rich, but they have kept a small home when most of their acquaintances have gone bankrupt.

"Grandma, have you seen my shoes?" Jessie yells from her bedroom.

Amy Larivee sighs, then chuckles. "Have you tried looking next to the couch where you were watching television last night?"

"Oh, duh," says Jessie. She runs by Joe into the living room, carrying her pack. She finds her shoes and stops to put them on. Then, grabbing her backpack from the floor, she runs toward the door.

"Whoa, little girl," says Joe, "you forget something?"

Jessie stops and walks back to Joe. He stoops over so she can put her arms around his neck and kiss him on the cheek. "Bye, Daddy, love you."

"Bye, sweetheart, love you, too," he says as she scampers out the door.

"What's got into her this morning?" snaps Jolene.

"She's presenting her science project. The one she's been working on since January," says Joe. "Christ, Jolene. She's been talking about it for two weeks."

"I've had a lot of things on my mind, Joe," says Jolene.

"You know, Jolene, you can always talk to family about your troubles," says Amy, who stands at the kitchen door.

Jolene shoots Amy an angry look. "I don't think you would understand, Amy." She picks her purse up from the table with a terse gesture and says, "Gotta go to work." Then she is out the door, too.

Joe looks at his mom, and he can see the hurt in her eyes. There has always been tension between them. Jolene has never liked his parents. When he confronted her about it once, Jolene said, "people are just different, Joe. You don't have to like everybody."

Amy turns away, goes back to her husband, hunched over a computer in the back bedroom.

And then the doorbell rings.

That was the last time Joe saw Frank and Amy, being led out the door in handcuffs, pleading innocence, Frank demanding, "What are we being charged with? We haven't been political since Joe was born."

DHS officers took Joe to an interrogation room where they told him to sign a statement. A statement already printed out and waiting. They said, "If you want to see your little girl again...." They made it clear it was Frank and Amy, or Jessie. What choice did he have?

And Jolene? What did Jolene say when they came to her? And they must have. He never found out, because she didn't return home that day. Before her recent call, he had only talked to her twice, the first time about two years ago when she told him she now worked for *them*, the Department of Homeland Security, some bureaucratic position in Seattle. He never broached the subject of that day. He was afraid of what she might say, what he refused to believe, that Jolene had turned in Frank and Amy as part of a career move. A part of him knew Jolene was a troubled, narcissistic woman.

Frank and Amy disappeared, dead or renditioned or held in an internment camp, it hardly mattered. They were gone now. He suspected Jolene had a role in all of that, but he would never know. What he would never forgive was her abandoning Jessie without a word of explanation. And here she was again, implicitly accusing him of being a poor parent. But he wasn't a terrible father. He was only trying to do his best for his daughter. It wasn't his fault that the world was so fucked up. He blinked, and something pushed from his gut up into his chest, his throat, the space behind his eyes.

"You were born on the eve of the Turn, Joe," Amy once said to him. "It was the end of the old world and the start of a new millennium, of new possibilities. And you, Joe," said his mother, "you are the hope of this new world."

What a fucking trip to lay on a kid. Yet Joe didn't blame Amy. She had to believe in something better for her kid, and this was not the world promised to him and to his generation by the spin-masters.

BRIDGE PUSHED UP THE MURPHY BED WITHOUT BOTHERING to make it and swiveled the couch out from the wall. It came part way before stopping short. Irritated at its stubborn refusal, she pulled harder, without success. She was about to give up when she noticed a shoe jammed in the mechanism. She cursed under her breath and pushed the contraption back into the wall. As she tugged on the stuck sandal, left over from the summer, it suddenly gave way, propelling her on her ass. Her head throbbed, no doubt from yesterday's marathon inworld session, and for a long moment she just sat there, immobile. She could take something for the headache, but it would go away as soon as she zoned. It always did.

When she had the couch in place, she sat down, cradling her head in her hands. The tea water was boiling, and she had an urge to scream. Calm down. Calm down and center yourself. Take a deep breath. Take two steps across the room. Shut off the boiling water. Pour a cup of tea.

She turned off the burner and pushing aside a week's worth of dirty dishes piled on the counter, grabbed the jar of mint leaves she had collected from the neighborhood, and put two large pinches in the tea strainer, before adding another generous pinch of St John's Wart. She poured the boiling water over the leaves, recalling a time when the kettle whistled and how handy that had been.

Bridge sipped her tea, and she considered her next step. She couldn't put off the visit to Stan, as much as she would like to.

When she finished the tea, she grabbed her jacket and the strings of captured code saved to a memchip and walked it to Stan Davies, a brick and mortar computer tech with a shop on Broadway, just around the corner from Yesler. The old geek lived in the same low-rent building as Bridge, on the floor below hers, which was how she came to know him. Stan's shop was a little hole-in-the-wall, and he made a living selling hardware mods and repairing and refurbishing customers' old equipment. His shop was full of electronic components and used parts scattered about in piles, which to the casual observer appeared a disorganized mess. In fact, it was all organized in such a way that Stan always knew where to find any particular item.

A confirmed pitter, Stan was once a top-level Microsoft programmer and innovator who had dropped out twenty years ago when he became fed up with the life of a high-tech professional. Bridge often came to him when she needed some special software coded or modification performed. He was more accessible than KT Willow, who always had more work than she could handle. Stan was efficient and confidential, and he was a hardware guy, something only a pitter could do.

Opening the door trigged an old-fashioned spring-activated bell. Stan flashed an enormous smile when she crossed into his domain. "Hey, Bridge. How's my favorite lady detective?"

"Well, you know, it's all work, so I guess that makes me a dull girl."

"Not for a moment, lady." Stan winked. "What you got for me today?"

"Stan, you have any citspec mods from DBT?"

"Sure do, Bridge. Had 'em for a couple of months now. Babies sell better than girlie magazines. You need 'em for a job?"

"Yeah, Stan. Can you tell me what they do?"

"Well, the product package says, I quote, 'These modifications provide an enhanced user experience on the new experimental sims from Mitologias, SA. A high better than drugs.' Must be true, the way they fly out of here. But, if you want my technical opinion… they're practically giving these things away, so I took one apart the other day. I've never seen tech like this before. Totally new stuff to me, but they have some kind of nanotech neurosensors in them; an API so you can program objects for taste, smell, touch, even simulate real gravity if you're clever enough; and possibly nano-factories to trigger brain chemicals—serotonin, dopamine, and so forth. Probably modifying the wearer as well as the citspecs, for all I know."

"How long to install?"

"No time at all, Bridge. Just have to pop 'em in."

"Thanks a million, Stan. How much do these things cost?"

"Nine ninety-five. As in nine dollars and ninety-five cents."

"Jesus. How can they make any money?"

"I don't know. I get them for almost nothing. They give out coupons to the kids, so they can get them free. Maybe they're trying to corner the market. You know how these big corporations are. They hand out swag to get you into their sims."

"Yeah. Well, go ahead and insert them, Stan."

"You sure you want to do this?" he said.

She nodded. "Put them on my account."

"Sure thing, Bridge." Stan put on an old-fashioned jewelers monocle and picked up one of the tiny components with a specialized tool. "Turn around and I'll pop your old ones out and drop these babies in."

Bridge turned so Stan could reach the mod slots behind her ear. A slight tug and he had the old MR mods out, then he nuzzled the new ones in. "Let me know how these things work. I'm curious about them. Anything else?"

"I have a couple of pieces of code here. I need you to look at them and tell me what you think."

"You want to wait while I have a look?"

She handed him the memchip. "Yeah, I'd like a first impression. Then I'll leave them for you to examine more closely."

Stan took the memchip to what he called his flat-world computer and plugged it in. He refused to have anything to do with New Life. "You're living in a fantasy," he once told Bridge. "I got enough of that back in my Microsoft days." Stan's flat-world computer, he proclaimed, was as capable as anything out there in the corporate simverse. And a hell of a lot more secure.

Stan opened the first program and scrolled down. "There's quite a volume of code here," he said. "I'd say, right off the top, it's controlling cyber immersion devices, some citspecs mods. Probably those mods I just installed for you. I'd have to look more closely to be sure. That's the file you've labeled 'sweetland.'"

He opened up the other file, the one she had marked "skyrmion." This was the string she had captured in the sim's back end just before they had ejected her.

"This one," he said, frowning, "appears to be related to the sims... hmm... and the Grid. I need to look more closely. Might take me a couple of days or so."

"Okay, Stan," said Bridge, "I'll be home as usual. Call me."

OUTSIDE, THE RAIN HAD PICKED UP AGAIN. SHE PULLED HER coat tight around her neck and briskly walked up Broadway. Another storm was gathering and few people were out braving the weather. An occasional commuter passed on a bicycle, dressed in slickers. The Capitol Hill bus went by. A man took cover in a doorway, his blue slicker pulled up around his head. Had she heard footsteps behind her? When she turned the corner on Yesler Way, she stopped and waited. The footsteps continued for a moment. Paused. Then started again. Bridge's heart was racing. The man in the blue jacket came around the corner, stopping short as he confronted her.

"Sorry to startle you." He tugged on his neat blond beard as he backed up a step. "You know where the stop for the University bus is?"

Bridge exhaled. "One block to the north." She hadn't been able to get a good look at his face. Had he been following her? It seemed unlikely. Just a stranger looking for a bus.

"POLICE ROUNDED UP MOST OF THE PARTICIPANTS IN A CELL OF nine suspected terrorists this morning. The arrests followed a months-long investigation, after the husband of one plotter became suspicious of his wife's activities on the Grid and called the Department of Home-land Security office in Seattle… meanwhile, an increase in the number of reported missing persons has the government worried and local police stumped…."

Pulled back into the moment, Joe removed his buds and laughed. When has the government ever worried about poor people, unless they're rioting? Aware his co-workers were looking at him, he lowered the volume of the Gridcast and tried again to concentrate on the endless forms before him, all needing to be entered into the database by five. Each time he tried to accomplish something, his thoughts only raced from Jolene to Jessie and back, until he shut down his screen in frustration.

He hadn't been able to push Jolene's call from his attention. He grudgingly admitted her point. So, what could he do about Jessie? What did she need from him? He couldn't ignore her cry for help. He needed to find her counseling, but he had no insurance coverage.

He wondered if maybe Anya might agree to talk to her. Would that kind of request offend her? He didn't think so. Was it too late to ask her to go out to lunch with him? It was nearly one, but maybe she hadn't eaten yet. He didn't recall seeing her in the office this morning, but that wasn't unusual.

He wanted to address other things with Anya, as well. He wanted to scold her about Friday night for one. It was a stupid thing that Anya and her friend had done. Her rebel sympathies didn't surprise him. He shared many of them with her, but Disruption was a crime under the Anti-Terrorism Act, and she was risking her life and her career to drop a silly banner at a concert. Even if it was a virtual concert. Why had she confided in him, putting him in this untenable position? Maintaining a friendship with her could be dangerous now. Still, she was his friend, and he didn't give up on his friends.

He walked across the office and looked at the day's roster. She hadn't checked in yet this morning. He would have to leave a message on her mobe. Their talk might have to wait until tomorrow. Celia Greene would expect a home visit from him in the morning. It was too late in the season now to ignore the autumn chill, and her meager government assistance would have to be divided between heat and food. It left a hollow feeling to know he had been neglecting people who depended on him, even though he believed it didn't matter in the bigger picture. He was Sisyphus endlessly rolling the stone up a hill. And yet, Celia and her kids were individual human beings, not statistics; they depended on him, Celia Greene and her little girls, with the snot from their chronic colds dripping from their noses, and their big, sad eyes filled with mucous and troubling questions. Questions Joe couldn't answer.

.   .   .

When Anya returned his call at noon, he had forgotten his initial urge to reprimand her about Friday night. It wouldn't be a safe conversation to have over the agency line, and he didn't want to jeopardize their friendship. He confined himself to talking about Allison and setting up a lunch date with Anya so he could broach the subject of Jessie.

"She seems rather cynical, don't you think?" he said about Allison.

"That's just a front, Joe. Allie's one of the good guys. Really."

"How does she justify doing that kind of work?"

"We're all in the devil's employ, aren't we, Joe?"

"But, Anya, at least we are trying to help people."

"Are we, Joe? Or are we just trying to prop up something that's no longer working?"

There was pleading in Anya's voice. Were social workers like him fostering false hope? Was that what Anya meant? He couldn't tell if he was disappointed in Anya or himself.

"I don't know, Anya."

"Well, Joe, neither do I, really. It's just a question. Things are not always as they seem."

"Yes, that's precisely the problem with Allison. How many layers of skin to get to the heart beating underneath?"

"Ah, well, maybe Allison Marquam isn't meant for Joe Larivee. But she's a wonderful person. Really. And it was fun, wasn't it?"

"Yes." He smiled at his recollection of the evening. "I had a great time."

"I'm so glad, Joe."

Joe hesitated. He had so many questions for her. "Are you free for lunch, Anya?"

"Not today, Joe. Sam and I are preparing to move to a

new place, and I'm pretty busy this week. Do you need to talk?"

"I suppose nothing that can't wait. I wanted to talk about Jessie with you. It's this whole Sweetland thing."

"Look, I'll talk to you again soon. A day or two. Okay? In the meantime, I think you should consider trusting Jessie. I know that's difficult."

"What are you trying to tell me, Anya? Sweetland… it could be a dangerous delusion."

"I don't have time right now, Joe. Have a chat with Allison in New Life. You can trust her, too, and I think she can help you find some answers."

What was Anya trying to get at? He needed answers, not counseling, but he didn't want to argue with her. "Okay, I'll talk to Allison. Good luck with the move."

"Thanks, Joe. Take it easy. I'll call you about lunch."

"Sure, Anya. We'll talk soon."

STAN DAVIES PUT DOWN HIS CUP OF JAVA AND SETTLED himself into his comfortable old office chair. The code young Bridge had shown him yesterday intrigued him, especially the one labeled 'skyrmion.' But he chose to open the file labeled 'sweetland' first, get it out of the way. He noticed it contained too few annotations, poorly done, a fact which Stan blamed on the new generation of sloppy coders. These kids all thought that their product was the ultimate shit, and no one would ever have to go in and fix their mistakes for them.

After about fifteen minutes of scouring the code, Stan

had a good idea of its purpose. The trouble was, it was only intermediate code between the device, the citspecs mods, and some other program somewhere. Without seeing that other program, and without knowing what those mods did, he had no way of knowing what functions this little fragment might perform. But he could at least tell Bridge that these bits of code came from different coders. This one looked like a typical open source project, patched together from several routines. His friend Marina might help him figure out how it connected to the hardware.

He closed down the file and sipped his java. Bridge was allowing herself to be some kind of guinea pig by having him install those mods. He didn't like it. Those nano-devices could theoretically control her nervous system. They could attach to the cortex of her brain and trigger false sensations and even false memories. They could stop her heartbeat with the right signal. Such deployment was inevitable. Greed and technology were a deadly mix.

He had once believed that technology would be the savior of humanity. He'd been so young and naïve when he entered the field. And the recruiters from the high-tech companies all gave him their idealistic spiels about the unlimited future. He joined his starry-eyed colleagues, and then it all changed with the high-tech boom and the cocaine parties and the sex, and the expensive gas-guzzling automobiles, and overnight flights to Paris and London. It became about money and power and creating products whose only purpose was to pry open the wallets of consumers, those passive, faceless masses glued to the internet. Suckers for the corporate hucksters who wore their veneer of idealism like a flag. And when he realized it, when he saw his role in that process, it was time to get out.

Stan finished his java and opened the 'skyrmion' file, the

one which referenced the Grid and pages of lower level code. Unlike the 'sweetland' code, this one was elegant. He scanned it again, line by line, searching for something to verify his initial read. The Grid was a communications infrastructure which supported a network of several thousand q-servers worldwide that made up what the old school crowd called Web 4.0 and the general consumer knew as New Life. The Grid depended on the cooperation among numerous political jurisdictions and redundancies built into the system to prevent breakdown. Many high-tech engineers considered it to be fool proof, invulnerable to massive failure. Stan laughed at these claims. No system was invulnerable. You could render the Grid inoperable for an indefinite period with the right combination of overload and sabotage. Some localized nodes might still function, but, theoretically, you could destroy the world's biggest economy, and it might take years to build it back up from the bottom.

After an hour of marveling at the sophisticated code, Stan shut down the file and removed the memchip. His hunch had been correct. This program crippled the Grid. And if launched from enough sites simultaneously, it would be very efficient in its job. The purpose of the project, code-named *Skyrmion*, was to crash the world's largest economy.

But, there was something else going on here as well. Some anomaly had struck him as he scrolled by. Someone had written stealth coding to spare certain nodes. Dark matter hidden in the Grid's fabric. An elusive skyrmion. He wondered what role the hypothetical magnetic particle played in this scheme, if any. It was likely nothing more than a code name.

He would have to warn Bridge about the danger she had just stumbled upon. But first, maybe he should call around to a few people and see if he could verify his own theory.

And he needed to find out who owned those nodes and what their game was.

Joe arrived home from work still preoccupied with Jolene's surprise call, and his own inability to do something for his daughter. He wanted to lash out at the world, get drunk, or both, but Jessie held him in check. They needed to talk about this Sweetland business, but he feared his own pissy reaction. If he brought up the conversation with her mother, would that drive a further wedge between them?

He stacked the morning's breakfast dishes, still on the table. He picked up the empty cereal carton Jesse had left on the counter and took it to the recycle bin. A discarded letter stuck out between the folded cardboard. The Benson High School letterhead was distinctive enough to recognize even backwards through the back of the page. He lifted the letter from the bin and turned it over.

"Dear Mr Larivee: We are concerned about Jessie's attendance and academic performance. Jessie has missed several consecutive days this term, including three test days..."

Joe cursed and threw the letter down on the table. Forgetting his caution, he strode to Jessie's room and pounded on the door.

"Jessie, come out here, right now."

"What do you want?" she yelled back.

"Open this door and come out here. Now!"

"Jeezus." Jessie stomped across the room and threw open the door. "I suppose you found..." She caught herself.

"Found what? What do you think I found?"

"I don't know." Innocence.

"Jessie, I'm getting tired of lying and secrecy. And missing school is going to end. We have only two more years of free public school, and, goddamn it, we're going to make the best of it."

"Why, Dad? What difference does it make? The fucking world is over. Don't you get it? Why don't you get it?" Jessie was on the verge of tears.

"Get what, Jessie?"

"Did you know that there are no wheat or corn crops in the Midwest this year? There's won't be enough food to feed everyone, and scientists say the drought is so bad they won't grow anything again for a long time. But the stupid fucking school… do you know what we study in school, Dad? We study football and how to make Grid games. That's how bad it is."

"I thought the Teachers' Coop was more aware than that. Aren't you exaggerating?"

"They're all in fucking denial, Dad. Just like you."

That stung. "I think we're all trying the best we can."

"It's not good enough, Dad. It's not fucking good enough."

He put his arms around her as she sobbed. "Sweetheart, I'm so sorry. I didn't know you were thinking about these things. It's going to be okay, darling, we'll make it."

"I don't think so," she said.

He held her in his arms and tried to reassure her. After a moment she said, "Dad, do you know about Sweetland?"

She didn't wait for him to answer. "I'm going to Sweetland."

"Baby, there is no Sweetland."

"Yes, there is, Dad. I'm going. I want you to go with me. There's no future left here."

He wanted to tell her, No Jessie, sweetheart, it's all just a mirage, but he couldn't do it. How could he do that?

Jessie gave him a look of dismissal, disappointment, resignation, he wasn't sure which. She stepped back into her room and closed the door between them. Outside, the drumming had begun, louder than usual, and its insistence drew him toward the window. He looked out into a foggy night, seeing nothing. He just wanted the noise to stop.

WHAT COULD SHE DO WITH HER FATHER TO GET HIM TO believe that Sweetland was real? How would she convince him of the hopelessness of trying to make a difference in this fascist world? Even after she'd broken down and let her genuine feelings out, he still didn't get it. He wanted to heal everyone, but no one could do that. And it would only get worse before the end. Much worse.

She felt guilty for not being able to convince him and, for wanting too hard. If he didn't want to go, if he needed to stay here and help the suffering, shouldn't she honor his feelings? It didn't mean he didn't love her. She knew he loved her. But he had his own life. It was just that he didn't even realize he had a choice. That made her so sad.

Orientation Week began a week from Monday. A short time after that she would leave for Sweetland. There were only a few weeks left to convince him. And here he was, at a crucial moment, going out on dates. What if he fell in love with this mysterious person? What if she lost him? Could she handle that?

One more time, she thought. I'll try one more time to convince him. I'll tell him everything. Then if he still doesn't get it, I can at least tell myself that I tried.

She waited in her room until she decided he was asleep, then took the recycling out, hoping to see Alan. She'd planned to search for him this afternoon, but she'd let the time slip by. Dad said he would try, too, but she didn't really trust him to do that. He had a lot on his mind with his horrible, thankless job, yet she couldn't help feeling angry at him for being so thick-headed. If he only paid attention!

She encountered only crows and litter and the stink of decaying food in the dumpster cage. She put the empty bins on the back steps and walked up the street a few blocks and peered into the alleys and doorways. It was foolish. The hope of finding Alan, now, dwindled with each day, but at least it gave her the illusion of doing something.

Returning to the apartment under a heavy weight, she replaced the recycling bins, careful not to disturb her dad, now zombied out on the couch. Back in her room, she curled up on her bed and closed her eyes, listening to the drums coming from the park.

The Revolution was almost here. Just a matter of weeks, and she would be on Sweetland, building the new world. Nothing would stop her now.

ON HIS WAY TO CELIA GREEN'S IN THE MORNING, JOE stopped at the grocery, picked up some canned vegetables, beans and rice, a couple of lollipops for the girls. He shouldn't have; it was a mistake to buy food for the clients, and his October food stamps were going fast. He was violating professional boundaries, but he realized he didn't care anymore. He always felt helpless when little Gwendolyn opened the door, gripping her toy bear, and smiled at him with that gap-toothed smile and four-year-old innocence.

"Hi there, Gwen," he said. "How are you, today?"

"Fine, Mr Larry." Her voice no more than a whisper.

"And how is Finnegan?" Joe reached out and touched the bear.

"I don't know, he doesn't talk anymore."

"Let me see if I can fix him." Gwendolyn handed him the bear. Holding the sack of groceries in one hand, he popped open a compartment behind its ear with the other. He pushed the dislodged memchip firmly back into its slot. The bear came to life, but instead of greeting Gwen as programmed, it uttered incomprehensible grrs and gwaps.

Gwendolyn frowned, but it was resignation, not disappointment. "Mommy said he's a sorry piece of junk."

"Is your Mommy home?"

"She's in bed. I think she's sick."

"Are you and Carolee okay?"

"Carolee made a mess in the kitchen," said Gwen. "I tried to clean it up, but she spilled cereal all over the floor. I told her she had to clean it up herself. But I don't think she listened."

"Gwen, could you go tell your Mommy that Mr Larry's here?"

"Okay, but I don't think she'll answer me. I tried to wake her up already."

Joe's stomach dropped. He pushed inside and put the

groceries on an end table, then hurried down the hall to Celia's room.

"Celia," he called through the closed door. "It's Joe Larivee, here for our appointment." No answer. He knocked, but still no answer. He pushed the door open to see Celia sprawled on the bed, citspecs over her eyes. No drugs or drug paraphernalia in view, but the signs—it had to be drugs. He walked over to her and checked her pulse. Her skin was cold against his hand. Shit, Celia, you checked out with these little girls still in the apartment. What the hell were you thinking?

Joe turned to find little Gwen behind him, question marks in her eyes tugging at him. He took her hand, guiding her out of the door, and closed it behind them. He told her to go see to Carolee, and then he called 911 on his mobe. After he finished reporting Celia's death, he called Children's Services. As much as he hated to involve the state, Celia's only family was a sister, more messed up than Celia.

"Gwen, bring Carolee, please. I want to talk to both of you."

When Gwen returned with her three-year-old sister, he seated them on the couch. "Girls, Mommy is very sick, and you will have to stay with some good people who take care of children like you."

"Mommy," said Carolee.

"When will Mommy get better?" asked Gwen, her eyes watery.

"I don't know, sweetheart," said Joe, feeling sick to his stomach.

"Could we stay with you, Mr Larry?" her voice pitched high on the edge of a whine. Now the tears were splashing on her round cheeks.

"I'm sorry, Gwendolyn. I wish I could let you stay with

me, but I can't take care of you."

I can't take care of my own little girl, he thought. His hopelessness was complete. They were all in a trap. The world was caught in a spinning funnel, being sucked down into a storm drain, and there was nothing *anyone* could do about it.

JOLENE PARKED ON HER COMFORTABLE LIVING ROOM CHAIR and zoned into the office for her usual Saturday check-in. SUATO7 and SUATO3 were scheduled for duty today, but Three was out in the field, aka the Pit, performing PR work. As much as she hated it, there were still tasks that had to be done out there in the Real World, but fortunately she had underlings to do the unpleasant grunt work for her. How had she grown to hate meeting people face-to-face? It was like the whole Grid thing had some kind of addictive hold on her. Of course there had been studies suggesting such an effect since the days of the old internet, but she preferred to think of herself as immune to such forces. That bullshit pop psychology only applied to the cattle.

Unsurprisingly, SUATO4 sat at his virtual desk entering data. Like her, he was a certified workaholic. She admired his avatar's broad, masculine shoulders, thought about an old Johnny Cash song she once heard about a boy named Sue, and smiled with a slight edge of cruelty—her own personal joke. Most of all, she liked the way he reacted to her use of it. Soon she would be SUATO1, and she could openly smile that smile at all the fools below her. These men think they are such hot shit.

"Hey, Su," she said, "do we know the IDs of the target's associates yet?"

Four turned to her and glared. "Yeah. Cedar Bark is Felicia Ibanez, of Albuquerque, New Mexico. Age 22, a young woman with connections to known terrorist networks, one of the little guys, but a staunch ideologue, dedicated to the Bolivarian project."

"And...?"

"Pox Americano, aka Michel Boulé of Montreal. A programmer and systems engineering student. At age 17, a very bright boy. His sister, Thérèse Boulé, is a 21-year-old graduate student in Forest Ecology at the *Universidad Simón Bolívar.* She is Gretel deVoid's tutor. Goes by Toxine. Neither of them appears to be particularly ideological. One recent addition," said Four. "Melissa Monroe, Portland, Oregon. She might be a real world acquaintance. Parents were Maoist radicals in the nineties, but she doesn't seem to be an ideologue, either."

How could such bright young people fall for this Sweetland shit? It was shit, wasn't it? She guessed that she would soon know.

She leaned back and surveyed the office. She hadn't seen One in three weeks. The others had no idea where One spent his time, but she knew well, she had made it her business to know. That was why she would be sitting in the Director's chair when the agency was finally Privatized. One was on a gambling and whoring binge, carousing on Inferno or SinWorld or another of the dozen mob-controlled sims. The corrupt little asshole's days were numbered. She was checking them off dutifully on her private calendar.

She could always count on Four being there in the office, when he wasn't in the field, the climbing little bastard. She admired that about him, actually, but no way was some ambitious little jerkwad punk like Four going to climb past her. *Fuck that.*

Seven, on the other hand, was a sweet kid who talked like a school boy. Sweet guys made good tools, if you knew how to use them. Joe had been a sweet guy, and she had spent nearly twelve years mastering the art. The problem with nice guys was that they were going nowhere. You eventually had to dump them. She had learned that too from Joe. She didn't really regret the years spent with him. It was a bit like going to college.

She rose and crossed the room to Seven's cubicle, swinging her hips a little, smiling as she approached. She loved the way he reacted to her. Her own puppy dog. Pant. Pant. She could see right through his cool filter. No sophistication at all. He would have to learn to tweak his algorithms if he ever wanted to be assigned undercover.

"What you got for me, handsome?"

"One thing," he said after a brief pause. She could almost see the blush on his face. Except, of course, these government issue avatars weren't capable of that. "You're not going to like it."

She raised her eyebrows. What the hell was it now?

"Your ex was just flagged on HATHOR. A social connection to someone on our watch list. Minor. But thought you might want to know."

Fucking hell. She'd have to talk to her pitter guys down in PDX. Maybe put a little scare into Joe and Jessie both. Then she needed to find out what this *Universidad Simón Bolívar* shit was all about.

☼

Joe retrieved his citspecs from the drawer where he had stashed them. Whatever was going on in Jessie's mind, it all seemed to lead to New Life. The answer had to be there somewhere. He hesitated, thinking about the nanos and the brain chemicals, the addictive quality of this tech. But, he needed to do this thing. He could make no excuses. He recalled the note on Jessie's desk a few weeks ago. She'd scrawled Old Paris there, along with that Le Guin reference. He was pretty sure it was a sim on New Life. Some place she spent time.

He donned the citspecs and zoned "home," which he still thought of as Kali's space. She had rearranged the room. A desk now stood in the corner with an old-fashion computer and telephone. The computer had an annoying brand name and price tag attached to it. Against one wall sat a dusty blue couch overlaid with subtle floral patterns, a chair and a reading lamp placed nearby under the picture window. On the walls hung various pieces of Chinese water-colors. Kali sat on a rug in the middle of the floor. She appeared to be meditating. He cleared his throat, and she looked up at him.

"Good evening, Joe Justjoe. How was your day, today?"

"Lousy," said Joe. "Concerned about my well-being, are we?"

Kali looked indignant. "You may change my personality, if you don't like the current one, Joe Justjoe."

"Sorry. I'm cranky is all. I like you fine, Kali." Did he need to apologize to a computer program? Then he added, "I prefer to be around independent women. You could be a little more uppity and a little less fawning, for god's sake."

"I am not a woman, Joe Justjoe. I am a Programmed Digital Assistant." Well, there it was.

"I like my Programmed Digital Assistants that way, too.

Groveling destroys the illusion."

"As you wish, Joe Justjoe. I will try to adapt to your desires to the best of my ability. But I should point out that I am programmed to please."

"I would be pleased if you didn't try so hard to please me."

"I see Joe." Kali looked perplexed. "Would you like anything more from me?"

"Can you send me to Old Paris, Kali? Is that a sim?" She looked up from her magazine. Her smile revealed a hint of disapproval. Was she adapting already?

"Yes, Joe. Are you sure that you want to go to one of the Bolivarian Alliance sims? They are programmed by the enemies of freedom."

"I suppose you have plenty of alternatives to suggest?"

"There are several very nice shopping malls, and some scorching porn sites. Or the casinos are quite popular. There are also many nice tourist destinations. There are fun ocean cruises, or the Disney sims are very popular, especially Adventure Land and Fantasy Land and Trump Land. Then there is Lukas World. Very artistic. You can fight Darth Vader alongside Luke Skywalker."

Should he laugh or scream?

"Kali, that was a rhetorical question. I really don't care for a list of our sponsors. Take me to Old Paris, please."

"Very well, Joe, but I'm required to issue a warning. You risk being flagged."

"Flagged by who? As what?"

"As a terrorist sympathizer by the DHS, of course."

For a moment Joe froze, unable to respond. But this was his daughter. If Jessie had somehow become involved in something like this, then he had to know, didn't he? He had no choice.

"Just send me to Old Paris, Kali."

JOE EMERGED FROM A CHANGING ROOM ONTO BRICK AND stone streets, a long, wide boulevard of an old European city. The street sign said Boulevard St Germain. Throngs of students milled about, some in small groups, engrossed in animated conversation, some danced wildly in the street, others hung off of balconies, shouting things like, "Vive le Révolution." A couple of girls swung one another down the street, laughing and nearly colliding with him. They had transported him into some leftwing Disneyland.

Words in English drifted toward him from a small group of young people nearby. Two women and three men appeared to be engaged in an intense political argument. Joe moved toward them, hesitant to butt in.

"… but do you really think that we are ready, Michael?" one woman said in broken English.

"Hell yes," Michael replied. "If not now, when? I've heard that the corpos are close to discovering the Sweetland technology. At least, that's what they are saying in the spokes council…"

Sweetland. They had his interest. He moved closer, offered a tentative, "Hi."

"Greetings, comrade." The young woman appraised him. "Are you here to enjoy the celebrations?"

Joe hesitated. "I didn't know about the party. I'm interested in Sweetland, actually. Are you going to Sweetland?"

The woman shook her head, as did her friends. "Sorry," she said. "We are all staying behind to fight. But if you are interested in going, you haven't much time. The gate is closing soon."

"What did you mean about corpos?"

"Corporate spies. They are everywhere. If they find a way to Sweetland, then it is all over for the grand experiment, yes? They will bring their capitalist exploitation with them. But the end is near for them. It is too late to stop what is coming."

"What is coming?" said Joe, still not understanding if this was a game or something else. One man shook his head and glared at the woman in warning.

"Chill, René," she said. "If he is an agent, it is too late for him. Are you an enemy agent, Citizen?" Her smile was seductive.

Joe laughed. "I don't even know who the enemy is." He extended his hand to her and said, "My name is Joe," The gesture was more an afterthought than anything else.

"I am Marin," she said, holding on to his hand for a little longer than felt comfortable. She didn't bother to introduce him to the others, and they didn't offer.

"Are there really this many people out today, or are some of these bots?"

The young man named Michael pierced him with skeptical eyes. "Do you have so little faith in The Revolution, comrade citizen?" Joe noticed the Boston accent.

"It's my first time here. I didn't realize… so many people on the sim."

"Ah, you are a virgin," The first woman winked at him. "It is amazing, is it not?"

"Yes. Are you all college students?"

"Not me," said Michael. "I am a proud member of the proletariat."

"Bullshit, Michael," said Marin, "If anyone here is a bourgeois poseur, it's you." The others laughed and Michael feigned hurt with a dramatic *who moi?* gesture.

"Yes." Marin's words now directed to Joe. "We are all

students here at The Sorbonne. You must think we are silly children. When not in class, we rather delight in role playing, it is the way of the sim. So, welcome, comrade virgin." Without warning, she kissed him on the mouth. An intense feeling of pleasure spread across Joe's lips and teased his loins, not an actual kiss, not like the kisses he had shared with Allison, but electrifying nonetheless. *The DBT mods,* he thought. He was understanding the allure of New Life, especially for his client's kids stuck in their hopeless existence. He wondered if he dare press the Sweetland issue, decided against it. Instead, he smiled at the young woman who had kissed him, then turning to face the others, he said, "Thank you, comrades. *Vive le Révolution.*"

Joe found a chair at a small sidewalk cafe nearby and sat to watch the spectacle. After a few minutes, a server, dressed much like the young students, offered him a menu which he perused absent mindedly. When the server came back with a plate of pastries and coffee, he shook his head. "I'm sorry. I really can't afford—"

"No, everything's on the house today. *Vive le Révolution.*"

"What are we celebrating?"

"It is the tenth anniversary of 18 October, of course. The Bolivarian consolidation." Now Joe understood. October 18, 2028. The day that the revolutionary forces in Peru stormed the palace and overthrew the six-year-old dictatorship of Luis Tejada, installed with the help of the CIA. Historians considered it the defining moment for the Alliance of Bolivarian States. The ABS confederation now included every nation in South and Central America and most of the Caribbean. Nine months ago Mexico joined, triggering a bloody civil war south of the border and inflaming tension between the US and the Bolivarians. But the US, involved in its own wars in Africa and Asia, was in no position to risk another so close to its borders. Especially a war it was likely to lose.

Joe thanked the young man and turned to view the street circus. The smell of coffee and pastry teased his senses, and he reached for the cup. It felt warm to his touch, and when he put it to his lips and sipped, the pleasant taste of real coffee enveloped his mouth, flooding him with the pleasurable sensation of caffeine. But when he swallowed, of course, nothing slipped down his dry throat.

A flash of light, like a laser, burst from across the street, its beam striking somewhere on the next block, out of Joe's field of vision. A virtual concussion followed, sending bystanders flying away from the point of impact. Then everything stuttered and went black. Disorientation and a slight nausea gripped him for a moment before the sim came back online in jerking strobe light flashes. He turned in time to see a man on a balcony vanish with some sort of device in his hand. The server, now standing behind him, said, "God damned griefers."

Shaken, Joe turned to face him. "What just happened?"

"Griefer attack. Happens every few weeks."

"Why did everything go black?"

"A rupture. A surge disrupted the local Grid."

"Is it some sort of game?"

"Could be a game. Could be an assassination. Either way, it's seriously messed up."

"I don't get it. How can you assassinate an avi?"

"The Sassis don't kill *you*, of course—just your avi. They can seriously mess up your data and keep you in the pit for weeks, or months, however long you take to re-establish your identity with the authorities and put your shit back together. It's serious stuff. Some governments actually can kill the real you, so they say—they just don't use it often, I guess, or we don't hear about it or something. Otherwise, I suppose people might stop coming inworld and spending their money if they thought it might be so dangerous. Of course, that will all be meaningless in the next week or so when everyone moves to the enclaves. Understand, there is a real war going on here, just as it is out there. It's just beneath the surface."

STAN SNAGGED HIS MOBE FROM HIS POCKET AND CALLED HIS old friend and colleague from his Microsoft days, Dr Marina Waterman, a specialist in cybernetic UI design, who now taught at the U of W. Which, he thought, dwelling for a moment on the irony, would soon be a solely owned subsidiary of Microsoft after full privatization arrived.

"I'd like to speak with Dr Marina Waterman," he said to the receptionist, who answered. A real person, he marveled. Although you could never be certain these days. "Is she in?"

"Just a moment, sir. I'll connect you to her office. May I say who's calling?"

"Tell her, Stan Davies."

The phone rang several times before she answered. "Stan. It's been a long time. How are you doing?"

"I'm getting by, Marina." His standard answer to this question.

"You still running that little hardware shop on Broadway?"

"Sure thing, Marina. That's what I'm calling you about. A hardware UI problem I'm researching for a friend." He knew he should go through the social niceties and ask

Marina about herself. But he hated chit chat, especially on the phone, and this problem perplexed him beyond distraction. He feared those DBT mods he had installed for Bridge might actually put her in danger.

"Sure, Stan. Whatcha got?"

"I have some new hardware and a chunk of the proprietary code which runs it. I was wondering if you might look at it."

"Proprietary, you say? I don't want to be involved in violating intellectual property. That could cost me my reputation, as well as my job."

"No, that's not what this is about, Marina. I wouldn't ask you to do that. I don't want to discuss it on the phone. Could we meet somewhere over in your neck of the woods and talk?"

"How about lunch at that Mediterranean restaurant in the U District? You know, the one on 45th? About 12:30?"

"Thanks, Marina. I'll see you there."

MARINA WATERMAN STILL LOOKED LOVELY. SHE WAS CLOSE to his own age and he would be seventy next February. But she was trim and fit, unlike himself, her silver hair cut short in a kind of pageboy, bangs covering her forehead down to her eyebrows. Last time he had seen her, about ten years ago, she had worn it to her shoulders, black and swooped back over her ear on one side. He liked this look. It fit her better.

Marina rose from her chair as he approached, and they hugged. "So, my old friend, you have a hardware puzzle?"

"Yeah. But why don't we eat some lunch and catch up on each others lives a bit before we get into all that stuff."

When the server came around, Stan ordered a falafel

and hummus. Marina had tabbouleh and spinach pie, along with a glass of red wine.

Her husband had died five years earlier, she told him, and she lived alone in a university-provided apartment near campus. She had a small cancer scare a few years before her husband's heart attack, but it turned out to be a benign tumor. Nothing to worry about.

Stan was reluctant to open up when it was his turn to reveal. A benign tumor is not so benign when you have no insurance and could lose everything you own to the hospitals. Including your only means of making a living. His apartment on Yesler Way was essentially an indigent hotel. But he had made his choices and Marina had made hers, and, well, that was that. So, he kept his remarks general. To Marina's chagrin, he could see.

It was time to get down to business, and Stan pulled the package of DBT mods from his briefcase, along with a memchip which held a copy of Bridge's "sweetland" file and his notes on both the hardware and software. "These are new citspecs mods from D-Brane Technologies. And this is a piece of the code that runs them. I'm doing some work for a friend—an investigator on contract with New Life Corporation."

"We're not talking about corporate espionage, Stan? I can't—"

"—No, no. New Life just purchased Mitilógias and D-Brane Technologies. But the Bols are partners in those subsidiaries, and the big brass at New Life has hired my friend to make sure everything is on the up-and-up. No hidden agendas, etc. But I came across some odd things in this code."

"Such as…?"

"These mods have nano factories. All the new mods do these days."

"Yes," she said, "they create mood chemicals and improve synaptic function, and so on."

"Yeah. At first I thought that was all these did, too. But I plugged these into a dummy setup and ran some subroutines. One routine in particular made the flags go up. I'm not a biologist or a neuroscientist, but I'm guessing that they have a potential to mess with a wearer's more complex biological systems."

"How so?"

"There are eight nano factories in these two mods. Other mod brands have one or two. I noticed that this subroutine accessed some of the 'extra' factories. So I ran the subroutine on the dummy and analyzed its product. The nanos manufactured guanine, and a couple of other substances my equipment can't analyze."

"Oh, my. Guanine is a component of DNA and RNA. What could be the purpose of that?"

"That's what I would like you to help me with, Marina. I mean, maybe some of my own DNA contaminated the results or something. My equipment is unsophisticated and not in a sterile environment. If you ran it through your labs here at the U… as I said, I'm not a biologist or a cyberneticist like you. I'm just a tinkerer. But it looks suspicious to me."

"Sure, Stan. I'll look for you. If what you are describing is accurate, it's certainly piqued my curiosity. I'll try to keep it under the radar, but if I end up doing anything more than a cursory look, though, I'll need to get a liability waiver from your friend."

"I understand. Thanks, Marina. I owe you big time."

☼

THURSDAY MORNING CAME AROUND AND ANYA STILL HADN'T checked in to work. Her office line went unanswered, as well as her mobe. Had they transferred her already? When she called on Monday, why hadn't she told him? Joe logged out from his computer, trekked to the other end of the basement, and peered into her cubicle. Still empty, as he knew it would be.

A small fear stabbed at his gut.

He consulted the office roster outside Chandra's office. No Anya. He popped his head inside his supervisor's door. "Chandra, has Anya already moved over to ABW? I thought she wasn't leaving for another week."

"I'm afraid I can't help you, Joe," said Chandra. "She hasn't checked in this week. ABW hasn't heard from her, either. Can someone else help you?"

Joe shook his head. "It's personal."

Chandra raised an eyebrow, but said nothing.

"Thanks," he said. It was going to be a shitty morning.

He returned to his desk and attempted to settle back in to work, but despite all of his effort, he couldn't get his mind off of Anya. Where the hell was she? People don't vanish like that, do they? Yes, they do, there have been too many. He thought about Susie Miller and most of the other colleagues who had disappeared, knowing Anya wasn't like them. The work hadn't burned her out—she was a soldier. Anya wouldn't have just quit without a word. Yet, the alternative was too horrible for him to consider. Did it have something to do with the stunt Anya and Samantha pulled?

Was Anya more involved in this rebel thing than he realized?

The paranoia fought for control, and he pushed back. Calm down. Would the government really waste resources going after someone like Anya for something so benign as dropping a banner at a concert? Get a grip on yourself. Take a deep breath.

He breathed in deeply, and his racing heart relaxed just a little. Anya found a better job. She decided ABW wasn't what she wanted. She just forgot to call and tell me is all. It's not like I'm anything to her, just one colleague out of many.

Just as Joe was about to dismiss his paranoid worst, two expensive suits walked in and headed straight for his cubicle.

"Joe Larivee," said the one in deep blue, African-American, about 6-foot-2. He stood a good head taller than the Latino bulldog wearing black. "We would like to talk to you about Anya Dorena Kerenskaya. I'm Matt Dillon, Federal Bureau of Investigation." He flashed an ID at Joe. He nodded toward his partner. "This is Pedro, my sidekick."

Pedro shot a homicidal arrow at the back of Matt Dillon's head.

"Go ahead," said Joe. He hoped Anya was some place safe.

"How long have you known Ms Kerenskaya?"

"She started work here about two years ago."

"You didn't know her prior to the time she became employed here?"

"No. Could you tell me what this is about?"

"Maybe… we'll see." said Mr Dillon. "So, Joe, I hear you two are close."

"We're colleagues. We have lunch together sometimes."

"Sure it doesn't go a little further than that, Joe?" said Pedro. "Some of your coworkers here think maybe the two of you have something going on. You know, a little bouncy-bouncy in the broom closet. Who'd blame you, Joe. You're single. She's a hot little toddy. Roger over there says she gives mouth like a pro." Pedro winked at him.

His face grew hot as his fear turned to anger. He attempted to rise, but Dillon put a hand on his shoulder, pushed him back down.

"Roger doesn't know a mouth from a cocker spaniel's ass." Joe said it loud enough for Roger and everyone in the office to hear. "As for you, Pedro, it's none of your damned business what's between Anya and me."

"Joe, Joe," said Dillon, "no need to get hostile. You see, we've got a bit of a predicament here, Joe. Your sweetie Anya may be part of a terrorist cell."

Joe shook his head. "You're full of shit."

"We're all full of shit, Joe," said Pedro, "until someone comes along and rips our guts open. You ever seen someone's intestines, Joe? I have, and let me tell you, it ain't pretty when your shit's all over the fucking ground. Now you listen, shit head, your Anya Bananya has disappeared. We need to know her whereabouts. We need to know who she knows. Comprende?"

The cold trembling traveled from his hands to his arms, moved up to settle between his shoulder blades, until a chill gripped his core. He felt the way he had the day they took away his parents. Helpless and angry. He shook for a few long seconds before he pushed away the fury.

"Sorry." Was he selling out again? "I'm sorry. Anya and I confided sometimes. You know, personal things."

Dillon raised an eyebrow.

"I mean… I talked to her about trouble I was having with my daughter. That sort of thing. Not anything that would help you—"

"You let us be the judge of that, Joe," interrupted Dillon. "So, did she mention friends outside of work, anything like that?"

He thought of Sam and Allison and felt the blood leave his face. "Not that I recall."

"Well," said Dillon, "I'll tell you what, Joe. We'll leave now, let you get back to work. You see if maybe you can exercise that flabby memory of yours, and we'll visit again in a couple of days. Nice chatting with you, Joe."

He glared as Dillon and Pedro walked out the door, shivering at their nasty little Laurel and Hardy act. Stay calm, he told himself, keep level, rational.

For the rest of the day, he fumed about the agents and fretted for Anya. Whenever he brought her name up, his coworkers remained silent. She'd been involved in a reckless but harmless prank. Why would the FBI think she was a terrorist? He couldn't think of a more unlikely extremist than Anya.

MATT DILLON THREADED THE OILED CHAMOIS CLOTH through the cleaning rod, then picked up the antique Colt.45 that he had placed lovingly on his lap. He flipped open the cylinder and gave it a gentle spin, letting the cartridges fall into his lap, then he removed the one in the chamber and inserted the rod into the barrel. In and out in a smooth motion, he twisted the cloth a quarter turn with each thrust, two times around, then he removed the rod and pulled the chamois from the slot. He replaced the rod in the kit and wiped down the surface of the gun, carefully, to not miss any of the parts. The revolver wasn't on the Bureau's approved firearms list, and Dillon was about the rules. But he made a singular exception for his baby.

Dillon couldn't figure out why Jolene Cheng wanted to harass this Larivee schmuck. The guy was obviously not a player. Probably somebody had a hair up their ass about Larivee's subversive parents or something. Unless it was a personal thing, exes and all. Anyway, if she wanted him to push this guy around a little, then that's what he would do. Just another job. He didn't get the pleasure out of it that Pedro did.

"You know," he said to Pedro Blasón, who was sitting across from him in the living room of Pedro's apartment, "I don't know why we don't just let the Bols have it all. Let them try to control this zoo. Shit, they'd run like hell in a year's time."

"Bols are for smoking, Dillon." Pedro grinned. "You know those assholes want to give it all back to the Indians. Fuck that shit."

Dillon looked at Pedro's dark Mayan features and laughed. "What the fuck do you think you are, Pedro? A Swede?"

"I'm an American, and I'm proud of it. You know what *you* are, Dillon? You're a fucking pussy."

Dillon picked up one cartridge from his lap and placed it back in the cylinder, then closed the cylinder and gave it a spin. He pointed it toward the window and looked down the gun sight, slowly pulling back the hammer. Then, with a smooth motion of his arm, he swung the gun around and pointed it at Pedro's head.

"Hey don't fuck around with that shit," protested Pedro.

"Who's the pussy now?" Dillon eased the hammer back down to rest and returned the gun to his lap.

"You're a crazy fucker, you know that, Dillon?"

"So says the fucking pot." Dillon gave Pedro a hard, haughty stare. "Speaking of pots, what the hell's for lunch?"

Pedro thought about it. "My aunt Maria brought over some homemade menudo last week."

Dillon placed the .45 in its shoulder holster. "You know what that shit is, Pedro? It's fucking guts. How can you eat that disgusting shit?" Dillon put the cleaning kit in his overcoat pocket, then stood and moved toward the door. "Think I'll go get myself a hot dog."

LITTLE GWENDOLYN GREENE STANDS OVER HER MOTHER'S body, which lies on the deathbed, a needle dangling from its arm. The dead woman gazes back at her with open, staring eyes. Gwen wipes tears from her face with the back of her tiny balled fists. "She's gone to Sweetland, hasn't she, Mr Larry?"

"Yes, Gwendolyn, she's gone to Sweetland."

Darkness descends on the room, a room of deep shadows, ghosts, fragments of horror. Panic grips him. "Run, Gwen. Run as fast as you can away from here."

Of course Gwen can't run. She's only five years old. Where could she go? He attempts to move, but he's paralyzed by fear.

Then he is sitting in his cubicle at work. On the other side of his desk, little Gwendolyn holds Carolee's hand, sobbing. "Can we stay with you, Mr Larry?"

"I'm sorry, Gwen. I can't take care of you. But there's someone

here who likes little girls very much. He will take care of you." Joe feels a mixture of shame and grief as he signs the paper.

He turns to a figure standing in the shadows. "Here's your lunch, sir. Feed them and let them get a little fatter before you eat them."

The thing steps from the shadows. A hideous thing with four arms and a face like a crocodile, green and knobby, and dripping great gobs of slobber on the floor. Gwendolyn and Carolee scream.

JOE WOKE FROM THE DREAM WITH A START, SWEATING. IN the kitchen, he could hear Jessie rattling around. He should remove himself from the couch, go join her, but he stared at the wall for a long time until he began drifting back into the darkness.

"Sweetland, Mr Larry. Maybe we should go to Sweetland to see my mommy."

Joe's eyes shot open again.

He needed to get himself ready for work. He got up and dressed himself, but froze halfway through tying his shoes. *Allison,* he thought. Anya had suggested contacting her. He had Allison's card, the address of her New Life persona. Could he find some answers, there? Answers about Jessie, about the missing Anya? About what the hell was going on?

He picked up his mobe and called into the office, telling them he was going to be working from home for a few hours. It was only a small lie. Jessie sounded a bit put out when he told her, raising alarm bells. Had she been planning on skipping school again this morning? He decided not to confront her and waited until she left the apartment.

On the coffee table his new citspecs lay folded, enticing him. He made no move, resisting for another moment, thinking about nanotech and neurostimulators. Then giving in, he slipped the devices over his eyes, and felt that uncanny numbing sensation overcoming his body.

Kali was lounging on the couch, legs crossed, her hands cupped around a steaming mug of java. A jar placed strategically on the coffee table said that it was JavaWorld Premium Exotics brand.

"It's delicious," cooed Kali, as the aroma wafted by Joe's olfactory sensors.

"Is that really necessary, Kali?"

"Is what necessary, Joe Justjoe?"

"The commercial."

"I'm programmed to remind you of your favorite products, Joe, and possible alternatives."

"How do you know my favorite products?"

"The nanocoms inform me, of course. Every product you purchase has a nanocom."

"Can you *not* remind me of products, Kali?"

"If you so choose, Joe Justjoe. I will change your settings. However, I must disclose that certain paid product placement will continue to override these settings."

"Fine. Just minimize it."

"As you wish, Joe." The JavaWorld Premium Exotics can vanished, but Kali continued to sip from her cup.

"Why am I able to smell that stuff?"

"Nano-neurostimulators, Joe. They are from your DBT mods. Our programmers have recently incorporated new routines which make use of the cutting edge D-Brane API. Soon you will also be able to experience touch and taste as well."

"Wow, so this is progress." A quiet anger stirred in his gut. The damned advertisers were playing with his nervous system. What other tricks could they perform?

"Kali, would you contact Lindsay Lane and find out when she might be available to meet with me?"

The reply was immediate: "Ms Lane is available to meet you in fifteen minutes. Shall I tell her secretary you will be there?"

Could they have communicated that quickly? Of course they could.

"Yes, please, Kali. And transport me to a privy room—or whatever you call it—near her office. And directions, I'll need those."

"Certainly, Joe." Kali vanished.

JoE STOOD IN A SMALL, FEATURELESS ROOM WITH A SINGLE door and several hooks on the wall. He stepped out of a changing room into a department store men's section, indistinguishable from any clothing store he had ever seen in an actual mall, except it was busier here, and the clothes more upscale than anything he'd seen in Portland, with aisles of skins, complete digital bodies, ranging from Ruddy Blond to Vaguely Ethnic, all tall, suntanned, and uniformly handsome, a look once called metrosexual; ethnic like that old actor Keanu Reeves, but if you wanted short, dark Vietnamese, you were shit out of luck.

Nanobots whispered their subliminal language, "Buy me, buy me," as clerk bots ran their hands over products and beckoned him with broad smiles. A clerk approached, and he turned to flee, only to be confronted by another attacking from his right flank. The snazzy-suited bot, which he now recognized as Mediterranean Macho, appraised him, his eyes settling on Joe's crotch. "Sir, May I suggest an upgrade? Personal Enhancements are discreetly located in the back room."

Panic replaced embarrassment, and Joe rushed toward the exit. Outside, he took a deep breath. A skater punk thrust a flyer into his hand. *Bots are taking our jobs. Join the botcott.* The kid vanished before his eyes, and a man in a suave business suit sidled up next to Joe. "Fucking disruptors," he growled, giving Joe a look that might have been accusatory. "I wouldn't get caught with that, buddy, if you know what's good for you."

Joe tossed the flyer in a receptacle, then proceeded up the busy street, following Kali's direction. The window displays reminded him of Hawthorne Street or Mississippi Avenue—a street of cafes and boutiques with manikins behind glass, virtual SmartSpots advertising clothing brands tailored to the reader, flashing clips of sexy, hip-looking models. But the clothes here, like those in the department store, were far more fanciful than the real Salvation Army Wear now found in the shabby shops of his real life hometown.

He passed a small bookshop and stopped to glance at the titles—books about science and religion. A title caught his eye: *What is Sweetland?* He didn't have time now to check it out, so he searched for the name of the shop. A sign on the door said, "Temple Reading Room." In the corner of the glass he saw a decal, an ancient navigation instrument he recognized from a college history course. What was it called? An astrolabe, that was it. He made a mental note to return here later when he had time.

Lindsay Lane waited for him in the lobby of New Life, Inc, a look of concern—or perhaps distraction, he thought —on her face. She invited him into her warm, minimalist office. Logos and commercial advertisements, artfully placed, spanned one wall; on another, a monitor covered the entire surface, displaying a slide show of various public relations campaigns.

"So, this is where you do your design work?"

"All the tools of design and multimedia creation, right here. I can be anywhere in the real world and work out of this office."

"That's amazing. That could never happen with my job." He thought about Celia Greene and her little girls.

"I don't think you would want that." Lindsay smiled. "But it's going to happen anyway, you know. You'll be talking to your clients inworld, and you'll be selling them virtual fixes—those who can afford it—if something doesn't change."

"Yeah, I suppose. As long as you have a dime, they'll squeeze it out of you."

Lindsay appeared to be assessing him.

"We shouldn't be talking about this here," she said.

"Look," said Joe, "I wanted to tell you, I really enjoyed the other night."

"I had fun." Her face was distant and cool. "So, what can I do for you, Joe?"

"A couple of things. I have a problem with my daughter and our mutual friend suggested I talk to you. And I am also concerned about our friend's wellbeing—"

"Joe, say no more. Why don't we go for a drink?"

"In the actual world?"

"Not the pit. I know a place inworld with topnotch encryption."

"Oh, then, lead on."

Lindsay touched his hand, and they were standing in a crude restroom. He could see a condom dispenser out of the corner of his eye and in the mirror a piss-stained toilet. It struck him as ridiculous, and he laughed. Lindsay flashed a sly grin and led him out into the smoky bar, a dive straight from some noir film set, sawdust on the floor, lots of neon, a counter of crafted mahogany, or virtual mahogany, he had to remind himself; Big Joe Turner on the box singing *Low Down Dirty Shame*. An attractive redhead sat at the end of the bar, eying Joe. She looked as though she were part of the scenery, dressed in a pretty green dress and hairstyle that matched the bar's forties motif. Maybe his grandmother looked like this in her youth. He smiled at her, and she gave him a long, wistful look before turning away.

Lindsay approached the bartender, a short, stocky black man. "Jasper, bring us a couple of single malts. We'll be taking one of those privacy booths in the back."

"Sure thing, Ms Lane."

Joe sat down, facing the bar. The redhead was leaving, and she threw him a quick glance before putting on a black trench coat and slipping out the door.

"Are you somewhere… real world alone?"

"Yes, about as alone as you can get." He hoped that didn't come off the way it sounded.

"I think we should go into privacy mode, Joe. Use your hardware encryption so your concierge doesn't hear. You can't trust them."

Joe wondered if this was a you-can't-trust-the-help moment. Just then, Jasper set two drinks on the table. "Enjoy."

"Thank you, Jasper," Lindsay replied.

"I don't understand," Joe said, when they were alone again. "Why shouldn't I trust my concierge?"

"Because someone programs Personal Assistants some-where in the corporate world, Joe. And people and compa-nies have motives. Your concierge provides its master with information about you, your shopping and travel habits. And maybe other information, as well."

Joe said nothing; she had only reminded him of what he already knew. His real world double pushed the tiny encryption button on the inside of his citspecs.

"Okay, Joe, we're locked. You want to talk about Anya."

"I haven't been able to get in touch with her all week, and after that stunt at the concert… I think maybe she's in trouble. The FBI came around asking about her. I thought maybe you might—"

"—Joe, drop it. Think about it. If I knew—which I don't —and I told you where Anya is, if the feds come around again, you will be an accomplice or an informer. Trust me, Anya is safe. I know nothing more. And it's best if you don't, either."

"But she's the only friend I have. My daughter is mixed up with something I don't understand, and Anya might talk to her."

"Your daughter? Is that what you were saying earlier? I'm sorry, Joe. I wish I could do something."

"Sweetland. I was in a fight with her a few days ago. She was talking nonsense about moving to Sweetland. And just a week ago, I interviewed a kid whose brother ran away. Gameliel said his brother was going to Sweetland. What the hell? You know? There are kids going missing and I don't want Jessie to be one of them. I was hoping maybe you knew someone who could help me get to the bottom of this."

A long silence ensued before Lindsay said, "Joe, things aren't always as they seem."

"That's what people keep telling me," Joe snapped back. "You think I don't know that?"

"Maybe these kids… maybe they're involved in some-

thing bigger than us, bigger than we are willing to dream."
Something in her face, in the way she spoke the words, said
she knew about Sweetland, about this total mystery that had
him stumped.

"What do you know, Lindsay? What is it you just can't
come out and say?"

"Look, Joe. Look around you. We have the technology to
create any kind of world we want, and what do we do with
it? We recreate the same fucked up mess we started with.
This will happen again and again until we make a break
with the past."

"I don't understand. Why are you speaking in riddles?"

Lindsay fished in her purse and handed Joe a business
card. "The redhead who was in here earlier at the bar. This
is her card. She may be able to help. Now I must get back to
work. Bye, Joe."

Lindsay Lane vanished, leaving Joe flustered. He looked
at the business card's plain gothic typeface: *Claire Deluna,
Private Investigator.*

JOE RETURNED HOME FROM WORK EXHAUSTED. THAT IT WAS
Friday night should have been a relief, but things were
unsettled. His morning's talk with Lyndsay Lane—Allison,
he reminded himself—had left him frustrated. Why weren't
his friends straight with him? Why were they passing him off
one to another? Was it because no one had the answers? Or
because they didn't have the courage to tell him the truth?
Or maybe they didn't trust him?

What did he have to lose talking to Claire Deluna? He

set himself down on the couch and slipped into his citspecs, allowing the virtual world to settle around him.

He could go to the address on her virtual card, but on a hunch, he had Kali deposit him at The Downbeat. He stumbled from the restroom as sad blue notes slipped furtively into his consciousness, dragging him down the hall toward their source. Beyond the smoky haze, the bartender —Jasper, that was his name—and the redhead detective chatted at the end of the bar. She turned as he entered, the faintest smile on her red lips. He smiled back and sat half-a-dozen stools down. He ordered bourbon on the rocks, thinking of his father. Frank drank bourbon. He would say, in the disdainful way he did, when he spoke of such things, "Scotch is the rich man's drink. Bourbon now, that's the common man's whiskey. If you're going to drink whiskey, son, drink bourbon." This was usually after he had consumed three or four of them.

Jasper put Joe's faux bourbon in front of him and the ice clinked against the glass.

"Saw you in here yesterday with spinning Jenny," said Claire Deluna. "Do you work in the lie industry, too?" There was no hint of irony in her question.

"No," he said. "I'm a social worker."

"Didn't think so—the clothes, the skin, not nearly flashy enough."

"Oh?" Did he just receive an insult?

"I don't mean that in a bad way," she clarified. "You're a noob. A pitter." It wasn't a question.

"Yeah, pretty much. I've only been doing this New Life thing for a few weeks."

Claire Deluna vanished for a split second and reappeared on the barstool next to him, causing Joe to jump in surprise. She thrust her hand toward him. "I'm Claire

Deluna. Sorry about that. I'm a bit impulsive—always scaring people away."

Joe smiled, taking her hand. "Hi, Claire. I'm Joe."

"Is it just Joe?"

"Yes, Joe Justjoe." He laughed. "Really."

She giggled. "That's funny. No need to explain. You know, you can change that."

"Yeah. I've grown to like it, actually."

"So, Joe Justjoe, what does a social worker do?"

"I'm a case worker. I keep struggling families on the path to recovery. Or so says my job description. I fill out a lot of bureaucratic paperwork, mostly."

"That's very admirable. Helping people, that is—not necessarily the paperwork part. I like to think of *my* job as uncovering the truth. But I don't know if that's accurate, really. Sometimes I think I'm in the same business as Ms Lane when it comes down to it. I find the truth my clients want me to find."

"You're a private investigator."

"Pretty obvious, I guess." She laughed and gestured toward her surroundings. "A bit of a stereotype."

He could have told her that Lindsay Lane had given him Claire Deluna's business card. But he didn't.

"It started as a game," she said, "the lady detective. You ever do RPGs?"

"Sure, when I was a kid. Hasn't everybody? But they had nothing as realistic as New Life back then."

"Back in the dark ages, eh?" Her laugh held a sardonic edge.

"Yeah, I'll take the dark ages any old time." A heaviness tugged him downward.

· · ·

Joe considered Claire Deluna. What attracted him to this person? Did he recognize a yearning? An aching similar to his own, perhaps? Or was that just projection?

"Yeah, the good old times." She chafed, exposing an edge of bitterness. "We won't be seeing those again. At least not in the pit."

"I suppose not," he said. "Do you really make a living at this private eye business?"

"I pay the rent. And I give to my favorite charity." She nodded toward Jasper. "It's not much of a living, but I survive. And I get to spend my time here, instead of out there tripping over starving people in the street." She cringed, and Joe sensed a wall going up.

"But starving people need our help. We can't just ignore them or pretend they don't exist."

"I don't mean to be so cold. I really do admire what you do, Joe. I just can't deal with it. Life seems so futile most of the time."

"I admit, it feels that way to me, too, sometimes. I had a mother a few days ago, OD'd with two little girls in the apartment. It breaks my heart."

Claire looked as though she wanted to cry. *You go to a bar to forget about the sadness out there, don't you? This entire conversation tasted sour.*

A long moment of silence ensued. *I've got these memories, she's got you*—Patsy Cline's unmistakable voice dropped into the space, giving them both an excuse for not speaking. This would be a good time to get out, to say, Nice meeting you, Claire. Have a nice day. Except something held him, some purpose he had now forgotten.

"Would you like to get out of here and go dancing?" she said with no warning. "We could visit some hotspots and forget about all this sad stuff for a while."

He took a minute to mull it over. What could it hurt? It was the virtual world, and an evening dancing could be fun. Even if it wasn't really dancing. "I'd love that," he said.

J OE COULDN'T BELIEVE THAT THE LOVELY LADY DETECTIVE had just picked him up. He liked Claire Deluna. He recognized the tough-girl act. How many hard-shelled little girls had he dealt with on the job? And behind most of them was a big hurt. Claire didn't even hide it that well. It appeared right there beneath the surface, trying to escape through the pores, if an avatar had pores. But while the vulnerability attracted his male protector genes, he had also detected in her voice some quality of compassion and intelligence. He thought he might like to get to know her, if she were open to it.

She took him to a nightclub on a sim called Ambient. The nanos kicked in the moment they arrived, and he forgot his real world body, feeling present somehow in a way he hadn't before. Weight, like gravity, but not quite. Claire touched his arm, and he felt—what? It was a tingling something—not touch, but something. Like the gravity, it wasn't quite the real thing, and, yet, it was thrilling. But if he stayed here long enough, he would forget how real gravity worked, and it scared him, how much he wanted to forget.

Claire ordered up some green drinks called Liquid X, and Joe took a sip. Immediately, the muscles throughout his entire body danced with small, pleasurable spasms to the beat of the music, inhabiting the cells of his body.

"My god. This is incredible."

"You like the music?"

"The drink. The programming. Whatever the hell it is. Wow."

"Oh, it's the mods. I didn't realize… I should have warned you. I just had those toys installed myself. Not sure what I think about them yet. They seem to be kind of addictive. Shall we?"

Claire nodded toward the dance floor. Joe rose and offered her his hand. He led her to the edge of the dancing hive, where his feet moved without volition to the beat of the music. Soon he was in a groove, and he smiled at her as she danced beside him, his eyes locked to hers. How long had it been since he had gone dancing? Not since Jessie was a little girl. He remembered how much he loved to dance, to move to the sensual rhythms, to be part of the mass of communal ecstasy. A pattern of colors pulsed in his brain and Joe forgot about Anya and work, and even his problems with Jessie. Holy shit. Purple he could feel on his retina, so deep it went through him like a wave rolling across the dance floor; orange yellow blue light swirling and pulsing to the beat of loud, dissonant music; a hypnotic tribal beat. Heat rose through his body, spreading from his groin. Every move was brilliant. Claire was brilliant. The three raver boys whirling around each other were brilliant. Everybody's heart beating together. And then, without warning, the music ended, the colors turned off, and for just a moment he realized where he was, in the actual world, lying on his couch in his little apartment all alone with a pair of citspecs over his eyes. And this beautiful, digital creation whirling with him on the dance floor was someone's dream. Someone somewhere, just like him, all alone.

"Claire," he asked when the song had finished, "do you only go out with men in-world?"

"This way you don't get your heart broken." She said.

Joe regarded her for a long time, then he said, "I'm not so sure about that."

Claire looked away. "Joe, I… you're a nice man, and this has been a fun evening. I… I've got to go," and, just like that, she disappeared.

Dumped again, it was the story of his sorry, fucking life. He took off his citspecs, and looked at his drab, messy apartment. Then he closed his eyes and watched the neural ghosts play across his retina until he faded into sleep and dream.

PUSHING ASIDE A HALF-EATEN APPLE, BRIDGE WHITEDEER propped her elbows on the table and cradled her face in her hands. Raindrops accumulated on the window glass. She focused on one particular drop, seeing in it a reflection of her entire world. In the middle of that drop a tiny black hole the size of an atom. That void with the capacity to hold the universe multiple times over. To go near its gaping maw was to be swallowed, to be lost forever.

"God damn him." She said aloud, as she refocused her gaze on the Seattle rain. "God damn him to hell."

He had no right coming into her life, trying to worm his way in and make a fool of her. I won't let it happen, she thought. I've got work to do. I'm too busy to let some guy get under my skin. It was the middle of the night. She was exhausted, but she couldn't sleep. There was a dull pain in her gut. She tried to convince herself it was hunger, but she knew better.

God damn him.

Part Four

Sorrow's Spy

"Since knowledge is but sorrow's spy, It is not safe to know"
    —William D'Avenant

"We are never deceived; we deceive ourselves."
    —Wolfgang von Goethe

She admired her new persona in the mirror. Beneath the shock of turquoise hair, a pretty face with glitch nose ring and subtle pink freckles smiled back at her in self-satisfaction. Yes, Penny Fortune would do nicely. Perhaps a slight change in skin hue to complement the hair. Set the freckles further into the background. Just a smidge. And then, it will be perfect.

Penny Fortune left the New Bohemia Boutique wearing the latest in anti-fashion. New dress, new hair, new skin, new hip sandals. Funny how these fancy Skins seemed to carry with them an actual personality, independent of her own. How did that work? Was it just psychological? Whatever, it was useful.

Already she had second thoughts about her purchases. She hoped it wasn't *too* perfect. Most university kids come from the comfortable classes, don't they? Of course they do. Penny Fortune certainly did. So I like nice clothes. So fucking what?

Outside, on the street, a long-haired, bedraggled man sat on the curb, smoking a doobie. He wore a retro, tie-dye tee shirt and jeans ripped down the seam. He leered at Penny.

"Hey, babe," he said, "wanna get high?"

"I don't get it," said Penny. "Why the hell do you dress like a bum? What's with that?"

"Do I offend your reality? I do so apologize. *Not.*" He paused, continuing to fix his gaze on her. "So, you wanna get high or not, babe?" he repeated.

"What you got?" she asked.

"Depends on what kinda mods you wear. Got different patches for different mods."

"What do you have for DBT mods?" Penny asked.

"Got lots of glitch vintage candy for the DBTs. Blow,

horse, uppers, downers, X, twelve kinds of acid. Some of the newer highs, too. I got fuckin' shit that'll blow your brains away in orgasmic delight, sweetheart." He flashed her a lascivious smile, and she noticed the enormous gap in his teeth. Some people just wanted to offend.

"Sorry, not interested," she said. As she backed away, he let go with a loud, nasty-sounding fart, which exuded a mind-numbingly horrible odor. Penny retreated down the sidewalk until she was out of range of the foul smell.

As she retreated down the hill toward downtown, she released a deep sigh. That was one sorry ass she wouldn't mind hauling in for illegal patches. But it wasn't her jurisdiction, and she had other priorities at the moment.

She was in no hurry. It was Saturday and she could use a little personal relaxation before she zoned to the *Universidad* this afternoon. She wondered once again if she wasn't on a wild-goose chase, spurred by some uncomfortable emotional attachment to the girl. Pitter pity. Then she remembered that young, carefree Penny Fortune would never be distracted by these kinds of thoughts. Get in character, Jolene.

Penny zigzagged through the virtual San Francisco streets, smiling at the young men she passed as she navigated toward Market Street, passing by exquisitely recreated Victorian houses. She stopped at a Thrifty Mart and bought a chocolate bar. It was okay, but the programming could use some tweaking. She continued toward Chinatown and the Embarcadero, where she knew a great seafood restaurant on Fisherman's Wharf. Exclusive. They served five-star tasties.

The significant thing about tasties, you could eat all you wanted and not worry about getting fat. The technology was new, and it was only a matter of time before the low-lifes moved in, before McDonalds began hawking Big Macs on the waterfront. But right now the quality of the virtual food was superb. High-class establishments could afford high-class techies. But the clientele made a place top-drawer. Those who appreciated—and could afford—the best.

Penny ambled along the streets of Chinatown, browsing in the shops, window shopping. She could spend hours doing this. But a sense of urgency tickled at her, and she boarded the Mason trolley for Fisherman's Wharf. At the restaurant, they told her that the wait would be about 45 minutes, just enough time to make a pit stop, get some actual solid food and piss.

Universidad Simón Bolívar didn't seem all that different from a typical North American university. Not that Penny had expected it to be. Young students and egghead academics were the same everywhere. Administrators, no different. Designers and architects and 3D artists, all schooled in the box of western tradition. Tucked away behind a tall eucalyptus grove, the large, U-shaped *Colegio de la Ciencia* featured a courtyard with picnic benches and several shade trees. The building itself, designed in a historic Spanish colonial style with arched windows and doors, appeared to be constructed of centuries-worn, ivy-covered brick. Penny laughed at the postmodern conglomeration of college stereotypes. Nothing revolutionary here, she thought, an observation which didn't necessarily apply to the minds within. Although, in all probability, it did.

The halls were quiet. Physics. Math. Astrophysics. Chemistry. Biology. Here we go. She opened the door to the Biology Department and entered a second corridor. She continued until she found *Ecología y Sistemas Biológicos*. This would be the girl's bailiwick.

Penny entered. A young woman about her own virtual age sipped a cola as she graded exam papers. She was probably a graduate assistant. Penny cleared her throat, and the girl looked up.

"May I help you?" she asked in French-accented English.

"Yes," said Penny. "I'm thinking about joining the ecology program."

"Wonderful." The graduate student extended her hand toward Penny. "I'm Toxine."

What luck. Sometimes things just fell in place.

"Penny Fortune. Nice to meet you, Toxine."

Toxine looked at her, appraisingly, as Penny picked up a department catalog and thumbed through it. There it was, page four. Sweetland Studies.

"I'm interested in this." She pointed at the brochure. "Is that a tough program to get into?"

"Haven't you heard? We have terminated all the Sweetland programs. The last courses ended yesterday. If you're interested in studying Sweetland, you'll have to do it after you arrive."

"Do it there?" What was this girl talking about? She couldn't afford to get tangled up in confusion and explanations. "Damn," she said, "my friend just told me about these courses a few months ago. I guess I put it off too long."

"Sorry. Who is your friend?"

"Gretel. Gretel deVoid." She hoped that hadn't been a mistake.

"Oh, Gretel. Gretel is one of our most advanced students. I expect big things for her on Sweetland. You know, you can still go through the preparation at the Temple. Gretel's group starts next week. Most of this batch is pretty young—like Gretel. But, you know, it's better than going cold."

"How do I sign up?" asked Penny.

"I'll put you on the list. Meet us here Monday at sixteen hundred VT."

Penny thanked her and left. She couldn't believe her incredible luck.

The office building nested on a street of old-fashioned brick-faced structures adorned with gothic chimeras and gargoyles. The elevator looked like something from the 19th Century. Its cage door opened with a lever, and it creaked and squalled as it rose by jerks and jolts to the 4th floor. Joe marveled again at the amount of detail put into these virtual reality simulations.

He walked along a hall lined with dark wainscoting and single-light mahogany doors beneath dusty transoms, until he found the door with "Claire Deluna, Private Investigator," painted on the virtual glass. He hesitated, nervous about seeing Claire Deluna again after she had disappeared on him like that. Would she think he was a stalker? She dumped him, but never gave him a reason. She didn't tell him not to come back around.

He opened her office door, wondering why doors on New Life always creaked like they needed oil. In the reception room, a petite and very intimidating woman in a blue suit, with a short retro hairstyle and deep red lipstick, greeted him.

"May I help you?" she asked with a thick, southern accent.

"I need to see Claire Deluna," he said.

"Do you have an appointment?"

"No, I was hoping I could just pop in for a minute."

"Ms Deluna is a very busy woman. May I ask what this concerns?"

"It's a private matter."

"May I say who is calling?"

"Joe Justjoe."

"Just a moment. I'll see if Ms Deluna is available."

It relieved him when the receptionist returned and ushered him in, but the instant Claire saw him, she went ballistic. "God damn it, Joe. I don't need this. I am in the middle of a nightmare, I have nasty people following me, and I don't need a guy with some romantic bug in his pants stalking me, too. Please go."

"Claire," he protested, "I'm not a stalker. I just thought there was a connection between us last night..."

Had he said the wrong thing? He hesitated for only a moment. Just a blink. He found himself on his digital butt in the middle of a street, outside her office, looking around in confusion. Jesus, Joe, you screwed that up. What the hell is wrong with you, anyway? Why did he have to turn this into some romantic thing, anyway. He had come here wanting to find out what Jessie's Sweetland obsession was all about. Hadn't he?

JOE PICKED UP HIS BRUISED EGO AND STUMBLED DOWN THE street, aimless and defeated. When he heard an electric blues guitar belting out Muddy Waters, he realized The

Downbeat was nearby and waiting for him. The place buzzed with customers as he pushed himself up to the bar.

"Hi, Joe," said Jasper. "You have a good time with Claire the other night?"

"Too good," he said, thinking, damn this guy has an excellent memory.

"Uh-oh, do I detect a little heartbreak?" asked Jasper.

"Yeah. I think I really blew it."

"I wouldn't be too hasty in your conclusions, Joe," said Jasper. "The little lady came in late last night. Moped around for a couple of hours. Just a heads up. Can I get you something?"

"You got anything that will get me drunk, Jasper?" He released a weak, dispirited laugh.

Jasper mirrored his laugh and said, "Claire likes the vodka crans. But they won't get you drunk."

"Sure. Give me one of those."

Jasper poured a drink and set it down in front of Joe. "Hang in there, Joe," he said.

Joe payed, picked up his drink and moved to a booth at the back of The Downbeat, where he had a decent view of the band. He recognized the 1955 Muddy Waters singing "Trouble No More," laying down a sadness deeper than his own.

For a time he allowed himself to become lost in the music. But after a few more songs he removed his citspecs and took a six-pack of beer and a half-eaten carton of mac and cheese from his real world fridge.

He popped a brew and ate the cold, tasteless macaroni, washing it down with beer. Then he brought the rest of the beer into the living room. If he was going to drink imaginary drinks at an imaginary bar, at least he could get real world drunk.

☼

CLAIRE FINISHED ANOTHER PULP NOVEL, NOT SATISFIED WITH the ending, not satisfied with reclining on her ragged virtual couch, not satisfied with much of anything, in fact. It was early evening and her head hurt from too much time inworld and laying awake all night thinking about Joe and the way she had treated him. Now she had just made it worse. She thought about the night ahead of her. She should have changed, she thought, before she went out—she had spent the afternoon chatting with Mickey Nines and she still wore her Kick-Ass outfit—but she was too tired and depressed to make the effort.

She informed Maxi that she was checking out for the day. Time to go unwind at The Downbeat. Maybe Jasper could pull a few laughs out of her.

The problem with Joe, he was smitten with her. That was obvious. But it wasn't her, Bridge Whitedeer, he was goo-goo-eyed over. It was the glamorous Claire Deluna. What is this, she thought, jealousy? Was she jealous of her own persona? How the hell can you envy a bunch of ones and zeroes on a microchip?

At The Downbeat, she sat at the bar and waited for Jasper to serve her. When she caught his eye, he raised an eyebrow.

"Nice outfit," he said as he made his way down the bar toward her. "Out cruising the undernets again?"

She blushed. "Yeah, just chatting with an old friend."

"You want the usual, sweet cakes?"

"Sure, Jasp. Give me the usual."

"You sound a bit down tonight, girl."

"I'm weary, Jasper. I'm tired of it all. I have people following me, and I don't know why I'm doing this anymore. And I got nasty to a really nice guy who doesn't deserve to be treated like that—ejected him from my office. Pushed the eject button, and bam, he was lying out on the street. How do you like that?"

"You mean that guy over there?" Jasper pointed to the booth where Joe sat listening to the band, unaware that she had entered. "This is the second time he's come in today. He seems to be looking for something. Why don't you go over and apologize to him?"

"I don't think I can do that, Jasper."

"And why not, sweet cakes?"

"Because he's attracted to this." She jabbed her forefingers at herself with both hands. "Claire Deluna. But that's not who I am, Jasper. I'm not this fucking Persona. I'm a skinny little flat-chested half-breed who ate too much ugly fruit as a kid."

"Well," said Jasper, "you don't know what Joe is like in the real world, either. Or what he appreciates in a woman. That's all just projection. So, it seems to me, the two of you are even. You'll never know if he's looking at the pixels or listening to what's behind them, if you don't go ask him."

Claire put her elbow on the bar and propped her head on her hand. "How do you do it, Jasper?"

"Do what, sweet cakes?"

"Always have the wise thing to say? And don't tell me some crap about sixteen million lines of code. That's not wisdom."

"I guess I must have inherited it from my wise and wonderful programmer, then." Jasper winked.

· · ·

She had no reason to be angry with Joe. She could have left it the other night; instead, she had invited him to go dancing, and ran from him the instant he came too close. She took her drink and ambled over to Joe's table.

"Mind if I join you?"

He gave her a who-are-you stare, then he smiled as recognition came to him.

"Claire. No, please sit down. Great outfit, by the way." It didn't seem to be sarcastic or ironic.

"I call her Kick-Ass Claire. I was out in the field today."

He laughed. "Lady of a thousand disguises."

"Look, Joe, I owe you an explanation. It's just when you came into my office… it's been a rough day… and when you came into my office… I can't deal with personal stuff at work… I'm sorry, Joe."

"Claire, I'm the one who should apologize. I should have told you right from the beginning, you see. I came to The Downbeat the other day because Lindsay Lane gave me your card." He pulled the card from a shirt pocket and laid it on the table. "And talking to you at the bar, I just forgot—I forgot why I came. I just thought we had something going, and I got carried away. I'm not the kind of guy who just falls all over a woman, you know. I've been alone for five years. My daughter Jessie and I get along just fine. Or did. I really need your help and advice. I'm afraid she may be in some serious trouble."

"So, you came for my professional help? You really should have said something, Joe. I'm not taking any fresh cases. I may even be getting out of the business."

"I don't know if I could pay you what you need, in any case."

"Why don't you tell me about it. Maybe I can give you some advice."

"What is Sweetland, Claire? Do you know what this is all about?"

CLAIRE STARED AT JOE, DUMBFOUNDED. WHY WAS THE universe orbiting around this Sweetland crap? Officially she was still deciding, but in her heart she knew she was getting out of the business. If she changed course now, she might never get away. It would take all of her energy to resist the addictive lure of New Life. Could she go cold turkey? Just pull the plug? On the other hand, what if all this Sweetland stuff was somehow connected? What if it had something to do with the Bolivarians and Mitilogías? What if there was no way out of it, but further into it?

"Claire, are you there?"

"Yeah, I'm here. Joe, what do you know about Sweetland?"

"As far as I know, it's a marketing campaign for New Life. Allison… Lindsay Lane is part of the Tollgate Group. She told me about it. But kids are really getting messed up by it."

"Maybe that's just what it is, a marketing campaign. Maybe it's more. I'm not sure. I don't know if I can help you, Joe."

"What do you mean, 'Maybe it's more'?"

She couldn't say it, tell him the sad and real possibility of it. It was lousy of her. But she just couldn't go there.

"I might give you some advice about diverting her from this Sweetland thing. But I think I'm leaving the PI biz. I don't have the stomach for this anymore."

"You said earlier that people were following you?"

She looked away, toward the band on the little corner

stage, at the smattering of patrons. She wanted to change the subject.

"Well, actually," Joe said, giving her a reprieve, "I'm not in prime condition to talk this evening, anyway. I think I might have sucked down a few too many of those vodka crans."

Claire laughed. "Joe, I'm sorry. So you like vodka crans, huh?"

"Jasper said, 'that's what Claire drinks.'"

"You've been talking to Jasper about me?"

"Yeah. He brought it up, honest. Jasper's a great guy."

Just then, as though conjured, Jasper appeared. "Can I get you kids another round?"

"We were just talking about you, Jasper," said Claire. "I was about to tell Joe that you're an AI."

"You're kidding," said Joe.

"All six hundred million plus lines of me," said Jasper. "Unbelievable, huh?"

Claire giggled. "He's also modest. We'll have another round, Mr Unbelievable."

"Coming right up, sweet cakes," Jasper winked and returned to the bar.

"That's amazing," Joe said.

"Yeah, ain't it? That's why I support this place; one reason, anyway."

There was a long pause in the conversation as they listened to the band's female singer belt out, "... sometimes I feel like a motherless child..."

Claire broke the silence. "I feel like I owe you an explanation about the other night, too."

"It's unnecessary, Claire."

"But it is. You're a nice man, and I'm just scared. It's been so long since I've had anyone in my life."

"I understand. Really, I do. I would like to know you, Claire Deluna. And whomever you are out there in the actual world. But I know you have another life somewhere, and there's probably not room in it for some new guy. I mean, you haven't even seen me. And what do I know about you, except that you are bright and have a witty sense of humor, and I thoroughly enjoy your company. And you know how to build a gorgeous avatar."

Claire laughed. She had an urge to say something self-effacing, but held it in check.

"God damn it, Joe. You know how to pull at a girl's heartstrings. You know, it's not just an avatar—it's a complete persona."

"What's the difference? We all have our public personas, don't we."

"It's more than just putting on a face, you know. It's coded into your avatar. A voice. A way of speaking. A style."

He smiled, still not understanding the difference. She paused for a moment, then reached across the table and touched his hand. He felt a slight tingle from the contact, longed for it to be real.

"Say, would you like to go to the fair with me tomorrow? We could talk about this some more."

He laughed at her sudden change of mind.

"It's not exactly fair season, is it?"

"This is the virtuality, remember. It's always fair season. I know a sim where it's High Summer all year around. It's not New Life, at least not the adult version. It's called Kid's Life. It's a family kind of place where people take the kids, just like a real fair, and the programming is extremely good."

"You won't disappear on me again, will you?"

"I promise. You'll love it."

CEDAR INSISTED THE TEMPLE WASN'T RELIGIOUS OR political indoctrination, despite the weirdness of it all. But then the whole idea of going to Sweetland required serious mental adjustments. So these were just hoops you had to go through, like immigrants having to learn who the third President was or who shit out the crap about the free market.

When Gretel arrived at the university labs, the others were waiting, and she was surprised to find a stranger with Toxine. Toxine caught Gretel's eye, and her conspiratorial smile left Gretel confused.

"This is Penny Fortune. Penny will go through the Temple courses with you."

"Hi, Gretel." Penny walked up to Gretel and hugged her like an old friend. Gretel shrank away. Who was this person? She couldn't recall having met her. It must have shown on her face, because Penny stepped back and placed her hands on Gretel's shoulders. "You remember, we met back in August. I have you to thank for telling me about Sweetland. I guess I've had a bit of a makeover since then…"

Gretel had no such recollection, but then maybe she'd just forgotten. She talked to several people back then when she was new and super enthused. There was something odd about this scenario, though. And something wrong about Penny Fortune. She needed to talk to Toxine about it later — now it was time for class.

"Yeah… Penny… hi… glad you could make it."

·   ·   ·

"I'M SISTER ALICIA. YOU ARE IN THE HALL OF CULTURES. New Initiates must choose a familiar environment in which to enter the Rites. The Paths, as we call them, are categorized by language and religious tradition. For the non-religious, choices also exist, but everyone must choose *a* path. You are young, and a minimal education is required of you before you enter the final stages. All potential immigrants are encouraged to attend the Rites, but older candidates with more life experience," — she looked at Penny — "may be sent directly to the Path of Atonement and Reconciliation, the ultimate path we must each take, a journey through the sim Chaos. It is Final Judgment."

"How do they decide?" asked Benson.

"Don't worry, students," said Sister Alicia. "As long as you are healthy and psychologically fit, you will not have a problem.

"The Rites will last for an intense week, ending with First Crossing. During that period you'll learn the Tenets and the skills to help you get along in your new home, as well as history to teach you the lessons of the past."

Gretel's small group of students chose the Path of the Revolution. It appeared exciting and romantic to Gretel, and maybe a little dangerous even. And none of them were religious. This was one of a half-dozen secular paths. The new girl followed along with no questions or objection, and Gretel found that suspicious, too. Though maybe Penny Fortune was taking the Path of Least Resistance.

"I will be your mentor and guide," said Sister Alicia. "For your first days on the Path of the Revolution, we will study the lessons of history from the perspective of the great social movements. We will go to Old Paris, Soweto, Birmingham, La Paz, Kolkata; we will speak to Gandhi, Mandela, Bolivar, King, Luxemburg, Tecumseh, Morales, and others and analyze their words to help us build our better world."

"But why do we need to study these moldy old dead people?" asked Penny Fortune. Cedar rolled her eyes. Then Benson chimed in, "Yeah, weren't they part of the problem to begin with?"

Penny turned and stared at Benson, fixing on her as though she was a homing device. It gave Gretel a chill.

"Yes and no," said Sister Alicia. "Many good ideas are used for destructive ends, that is true. And many of these individuals held onto dogmas and superstitions we now reject, such as the Inevitability of Progress or Dialectical Materialism. These were people who were seeking solutions to the problems of inequality, oppression, and exploitation. Students, new ideas are built upon the knowledge of history. Just because we may reject certain tenets of dialectical materialism doesn't mean Marx didn't have many important things to say about class struggle and change.

"At the end of the week we shall study the Three Tenets of Justice: Equality, Redemption, and Reconciliation, followed by the Tenets of Rights and Responsibilities: Vigilance, Respect, Citizenship. The final and most important of the Paths comes Saturday.: First Crossing. When you arrive on Sweetland for the first time, you will know with certainty that the ground beneath your feet really exists. The dream will be manifest.

"But first you must walk the Path of Atonement and Reconciliation. This is the hardest path for many. You will be on your own. It is a role playing game which needs a cool head, but a game which also requires honesty with yourself. Your goal is to reach the gate to Sweetland. We call this gate The Eye of the Needle. The path you will walk, we call

Truth and Reconciliation. Think about what that means. It's the key to your success."

"You mean it's going to be a different experience for each of us?" Pox asks.

"Yes," says Sister Alicia, "each of you must walk your own path."

"What do you mean by truth and reconciliation?" asks Gretel.

"The guilty must face their accusers, and confess and atone for their crimes. None are without guilt, or sin if you prefer that metaphor. Confession is the first step in reconciliation. The next is to forgive and be forgiven. We all share guilt in allowing things to reach this monstrous condition on Earth. We must be sure that only those who understand this may proceed. Sweetland must begin with a fresh start."

It seemed right, and yet Gretel felt uneasy. "So, how will you know who is guilty?"

Sister Alicia replied, "Your conscience will speak for you."

"What happens if some make it over to Sweetland, unatoned and unreconciled?" asked Cedar.

"It is inevitable," said Sister Alicia. "And even if it were not, their ideas will arrive, uninvited. Does anyone remember the First Tenet of The Responsibilities, students?"

"Vigilance," shot Gretel without hesitation.

"Very good. The most important defense of the Community is Vigilance. We must remember this, always, and not let the old ideas take root. They must be pulled like weeds, the moment they sprout."

☼

THE FAIR PORT-A-POTTY SMELLED LIKE LAVENDER. JOE WAS pretty sure it wasn't the scent of Claire's hair, although his face was pressed into her head. Did he imagine the press of her body and the softness like real hair? He flushed with embarrassment. It wasn't just his proximity to her. What would people think when they walked out together?

Claire giggled. "It happens, sometimes."

They stepped out into the midst of a huge, spirited carnival. Joe was reminded of childhood trips to the State Fair, but, there were fewer adults here, and children of all ages ran out of control. "Come on over here, kids, win a genuine vintage child-star persona," yelled a barker, and a dozen children changed direction in front of them. One of them, a little girl, stopped short at Claire's feet.

"Wow. Are you a Hollywood star or something?"

Claire shook her head, but then her face turned red. She looked down at her skimpy leather Kick-Ass Claire outfit. "Uh-oh, this identity might not be so appropriate here."

Claire was surrounded by a growing pack of children demanding to know who she was and what movie she was in. "Are you a pirate? Or what are you?" asked a young boy.

"Well," said Claire, "I'm not in a movie, actually."

"You are too," the boy insisted, "real grown-ups don't dress like that."

Joe, still holding Claire's hand, kneeled and beckoned the boy closer. "Do you know that new Griddie, *The Space Pirates of Neptune?*"

The little boy shook his head, but the girl standing next to him said in a tiny voice, "I think *I* might have heard of it."

"Well," said Joe, "This is the famous star, Claire Deluna, who plays the pirate queen. But she's hungry right now, and she's late for her important luncheon date. If you come around later this afternoon, she'll be giving away laser swords at the pavilion over there." Joe pointed up the midway toward a large domed building.

"Oh, okay," said the boy, "we'll be there."

"Bye, Ms Deluna," said the little girl, and the kids ran off laughing.

Claire gave Joe a mock frown. "Do you always lie to little kids with such ease?"

"Every day." He gave her a sly grin, but he felt the truth behind it. "They're too young. They won't remember. And now they can tell all of their friends they saw the famous actor, Claire Deluna."

"And they'll wonder why *The Space Pirates of Neptune* never came to a sim near them."

"Well, it was a horrible vid, anyway. Now, I think it might be wise if you changed into something more… uh… normal."

"Yeah," said Claire. "Back to the restroom."

Claire moved out of sight down the midway. She was the same vulnerable girl underneath that Kick-Ass Claire persona, stumbling and blushing. What was her actual life like? Joe wondered. Was a relationship possible? It seemed unlikely. He didn't even know where she lived. Even if it was on the West Coast somewhere, when would he have the time to make a relationship work?

Two teenage girls with cotton candy passed by, and the sweet sugar smell sent him into nostalgia. Cotton candy and popcorn and sodas. Hot August afternoons at the State Fair. He had taken Jolene once, that last year before the virus. Before Jessie was conceived. They walked hand in hand, two young lovers viewing the exhibits and the farm animals, riding the carousel, making out on the Ferris wheel. They stayed into the warm summer evening, sitting in the grass listening to an aging Sarah McLachlin sing "Adia" from outside the gate to the rodeo grounds because they couldn't afford the ticket to get inside.

A pretty young woman in a bright yellow summer dress walked toward him, a lilt in her step, her black hair in French bangs and a ponytail. Claire, her same pretty face, but younger, like a college girl. What was her actual age? The thought had never occurred to him. This was another one of her personas.

She spread out her arms as though they were wings and performed a pirouette. "What do you think?" she asked. "I call her Cutie Claire."

"You continually amaze me. She seems a little young, you know, for an old guy like me."

"I hope not, 'cause you're stuck with me, Pops. I'm your date whether you like it. Now, would you take me on the Ferris wheel, Daddy-O? Please?"

He wondered what this sudden, weird role reversal was all about. But he was smiling and feeling happy about it. "Do we have time?"

"We have all afternoon," she countered with an exaggerated frown, "and I've never been on a Ferris wheel. I'd really love to go. Won't you indulge me, *please?*"

"Okay," he said, "but first some cotton candy."

Claire didn't understand what had happened back in the restroom. She had meant to put on Everyday Claire. But she couldn't. It felt like the thing she should have done, but it wasn't what she wanted to do at all. It came on without warning, this compulsion to be the young woman-girl she hadn't allowed herself to be for the past six years. She was the sophisticated, street-wise Claire Deluna, Private Investigator, and to be anything else would reveal some mortal weakness. Cutie Claire had just been a secret whim. An impulse purchase. She never thought about ever wearing her. But it felt good. It felt damned good. For one day, she could just be a girl and hold a guy's hand and ride on the Ferris wheel with him. To hell with everything else. And when she saw Joe and the smile on his face, she wanted to fall into his arms. She wanted to dance. She wanted to leave New Life behind and find the real life Joe and take him away to her forest. Today, she would not let the fact that there was no forest slow her down. Today, she could dream a forest for the two of them.

She saw him melt under the weight of her "*please.*" She imagined his daughter had him wrapped around her little finger. Joe took her hand and led her to the Ferris wheel as they ate their cotton candy, feeling its sugar high. Stalled at the top, the bizarre, make-believe world spread before them, Joe gazed out across the landscape, deep in thought. She laid her head on his shoulder and sighed. "What are you thinking about, Joe?"

"My life, and this *Through the Looking Glass* world we're in. How the hell did we get here, Claire? You know, a guy thinks he's fallen for a girl, but he can't even kiss her. Not a proper kiss. He can't touch her flesh-and-blood hand, or caress her hair. Isn't that messed up?"

"But we're still here, together. Can't we just enjoy that for now? Then maybe… who knows? Maybe there's a way."

She didn't believe it herself. It wasn't so far between Portland and Seattle, but Claire lived in New Life, not Seattle. The gulf between Claire Deluna and Bridge Whitedeer was bigger than the ocean.

Joe rested his head on top of hers, wishing he could feel her actual body, like he had that night with Allison.

"Yeah. Maybe we can find a way."

A VAGUE FEELING OF ANXIETY NIBBLED AT JOE. THE virtual sun—one which mirrored the actual sun in his part of the world—would soon be down. The afternoon had gone by in slow motion until he had forgotten that time was moving at all. He had a sense of déjà vu. He felt like a teenager on magic mushrooms. The heightened intensity of the world. Sounds echoing long after they had gone. Time stretched out, so that tomorrow seemed like an eternity.

Some schmaltzy romantic voice said, *It's love, Joe.*

But a more rational one said, *It's the cotton candy, fool.*

It was drugged. Cotton candy programmed as a hallucinogen. He ought to alert Claire, but his senses once again became overwhelmed, and he lost himself in her voice as she was telling him about seeing a bear and having picnic lunches when she was a little girl, and her love for the forest. And then he talked about Jessie, and his childhood in Portland in a household of radical activists; the first time he had come to the State Fair. Through it all, the nagging thoughts kept returning. Cotton candy. Jessie. You need to be spending more time with Jessie. You need to be winning her back from this Sweetland nonsense.

They wandered through the midway when he crossed the threshold, coming down, his mind no longer caught up in the moment, and he relaxed back into the flow of past and present.

"Claire, this has been a wonderful afternoon."

"I know," she said, "I don't want this to end, Joe. I never want it to end."

"Claire, the cotton candy. It's hallucinogenic." He thought about the cotton candy, and the unsuspecting children being fed this stuff.

"Yeah." A sadness came over her face. "That's what I thought, too. We should tell someone. They shouldn't be selling this stuff here."

His anger rose to the surface. "We can't even construct a virtual reality where kids can be safe. This really sucks."

"There's no place that's safe for most of them, Joe. For any of us, really. Not in this world."

"Jessie," he said. "I have to think about Jessie. This world is her future. I can't fall into that kind of despair."

"Joe…" She needed to stop this now, to tell him 'no,' but where were the words?

"I know what you're going to say. Please, just hear me out—"

"—It's going to be alright, Joe. She's just a fourteen-year-old girl. They all act out and fantasize." She hoped her words were true. If they weren't, what could she do about it, anyway?

"Yeah, you're probably right. Maybe I just need to be a better father. "

"I can't imagine that you're not a great father, Joe. But the world… the actual world is so god damned hard."

Once more he felt an overwhelming urge to hold her right then—in the real world. He wanted to put his arms around her and hold her. And he wanted to hold Jessie if she would only let him. It was so fucking unfair.

Claire scrutinized him with a little sadness, a little trepidation. "Do you want to go somewhere and talk about Jessie?"

"Yes. Thank you, Claire."

"You know this can't go anywhere. You and me. How could it?"

He could have said he'd find a way, but he didn't know if it was true. "I understand. But you can still help me with Jessie."

He half expected a no, but she said, "How about we go to a safe place I know."

"MAKE YOURSELF AT HOME, JOE." CLAIRE GRINNED AND showed him a patch of virtual meadow grass. "Too bad we don't have a basket of sandwiches and a bottle of wine. Maybe some apples and cheese. We could have a picnic."

Joe scanned the Borealis sim, taking in its rich design. "I hear longing in your voice."

"When I was a kid," she said, "my parents used to take me to places that looked like this. Real picnics. It was magic."

"I remember a camping trip once near Opal Creek," Joe said. "The sun filtering down through old-growth trees. It was the closest I ever came to believing in God. You know, I grew up in one of the largest and most beautiful urban forests in the world. I would wake up in the morning to the sound of songbirds in the hedge, and ravens calling outside my window. Hundreds of ravens squawking and bickering and talking to one another across the treetops. Squirrels everywhere. Most adults thought they were a nuisance, but not me. I loved them. Portland's forest is gone now. It took less than two decades."

"Well, that's the past," Claire said. "I have Borealis. It's my private little hidey-hole. And there are no ants or mosquitoes."

"And no breeze in your hair or smell of wildflowers. No picnic lunch."

"Maybe the DBT mods will change that when they get programmed here. I guess if you have enough money you can buy your own sim and have all of this stuff coded yourself."

"The rich can have their sims. I've got to eat. My little girl has to eat. Millions of people have to eat and stay warm and find a little freedom to smile, and, to tell you the truth, Claire, I don't give a rat's ass about the rich and their toys."

Claire studied him, surprised by the outburst. A man with passionate convictions.

"It's Bridge. Bridge Whitedeer." Why did she tell him that? Wasn't that all settled?

"Bridge. Is that short for Bridget?"

"Everyone asks me. No, I was born in the middle of the Hood Canal Bridge as my dad tried to get Mom to the hospital in Bremerton. So, they called me Bridge."

"You're from the Peninsula. I remember going up there a few times before the flooding. It was beautiful. Do you still live on the Peninsula?"

She had already told him more than she should. Now she couldn't believe she had just told him, not only her proper name, but where she was born as well. "Look, Joe. Please. I've told you too much. Please don't—."

"—don't worry, Claire, I'm a social worker. I know about confidentiality. I promise not to blow your cover." He studied her image. Just the right amount of glamor. Just the right amount of pathos. "Bridge, what are you running from?"

She should have been angry, but she choked up and went silent. The only anger she could dredge up was anger at herself. She had invited this, hadn't she? She never took clients to Borealis, it was too informal and too private—it was her personal retreat. And yet here she was with Joe. What was happening to her? And why did he have to keep going there, to that personal place? Change the subject. We're here to talk about Jessie and Sweetland, and whatever the hell this is all about.

"I'm sorry, I had to check out for a moment," she said, breaking the silence. "Tea water boiling, you know. I'd offer you a cup if I could."

"I'd love that. Couldn't you res a couple of tea cups?"

"Joe, please.… "

"Okay, okay. Let's get down to business."

"I'm sorry, Joe. It's just that this job I'm doing has really rattled my nerves. I think someone's been tailing me, and I don't want to get you entangled in that."

"Oh, hell, I'm sorry." Joe recalled Dillon's and Pedro's visit to the office. They had let him know they would were watching. He wondered for a moment if he wasn't putting *Claire* into further danger.

He told her about Anya and the grilling they had given him.

Christ, she thought, this adds a whole extra layer of complexity. She hated it when things started getting political. Political always meant trouble, especially the radical kind, and this total mess had been going all political for some time.

"They accused Anya of involvement with terrorists? Can there be any truth to it?"

"I trust Anya, Claire. I don't think she could be involved

in political violence anymore than Jessie could. Do you know something about this Sweetland thing?"

"In my current investigation, I've discovered this cult, the Temple of New Life. They claim that paradise is on a world called Sweetland. Nutty, huh?"

A numbing chill gripped Joe. "Yeah, that's really crazy. It scares the hell out of me. The thing is, Jessie doesn't have a superstitious, religious bone in her body."

"It's as though it's some kind of mass delusion."

"But, what if it's not? What if it's something real—in the actual world. That's what Jessie told her mom. Bolivia, somewhere. But, she told *me* it was a planet a person could somehow teleport to, out in some unknown reaches of the universe. That's more than I can believe. But it could be some place real, couldn't it?"

"It could be. These cults have a tremendous pull, Joe. They take lonely young people, vulnerable people, and promise them community and love. You don't have to be religious to get sucked into that. What puzzles me is how the Bolivarian radicals fit into all this."

Then there is Mitologias and its mysterious projects, Bridge thought. She couldn't talk to Joe about that, it was confidential information. But how did Jessie fit into this puzzle? Did she? And Joe's friend, Anya?

"Can you think of anyone else who might associate with rebels or the feds? Anyone at all?"

"My ex-wife, Jolene. She works for the DHS in Seattle. I think she's a low-level bureaucrat there or something. I'm not really sure what she does, but she was just a County drudge when she left. We don't communicate much. But she called me a week ago and said that she had been talking to Jessie. That's when I learned Jessie had told her that story about going to live in some commune."

"She go by Larivee?"

"No, Cheng. You think she could be involved?"

Jolene Cheng. The name wasn't familiar to Bridge, but you have to watch out for ex spouses. Especially exes who work for the government.

"Just covering the bases, Joe. I have some business to follow up in the morning; I know that you're feeling frustrated. Just be patient, and meet me at my office again at 11:00 tomorrow. I may know more by then, if it's not a false lead. I'm meeting with someone about Sweetland. In the meantime, I think you should stay offline until I can get you some protection."

STAN WAS JUST ABOUT TO CLOSE UP SHOP WHEN THE PHONE rang. Marina Waterman. "Stan, can we meet for coffee over in your neighborhood somewhere?" She sounded somewhat frantic and out of breath. "It's about your devices."

"Of course," said Stan. "Is everything okay?"

"Not entirely. I'll fill you in when I get there.

"There's a place nearby on Broadway. Come by the shop and we'll walk over. How soon?"

"I can be there in a half-hour."

Marina hung up and Stan mulled over the conversation. What had his friend discovered that spooked her? He didn't believe there would be enough code on that memchip that she could do much more than verify his own suspicion that the mods manufactured some DNA base chemicals. That would be a curiosity, but nothing more. Had she done some digging of her own?

Marina arrived in 30 minutes as promised. Stan closed up the shop before taking her around the corner to the Mug, a former hipster coffee joint that now just survived, like all the other businesses in the neighborhood. He could feel Marina's hand trembling in his as he led her through the door and to a quiet table at the rear of the shop.

He didn't hurry her, but let it come out on its own. "Stan," she said, "I don't know what this is, but I think it's not safe. I don't know what you've gotten me into."

Alarmed, Stan put his hand on hers. "What's not safe, Marina?"

"Stan, where the fuck did this technology come from? This is not possible. Not with our current state of knowledge. This is so far beyond anything we can produce it might as well be from outer space."

"You can tell that from that little chunk of software code I gave you?"

"No, we can tell that by reverse engineering those mods."

He hadn't expected this. "You reverse engineered it?"

"Well, yeah. At least Dr Mbili and his assistants did. As much as they could."

"But I thought you were only going to take a cursory look?"

"I'm a scientist, Stan. I had to find out what I was looking at. And what we saw are some kind of nano factories that produce all the components of a DNA-like structure. It's some kind of nucleotide assembler. But its not PNA, which was my initial thought. It's an XNA structure we still need to analyze. It uses different nitrogenous bases than DNA, and Dr Mbili suspects it can assemble a quadra-helix structure by modifying a wearer's own DNA. Or possibly a triple helix structure. But Stan, this should not be possible."

"Wait. So the wearer is having their DNA modified?" He thought about Bridge and all the kids who had been buying these things.

"Not necessarily. We tested one of our lab girls who's been wearing these mods for a couple of months. Her DNA is normal. So I guess the factories might need to be triggered somehow. Perhaps by some special Sim software."

"What does this mean, Marina?" He wondered if he should tell her about skyrmion.

"I don't know, Stan. But the phone call frightened me."

"Phone call?" *Oh, fuck.*

"Someone knew. They knew what we were testing, even though no information from the lab is ever exchanged online, and our labs are secure. They're swept daily. All staff must leave their personal devices outside the lab."

"Maybe one of your lab rats spilled the beans in their off time."

"Or maybe they're following *you*, Stan."

Oh, double fuck. It wouldn't be safe to tell her about skyrmion, now. For her own sake.

BRIDGE SHOULD HAVE FELT BETTER, BUT SHE DIDN'T. SHE had just had a lovely afternoon with a man she really liked, but it left her disheartened—nearly as empty as those virtual one-night stands. She didn't want this to be another one of those brief encounters, and yet how could it be anything different? It had been so long since she had held someone real. What would that be like? What would it be like to be in the real world with someone like Joe? She didn't want to hope, couldn't let that worm into her heart. But still she wondered.

She didn't bother to fold up the Murphy. Just enough time for some tea before returning inworld to meet with Brother Dave. This chase was all so pointless. These wars between the ideologues and the corporations, and the destruction of young lives. And she was one of them, one of the young lives, a girl who had grown up much too soon. Joe's daughter was one of the lucky ones who still had a father who cared about her. Her own parents were both gone by the time she was fourteen. And yet she too was so much more fortunate than those masses of humanity who survived on the streets and in the abandoned buildings. And those children with so little hope that they ended up dead in warehouses.

Now she had to jack back into New Life and do something she knew she shouldn't do. But she had to be sure, didn't she? She had to know what she was playing with.

"Are you certain you want to do this, hun?" Maxine said, curling a lock of chestnut hair around her index finger. "Just googling a federal agent can trigger tracers. I can try to use a back door, but anything we attempt to route through an encrypted proxy will be blocked. That leaves us kind of vulnerable."

She considered it again, for just a moment, but she had already decided. "Cheng's a bureaucrat, not an agent. I just want to know what department, where she works, that sort of thing. No need to go deep."

"I'll see what I can find out. Hang on." Maxi disappeared into her magic chamber.

Claire gazed through the half-open Venetian blinds at the nineteenth-century brick office building across the street. She noticed how the colors shifted when she stared at them. If she looked long enough, would she see through the edge of the illusion? But what was strange was that when she was tired, back in the pit, she could see those same moving patterns of color on her apartment wall. Maybe it's an eye-to-brain thing, she thought.

Her thoughts returned to Joe. What sort of complication had he brought into her life? Why was she letting it happen? When she found out that he had been questioned by the F.B.I. she should have dropped this whole business. Why hadn't she? Why was she asking Maxi to check out his ex-wife instead?

Maxine Magnolia appeared in the doorway, interrupting her thoughts.

"Darlin' now don't say I didn't warn you."

Oh, shit. "What did you find, Maxi?"

"Jolene Cheng is second-in-command at the Seattle Unit of the Anti-Terrorism Office," said Maxi.

Jesus fuck. "This isn't good, is it?"

"It gets worse. They got a tracer on us."

She wanted to kick herself. This was another blunder of cosmic proportions. She didn't want to believe she had been set up, but that was her heart thinking, not her head. "Okay, Maxi, we need to perform a deep background on Joe. We need to know that this will not be a problem."

☼

Seven sat alone in his cubicle solving sudokus. An activity which had earned him the nickname Sudoku7 among some of his colleagues. SUATO2 had arranged for him to work late in order to meet with her, free from Four's prying ears. Although the office was otherwise abandoned, she motioned him into the encrypted conference room.

"What do you have to report, Seven?"

"I built that portfolio on Whitedeer. Trace info's sporadic; she's got some glitch evasion software. Anyway, I found something you might be interested in."

"Go ahead," urged Two.

"Her current employer is Mitologias, SA. Connection to the Bols. You probably know all of that."

Two nodded.

"Well, last night," Seven continued, "she was snooping around in the company database and trigg'd an auto-tracer. Guess who she was looking up?"

"I don't have a clue."

"You."

"Me? What the hell?"

"That's what I thought, so I looked at Ms Deluna a little more carefully. It seems she's got a new acquaintance—your ex, Joe Larivee. Goes by Joe Justjoe, inworld. He's also come up on the radar a couple days ago, traveling to one of the Bol sims."

"Hmmm. Any idea what they're up to?" That old irritation returned; Joe was a mistake that just didn't know when it was over.

"Like I said, her evasion software is glitch. But today she was traced to the undernets."

"Send me over your report," she said. "Have the lab geeks take a good close look at Bridge Whitedeer. Find out who else she's tied to, any aliases she might be using. Go deep. We can't bust Whitedeer—at least not yet—but I need you to get some pitter heat on her. Whatever it takes."

"I might be able to help there," said Seven. "Did Four tell you about the call that came in? The Grid thing?"

"Yeah. Something about some crank call or something?"

"Well, I took that call. I didn't think it was bogus myself. This chuck is an old computer geek here in town. A pitter. I checked him out, and he looks legit. Turns out he lives in the same apartment building as Ms Whitedeer. Four says he'll do the follow-up and I don't think much about it til the next call comes in. I take that one too. I recognized the voice. It's that chuck, Bernard. He's back in Little Beirut. He's been seen down on Swan Island."

Seven was talking about a shadowy character they had been tracking for a few years on HATHOR. Bernard had connections to both the mob and the Bols, but HATHOR's all-seeing eye had cataracts; it couldn't see far into the rebel enclaves or foreign sims protected by quantum firewalls, although it could read ordinary packets coming back into North America.

"I've been trying to get a fix on him," said Seven, "but I swear that fucker, Four, is sabotaging me. I can't prove it. Every time I get close to something, the son of a bitch takes over my investigation."

"About the phone call…" Su prompts.

"So I give the call to Four and monitor the son of a bitch. Bernard says something like, 'This techie chuck up here has some of our code. He may be trying to leverage it,' and Four says, 'How much?' and Bernard says, 'Enough. He's figured out the Grid's going down. He knows about our client. You want me to contact the boss?' and Four says, 'No, I'll contact him. He can take it to the New America guys if he wants.

You deal with this techie chuck.' Then the mole says, 'There might be some PI named Claire Deluna involved. You want me to take care of her, too?' Four says he'll have Ms Deluna watched. He doesn't think she'll be a problem."

"Do we know who he meant by 'the boss?'"

"No idea."

"Is that all you've got for me?"

"Yeah. It just didn't sound kosher, so I thought you ought to know about it."

"Thanks, Seven. That was the right thing to do. We're going to nail Four, that bastard. Keep digging on Bernard. And add this information to the portfolio on Bridge Whitedeer, would you?"

Upper brass had been monitoring rumors about plots against the Grid for several weeks, but New America Corporation? What could they have to do with this? Maybe her trip to St Louis was turning out to be work after all. Her feelings about that were mixed.

"I'll get right on it, boss."

"And Seven," she said, "you've got to cultivate your own informants. Loyalty is everything."

"Chuck, I have. Two of my snitches have gone zippo since Four took over. I swear, if he had something to do with that, I'll go to his home and I'll strangle the fucker with my own real world hands."

"Calm down, sweetheart. You've got to learn the game. And don't tell Four more than necessary. Do you still have assets on Swan Island?"

"Yeah, I have another snitch down there, but I don't want Four to find out about her."

"That's the attitude. Use her. I'll give you a level three encrypt. You'll be able to com right in Four's ear and he won't know you're not talking to dear old Mom. And Seven, don't report to anyone but me."

"Yes, ma'am."

JOLENE ZONED HOME. WHO THE FUCK DID THIS WHITEDEER bitch think she was, ferreting around in the DHS database, looking up high-level agents? It's called criminal hacking, now, sweetheart, not googling. A felony. It took a lot of fucking cheek. The chutzpa Jolene might have admired in other circumstances. Of course, she couldn't charge Whitedeer, since she had no warrant, and her tracers, themselves, were a no-no without one. Not to forget the minor fact that she couldn't prove it in court, even if she had a warrant.

Bridge Whitedeer was definitely trouble. But she was also an opportunity. The boys and girls in the lab had traced Claire Deluna to some fascinating persons of interest. At least her connections had very intriguing associations of their own. KT Willow, aka Imogen Kovacs, performed high tech work for various individuals behind the Jalapeño Curtain and certain mob and PI types. A major talent in the black hat universe. She was undoubtedly behind Whitedeer's sophisticated PA software. Mickey Nines also had his shady tentacles into the mobs—gambling, mostly. In addition, he had ties to the Chicago financial sector and various high rolling traders in the world stock markets. In the RW he was Gustav Schneider, a former hedge fund operator about two decades past due for the grave.

So, the mob, the Bols, and the financial sector. Put all that together with the Sweetland suicides, rumors of the Grid going down, preparation for riots in the cities, it all added up to something once inconceivable in Jolene's mind. Things were about to blow sky high. Worldwide. And it wouldn't be good for the likes of her. All you had to do was take a walk around the real world streets of Seattle to see it in the faces you met.

Insurrection. Revolution. This was what Sweetland was about. Her bosses were ignoring the warning signs. Even if her side came out on top, they were going to lose the West Coast, if not the whole god damned ball game. The so-called government she worked for had already been hollowed out to an empty shell. Another reason to get out and take this New America Corporation offer seriously.

Bridge Whitedeer must have some actionable knowledge about all of this. Every time Jolene turned around, there was Claire Deluna with her nose in shit. Jolene was in no fucking mood to be charitable. Bridge Whitedeer was going down, and her connections were going down. Including Joe Larivee. Even if she had to have the lady renditioned, if that was necessary, she wouldn't hesitate.

She had one consolation: she would soon be on her way to St Louis. And maybe a new job. But two thousand miles from home wasn't damned near far enough.

THE FOUR FRIENDS MET UP FOR COFFEE IN OLD PARIS. They'd planned this foray the day before to debrief. That was Cedar's word, *debrief,* and Gretel thought it silly as if they were some kind of secret agents or something. Pox said he knew a great place to hang. They made a point of not inviting their newest classmate, Penny. The skepticism about her unanimous.

The little sidewalk café on Boulevard St Germain was

quaint and in keeping with the period. It was in the hub of radical activity, a few blocks from the Sorbonne.

"So, what do you think of the lessons, Benson?" Cedar said as they pulled out chairs and seated themselves.

"I'm not sure," Benson said. "It all seems kind of… uh… dogmatic or something. Like I just joined some kind of Maoist personality cult, or something. You know, like they had back at The Turn."

"What the hell do you know about Maoists, Benson?" Gretel said, even though she kind of knew the answer to that.

"Well, not a lot, really," Benson said, "except my dad once belonged to some group called the RCP, until he got disillusioned and became a Green or something."

"This isn't anything like a Maoist cult, or any other kind of cult." Cedar was irritated. "It's about democracy and learning to live in community."

"It still feels kind of stiff and dogmatic," said Benson, "but don't get your shorts all in a twist, Cedar. I'm giving it a fair chance. You know, if I decide to go it will be because I think life will be better with you guys. And it won't take *much* to convince me of that."

"I don't get you, Cedar," said Pox. "You say it's all about democracy and community and all of that, so why are you so pissy and defensive about Benson speaking her mind?"

"Sorry," said Cedar, but the curt apology seemed insincere to Gretel. Cedar had been on Benson's case since Gretel first introduced her. It was almost like there was some kind of jealousy involved over Gretel's friendship. There was a too long silence before Cedar said, "Look, I gotta go. But first, Gretel, what's with Miss Ditz-head Hip Fashion Statement? Where the *hell* did you find *her?*"

Penny. It had been bothering Gretel all day. "I don't

know. I don't remember meeting her at all, to tell you the truth."

Later, Gretel arrived at the Ecology Lab to find Toxine polishing up her end-of-term reports. "Bureaucratic tomes for the department," she told Gretel with a dour smile. "I don't really give a damn about this stuff. I will be gone in a few weeks, and all of this—recommendations, advancement, pleasing professors—all of this will mean nada. And yet…" she shrugged and turned back to work.

Gretel watched Toxine for a while, trying to formulate the words. She felt a bit like a snitch. She hadn't yet decided what to tell Toxine when the older girl turned back around. "There then, that crap's out of the way. So what's on your mind, Gretel?"

"I don't know where to start, really. It's about Penny."

"Ah, Penny, yes. The US government agent."

"She is?" How had Toxine figured it out? And why was Penny still in the program? The thought crossed her mind for the first time that Penny might be Jolene, or someone sent by her? Yes, she was sure of it, the longer it sat there. Wouldn't it be just like her mother? Was this all her fault, inviting the woman back into her life? "I just thought something was wrong with her. She really doesn't fit in, you know. But why are you… they… letting her stay, Toxine?"

"Because it doesn't matter," said Toxine. "There is nothing the enemy can do now. It is over for them. And our screening is like a fine sieve. You will see."

"You aren't afraid that Penny will learn about… you know?"

"On the contrary, my dear. She will soon be more confused than ever."

☼

"GOD DAMN IT," CLAIRE MUTTERED UNDER HER BREATH, adjusting the edge of her skimpy costume upward to cover the bare nipple. She had never met a man who made her blush like this. It was just a damned tit. An avatar tit at that. But the thought of Joe arriving and seeing her bare-breasted embarrassed her for some reason she couldn't quite get a grasp on. What was happening to her, anyway?

She appraised herself in the mirror and confirmed that she was still the tough, formidable, Kick-Ass Claire. The girl with the best toolkit in the biz. Especially for dealing with the criminal classes. Some of her multiple identities had been purchased for a considerable sum of money from these same fine business types.

She felt guilty about having Maxi do a background check on Joe. She knew she shouldn't feel this way. With any other client, it would be more or less routine. But it should have been done first thing, god dammit, before she had fallen for the guy. Now she had to confront him, tell him what she had done and what she had found out.

MAXI'S VOICE CRACKLED THROUGH THE INTERCOM. "CLAIRE, Mr Justjoe has arrived."

"Thanks, Max. Send him in."

"Claire?" Joe froze in mid-step as he came through the door. He looked as though he had walked into the lady's restroom by mistake. "I see you're wearing Kick-Ass."

"We're traveling into the undernets, today."

"The undernets?"

"Yeah. Those are the alternative sims run by hackers, Bolivarians, mob types, people who don't like the strict rules you have to play by in New Life."

"So, it's that sort of place. Shall I put on my James Dean motorcycle jacket? I think I have one here, somewhere."

A scuffed black biker jacket appeared on Joe, and Claire scrutinized him. She liked the leather look. "Yes, that will do nicely."

"Where are we going?"

"We're getting some backup. Then we'll talk to my friend, Mickey Nines and find out the latest on Sweetland and missing kids."

"Backup? What sort of backup?"

"The geeks involved in this stuff are some of the most sophisticated programmers and engineers on the planet. We'll need some protection."

"I don't understand," said Joe. "What can they do to us?"

"For one thing, they can probably track you to your real life identity in a microsecond if we don't get you patched. These are dangerous folks, Joe. But I know someone who is the best damned hacker in the known universe, and when she's done with you, even HATHOR won't be able to find you."

"Hathor? What's that?"

"That's the big government computer system. Started out years ago as ECHELON. Total Information Awareness. It reads every packet going in and out of every American connection to the Grid. It's the same system that stores your iris scan and follows you on those little web cams that are everywhere in the pit."

"Shit, Claire. I hope I'm ready for this. I'm putting my trust in you."

"Speaking of which, I ran a check on your ex." A hint of anger had crept into her voice, before she put it in check.

"Oh. Why?"

"I had to know what I was getting myself into. In my line of business, knowledge is everything." Claire crossed her arms over her chest. "Joe, your ex-wife is a real spook."

"Yeah, she always scared the shit out of me," he quipped.

"No, God damn it," Claire snapped. "She's an operative. A high-level DHS agent. She's with the Seattle Anti-Terrorism Office. She's about as fucking dangerous as it gets. Please tell me again you didn't know this."

Joe had a sense of collision between his physical self and his other self. His physical body felt as though it was falling, his fingers jerked, and his avatar swayed. "Shit. I've put you in danger. I swear I didn't know, Claire."

"Joe, I don't know how to tell you this. I hope you'll understand. But I had Maxi run a deep background on you after I found out about Jolene."

Joe looked a little surprised. Maybe a little hurt. "So you know about Frank and Amy," he said. "Claire, that was years ago. I can't see how that should matter."

"Joe, I told you I'm working on a very sensitive case. The kind of case where I might be a target. Do you understand why I had to do this?"

Joe looked pale. As much as you can look pale on New Life. Maybe it was her imagination. "I understand," he said. "But about Frank and Amy. I feel like shit for that. They threatened to take away Jessie. She was only nine. I didn't know what else to do."

She wanted to cry. Of all the horrible things people have been forced to do to survive, making someone turn on their parents to save their children had to be the most evil thing she could imagine.

"Maybe we're not important enough to be on their radar." She didn't believe it. Homeland Security didn't care whether you were important. If they saw you, you mattered. "Let's go visit my friend KT on Fitzgerald's Pipe. We should be safe as long as we're in the undernets. KT will patch you up."

JOE PAUSED IN THE DANK STONE OUTBUILDING ON Fitzgerald's Pipe, still trying to grasp the significance of Jolene's role with DHS. The smell of excrement drove him out of the privy onto a narrow stone walkway in a dark wood. Some sort of rainbow-winged creature like an over-sized dragonfly circled Claire, who was waiting for him on the trail. A tangle of ivy and morning glory vines defined the borders of the path, and on either side grew thick groves of giant oak and walnut trees as far as he could see. The winding path led to an old stone bridge, and on the other side of the bridge, a cob cottage. When the little creature circled his head, he swatted at it, but it deftly avoided his hand. It came to a stop in front of his face and hovered for a moment. He saw the human shape of its body and realized that it was a fairy. It looked at Joe with curiosity and flew away toward the cottage.

Claire laughed. "One of KT's surveillance devices. I think we were just given the go-ahead."

"What if she hadn't approved of us?"

"We would have found ourselves buried in ice on

Dante's Inferno," said Claire, walking down the stone path to the cottage.

Joe laughed. "The Ninth Circle of Hell. The fate of the treacherous."

"You've been there?" Claire asked with earnest curiosity.

Joe laughed. "Not the Ninth Circle, personally. I just read the book, a long time ago in college."

"Oh, it's from a book?" Joe noted discomfort in her voice.

"One of the classics. You should read it sometime."

"Yeah," she said, "maybe I'll do that one day."

The door to the cottage creaked open, and before them stood a disney-cute pixie, about a meter tall, with pointy green ears, electric blue eyes, and a mischievous smirk on her face. Joe felt the pixie's blue argon eyes penetrate him, hostile for just a brief second before turning to Claire. Then, a broad smile came over her face. "Claire, my love. All dressed up for a little s and m, are we?" She grinned up at Joe. "Shall we make it a threesome?"

Claire smiled, "No KT, not today. I need to get Joe here patched for security. And maybe a little scan of my code."

"Ah." KT looked disappointed. "You're on a case. Who are we protecting against?"

"Maybe the Bols," said Claire. "Maybe the DHS."

"Hold it there, sweetheart. You're not serious?"

Claire nodded and told KT about the blunder with Jolene.

"I sent the tracer packing off to Jupiter, but I'm definitely now on their to-do list."

KT ushered them inside. Joe had to duck his head to avoid the low doorway, but once inside, the room opened into a spacious cavern. A phalange of goddesses and nymphs and pagan icons stared at him from niches, shelves, and pedestals. Against one wall, a glass case filled with rows of jars sparkled with brightly colored pixels of light. In old-time script, a label on the case read, "KT Willow's Faerie Dust."

"You know it's an all-new game out there now?" KT motioned them to sit, and Joe pulled up a mushroom-shaped stool, straight out of some Alice in Wonderland set.

"What do you mean?" asked Claire.

"Since those DBT mods came out, all the popular manufacturers have adopted its open architecture and API standards. Those babies are nano factories, Claire. They assemble hormones and other things from your body chemistry. Theoretically, with the new programming, they can zap you. The real you, sweetheart. You know, zap, as in dead meat."

"Jesus," said Claire. "I heard rumors, but I didn't take them seriously. I guess I should come round to visit more often."

"Damn straight," KT shot back.

Joe didn't like what he was hearing. Not at all. He had an urge to take off his citspecs, find the DBT mods, and remove them. Why don't I? I'm like an addict, he thought. I should just flush the shit down the toilet.

Wait, a hundred nano voices replied in unison. *Don't be too hasty, Bud.*

What are you doing to me?

Just my job. You should do yours.

Which is?

Find out about Sweetland. Jessie. Remember?

Oh. Right. Jessie.

"Look," he said, trying to shut off the voices in his head, "maybe this isn't such a good idea."

"Don't worry, darling." KT had a twinkle in her eye. "We'll take care of you." Was he being patronized or threatened? He looked at Claire, imploring.

Claire put her hand on his arm. "Joe, If KT says she can protect us, she's good to her word. You can trust her."

Joe gave Claire a weak salute. KT walked over to the glass case and opened it. She pulled out two jars and returned, putting them down on a small wooden table carved with intricate Chinese dragons.

Joe laughed. "You're going to protect us with Faerie Dust?"

KT's look penetrated him like a knife. "What would you like? An Uzi? An armored tank division? Or maybe a condom for your big, hard penis? Men!"

Claire laughed. He felt his face flush with embarrassment.

"I'm sorry," stammered Joe. "I really didn't mean to insult you."

"He's a pitter," chortled Claire. "Joe's not like that, KT. Really." She continued to chortle.

"It's a program." KT still sounded irritated. "Inworld, despite the 'interrupting the aesthetic' bullshit, a program can look like anything. This is how I happen to like it. Now I'm going to give you a pinch of this Yellow *Faerie* Dust. It's a super-encrypted anonymizer. Your PA, or concierge, or whatever you call it, will ask you if you want to accept this gift. Say yes. Then you will be asked if you want to install the patch, *Yellow Faerie Dust 17*. Again, say yes. This patch will anonymize your identity to most types of tracers. I don't guarantee it against any and all comers. It's not as foolproof as a fake ID. The hacker game is an endlessly evolving process. But I try to keep my stuff up to date."

KT put her hand in one jar, and when she pulled it out, she held up a tiny ball of sparkling yellow light. Joe touched it. When he accepted it, as KT had instructed him, showers of yellow glitter burst around him like a Fourth of July fireworks display.

KT picked up the green jar. "Next, you will both need this patch. This will protect your mods from covertly placed trojans, the kind that might kill you. It will also screen stimulus object programming, which might trick your nano factories into producing a physically harmful chemical in your body."

"The mods can do that?" It sank in, all of his fears verified. Joe felt his physical self reacting, heart pounding, a sudden rush of blood.

"Yes," said KT "As soon as the DBT mods were released, the bad guys started working on them. A breakthrough came a few weeks ago. The feds have it. The Bolivarians have it. And the Silicon boys and girls, and maybe some of the other syndicates. But don't worry, you're now protected from the worst they can throw at you as of yesterday."

"You mean—" Joe started.

"Yeah," said KT "I mean yesterday. Who knows about today."

They spied Mickey Nines at Danito's, where Claire recognized his square profile in the window, topped by his trademark fedora, sipping on a cup of coffee. Mickey smiled at her as they entered and nodded them over.

"Joe," Claire said, "I'd like you to meet Mickey Nines."

"Nice to meet you, Joe. And to what do I owe this second visit in a week, my dear?" Claire leaned over and kissed Mickey on the cheek.

"Joe's a friend. His daughter might be in danger." They slipped into the booth across from Mickey and Claire explained.

"So the mom's DHS, you say?"

"Anti-terrorism."

"Careful, Claire," Mickey said. "You're on dangerous grounds, you know."

She nodded. She knew all too well.

"What about my daughter?" said Joe, impatient.

Mickey looked at Joe without speaking. He turned to Claire.

"There's some mysterious Bols working the West Coast. Stirring up shit. Pardon my French, Claire. But word is they might not be Bols at all. They travel between the camps, Stanley Park to U-dub to Swan Island to the Bay Area and LA. I'd start my search in the camps. Don't have much more than that, I'm afraid."

"Thanks, Mick," said Claire. "That's a start."

"One more thing, kiddo. About that stuff you asked me to look into before." Mickey nodded toward Joe, indicating what he had to say was confidential.

"Think I'll go outside and get some fresh air." Joe grinned, half-hearted, and headed for the door.

"Okay, Mickey," said Claire, when Joe was gone. "What have you got?"

"Word in the back rooms is all this Sweetland buzz—the guerrilla ads, maybe even this Temple thing—is some kind of smokescreen. Some huge technology breakthrough by the Bols. It's so big that an outfit like the New America Corporation is going to extraordinary lengths to get their hands on it."

"Extraordinary lengths?"

"The Silicon Mob. Buying federal agents. Adding their own smoke to cover up what this thing really is. Evidently, the Feds are as much in the dark as you and I."

"Shit."

"Yeah. And New America may already have their hands on the tech, according to my sources. Things may come to a head."

"Any idea how this might connect up to dead people in warehouses, Mick?"

"Nada," said Mickey. "But you asked me about the Temple of New Life. They're involved in this thing, too. Maybe playing both sides. And the Bols have been cautiously recruiting volunteers through their sims. That's part of what this Sweetland buzz is about. Maybe they're putting together a cyber army. Hell, I don't know. If I were you—which I'm glad I'm not—I'd be trying to locate those warehouses or rebel enclaves. Ten-to-one, that's where your friend's little girl may be headed."

Mickey had pinpointed the fear that had been on her mind. That would explain the FBI and the so-called terrorist link. But it still didn't quite add up. Something about these rumors of another world. Joe's daughter and her certainty that she was going to a new world. If this was all part of an elaborate hoax, to what end?

She lingered for a moment without speaking, thinking about Joe. She stood and said, "Thanks, Mickey. I owe you one."

"Anything you need, Uncle Mickey's here." Claire kissed

him once more on the cheek and put 20 dineros on the table for the server. Then she walked out of the café to Joe.

She couldn't tell Joe what Mickey Nines had said about the warehouses, and that put her in a dilemma. She didn't want him terrified, but she wanted him to be informed. In the end, informed won out, and she dragged him off to Borealis so he could let out his anger and grief in anonymity.

When Joe had calmed down to a reasonable state, Claire said, "We need to go about this systematically. My sources tell me that there are at least three large encampments in PDX, and several more in the surrounding hills."

"You mean the homeless camps?" said Joe.

"Yeah. If they're like the ones in Seattle, they are much more than homeless camps. They are self-contained communities with their own police forces. They are armed, politically radical enclaves. Does that sound about right?"

The light went on in Joe's eyes. "Yeah," he said. "That's pretty much my experience. The city is afraid to go anywhere near them. They're alternative governments with pretty sophisticated tech, according to the grapevine, directional EMPs that can take out drones and anything electronic. They're also pretty much unapproachable."

"Without an invitation," said Claire.

"Yeah. That's about it."

"Look, Joe, I think you should lie low for the rest of the day while I see someone about this case. Then let's check out Malafreña and see if we can find out what Jessie has been up to. I'll let you know when I'm ready to go."

☼

THE FLIGHT LEFT FOR SEATTLE AT 11:00. DILLON'S CAR should be at the University by 13:00. The campus cops would have enjoyed a good four hours of messing up the crime scene prior to his arrival. Solid police work had gone all to shit since this Privatization crap. No proper training, a gazillion jurisdictions all involved in pissing wars with each other. Security guards with armored humvees and automatic assault rifles. A fucking zoo.

He would be on his own this afternoon, and that, at least, pleased him. He didn't need Pedro's cowboy attitude. It was bad enough that Jolene and her ATO snowflakes would be nattering in his ear from their high New Life cloud castle. How the hell could you keep away the bad guys, if you were too pansy-assed to walk down the streets of your own city in the flesh and blood, like ordinary people.

He activated the siren as the crime scene came into view, scattering the gawking pedestrians and bicyclists who scurried to get out of his way. He cursed as someone threw a shoe at his windshield, and he watched it bounce off on its journey to the gutter. He didn't have time time for this shit.

No group had yet claimed the bombing of the U of W Cybernetics Science Center, but the ATO guys were already leaning toward the Bols. Dillon wasn't so sure about that. He arrived at the scene mulling over several other possibilities, including the government and various corporate players. A CSI pointed him toward the Officer-in-Charge. After showing her his ID, he asked for a rundown.

"It was an extremely powerful explosion," she said. "At least five bodies inside, and another out on the sidewalk. We don't know if the vic is the perp or a passerby, but I would guess a passerby. The perp wouldn't have left much of himself or herself on the sidewalk." Too much information, thought Dillon. Why did everyone have to give you their pet theories? The OIC was Marcella Willard, a lieutenant with the U of W campus police. At least she was real police and not a rent-a-cop.

"Any tentative ID on the other vics?" asked Dillon.

"We think one of them is Dr Marina Waterman, head of the Department. Another one appears to be Dr Kenneth Mbili. The rest are probably post-grads or graduate assistants. They're all pretty young."

"Any idea if the two Docs might have been working on something together?"

"Too early to say, Sir. Possibly."

Dillon thanked her and circled the ruins, trying to pick up on anything that might be a clue to this mess. He wasn't having much luck when a call came in from the ATO. It was Jolene Cheng, or whatever the fuck her fairy name was.

"Dillon, I have something I need you to check out. You know that computer guy we talked about, Stan Davies?"

"Yeah, I remember. He had some piece of code or something and claimed the Grid was going down."

"He's the one. Well, it might be related to this bombing. We traced a couple of his calls to the Cybernetics Science Center. To a Marina Waterman."

"Yep, sounds like they're connected alright. Waterman is tentatively IDed as one vic."

"I think you need to pay a visit to Mr Davies, ASAP."

"I'm on it, Boss."

DILLON TOOK ONE LONG LAST LOOK AT THE RUINS OF THE Cybernetics building, thinking about his onetime dream of studying physics. He'd been more interested in the theoretical side of things than this applied science stuff, but it was a shame that someone would take out an entire building full of bright people, people who might have been able one day to turn around this world's slow slide into apocalypse.

He directed his car to take him to Broadway and Yesler, where he found the old guy in his hole-in-the-wall computer shop. Stan Davies jumped when Dillon opened the door. Dillon laughed and showed him his ID. "I take it you don't get much traffic through here." Dillon hadn't seen such a collection of obsolete electronics since he tinkered around in high school.

"Oh, god." Stan let out a deep sigh. "I'm glad to see you."

"Something happen since you called the other day?" He wondered if the old man knew about the bombing.

"When you guys didn't come by right away, I took that code to a friend at the U."

"Dr Marina Waterman."

"Yes. How did you... oh, yeah... well... Marina received a threatening call."

Shit, thought Dillon, he hasn't heard, yet. "Don't you listen to the news, man? The Cybernetics building was destroyed in an explosion this morning. Your friend may have been killed in the blast."

Stan sat down hard and put his head in his hands. "Oh, fuck. This is all my fault. Fuck. Fuck."

"Wait a minute," said Dillon. "You think this is your fault? Maybe we need to have a little talk."

☼

THE STREET SIGN READ *RUE-DE-LA-RÉVOLUTION*. AN OLD Paris alley paved with virtual stones and lit with virtual gas light. Behind a transparent cafe door, a candle-lit room and a small table at which sat a man in a black monk's robe, reading. A large medallion hanging from his neck appeared familiar—similar to, but different from, the one Carlos Seguda wore.

Claire opened the digital door, stepped in. Brother Dave looked up.

"Ms Deluna." It wasn't a question. Accented English. Portuguese, maybe—but a variation. Brazilian, perhaps. "Glad you could make it. You're interested in Sweetland?"

"Yes. Some friends were talking about it, and it piqued my interest. None of them knew too much, so I volunteered to find out. If it's what they say it is, then I'm definitely in."

He looked at her with a half-amused smile. "And what do they say it is?"

She had the uneasy feeling he was playing with her. But she could go along with the game. "There is a bit of disagreement on the details, but the consensus is that you are looking for people to take part in an ecological commune."

"Well, that's correct, as far as it goes."

"How does this work? Do I need to join your church or something?"

"Only if you wish, Ms Deluna. Are you religious?"

"Well, not really, but —"

"I see you have some confusion. First, let me say that it's a common misconception on the street that Sweetland is Paradise or some such thing. This is nonsense, of course. Nor is it a religious colony. But it requires a leap of faith of sorts. And the spiritual ritual helps some to take that leap, you see. For most, our process is simply a role-playing game with certain therapeutic — and let's be honest — screening value."

"For us non-religious folk, what do you say? I mean, if it's not Paradise, then what is it? A commune?"

"It is several communes, actually. Of course it started with just one, but now there are nearly seventy. But they are not religious communes, although there are many religious people involved. The Communities are secular and democratically run."

"And it is where? In Bolivia or somewhere else?"

Brother Dave laughed.

"You mean it's not in Bolivia?"

"It's another world, Ms Deluna."

"You mean another planet. Like in another galaxy or something? Or do you mean a sim world? Because I don't think we can survive in a sim world."

"We haven't figured out exactly where Sweetland is— not in relationship to Earth. The scientists will tell you about quantum transference, and string theory, and all of that, but nothing in Sweetland's sky is familiar to us. The only way to convince you is to show you."

"I can return?"

"Only once, Ms Deluna. Unfortunately, only once. You will have about four hours. If you were to stay longer, then you couldn't return to Earth. The process will have gone too far. When you come back, then you must decide within four days, or your connection will deteriorate, and your body cannot survive another attempt. It's about physics, entropy, all that. You see what I mean by a leap of faith?"

"Something I don't understand. If this is all true, then why isn't it common knowledge? How do you keep something like this quiet? I mean, you freely told me —" He put up his hand to cut her off.

"Because you have already been psychologically screened, Ms Whitedeer." She felt the blood drain from her real-world body at the mention of her real world name. How the hell had they traced her without alerting Maxi?

"You see," Brother Dave continued, "our servers run a very sophisticated psychological profile which determines your compatibility with the Sweetland project. We also run a background check. Takes only a few seconds. Despite these safeguards, I'm afraid that after six months of intensive recruiting, the word *is* getting out, which is why we must close shop soon."

"I don't understand. Why don't you want the world to know about this wonderful opportunity?"

"Claire, there are eight billion people. Sweetland is a slightly smaller planet than Earth, with less land mass. For that reason alone, we would overrun such a place. Then there are the violent, the power-hungry, the greedy, the people and ideas that have already destroyed *one* planet. We only want those who will protect Sweetland and live with each other in harmony."

"And I'd be one of those people?"

"So our profile says."

"What would be required of me if I went?"

"We have another screening process and an orientation. If you decide to go, you will embark on an extraordinary journey. Like your first ancestors who crossed from Asia to the Americas, you will go to an unknown country. We must make sure you are prepared. We have a small group leaving in a few days. If you pass the screening, you could be one of them."

She wanted to believe the truth of it, and it disturbed her. "So, what is this screening? How does that work."

"We take your memories, and with those we create a virtual reality, and we test your reactions to it."

"Wait, how is that possible?"

"You just have to trust the process, I'm afraid."

She gave him her most skeptical look. "Have you been there yourself, Dave?"

"Yes, Ms Deluna, I have been there. But I will not be going back. I'm ill and would not survive the journey. I prefer to help others."

"That's an interesting medallion you're wearing. It looks familiar, somehow."

"The astrolabe is an ancient navigation instrument. It's the symbol of the Brotherhood."

"The Temple?"

"Science, Ms Deluna. The Brotherhood are followers of the scientific method of inquiry." He smiled. "Now, shall I schedule you for orientation?"

"I think so." She smiled. An orientation. A screening process she couldn't take seriously. It didn't sound so threatening.

"Good. Now, if you will meet me back here next Friday, eleven-hundred UT, we will begin the process. If all goes well, and there is an opening, then First Crossing may only be a day or two away. Of course, you will have an opportunity to back out if you need more time. It's better to do most of the thinking *before* you go on First Crossing. Remember, only four days to decide once you have crossed over.

"And one last thing, make sure you are in a safe and comfortable real world space where you won't be disturbed for several hours. Your body will be unconscious."

☼

GRETEL DEVOID'S HOUSE ON MALAFREÑA WAS A SMALL bungalow on the edge of an evergreen wood. The house had a different setting, but Joe recognized it immediately. The house Jessie had grown up in, and the house that he was himself raised in. Frank and Amy's house in Montavilla. There were some things about it that were not quite right, things which Joe's memory would have placed a bit differently, the porch swing a little more to the right, the wisteria on the left side of the steps. But it was the way he remembered it. How many hours had Jessie spent recreating this childhood home? Is this what she had been doing the past several weeks? Luddite that he had become, he recognized that this had taken hours and hours of obsessive modeling to build. If only he had known, but Jessie had given him no clue.

His surprise must have shown because Claire said, "You recognize it, don't you?"

"It was our home in the Montavilla neighborhood. Where Jessie grew up. I didn't know…" He felt Claire's hand touch him. "I didn't know this had meant so much to her. That house was poisoned for me. I had put it out of my mind. It makes me so sad."

"We remember our childhood strongly at her age, I think. I do. It's a magical time…"

"Yeah, I suppose. I just wish I'd known. Her grandparents. She loved her grandparents."

He walked around the side of the house, noticing the holly bushes and the rolled up hose attached to a faucet. He expected that if he turned it on, something that looked like water would come shooting out the end of the hose. In the back, the compost bins and the clothesline, hung with shirts and trousers. In his mind, he saw Amy and Frank, hanging out the clothes together, chatting the way they did, about current events or extended family.

Returning to the front porch, he paused for a moment at the top of the steps to watch a brown eve spider build a web between the wisteria and the shingled siding. She constructed it, a strand at a time, her legs quick and efficient, dropping a new string of silk, tying it, climbing, dropping again, in an endless pattern. He wondered if the task would start all over again tomorrow, or the next time a passerby became snared in its ritual. Or could it be some kind of spy, planted here to track traffic or visitors? How did this world work?

He left the spider behind and entered the house through the aluminum screen door, Claire at his heels, observing. The rooms were laid out just as he remembered them, the couch and the rocking chair, and the round antique table in the dining room. The kitchen cabinets that Frank built. He went back into the living room, and sat in the rocking chair, rocking, hearing the squeak of the rails on the wood floor. A little black and white tabby rubbed against his leg. The cat looked up at him.

"Mr Justjoe," it said, "May we speak in private?"

It was the voice of a young woman. He looked at Claire, unsure of the wisdom of going off into private mode, not trusting this feline messenger. Claire nodded encouragement.

"Uh… yeah… sure," Joe stammered. He set his encryption, and Claire disappeared.

The cat hopped up on his lap. "I have a message from Gretel," it said.

Joe vacillated between anger and confusion. "Look, who are you? Is my little girl alright?"

The tabby purred and looked up at him. "I am no one. I am a message bot, trigged by your arrival. Gretel is okay. You have to trust her."

"Jessie is a fourteen-year-old, for christ's sake. I have to trust her, you say, when she has done nothing but lie to me for the past how many months. Who the hell are you, anyway?"

"I am only relaying her message. You must go through the Temple to get to The Eye of the Needle. You need to go soon, because they are shutting down the Grid. Go to the Temple of New Life. They will tell you everything you need to know."

Joe was about to protest. But the cat had vanished.

Snatches of voice drifted to his ears from outside. Others had arrived. He returned to the front yard, where two young people were talking, both about Jessie's age. One a very fem girl, with a short skirt and big eyelashes. The other of indeterminate gender, her wardrobe very unisex.

"Hi," he said. "You're Gretel's friends?"

"Hello," said Unisex. "Yeah, we're Gretel's and Cedar's pals. Do you know her?" They looked from him to Claire, and back.

He hesitated before saying, "I'm her father."

"Oh, glitch," said Fem, "that girl is always talking about you."

"I hope she has good things to say," he said.

"Oh, entirely," chirped Fem, "Gretel's a real daddy's girl."

Fem's revelation caught him by surprise. What had happened between them he and Jessie could no longer communicate?

"Are you going, too?" asked Unisex.

"Pardon me."

"Sweetland. Are you going?"

"I don't know. I haven't decided." He might as well play along.

"Yeah," said Fem, "it's a hard decision to make. You know, things are really messed up, but Sweetland is like stepping off into the void or something."

"Do you know where Gretel is? She invited us here." He hoped the lie wouldn't backfire on him.

"I think you missed the train," said Unisex. "Gretel is making First Crossing tonight or tomorrow, I think. It's Temple Week, and I don't suppose she'll be around on the sims anymore. Cedar might be somewhere, though."

"Temple Week, what's that?" said Claire.

"It's like preparation for crossing over to Sweetland. Everyone goes through it. At least all the kids do."

"Crossing over tonight?" said Joe, his dark thoughts catching up with him. "I don't understand."

"Wow," said Fem, "you don't know? Yes, they're crossing over in the next few days. In a week or two, these sims will be empty. If you're going to Sweetland, you don't have much time left. The Grid's going down. Everyone is going real world so we can beat the fascists to a bloody pulp."

Stunned by the girl's words, Joe didn't reply. *The enclaves,* the barista in New Paris, had said, and he hadn't understood. They were going to some enclaves in the actual world. Like Claire had told him. They were planning to take up arms against the oligarchies that ruled the world. And the ones going to Sweetland—they had gone where? Jessie had been trying to tell him, hadn't she? But he hadn't been able to get his head around all that craziness.

Joe turned away and climbed the steps to the front porch, where Claire waited for him. He heard Unisex say, "Nice meeting you, Gretel's dad. Gretel's dad's friend."

☼

THE VISIT WITH BROTHER DAVE HAD UNSETTLED HER IN
some fundamental way. She couldn't believe his fantastic
story about another planet, but, at some level of consciousness, she *wanted* to believe it. What did that mean about her,
and about all the others who wanted to believe so much that
they will risk everything? *Everything*.

She couldn't help but think about the warehouses and
the dead children. She didn't know what was real anymore.
The world had flipped over, had become something absurd,
that even this offer on the table, this offer of heaven—that's
what it was, wasn't it?—seemed like a rational bet.

She examined the deep longing she recognized in Jessie's
Malefreña, the loving obsession for something that was and
never was yet could be, here in this virtual place, and she
placed it next to the real empty world that awaited, and she
understood. She understood the desire behind Sweetland,
and she understood why these young people would lay their
lives down for it. What was there left to lose?

SHE TOOK JOE'S HAND, AND THEY ZONED TOGETHER BACK TO
her office to discuss the next steps. The room rezzed around
them with an odd stutter.

The first thing Claire noticed was the office floor lamp
protruding from the center of her couch, giving a whole
new meaning to the term, overstuffed. The coffee table
hung upside down in midair, and walls merged in odd
places. Someone was messing with her geometry, and it
would take hours to put it back in order.

"God damn it," she yelled, but already fear replaced the anger. This was the work of the Feds. Or the Bols. Someone had it in for her, and that meant real world danger.

"Maxi," she beckoned, and her assistant appeared in the doorway.

"Yes, darlin'?" said Maxi.

"Will you check the logs and find out who has been playing with my geometry?"

"I'm sorry, hon. Can't do that."

"Why can't you?" She watched in horror as Maxi's face transformed into the image of a snarling bulldog.

"Level Eight Emergency Protocol, Darlin'," said a gruff male voice. "Official State Secret—computer malfunction— the dog ate it, the cat shit in your shoe, hon. Maybe you can suck my dick for the answer to your dreams—oh wait, *you're* the dick. Well—whatever—you've been had, Ms Whitedeer."

Claire backed away from her personal assistant. Who the hell had the chops to get through Maxi's megaqudit quantum encryption? Unbreakable, KT said! If it was the DHS, it wasn't official, or her office would have been replaced with their "This Property has been Seized, under blah blah blah" seal. This was more like vandalism than a confiscation of her software. But the result was the same.

She saw the shock on Joe's face. She needed to get him out of here. Now. Somewhere they would be safe and she could process this. Maybe Borealis. But before she could act, the stuttering began again, and her head exploded. Her world went dark.

☼

SHADOWS DANCING ON THE WALL AND THE FIRST TENTATIVE drums told Joe that he had been out for several hours. A ferocious throbbing like the worst hangover ever pounded the inside of his skull. Through the pain and the haze, he remembered Claire's trashed office and the bizarre behavior of her concierge or PA or whatever Maxi was called. He remembered the stuttering—a rupture. Something had knocked him out of New Life. And out of consciousness.

He didn't know how long he'd been out. It was already midafternoon, so it must have been most of the day.

He tried not to think about Bridge. Jessie was the one who needed his attention now. He listened for a sign of her presence, but he could hear no sounds in the apartment. He knocked on her bedroom door. No answer. "Jessie," he called, but she still didn't respond, so he pushed the door open, expecting to find her at her desk with her citspecs on. She wasn't there. She's crossing over tonight, said her young friend. His heart skipped a beat and his stomach muscles tightened, but he refused to panic.

He grabbed his jacket and ran down the apartment stairs. He rushed down the street to François' Café, and by the time he arrived at the little coffee shop he had calmed somewhat. Jessie was late coming home, that's all. It didn't mean the world was ending. But the knot in his core failed to ease.

Full of wolf men, witches, and wackenhuts, the line at François' was longer than usual for a late afternoon crowd. Halloween season, he remembered. He scanned the community bulletin board as he waited in line, and his eyes fixed on a tiny slip of paper not much larger than a business card. *What is Sweetland?* it asked. *Come to an informational gathering on Saturday, October 31st at 5 pm.*"

Joe pulled his mobe from his pocket to record the

address and realized it was already Saturday. He had been out for over 24 hours. That meeting was only a few hours away.

At the counter François took orders behind a comic book superhero mask, one Joe didn't recognize. "Give me a cup of java, François."

"Sure thing, Joe."

"So, where's Marnie today?" He referred to the young barista who worked the Saturday counter.

"Just stopped coming to work about a week ago." François handed Joe his cup of java. "These kids, you just can't count on them anymore."

"Have you seen Jessie today?"

"She was outside a few hours ago with a skinny little black girl." Melissa Monroe. He let out a sigh of relief. It felt as if the puzzle was coming together; maybe a talk with Melissa's mom would clear this all up.

"Jessie says you're leaving," said François.

"She did? What did she tell you?"

"Only that she was taking immigration classes."

Joe breathed deeply, trying not to let his distress show. He searched for something to say.

"You know how kids fantasize."

"She sounded very serious."

"Hmmm. Did you happen to see which way the girls went?"

"They headed up toward Twelfth. On their way to the mall or something, I suppose."

Probably going to Melissa's, he thought. "Well, if she comes back by, tell her to get her butt home, would you? Have a good Halloween, François."

"Yeah, I pray again this year they don't burn down my house. See you, Joe."

He found the Monroe's number in his mobe directory and gave it a ring. No one answered, so Joe left a brief message inquiring about the girls. He took a sip, then dropped his ersatz coffee in the waste bin before heading down the street toward Twelfth. He didn't believe they were going to the mall at this time of the day, but he'd check the park. Maybe he could catch them, find out what was going on. Maybe it wasn't what he feared at all, but in his heart he didn't believe it.

As he approached the intersection with Twelfth, he slowed down to take in his surroundings and think about what he was doing. Everywhere SmartSpots flashed their commercial messages at him. Buy this. Buy that. Through the shop windows he watched hologram sasquatches and Frankensteins pushing their wares. In one window he even spied a Santa all decked out in red, Halloween already giving way to another dismal Christmas. Was it any more crazy to believe in an online hereafter, he wondered, than a 2000-year dead Jewish guy who claimed to be the son of God?

☼

Part Five

The Edge of Doom

"That's right, little children, there's a train a-comin', it's time to get on board, we'll make the journey to that sweet, sweetland; you know the devil, he is on the clock twenty-four seven; you know what I be sayin' here, now. You hear me out there in Delta Park? You hear me out there on that river, my ugly ducklings? You hear me up there on The Rock? You hear me what was once my America the beautiful; what was once our sweet land from shore to shore, but ain't no more? Get on board before it's too late, before they close that gate forever, children. Don't wait; the devil is on the move today.

"Now here's another tune from before The Turn, a little rasta reggae love for you. Bunny Wailer, singin' Johnny Too Bad."

—Brother JayJay, Radio Free Earth

"Love bears it out even to the edge of doom."
—*William Shakespeare*

Bridge awoke in serious hurt. A bomb had gone off inside her head. She scanned the clock on the counter and realized she had been out for at least eighteen hours. She should jack back inworld, let the mods take care of the throbbing pain, but as previous events returned to her, she reconsidered. How seriously had she been compromised? Was she even capable of returning inworld? It depended upon how badly they'd fucked her up. She had a backup identity, but it was her only one and needed to be used with caution.

Her thoughts turned to Joe. She bore responsibility for this complete mess. How would she be able to contact him if he lost his inworld identity, too? How would she be able to know he was alright? Would it be too risky to call him on his mobe?

She touched the jeweled mods behind her ear and popped them out, placing them on her table. She removed her ocs and their aud counterparts and grabbed a jacket. Descended the apartment stairs, she walked out into the Seattle rain. Fresh air. Maybe she could walk up to Capitol Hill or take a bus to the Arboretum. It had been ages since she had been to the Arboretum.

She made her way to Broadway and grabbed a northbound University bus, taking a seat toward the back. She watched as the empty commercial buildings passed in a blur, distorted by raindrops on the bus windows and the fog in her mind. Is there a reality, she wondered, and, if so, where can I find it? What does it look like? It wasn't here. Nothing felt like reality anymore. Images of a dead city flew by like dark winged things. Madison. Pike Street. The Starbucks Museum on Capitol Hill. On toward the University of Nothing, the bulk of its campus a refuge for homeless migrants, most of its classes moved inworld. The bus careened on toward that miserable camp, but she was getting off before it reached the University, at the north end of the Washington Park Arboretum.

She disembarked just before the old highway, thinking that she might walk the entire circuit of massive greenhouses, each connected to the next by a covered passageway, all the way back down to Madison. Over the years, the Arboretum had expanded to cover a vast swath of land, taking over the old golf course and stretching all the way up to the Lake Washington Ship Canal, a refugee camp for green things.

Bridge walked east along Roanoke to the Park, absorbed in thought. Or in half-thought. Shell-shocked like a soldier returning from the wars, trying to find her footing. Trying to find the world she had once left behind.

She paid the much-too-expensive entry fee, and the armed guard allowed her through. She hung the pass around her neck and surveyed the paths before her. There were few people out today. A small group of private school children, with their fine uniforms and armed escort. A couple of men talking or arguing, punctuating their conversation with animated gestures. The blond man in the blue raincoat she had seen the other day had followed her through the gate, some distance behind. That raised flags, but it didn't overly alarm her. He might just be a tourist. No one else came through. No one was interested in trees these days, except for a few botanists and the idle curious.

The Arboretum was kept alive by several universities and science foundations seeking a way to save the remaining forests. But funding was inadequate, more and more of it going instead into genetically engineering new species able to withstand disease and temperature extremes. The old trees were relics, and in the minds of many, this was a museum. But even the museum approach wasn't working well, because the admission cost was much too high for the ordinary person.

The Park maintained fifteen greenhouses at the center of the Arboretum, laid out in one enormous ring. Outside of that ring, most of the open-air trees were dead or dying. In the center of the ring, three massive geodesic domes towered toward the gray sky, each covering about twenty acres. Inside lived miniature experimental forest ecosystems, kept thriving in controlled environments.

Despite her earlier decision to walk the circumference of the Park, Bridge found herself drawn toward the center of the Arboretum, where she made for the conifer dome. Once inside the dome, the gently moving air felt cool on her face. The light wind swayed the tops of the living trees, and the trees sang the song of her childhood, as she inhaled the scent of pine tar and vanilla. It was like being in heaven. And when she found a place, a tiny refuge near the center of the dome, underneath the young ponderosa pines, she lay her head down on pine needles and gazed up at the baby giants, until her heavy eyelids could stay open no longer.

A HAND NUDGED HER SHOULDER. "YOU CAN'T SLEEP HERE, Miss. We're closing for the evening." She opened her eyes. A big dark-skinned man in a green parks department uniform loomed over her.

"I must have fallen asleep. It's so peaceful here."

"You've been here all afternoon," said the steward. "I came over a couple of times to make sure you were okay. When I saw you were just asleep, I figured, let the girl lie.

Not that many people anymore who appreciate these big old trees."

"Thank you," said Bridge.

"No problem. Say, I couldn't help but notice..." he pointed to the back of his ear, "are you one of those virtuals?"

"Yeah, my work is inworld."

He shrugged. "It's a shame people have to do that."

Bridge said nothing.

The ranger led her out of the Park, quiet beside her, saying only, "Goodnight now," when he had seen her through the gate on Madison. She bid him good night as the Lake Washington bus whizzed by. Damn, it was an hour between buses at this time of the evening. She would have to walk back to her Yesler Terrace apartment alone in the dark.

From somewhere toward downtown came a steady beating, boom, boom, boom, like a big medicine drum. Then, to the north, thud-pa-pa-pada-thud, and yet another behind her, from Lake Washington, rat-a-tat-tat, until she felt like the city was alive with a thousand drums shouting pain and anger at whatever gods they could name.

She shivered now in the cool air and pulled her collar tight around her neck. The waxing gibbous moon rose over the rooftops. Picking up her pace, she hugged the inside of the sidewalk and attempted to keep to the shadows. She knew how to take care of herself in New Life. But the pit was different. Here there was pain and brute force. And she was tiny and vulnerable. But she had her instinct for danger. And those mornings spent at the Life Center gym had kept her body and mind in shape.

Some cyclists flew by, and her heart fluttered. She heard a sound behind her and across the street, a stone rolling on concrete, a piece of rubble kicked by a passing foot. Every sound and moving shadow made her flinch. She paused a moment in the shelter of a tall juniper bush. Another scuffling sound from across the street. She turned to look. A man was stopped, his foot on a retaining wall, tying his lace. Or pretending to tie it. The moonlight revealing his blond hair and blue jacket. Then he looked right at her.

He was following her. And he wanted her to know it.

She was on the verge of panic. She knew she had to control her fear or it would get the best of her, so she tried to focus on the drums, lose herself in the rhythms. Just ahead lay the commercial district, most of its shops boarded up, but a few lights here and there promised safety. There would be bicyclists, pitters getting off work. She jogged down the litter-strewn sidewalk, toward the lights and traffic. It wouldn't do any good to look behind. He would follow her or not. But if he had wanted to harm her, he could have done it anytime during the afternoon while she slept.

She didn't bother to look for her tail. He was out there somewhere. There was nothing she could do about it. By the time Bridge reached Yesler, her heart had slowed, her head was clear, and she felt somewhat like a functioning human being once more. She had decided about some things. It was time to leave this P.I. business. She didn't know what she might do for a living, but it would have to be inworld. Her life was there. All of her skills were inworld skills. Maybe she could take some classes at one of the many universities and learn a new trade. Then she would find some nice guy, if one would have her. That was an even more frightening question. What if no one wanted her? Or what if Joe did? What would she do with an actual relationship?

Then another thought hit her. What if it were true? What if the Grid was about to go down? She couldn't think about that. It would drive her crazy. All she could allow herself to consider was finish up this Sweetland business. Make a graceful exit. Hope for the best.

A heavy rain was now falling, and she pulled her jacket up over her head as she ran down the last block to her apartment. In the lobby, she removed her wet jacket, dripping from the downpour. She could have taken the elevator for a buck, but she walked up the stairs to the seventh floor. She was still trying to shake off the excess water when she opened her apartment, nearly missing the piece of paper on the floor, lying where someone had slipped it under the door. Leaving it, she went to the bathroom and laid her wet jacket over the shower stall and grabbed a towel to dry her hair. Then she came back out and picked up the scrap of paper, which was folded neatly in half, and opened it.

"Ms Whitedeer," said the hand-lettered note, "we are advising you to cease your investigation of Mitologias. It will not be fruitful. You are touching dangerous territory, and it would be unfortunate if it were harmful to you."

They were threatening her life. Whoever "they" were. The man in the blue coat? Or someone else? They had gotten through her building's pathetic security. That shouldn't have surprised her, but somehow it did. She had never considered the real world danger of living in a rat trap apartment.

Her hands still shaking, she managed to lock her door and bolt it. Then, afraid her legs could no longer hold her, she fell into her chair and trembled.

☼

SATURDAY, AT LAST, THOUGHT SUATO2. JUST MAYBE SHE'D finally learn what this Sweetland thing was all about. Screening. First Crossing. Whatever this nonsense was. Then this miserable week would be over and she'd be on her way to St Louis. She checked out Penny Fortune one last time in the mirror, making sure that everything was in place. She trusted the tech guys had her back when she entered that Temple initiation. But it still gave her the chills. At least Jolene would be in a controlled environment, even if Penny Fortune was not. The techs would be ready to unplug her the instant her vitals faltered, or the electronics were compromised.

Seven stood by, waiting for final instructions. She could see his concern for her. Sweet guy. She'd have to do something special for him when she returned. If she returned, she corrected herself. If New America Corporation made her an offer she couldn't refuse, she might not come back to the ATO at all.

She touched her virtual nose ring, ran fingers through her bright red hair, a sardonic smile on her lips. Penny looked good this morning. Time to pull your nerves together. Steel yourself, Miss Fortune.

She zoned to the Temple.

THE WORDS OF A HYMN FROM CHILDHOOD DRIFTED LAZILY through Penny's mind. *You've got to walk that lonesome valley, you've got to walk it by yourself.* She tried to shut it out, but the song was stuck in a loop, *nobody else can walk it for you, you've got to walk it by yourself.* Why the hell is that damn song in my head? Concentrate. Concentrate.

She stood in the doorway of a church, the Catholic Church her mother had attended, to which she had been dragged every Sunday and every Wednesday evening, along with her brothers and sisters. Only the placard on this wall said, "Welcome to the Holy Church of Walmart."

Curious, she thought. She entered through the big wooden doors and into the Walmart Supercenter where her family shopped, where she worked her first summer job at age sixteen, before walking out the door one day and fleeing to Portland. Fleeing from a future of minimum wage, dealing with asshole supervisors and the trash who shopped there, being told, "You are now a member of the Walmart family." Jolene knew what family was all about. It is about being pushed into the mud by bullies, and having filthy man-things creep up under your nightgown as you lay in bed and cry. Fuck the Walmart family. I won't be another piece of trash.

"Miss Cheng," said a voice on the intercom. "Please come to the grocery department for a cleanup on aisle 67c. Miss Cheng to the grocery department."

It took a moment for her to realize that they were talking to her. Miss Cheng. She was Miss Cheng. Another strange name, Penny Fortune, hung in her consciousness like a long-lost sweater. Wasn't she supposed to be Penny Fortune? What an odd thought. Of course not, I'm Jolene Cheng. I must have been daydreaming again.

She looked for a mop and bucket and found them a few feet away, leaning against a wall. She grabbed the mop and wheeled the bucket through the aisles toward the grocery department, feeling the resentment she always felt cleaning up after sloppy, unthinking cattle. Why can't people mop up their own damn messes?

She rolled the bucket through Junior Clothing. Penny Fortune. She was supposed to be Penny Fortune, not Jolene Cheng. A cute little top dangled from a rack in front of her, all lacy and fine, like it came from one of those exclusive little San Francisco boutiques. I've never been to a San Francisco boutique. Penny Fortune has. Penny hates Walmart. I hate Walmart. Am I Penny, or am I Jolene?

She picked up the little pullover from the rack and held it up to her shoulders. The girl in the mirror was definitely little Jolene, sweet sixteen, a dirty work apron over her Walmart uniform. I'd look so sexy in this top.

"But it's Walmart," said a sneering little voice, "you can't possibly be serious."

Was that Penny Fortune?

Penny Fortune is on a quest. How did she know this? Penny is looking for something, and Jolene was pretty sure it *wasn't* a sexy new top. It had something to do with—

"Jolene Cheng to the Grocery Department for a cleanup," interrupted the voice on the intercom. Another familiar voice. But whose?

She tossed the little top back and grabbed the mop again, leaning on it for several seconds, thinking, trying to get her mind around her reality. Trying to remember about Penny Fortune and her quest. It's so close, why can't I remember?

"Jolene to the Grocery Department," the voice insisted. It was becoming a bother. She might as well get it over with. She rolled the mop through the candy section. Hundreds of varieties of sugar and chocolate and nougat, an island of sweets, a sweetland... was that the thing she was trying to remember? Penny Fortune was looking for Sweetland. Was Jolene Cheng looking for Sweetland?

"Jolene Cheng, please come to the Manager's Office immediately." The voice was sharp and angry now. She was in trouble. What was wrong with her? It wasn't like her to

tarry this way. If Jolene was anything, she was conscientious
and dutiful.

She left the mop and bucket at the end of the candy
aisle and headed straight for the manager's office. She would
have to be contrite and apologize. She hated being contrite.
She didn't feel contrite, just pissed.

Then it came to her. She had to find the door to Sweetland. That was Penny Fortune's task. The Eye of the
Needle. Would that be in the sewing section? She passed
Bed and Bath, bee-lining toward Fabric and Craft, with the
thread and the needles and the needle threaders. But that
was all wrong. There were no doors here.

She whirled around, confused. There was another
section there in the back of the store. A section she had
never seen before. A sign on the aisle said, "Truth."

What kind of truth can you buy at Walmart?

"And how much does it cost?" asked the little voice in
her head.

She walked down the aisle cautiously, a little creeped out
by it all. There were books here. A whole aisle of books. She
wondered why they weren't over in Books and Cards. There
were Bibles and Dhammapadas and Das Kapitals. Curious
that Walmart would have books like these. Bibles, sure. But
the others? She passed *The Kamasutra* and *The Koran* and *The
Principia Discordia*. Where was Sweetland? Yes, there, at the
very end. *Sweetland, Your Guide to Enlightenment*.

"Jolene Cheng to the Manager's Office. Now!"
commanded the familiar voice on the intercom.

"Shit, shit, shit." She ran down through the aisles,
clutching the book. She burst through the door to the
manager's office without bothering to knock. The man
behind the desk was familiar, but not who she expected. She
recognized the lascivious grin on his face. Daddy. Her step-

father, Aston, actually. But Mama said he had to be called Daddy. Daddy stood up, his face red with anger. He stepped from behind his desk and raised his hand as though to hit her. He loomed over her, licking his lips disgustingly. The hand didn't come down, it just remained there frozen in the air.

"You want to keep working here, you little bitch?"

"Yes." Wasn't she the model of contrition? Except maybe for that glare of hatred. She remembered those rough, awful hands on her body. That stopped when she and her sisters fixed Dwight. It all stopped, as though he knew somehow what she and her sisters had done. Was he afraid of them, afraid that the secret might get out? If only Dwight hadn't become like Daddy, pulling out his thing, putting his horrible hands up her dress, then maybe they wouldn't have had to do it. But she was fiercely glad they did.

Daddy reached over and grabbed a mop bucket, suddenly there, where a moment before had been an empty wall. He pushed the bucket and mop toward her. "You got a mess in the meat department," he snarled. "Clean it up. Now!"

She pushed the bucket, reluctantly, toward the meat department. She noticed the mess immediately when she arrived, a big fish flopping down the aisle. But it wasn't a fish at all. Lying on the floor was a boy, naked, screaming in pain, clutching his genitals. Only they weren't attached to his body. Blood covered the floor. She laughed. It was quite funny, actually. Dwight, the little son-of-a-bitch. He got what he deserved. But I suppose I'd better mop it up, she thought. That bastard, Dwight, really ought to clean up his own fucking mess.

Jolene watched impassively as two men in white arrived with a stretcher to cart off Dwight, moaning and crying like a little baby. Like everyone she met today, the men were oddly familiar. Something nagged at her, winking from the shadows. Some punch line from a colossal joke which Jolene just couldn't get. It infuriated her, and the angrier she became, the more irrational the world appeared. *Calm yourself, Jolene,* said a voice in her head. *You are in a dangerous situation, so you must become calm.*

Who said that? Her training instructor at SUATO. Yes. But what is SUATO? And who were those men? They would be from SUATO too, wouldn't they? SUATO3 and SUATO9. Yes, that's their names. Was this a training exercise?

She remembered the Sweetland book in her apron. She was on a quest. There was a puzzle she must solve. Something to do with Sweetland. Why couldn't she keep her mind on the task?

Jolene dropped her mop and retreated to Women's Clothing and Foundations, where she slipped into a changing room. She pulled out the book and opened it. *What are you looking for Jolene?* it said. She flipped to the next page. *What are you looking for, Jolene?* She ripped back another page and another, but they all said the same thing.

"Shit." She was about to burst with frustration. *Keep calm, Jolene.* "… think of it as a game." Yes. Who said that? Sister Alicia. Who was Sister Alicia? She had something to do with the game. But what was the game? And what was Sweetland? And why was Jolene supposed to find it?

Okay, it's a game. The book is asking me a question. So, Sweetland must not be the answer. Sweetland is a task I have to accomplish, but it must not be the goal. So what is the prize? Jolene was stumped. The book was telling her she needed to know the goal. She was sure it had something to do with SUATO. And maybe Penny Fortune.

It came to her like a burst of light, it wasn't the game at all. She was looking for the Game Masters. Was Sister Alicia a Game Master? They had taken control of her mind. She was Jolene Cheng, number two at the Seattle Unit of the Anti-Terrorism Office. She had fallen into this kind of trap once before. It wasn't supposed to happen again. The lab guys were supposed to have fixed things. She was furious, beyond furious, apoplectic.

The lab geeks had given her weapons. "Tracer, appear," she commanded. In her hand, a small device materialized. With shaking fingers, she activated it and waited while it sought the source, the person or machine controlling this sim, activating the nano-neurotransmitters, stimulators, and synthetic pheromone generators that had been moving her around like a puppet.

The tracer beeped quietly; the target pinpointed. Without hesitation, Jolene gave the kill command that sent a deadly string of code toward its intended victim. "Eat that sandwich for lunch, asshole," she screamed. "You don't fuck with Jolene Cheng."

THE ULTIMATE TEST COMPLETED, HIS PERMANENT PASSAGE to Sweetland ensured, Michel Boulé, aka Pox Americano, removed his citspecs and let out a loud whoop. He wanted to run and tell Thérèse, but she would still be inworld at university, finishing up her grading.

First crossing had been so awesome. It had been everything and more than he had hoped. The little forest community they were building, the solar collection farm and the big community hall, houses ready and waiting. And the New World, so mysterious and exotic and alive. In the end, he still couldn't believe it was real. But it was. The best part, he had met his friends and saw them for the very first time in the actual world. Or universe, maybe he should say. Jessie seemed a little young right now, but she was beautiful and maybe he was even more in love with her than Gretel deVoid. Well, he would see how that went. There was not enough time in First Crossing.

He considered slipping into Thérèse's room and taking off her citspecs, making her come home early, but it would probably anger her. She wouldn't be finished until 17:00, a full half hour away. Sometimes a little later, but he had made her promise to be on time tonight.

Maybe he had time to make the celebratory poutine. Just like he had promised. Some real homemade poutine with real potatoes, and real synthetic cheese curd, and real sauce, like his mother made back home in Quebec City. He had purchased the precious ingredients just for the occasion. Then they would go together to Old Paris to meet Gretel and Benson and Cedar for dancing and merriment. One last celebration in virtual reality.

He danced into the kitchen, where he grabbed a carton of St Hubert Poutine Sauce. He would have liked to have made the roux and the sauce himself, like his mother once did, but that required a stovetop, which no one had anymore because the electricity cost too much. He took the potatoes —a half dozen of them—from the cupboard and laid them on the counter, and he grabbed a knife, newly sharpened, and sliced them into large, thick fries. Then he dumped them into the fryer, one of the old-fashioned kind that heated through chemical reaction. He added a little oil. A small healthy amount. On second thought, he added some more. After all, this might be the last time they would enjoy the pleasure of poutine; might as well do it right. He turned on the fryer and grabbed the can of Kraft-Borden American Cheese Curd from the shelf. "Fresh from Elsie to You," it said on the can.

"Thank you, Elsie," Michel said, bowing, "This poutine is dedicated to you and your fellow factory workers. Long live the revolution."

He picked up the carton of poutine sauce and pulled the heat tab. Then, when the fryer's OLED flashed, he opened it and dumped the fried potatoes into two bowls, tossed on the curds, and opened the carton of heated sauce, which he poured over the potatoes and cheese. "Ah, beautiful," he said. "Thérèse will be amazed at her little brother."

Michel looked at the clock. A quarter past seventeen. It should be safe to go in now and pull her home from work. He grabbed the bowls of poutine, one in each hand, and headed down the hall to Thérèse's room. He tapped on her door with his foot, gently the first time, then louder. No answer.

"Thérèse, time to celebrate, dear sister." Still no answer. The door wasn't latched, and he pushed it open with his shoulder. His sister slumped on her desk. She must have fallen asleep, he thought. It had been a stressful week for her.

He walked up behind her. "Thérèse, see what I have made." He shook her gently, but she didn't move. He put the bowls down beside her on the desk and shook her again, a little more sharply this time. Her arm slipped from the desk and hung limply at her side. A tiny stream of blood trickled from her nose. He remembered the American agent she was guiding through Chaos today.

"Thérèse," he cried. He put his finger on her neck,

feeling for a pulse. No pulse. "Oh shit. Oh shit." Michel felt his legs give out, and he melted to the floor. "Oh, Thérèse. What have we done? What have we done?"

JESSIE HAD PLANNED TO MEET WITH HER COMRADES FOR A small celebration after First Crossing, to say goodbye to New Life and the friends they would leave behind. But no one had logged in since Orientation ended two hours ago, and she was considering panic. Mel, who would leave with her for the Enclave in the morning, hadn't planned on coming tonight—unlike the others, she had few friends inworld— but the others should be here. Could she go cold to Sweet- land without first wishing her friends luck? Somehow it seemed immensely important that they get together. This step was irrevocable; she might never see some of them again.

She was about to give up and call Mel real world, when Cedar materialized.

"I thought everyone was supposed to meet up this evening?"

Cedar stared down at the ground, contemplating her feet. Then, she looked back up at Gretel and simply said, "Thérèse," and Gretel knew the news was going to be some- thing horrible. You never ever used pitter names.

"What is it?" she said, trying to keep herself from freak- ing. "What's happened?"

Cedar looked as though she was about to cry. "They killed her."

"Killed Thérèse? Who killed her, Cedar?"

"The government, I think. Pox says that Penny Fortune was a fed, just like we thought. And Toxine—Thérèse—messed with her. They retaliated by zapping her somehow. Through the citspecs mods."

Unable to say anything, now panicking for real, Gretel mumbled, "I gotta go. I can't handle this."

"Pox needs us, Gretel," said Cedar, her voice pleading.

She logged out without replying.

Jessie threw off her citspecs and collapsed on her bed, bawling. The thought of the future without Thérèse was inconceivable. And what if this meant Michel, too? What would she do? It can't be true, can it? That's it, it must be all be a mistake. Cedar lived clear across the continent from Michel and Thérèse. Some kind of miscommunication, then.

But she knew in her heart that it must be true. One of her best friends was dead. No one she knew and considered a friend had ever died for the Cause before. And it was her fault. Thérèse died without ever knowing Sweetland, without knowing the end of the dream. And Jessie's own mother might be to blame for this. And if Jolene was responsible, then she, herself, was at fault. She had led her mother to the *Universidad*.

She was a traitor, and she didn't deserve Sweetland.

Pox needed her. But how could she face him now? How could she comfort him, when all of this was her doing?

She collected herself, wiped off her tears with her bed sheet. She comm'd Mel and told her what had happened.

"I feel so horrible, Mel," she said, breaking into sobs again. "This is all my fault. It's all my fault."

"You want to come over this evening and talk before we… you know…"

"I'll be right over, Mel. Thanks. But I don't know if I can go through with this, now."

There was a brief silence, then Mel said, "Meet you at François' and I'll walk you over. We'll talk about this when we get here."

Jessie grabbed her jacket and wound her way through the Halloween throng. The most popular costumes this year were Guy Fawkes masks and Che Guevara berets. Maybe she should stay and join the Revolution. The Revolution had its romantic appeal, although she knew in her heart it wouldn't be romantic at all. It would be hard and bloody, harder than Sweetland, even if they won and defeated the oligarchies of the world and their transnational allies. Even if they made their Free Cascadia a reality. But it would be something to see, wouldn't it? And her dad wouldn't be alone. She would have time to wake him up to the fact that there was nothing left to lose. And her first year training in Forest Ecology could be used here on Earth, too, couldn't it, to help restore the world?

But then, maybe she didn't deserve to see it at all. Maybe she deserved to die in the bloody war.

Mel was waiting for her at François' Café. On the sidewalk they hugged each other fiercely, not speaking, but allowing the touch to absorb each other's sorrow. They walked together to the apartment building where Mel lived with her mother. They stopped on the porch and hugged again before Mel led her inside. "Mom isn't home," she said as she held the door. "She never is. And Dad's in Eugene full time now, manning the barricades." Her laugh was small and nervous.

The Monroe apartment was austere, with sparse furnishings and bare, white walls, except for a tricolor, day-glow poster of Mao, an "ironic" hipster interpretation from around the Turn. Jessie was never sure if the poster was maybe some kind of double irony, or if it was just a good laugh at themselves.

"It's so horrible," said Mel. "I didn't know Thérèse very well, but I know you two were close."

"This is all my doing, Mel." Jessie felt the tears returning. She tried to blink them back, but they streamed down her face, anyway. "I think I led my mom to the *Universidad*. I was just trying to get her off my back. To let her know I was going to an actual school."

"Jessie, you can't think like that. You didn't know."

"But how can I face Michel? He'll never forgive me."

"You'll never forgive yourself if you don't, Jessie. If Michel blames you, that's his problem, not yours. You did the best you could."

"I don't know, Mel."

"We're all set to go on Final Crossing, Jessie. Don't give up now, after all the work you've put into it."

"But I'll have to face him, Mel."

"I know," said Mel. "But it will be alright. I know it will be alright. Michel cares about you."

Jessie wiped the tears from her eyes with the back of her hand. "Okay. If you'll hold my hand and stand beside me all the way."

Mel kissed her cheek. "Of course, *mon amie.*"

☼

JOLENE COULDN'T GET WALMART OUT OF HER HEAD. Fucking Bol technology. The lab crew had torn into the DBT mods—how many times, now? And they still didn't know how it all worked. It's the sim programming, they insisted, the software, not the firmware. But the firewall they'd patched in did less than nothing to stop the Bols. She didn't want to think that their tech was that much better than American tech. But it was pretty hard to get around. At least her revenge had been complete and effective. The weakness of these idealists, instead of going for the throat, they want to play with your head. Well, fuck them.

Now she had to get back on top of things before she left for St Louis. She had come no closer to understanding what this Sweetland game was all about. And the only thing she had discovered by masquerading as Penny Fortune: it *was* a game. She wondered how this could end well for Jessie.

She reminded herself this was not her problem, but only some misplaced maternal feelings. She had a higher calling.

SHE CHECKED IN WITH SEVEN FOR WHAT HAD BECOME THEIR regular weekend rendezvous in the conference room.

"What you got for me, Seven?"

"Picked up Four talking to that Bernard chuck again. Bernard said, 'I'm leaving for Seattle tomorrow to take care of that little problem we talked about,' and Four had like a frigging hissy fit, said, 'It should have been done a fucking week ago. If you want something fucking done, you got to fucking do it yourself,' Bernard was real cool. Said it would be done by Wednesday. Four said it better be. Then he called the boss."

"You mean One?"

"No. Some chuck named Dick Miglia. When I queried HATHOR about him, I got a national security block. Ever hear of him?"

Miglia. The CEO of New America Corporation, the very company trying to recruit her. A national security block? What the hell was going on here?

"Yeah," she said. "So, what did that conversation go like?"

"Well Four told him what Bernard said. And this Miglia said, 'Make sure he does it right. I think Ms Whitedeer will soon be out of play.' This mean anything to you?"

It sure as hell meant something to her. It meant that Four was the corrupt little bastard she had taken him for, and that she would have to be very careful with Dick Miglia. "Excellent work, Seven."

"One more thing, boss. It seems your daughter has been in contact with some suspected Bols—they might be planning a trip down to Swan Island with a Bol contact, and—" Seven paused.

"—And," she prompted.

"Well, the guys in Virginia have been doing some correlations. A warehouse on the Island may be tied to this citspecs thing."

The mass suicides. The most puzzling thing about this whole scenario. Unless you believed all of that Temple crap —and she was becoming more and more inclined to believe it at some level. But what the hell was it? That was the question eating at her. She felt a momentary pang for Jessie, but pushed it away.

Nearly as troubling, the lab boys and girls had also discovered some interesting things about those DBT mods after reverse engineering them. Thanks to the tip off from this Stan Davies dude. *Impossible,* the techs had said, but the devices somehow rewired DNA, maybe added a temporary extra helix somehow that was flushed out of the system after about four days. But what did it do? And where the hell did this kind of tech come from?

"Have your contact on Swan Island be on the lookout for Jessie—and let's see if we can find this warehouse. And put Dillon and Pedro on Joe's ass again—*hard.*"

THE KNOCK ON HER DOOR STARTLED HER AND, WITHOUT thinking, Bridge grabbed a kitchen knife from the counter. She held the knife in her trembling hand as she peered through the peep-hole. *Stan.* She released her pent up breath in a violent burst. Fumbling with the door bolt, her hands shook so badly it took several attempts to disengage it.

"Stan," she cried when the door finally opened. "I'm so glad it's you." Her voice quivered.

"Bridge." Stan stared at the knife in her hand. "What's wrong? Has something happened?"

She dropped the knife on the table and showed him the note that had been placed under her door. "Stan, I don't know what I've gotten myself into."

He read it carefully, then his eyes moved back to the top and scanned it again.

"My God," he said. "You better sit down, Bridge." He put his arm around her and led her back to her chair. "This ain't the half."

Suddenly she had a terrible feeling. "What are you talking about, Stan?"

"Couple guys from the FBI came by earlier today. A scientist friend of mine at the U was killed in a bomb blast, along with several others."

"Shit, Stan. I'm sorry. But what does that have to do with me?" Then it dawned on her. "You didn't give that software to someone…"

"I'm sorry, Bridge. I had to know what we were dealing with. I just wanted to protect you."

"Oh hell, Stan. Do I want to know what you've found?"

"Not if you had any sense in your head."

"Okay, we know that's not the case, so tell me."

"First, skyrmion is a trojan. It's a program designed to overload the Grid and knock it out for a very long time."

That was big. But could it be a good thing for the planet in the long run? She wasn't sure she cared anymore. "I thought you despised the Grid, Stan."

"The economy, Bridge. Nearly forty percent of the world's wealth is wrapped up in virtual money. In New Dineros."

"I didn't know. Can that be true?"

"It's true. But I've discovered a trojan inside the trojan, and its purpose is to keep some outfit called New America Corporation insulated from the damage."

"A coup?" said Bridge.

"Yeah, you might call it that. But that's not why my friend was killed."

Bridge stared at him, jaw agape.

"It's the sweetland software. Marina, my friend, was puzzled by it, so she had her lab reverse engineer the citspecs mods. They're built to fuck with DNA. Her theory was that they somehow had the ability to insert an extra helix or two into your DNA structure. It would likely be temporary and would be flushed out after a few days. But the tech is incomprehensibly advanced."

What had Brother Dave said? *You must decide within four days, or the connection will deteriorate.* Is that how it worked? By altering your DNA? This still didn't explain what it did. How could changing your DNA have anything to do with transporting you to another planet? If so, couldn't it just as easily upload you into some virtual world? Would you know the difference.

"What do I do now? It's all just been a game so far, Stan… it's never been real like this before. I'm scared."

Stan put his arms around her and gently pressed her head to his shoulder. "Let's think this thing through, sweetheart. What we need is a plan. I can set up a surveillance system on your door. You spend all day in this—" he looked around, shaking his head "—this pigsty on those damn VR sims, and you're completely unaware of your surroundings, Bridge. You're vulnerable here."

She backed away and surveyed her apartment, suddenly self-conscious.

"It's a mess, isn't it?" She laughed, nervously.

"To say the least."

"But a surveillance system won't do me any good against some terrorists or gangsters or whatever they are. They won't care about a little thing like a camera or an alarm."

"Yeah, I suppose you're right. Do you have anyone you can stay with for a few days while we figure this out?"

Bridge thought about that. She could think of no one. She shook her head.

"I would invite you to stay with me, but I'm afraid that might just be from the kettle into the fire. Look, I'll figure it out. I still have some friends out there. Lock your door and hang tight while I go over to the shop and make some calls."

☼

NO ONE HAD YET PICKED UP FROM THE MONROE'S. JOE
paced his apartment floor, dialed again, paced, dialed, until
he'd talked down his anxiety a little. There's no use going
off half-cocked, he told himself. It isn't a crisis, yet. But he
needed a plan, if he intended to find out more about this
Sweetland nonsense. Claire—*Bridge*—had been helpful, but
her revelations had only increased his worry. And now, she
seemed to be missing, too.

He remembered the number he had retrieved from
François' bulletin board. It led Joe to a house in the Alberta
District. A young man in his mid-twenties escorted him to a
large living room where a couple dozen people waited,
many standing. Silent anticipation filled the room. Behind
him, a woman in a green sweater observed the gathering
with a calm gaze. A nerdy looking guy, about thirty, jerked
his head about nervously, tapping his foot. He looked as
though he might bolt at any moment. To his left, a man
wearing a gray rain jacket over what might be a business suit
stared at Joe with steady, unblinking eyes. A young woman
pushed through the crowd to the front of the room.
"Cookies and juice in the dining room. We hope you'll stay
afterward and ask questions. Shall we begin?"

A murmur of agreement.

"Many of you are here today because you're interested
in going to Sweetland. Others have loved ones who are
considering or have already made the journey, and you're
eager to know what this is all about. I'll attempt to explain
as well as I can. My name is Sara Knowles. I'm one of three
here who've made the journey to Sweetland and will return

in the next few days. We cannot come back again. The immigrants call us messengers. I know that this is confusing, so please bear with me.

"Ten years ago, a little-known physicist, Dr Ian Chalderian, discovered what became known in scientific circles as the Chalderian Principle. To make a long story short, the Chalderian Principle led scientists to a new understanding of string theory and quantum entanglement, and eventually to a process which allowed them to manipulate the end location of an open string millions of light years distant. Theoretically, this manipulation could enable the exploration of space and time at the far reaches of the universe, utilizing a newly discovered relationship between quasiparticles, called skyrmions, and the Casimir Effect. It also opened up the possibility of teleportation by mirroring objects on another world, via what the scientists started calling a quantum chain. This process is called quantum transference.

"I should say that I am not a physicist, and I don't understand any of it very well. But I'll try to explain as best I can. The basic building blocks of matter can be 'entangled,' that is, intimately connected to other particles elsewhere in the universe, connected by a theoretical construction scientists call a quantum string. In nature, these strings of seemingly random entanglement are all over the place, determined by the same forces which created our universe. For more than a half-century we have known how to create entangled particle pairs in the lab, and in the early part of this century the entanglement and transference of the first visible object was achieved. But until a few years ago —except for quantum computing applications—this knowledge was more theoretical than practical.

"Eventually, the new theories led to creation of the quantum chain I mentioned before, a set of strings, bound in a quantum field, and duplicated at the far end of the entanglement. If anyone here understands any of this, you are welcome to chime in. I'm afraid I'm not doing a very good job. Four years ago, they transferred the first inanimate object, and the following year, a live specimen. Every particle has a pair. So this twin on the other end of the quantum chain is an identical twin in the fullest sense. The 'you' on Earth is physically the same 'you' which is on Sweetland. Then, about two years ago, the final break-through came, transferring consciousness. But it came at a price. The price is this: a subject can now be teleported to the other end of the chain, creating a host body on Sweet-land, but if the process is halted too soon, the transfer may cause permanent damage to the consciousness of the host on either end of the chain. We are not sure why this happens."

The room hummed with whispering and cleared throats. A hand shot up at the front of the crowd. Were others as skeptical of this bullshit as he was?

"Yes," said Sara Knowles, pointing to the raised hand.

"Does that mean there are two bodies?" asked a young man.

"I know that this is frightening for most of you. Yes, is the answer. I now have a body on Sweetland, identical to this body. A body which has basic motor functions but limited consciousness. It is lying in a type of incubator to keep it healthy. If I don't complete the transfer within a few days, that other body will die and I won't have another chance because this Earth body will be too damaged to start over from the beginning. When I make the final journey to Sweetland, then this body on Earth will lose its conscious-ness—and eventually its involuntary motor functions."

The murmur grew to a quiet roar.

"Are you saying my son is brain dead?" demanded a middle-aged woman.

"We have well-controlled environments mostly, ma'am. Over seventy-five percent of our travelers are successful. Ten percent back out before the second transfer."

"What about the other fifteen percent," someone shouted.

"Unfortunately, there are those who don't make it. About eight percent become frightened, or paranoid, or have the process interrupted by meddlers who don't know what they're doing. Many of these have irreparable damage. That's why we try to control the departures. Another seven or eight percent have serious health problems on the other side. There is a risk, a fairly high risk. It's important—if you decide to go—that you understand this. There is a fifteen percent chance of not making it alive or whole."

Joe's head was reeling. He glanced furtively around the room. Awe or anger filled most faces, but not the suit's. Not the woman in the green sweater, who continued to scan the room dispassionately. A few others appeared suspiciously unaffected. Suicide cult, Claire had said. Suicide cult, or population control?

"My daughter," Joe shouted above the din. "I need to know that she's safe? How can I be sure she's safe? Why haven't I heard of this before? She's only fourteen, for christ's sake. How can she be allowed—"

"Sir," said Sara, "We have a list for families of the emigrants. We will try to find out for you. It's difficult. Returnees are only on Sweetland for a maximum of about four hours, so communication is slow and unreliable. Please, come up and put your daughter's name on the list, and someone will contact you when we have some information."

"How can you allow a fourteen-year-old to take part in

something like this? I'm her father. Don't I have a say?" The room was looking at Joe, now, some shaking their heads.

"So you can force her to stay here," a young man shouted at him. "Screw that, man. Kids have rights, too."

"You people fucked us," said another teenager. "Why should we have to listen to you?"

"Please," said Sara, "this man is concerned about his daughter. Please, sir, come up and talk to me, and I'll try to explain. It's complicated."

Joe's muscles tightened and his face flushed. He pushed through the crowd toward the door, nearly knocking over the nerd. As he did so, the woman in green moved in his direction, intersecting his escape. He noticed the astrolabe around her neck as she sidled up to him at the door. "Swan Island," she whispered in his ear, before veering down the hall and disappearing into the bathroom.

The words haunted Joe all the way home. What could Swan Island have to do with Sweetland? He recalled Mickey Nines' words about fake Bolivarians stirring up trouble in the homeless cities. And Claire's mysterious matrix search. So many pieces to the puzzle. Is that where Jessie intended to go? Enclaves. Warehouses. There were warehouses on Swan Island. Was that the departure point? Or was this all about disappearing to join some revolution.

He didn't want to believe the girls would take that route. Jessie was a committed pacifist. But it was preferable to the alternative—some cult boarding the mothership for their new home in the sun.

New questions kept occurring, and as soon as he had his mind around one, another surfaced, dislodging the first. The biggest questions of all loomed in the background—what could he do, and who could he trust?

☼

BRIDGE SHUT THE DOOR AND LOCKED IT BEHIND STAN. SHE listened to his footsteps fade down the hall. She wasn't sure she wanted him making any more calls. He had her best interest at heart, but his protective words didn't comfort her. And she suspected Stan was still holding something back, but she couldn't guess what it might be. She pushed her couch up against her door. It might slow them down.

It was time to take care of a few loose ends before she could consider going underground. There was Joe for one. What would she do about Joe? He was the first man in a long time who had taken an interest in her—in the real her. And she had made a promise to help him find his daughter. At the very least, she needed to contact him and make sure he was alright.

She found her backup ocs where they should be, stashed away in her secret compartment behind the Murphy. They would allow her to go inworld with an alternative identifier. Alternative Claire was just enough different she might fool someone who didn't know her well, but it didn't change who Bridge was inworld or her access to her tools—only the iris scan that tied her to a new real world ID, the illegal kind sold by the Silicons.

She would meet again with Brother Dave. She hoped the Temple's sophisticated software could recognize her through her altered real world ID. If Maxi had been right, it was that good. She counted on it.

Why was seeing Brother Dave was so important to her? She had probably pulled all the information out of him he would give. And yet, she was determined to go deeper into the rabbit hole. The afternoon at the arboretum had only reminded her of her longing for meaning, for a future. Maybe Sweetland sounded like an option. Maybe she wanted to be convinced. Maybe she was that sick of this world.

First, she would visit Jasper, get some advice from her trusted AI. Then, she would have to make a choice.

THE DOWNBEAT WAS UNUSUALLY QUIET, ONLY ONE OTHER customer at a back table, checked out. *Apparently checked out,* she corrected herself, feeling a new edge of paranoia. But she didn't really care. She had already decided to make her exit, and if it hadn't been for Joe, she would have been gone. At least that's what she told herself, unconvincingly.

Could she leave without contacting Joe? She didn't know if she could handle a goodbye. She didn't owe him anything. Why did she feel so shitty about abandoning him? Then there was Sweetland. Could she really go through with it? And if it turned out to be real, and Joe's daughter was safe, would it be too much to hope she could convince him to go with her?

"You have a vodka cran for me, Jasp?"

"Coming right up, Claire."

Jasper went through the motions of adding ice, pouring, stirring, placing the drink down before her.

"You look down today, Sweetcakes. Your case not going so well?"

"Nothing's going well, Jasper. I'm getting out of this damned PI biz."

"Sorry to hear that, Claire. We'll miss your pretty face around here. You classy this joint up, lady."

"Pixels, Jasper. Pretty *pixels.*"

"It's all the same to me."

"Yeah, I suppose it is. Well, just because I'm getting out of the PI racket, doesn't mean I won't come around. Necessarily."

"What's it depend on, Sweetcakes?"

"I need to feel real dirt beneath my feet when I walk, Jasper. I want to smell real flowers and see the wind blowing through the branches of real trees, to be touched by a real man, not some digital sex machine."

"So how is it going with Joe?" said Jasper, picking up on her thoughts.

She felt suddenly glum. Those words she had just spoken had been Joe's words to her. Or something like them.

"Just another Joe," she said. But he wasn't, was he? That was the problem.

"I might leave Earth altogether. Remember when I asked you about Sweetland? I might go there. I'm considering it. It might be real."

"So, all that turned out to be legit?"

"I don't know, Jasper. I'm not sure I care anymore."

"Well, good luck, Claire. I hope you find your place in the sun. You deserve it, Lady."

Somehow, she didn't she feel like she deserved it.

THE GIRLS MET AT FRANÇOIS' TO BEGIN THEIR JOURNEY TO the Rose Quarter, a vast complex of high-density apartments occupying what had once been a large sports arena. At noon they would meet a woman from the Temple of New Life, Sister Barbelo, who would take them to the departure point, where they would prepare for crossing over to Sweetland. Final Crossing.

But noon was a good hour away, and Jessie insisted that they stop by some of the homeless gathering spots. "I need to say goodbye to Alan before we leave, Mel. I'll feel so much better if I know he's alright."

"Sure," replied Mel, "I think we have time to hit some of the nearby parks. We could even go down to the old waterfront, maybe. If you think it's safe." Mel looked doubtful.

"I won't say it's safe, Mel, but you're going to Sweetland, for crying out loud. Is this more of a risk than that?"

"Sorry, Jess, I don't mean to be so whiney. It's not really safety that's the thing, I guess. It's the hopelessness of all those people in those camps, you know?"

"I know, Mel. We can't let that hold us back. We need to look at it with open eyes, so we don't let the same thing happen in the new world."

"Do you think that's possible. Do you think we can really change things?"

Jessie examined her friend, taking in the question marks in her eyes. "I don't know, Mel. I just know I have to try. I couldn't live with myself if I didn't try.

THE GIRLS WALKED DOWN BELMONT STREET TOWARD THE river, cutting over to St Francis Park. There was no sign of Alan among the tarps, sleeping bags and inevitable trash, but Jessie spied Big Martha.

"Hi there, sweetheart," Martha said as the girls approach her. "I told Alan you've been asking about him. He was in a real bad way. Mouth all infected and shit. Don't think he wants to see anyone. I told him to get his butt down to a free clinic or something, but I doubt he'll listen to old fat Martha. Stupid fool."

"Thanks, Martha," said Jessie. "Do you know where he might be camping out?"

"Down by the river, maybe? Don't know, hon. You might try down under the Steel. But watch out for those clean-n-safe's if you girls go down there. They like to get the little girlies alone under the bridge. That's why most of us gals stay up here unless we've got a man to protect us. Even then, those fuckers have guns."

"Thanks, Martha," Jessie said again. "We'll be careful."

Jessie and Mel threaded their way northwest toward the Quarter, taking the back streets down through the old industrial area. As they passed under the Burnside Bridge through the old skatepark, an eerie silence added to the neighborhood's aura of menace; it was too quiet, too isolated, too dark beneath the autumn sky. They should have taken the long way around, but it was too late now. Any closer to the river they risked the clean-n-safe patrols. The kids told scary stories about this part of town, girls raped and killed, vicious beatings by the corrupt rent-a-cops. Most of it was just talk, Jessie thought, but usually that kind of talk had some sort of basis.

"You don't have to go with me," she said at last to the nervous Mel. "We could meet at the Rose Quarter. I would understand if you want to turn back."

"Of course I'll go with you, silly," replied Mel. "We're in this together, right? You can't go down there alone."

"Okay," said Jessie, "we're in this together, then."

JESSIE AND MEL SNAKED THEIR WAY ALONG THE RIVERFRONT until the Steel Bridge loomed before them. They slipped down broken concrete steps and across the railroad right-of-way to a makeshift fishing dock. Two men huddled under the bridge. Mel hung back, but Jessie made her way toward them along the muddy bank. "You guys know Alan?" she called out, when she was close enough for them to hear.

One of the men sucked deeply on a hand-rolled cigarette. "Badger hole up in the bushes, other side of the tracks. Not much you can do for him, sweetheart. Better get the hell out of here before the goons come around. They won't mess with us, but a couple of girls like you — it ain't safe."

Jessie thanked them and signaled to Mel that she was going to cross the Union Pacific tracks up the embankment to the bridge abutment where a small copse of scrub oak pushed through the ivy. Mel followed as Jessie darted across the tracks and up the hill, slogging her way through the garbage and mud, slipping back a step for every two she took, until she could make out a small space beneath the bridge overhang. "Alan," she called. No answer.

"Alan," she shouted again, as Mel caught up with her.

"Is he up here?" asked Mel.

"According to the guys down by the river. I'm going in."

Jessie climbed deeper into the dank hole, nearly retching from the smell of beer and vomit and rotting food. Finally, she came to a flat spot with a bit of grass, where the afternoon sun filtered in. Alan was lying on a piece of cardboard, a few shreds of ragged blanket covering him. She kneeled beside him and could see that his face was badly infected, pus oozing from his wounds and from his eyes, which were swollen nearly shut.

"Alan," she said softly, but he didn't respond. "Alan," she murmured again with tenderness, "it's me, Jessie."

☼

"I'm so glad that you decided to come, Claire," said Brother Dave. "Many people back out at the last minute, you know. But I had a good feeling about you. There is good news. There is a group making First Crossing this morning. If you're ready, we have an unexpected opening."

"Oh?" Wasn't this all a little fast? And what about her gave Brother Dave a *good* feeling? Her eyes focused on the medallion around his neck. Who was this Brotherhood, and what did they have to do with this? The feeling returned that maybe this was all just a game.

"I'd like to go through the application or initiation or whatever you call it. I'm not sure if I'm actually ready to go."

"Of course. We won't send you over without your final affirmation. Now, come this way, and I will explain a little about what happens next."

He led her to a hallway at the back of the cafe. On one side of the corridor were restrooms and on the other a door that read *Employees Only.* At the far end of the hall was yet another door. This was where he led her.

"Now, before you go through this doorway, I'm obligated to warn you. By entering this sim, you are giving implicit permission to install certain mod patches. These patches will put you into a trance-like state, a sort of blending of memory and dream, or perhaps a better way to put it, a sort of digital truth serum."

"You're asking my permission to administer a truth serum?"

"Yes, Claire, but not as you might think of a truth

serum. You may imagine you see people you know or have known in your real life. You may temporarily forget who you are and why you are here. For some troubled people, it can be a bit of an ordeal. For others—and I believe you are one of those others—it may be, let's say, simpler."

Claire hesitated. What was she getting herself into? Would KT's software patches protect her from malware she *voluntarily* allowed into her system? She tried to remember what KT told her. It would filter for trojans. Yes? Maybe?

"I see your hesitation," said Brother Dave. "I'm here to answer questions you have. We don't want to pressure anyone."

"If what you tell me about Sweetland is true, then I am risking a lot. I'm totally putting my trust in you. In your organization. And I don't really even know who you are."

"I don't mean to sound flippant, Claire, but isn't that what you do every single day of your life. The very food you eat comes from... do you know where it comes from?"

"It's not the same thing. There are protections. There are rules."

"Is that so?" asked Brother Dave. "I don't know. But perhaps this is more like putting yourself in the hands of a surgeon you have never met. A bit more scary. I understand."

"Yes, and I would never do that."

"Unless it was an emergency, of course," replied Brother Dave. "I understand your fears. They were my fears when I decided to go on First Crossing. One thing we will assess while you're inside that sim is, just how badly does this woman wish to escape this Earth? It's time to get on board, if you don't want to be left behind. Remember, First Crossing will only last four hours, and then you will have about four days to back out if you wish."

Claire held her breath and closed her eyes. She hoped KT's software had her back. The air in her lungs burst free.

"I'm ready to go," she said, and walked through the door.

DARKNESS. THEN A SMALL LIGHT, INDISTINCT. TREES TOOK shape out of the shadows, and the light became a fire. Behind the fire sat an old man, squatting, and around him a half-dozen children, waiting patiently. A little boy turned, and looking directly at her, motioned her to come forward and join the circle. Claire took one hesitant step at a time until she stood near the fire and saw the weathered face of the old man through the smoke. It was the face of her father, aged as he now might be if he were alive. The boy motioned her to sit beside him, and she did.

"Daddy." Her voice was barely audible, but the boy turned toward her, holding his finger to his lips. "Shhh."

A subtle change in the light. A prolonged silence. The mood set. The play about to begin.

"In the first instant there was nothing." Johnny Whitedeer's voice was worn and scarred like his face. "Only the Mist. And from the Mist was born Mother Chaos. And Mother Chaos spoke. And so was created the Word. But the Word was yet an Illusion, without substance.

"Then, in the infinite void, where Time did not yet exist, Mother Chaos slept, and she dreamed. And she dreamed all things, and she put them in order, and this order she called Reality. And Reality was still but Dream. Upon awakening, Mother Chaos recalled the Dream, and she pulled a thread from her gown. And one end of this celestial string she tied to the Illusion, and the other end she tied to the Dream, so at the bottom of the Illusion hung the Dream.

"Then Mother Chaos spat upon the Dream, and the Dream became manifest. And so, on the Earth, which she had just created, she could now recline, and rest, and admire her creation. And when she had rested, she told the Story, and from the Story was born Time, for a story must move from one moment to another. And so came from the Story all things which move in time.

"But all these fragile things, born to the Dream and to the Story, tied by a string to the Illusion, will recede back into the bosom of Mother Chaos. And this death she called the Entropy, and to this state all Information must return.

"So she gave to each of these she had created the power to dream dreams of their own. And these dreams are even more fragile than the Dreams of Mother Chaos. And so this is our gift from Mother Chaos, the gift to dream our dreams and tell our stories, which are tied by a string to the sweet land of our imaginations.

"And this we would do well to remember. In the end, when the true Gran Rupture returns all of creation to the static timelessness of the Entropy, there will have been the story, but it will be no more."

Johnny Whitedeer was silent. He looked at Claire with a long steady gaze, as though asking, "Do you understand, my daughter?"

"What does it mean?" asked Claire, though she knew the answer with a cold certainty.

"It means, my child, tell your story while you can. Tell the story of your world while you have a world."

"And now? What now?"

"It's time to go to Sweetland, daughter. Are you ready?"

"Yes, father." She surprised herself with her answer. She reached out and touched his hand.

Without warning, she was falling endlessly through blackness.

JOE AWOKE TO A STILL DARK SKY. HE HAD FALLEN ASLEEP ON the couch again, and the clock said it was 10:15 pm. The drums hadn't yet ceased their nightly rhythm. He listened in vain to detect any sign of Jessie in the apartment. Nothing. Did she come home last night? Did she spend the night at Melissa's? Why didn't he know that? He called out her name. No acknowledgment. It was too early. She would be asleep still, wouldn't she? He should wait to talk to her, but he was impatient. He needed to stop this Sweetland thing now. He called again. Again, no answer. An eerie silence had fallen, although he couldn't say why he thought that. It was as though he had suddenly grown an extra sense, a new faculty which measured the dimensions of his emptiness.

And where was Bridge? He still hadn't been able to reach her. Where was Anya? Where were all of his friends now that he needed them?

He extracted himself from the couch and stretched for a moment, adjusting to the ache in his back, to the lack of virtual stimulators. His mobe chimed, and he found it where he left it on the coffee table. He answered, hoping it was Jessie. He didn't recognize the excited voice, saying, "Joe, it's real. It's not a sim. There's ground beneath your feet. Gravity, Joe. And forests with real trees. And the breeze, you can feel the breeze on your face, and it's my real face, Joe. I'm not sure if that's a good thing, but I don't even care anymore."

"Bridge," it had to be Bridge, "slow down. What are you talking about?"

"I'm talking about Sweetland, Joe."

"Claire… Bridge… this is crazy talk. Are you high? You can't live on a sim. You said that yourself."

"It's not a sim, Joe. It's real. Sweetland is real. They say it's a planet somewhere—they aren't sure where. I don't know how we travel there—it has something to do with strings or quantum entanglements or something. I don't understand that science stuff, but—"

"How do you know, Bridge? How do you know it's not an illusion?"

"Because all the technology in the world couldn't produce a forest like that. It would be impossible, Joe."

"Think about what you're saying, Bridge. You're telling me that someone, whoever they are, has produced technology which can transport you across the universe. And, if they can do that, then what the hell *can't* they do?"

"I just know what I experienced, Joe. Take First Crossing and see for yourself. Jessie's safe—she will wait for you. *I* will be waiting."

"Jessie. What do you know about Jessie? Where is she? How can you have seen her, Bridge. You're not making sense."

"She's going to a safe place, Joe. We made First Crossing together. Now she's on her way somewhere her body will be undisturbed while she crosses over permanently. Please trust me."

Jesus Christ. Where her body will be undisturbed? Permanently? This is insanity.

"Where, Bridge? Where is she?"

"I don't know, Joe."

"Oh, God. Don't do this, Bridge. You don't know if it's

real. The things they can do now. They're manipulating your mind—those mods—"

"Joe, we can talk about this some more. I'll call again tonight, Joe."

Without answering, Joe put down the mobe. Things were going to shit. Everyone he ever touched disappeared or crazy. How did they get to Bridge? She thought it was a suicide cult, so, how did they convince a hard-headed skeptic that you can get to another planet through New Life? What did it all mean? And where was Jessie? She still wasn't home. He wanted to scream.

Oh Christ. Jesus fucking Christ.

His heart pounding, Joe banged loudly on Jessie's door one last time. The only answer was the drums, evidently no longer restricting themselves to the evening, their rhythm fully entering his consciousness now. He pushed open the door. She wasn't there. But more alarming, neither was her VJ. He couldn't recall ever not seeing it open on her desk. No VJ, no citspecs. Nothing else seemed to be disturbed. No note. No clue of her intent. He went through her things, dumping her trash on the floor, scrabbling through it. He found a scrap with "Mel" written on it, and today's date. "Sister Alicia—Sunday morning—the Enclave" was written on another. "Sister Barbelo" on yet another. Whose sister? Cedar's? Mel's? A nun?

On her desk, a photograph of Jessie with Frank and Amy, sitting on the porch of their Montavilla home, rested against a glass paperweight. Above it, tacked to the wall, hung a calendar, but there was nothing written on it but an asterisk on Sunday—today.

Joe grabbed his mobe from his pocket and called Jessie's

number. It rang several times before her message came on. "Hi, this is Jessie. Leave a message." Short and to the point.

"Jessie, this is your dad. Please call me and tell me what's going on. I love you."

He released a heavy sigh. The despair hit his gut first and stomach acid rose to the back of his throat, washing his mouth with a sour taste. It wasn't just that Jessie wasn't in her room, that he couldn't contact her by mobe—she had left the shelter of his reach, stepped through some door he wasn't prepared for her to step through.

Where would a fourteen-year-old girl go? And why did he know with such certainty that she was gone? He snagged his coat from the coatrack, threw open the apartment door, and bounded down the stairs.

François was cleaning his espresso machine when Joe burst through the door. The little coffee shop appeared deserted on the morning after Thanksgiving. He looked up from his work, a smile on his face. His house evidently didn't burn down. "Back again, two days in a row?" he said.

Joe didn't waste any time with small talk. "François, I still haven't seen Jessie. Has she been in this morning."

"Sure," said François. "She was in with that black girl again about 10 or so. Took off toward St Francis Park, I expect. She said you guys were leaving town this afternoon. Is that true?"

Joe muttered, "Oh, shit," and charged out the door. They would be asking around for Alan, looking for the encampments.

THE LARGE WOMAN SPRAWLED OUT ON THE SIDEWALK IN front of St Francis Park parted her long hair with her cigarette-stained hand, her cigarette ash falling on her ratty slacks. She looked skeptically at Joe. Taking a long drag, she blew smoke out the side of her mouth.

"What did you say you wanted them for?"

"I told you. It's my daughter, Jessie, and her friend, Mel. I think they're in trouble. They walked by here this morning."

"In trouble, huh?"

"Look, have you seen them or not?" That was too sharp, he thought, reminding himself that these people looked out for one another. But it was so damned hard to keep perspective when it was your own daughter in trouble.

"I'm not saying one way or another unless you can convince me you're legit."

Joe pulled out his ID. Then he showed her the picture he carried of nine-year-old Jessie with her arm around him. "My name is Joe Larivee. I'm a social worker. Jessie's my daughter. Please...."

The woman considered him for a moment. "I'm known around here as Big Martha. Look, I normally don't rat, you understand. Even on kids. But I talked to those girls a half hour ago, and I'm kinda worried about them. They headed down to the Steel to look for some crazy dude named Alan. He's in a badger hole by the east abutment. Them damned clean-n-safes are fucking bad news down there."

Shit. Alan Tolliver. Under the bridge. What did he have to do with this Sweetland thing? And why were they taking such risks? Images of rape and violent death flashed through Joe's mind. Without looking back, he broke into a run. It was a good mile to the Steel—maybe he still had time to catch them before they made it to the river.

☼

"Jessie," Alan whispered, "what are you doing here. You shouldn't be here."

"I needed to see you, Alan," she said. "I want to make sure you're alright."

"I'm dying, little girl. Can't be alright now. Unless you can take me to Sweetland. Can you help me go to Sweetland, Jessie?"

Jessie wasn't certain what Alan meant, was afraid of what he might be asking of her. Did he want her to help him die? Could she do that?

"I don't know, Alan. I don't know how to help you."

"Sweetland. Just want to go to Sweetland."

She turned to Mel, who had crawled into the hole behind her. Tears streamed down Jessie's face. "The citspecs," she said. "The nanotech thingies can help his pain, Mel. I can't let him die like this. I can't."

"But Jessie," protested Mel, "you can't do this. You've worked too hard to go to Sweetland.

Jessie stroked Alan's forehead. "I'll help you, Alan. I won't leave you like this."

"Sweetland," said Alan again.

Jessie bawled. Behind her, Mel rustled in her bag. Then Mel crawled up beside her and slipped her citspecs over Alan's eyes.

"Oh, Mel," Jessie sobbed, "don't. You won't be able to go if you do that."

"It's too late. I already reset them."

Alan relaxed, a slight smile on his face. "Oh, Mel," Jessie said, turning to her friend, searching.

"I did it for you, Jessie. You're the brave one. You were

ready to go all alone, and I could never do that. Not without you. This is the only way."

Jessie embraced her friend with a passion she didn't know she possessed, clinging to her fiercely. Then she turned back to Alan, and she gently touched his bearded cheek. At least he had some peace now.

Somewhere out of sight down the embankment she heard the crackle of gravel under boots. "Oh, shit, Mel. Clean-n-safes. They'll find Alan." And us, too, she thought.

"What'll we do, Jess?"

"Crawl all the way through this way, and run down the other side of the abutment, maybe they'll follow us, and not bother coming up here. We can get away up the hill on the other side."

Without waiting for agreement or argument, Jessie crawled forward past Alan toward the north side of the bridge, until she cleared the overhang. To the west the sun was setting, the clouds edged in a fierce orange glow. The way up the hill was blocked by a chain-link fence, so she scrambled to her feet and ran noisily down the embankment. She heard Mel following close behind. What she didn't expect was the other clean-n-safe coming up from the north. She ran right into his arms.

"Hey, what have we got here?" he said, a big grin on his bearded face.

"You find somebody?" came a gruff voice from the other side of the bridge.

"Got a coupla little sweeties here," said Beard. "One for each of us."

Jessie stood frozen, arms pinned behind her and barely breathing as the new guy approached her, his foul breath smelling of liquor. She flinched but froze as he stroked her face with the back of his rough hand.

"You little darlin's shouldn't be down here, you know, homeland security and all."

His laugh disgusted her. Behind her, Mel stopped cold, crying, "Oh, God. Oh, God."

"You girls wanna party?" said Beard. "Or should we make an example out of you?"

Jessie pulled herself out of panic mode and tried to recall her defense training. Divert his attention. Do the unexpected. But what? Options sped through her mind. Submit. Catch him unaware. She'd seen that in a half-dozen holoflicks. Men were idiots when their dicks were involved. She wondered if it really worked?

"That's such a hot beard." She tried to sound sexy, feeling supremely incompetent, uncertain of herself. How can she possibly be fooling him? Her heart trembled, and she pressed on. "We love to party. Let us go and we'll be soooo nice to you."

The bald guy with the gruff voice merely stared with his big, stupid grin. To her complete surprise, Beard relaxed and smiled. Jessie turned to face him, trying not to become nauseated at the smell of his breath. She looked shyly into his cold eyes, and as she did so, she brought her knee up into his groin with all the force she could muster. Beard doubled over in agony.

"Fucking whore. Fucking whore." The voice seared with hatred and pain.

Mel shot past the cursing Beard, still frozen in pain, as Gruff looked on dumbfounded. Jessie ran back up the hill toward the fence line, Mel on her heels. The Rose Quarter was only a few blocks away, if they could make it that far.

The fence at the top of the hill stopped her cold. But there was no turning back. She had to find a way through or they would never make it. Then she saw the gap where the homeless campers had pushed the fence apart for access, and she slipped through the opening. For a moment, her jacket snagged on the chain link and she became frantic.

"Hurry, Jessie." Mel's voice trembled behind her. Gruff had recovered and the two men were coming up the hill toward them, only a few seconds away.

"I'm trying," cried Jessie, giving her jacket a fierce yank, ripping it along the seam. She turned to help Mel through just as the two men topped the hill and headed toward them down the fence line. A frantic feeling seized her. They were too close now. They wouldn't be able to escape.

A clear path before them led to Interstate Avenue through a field of weeds and blackberry brambles, and the girls, nearly exhausted, shot across Interstate and the MAX tracks, the rent-a-cops right behind them. When they reached the apartments, they ducked through an alleyway and emerged onto a square on the north side of the complex. Jessie could hear the men's harsh breath just behind them. Then the sound of their running feet ceased.

"Halt, or you'll be shot." Beard.

It was all over. The girls stopped and put their hands in the air. Jessie's heart tried to free itself from her ribcage as tears welled in her eyes. Mel's face twisted in horror.

In the edge of her vision something flew through air. A shoe landed on the pavement with a slap and a voice called out. "Go home, fascists." Then more voices joined in. More objects rain from the balconies.

Without warning, a sudden, powerful explosion rocked the square, shaking the ground and showering pieces of stone. Jessie fell to a crouch, raising her arms to protect her head. Before the stunned clean-n-safes could regain their wits, scores of people poured from the low-rent apartment building, pelting them with debris, chanting, "Fascists. Fascists. Fascists."

A soft hand touched Jessie's shoulder, and she turned to see a tall, dark-haired woman, about her dad's age, standing behind her. "Hurry, girls," Sister Barbelo said, "we must leave before the blackwaters come. *Now.*"

Jessie, shaken, looked from the woman to Mel and back at the crowd, now kicking and pummeling the two clean-n-safes. It was all like a bad dream. She froze, feeling confused and remote, as Mel grabbed her hand and pulled her to her feet. Then they began running, the three of them, back down toward the river and Swan Island.

AS JOE DESCENDED ONTO THE RAILROAD RIGHT-OF-WAY, HE felt the chill of a strong, cold wind coming upriver from the north. The river was rough and full from the recent rains. The sun had now set, but behind him a nearly full moon was rising above the rooftops casting its light across the riverbank. Two men huddled beneath the Steel at water's edge. Joe approached them cautiously. The ones who camped down here between the Broadway Bridge and the Ross Island were tough, he had learned. They either worked with the clean-n-safes or they had come to some sort of understanding. Either way, it could mean trouble.

"Is there a guy named Alan down here?"

One man grinned. "Alan's a popular dude, today."

The other snorted and pointed up toward the bridge abutment. "Poor bastards up there. Don't think he's got long. There's a badger hole behind them bushes along the abutment."

"You said he had other visitors?"

"Coupla young chickees came by asking about him a bit ago. I warned 'em to get their asses out of here before the rent-a-cops come by, but they were determined."

"A bit? How long?"

"Don't know. Just a bit ago. Less than half an hour, I'd guess."

They could still be in there with Alan. He crossed back over the tracks and scrambled up the hill beside the concrete abutment, looking for the badger hole. "Jessie," he called. *Too loud.* He couldn't afford to draw the attention of the rent-a-cops. He finally found the hole, its entrance obscured by bushes.

He pushed aside the brush. "Jessie," he called again, this time a little softer. No reply. But he could hear a pitiful mumbling sound coming from within.

The crawl space barely left room to raise his head. He understood why they called it a badger hole. He pushed himself forward into the dark, trying to not retch from the horrible stench. When his eyes adjusted, he could see the vague shape of a man lying on his back. As he inched closer, he saw a pair of citspecs over Alan's eyes. He edged up next to his old school chum. Just enough light came through the cracks that he could make out the pus from an open wound running down his face, green and thick. Alan's breathing was halting and weak.

"Alan," he whispered, but Alan was in some peaceful bliss brought on by the citspecs. He clearly didn't have long to live, and Joe felt a sudden stab of guilt. There was nothing he could do now. Why had he abandoned Alan? Why hadn't he listened to Jessie?

Somewhere above he heard shouting voices and, gripped by panic, he pushed himself back out of the badger hole. Once out, he took off running up the escarpment, toward the noise. As he crested the hill to Interstate Ave and pushed through the tear in the fence, he heard a thundering explosion and saw smoke rising from the Rose Quarter. He broke into a full, all-out run, bounding through the busy transit stop, pushing away surprised commuters, forcing a path to the alley between the building. He came out the other side and found himself amid a crowd gone mad. At its center two bloody bodies were being kicked and trammeled by the outraged mob, who were shouting, "Kill the Fascists." For just a moment Joe's heart stopped as he saw the yellow vests of the rent-a cops, half ripped from the bodies.

No sign of Jessie, anywhere. Joe retreated, going back the way he had come, avoiding the Transit thugs whose attention was now fully focused on the apartment complex riot. He had failed to catch Jessie. He was sick to his stomach. Where had she gone? What could he do now?

Swan Island, he thought with a new confidence. The only thing that made sense. They were going to the enclave on Swan Island.

BELOW HIM SWAN ISLAND FLOATED IN A MIST OF FOG, THE abandoned industrial park now a huge armed camp of rebels and homeless people, where desperate men and women squatted by the tens of hundreds in tents and inside crumbling warehouses. The perfect place for them, city officials once said. The single access road had been destroyed in a firefight with corporate militia several years ago, collapsing the bridge which spanned the railroad tracks, effectively isolating the rebellious encampment. It was dangerous, practically impossible, for social workers like Joe to serve the people living there.

Portland once had a soft spot for the homeless, Frank had told him. One of the first cities to have an actual city-sponsored homeless camp. But there has always been a nasty side of the city, too, a constant pressure to push the poor and homeless away, to hide them during the festivals, to clean up the streets for the out-of-towners. Joe barely remembered those days. The days before the oil crises and the Depression, when the ranks of the homeless were swelled by mass unemployment and bankruptcy.

It had once been a real island, cutting the Willamette River into two channels, but when the river was dredged in the 1920s, the narrow east channel, the deep channel, was filled, connecting the Island to the mainland. The steep slope remained where the river once cut into the north Portland peninsula, isolating Swan Island from the rest of Portland. Previously, the home of the city's first airport and giant World War II shipyards, Swan Island morphed through industrial factories into service industry warehouses, finally becoming a refuse pit of outdated industries and discarded workers. The collapse of petroleum had made the industrial corporations and their post-industrial children obsolete.

Many of the old rusted metal buildings now stood on the brink of collapse, and at the north end of the Island jagged concrete and spears of rebar marked the spot where a tornado had touched down in '29, tearing away most of the flimsy structures in its path. No one knew how many people had died, because the residents refused to allow emergency vehicles inside, insisting they were better prepared to take care of their own.

Among the ruins sprawled a huge tent city teeming with people. Out of the city's sight, the homeless migration to Swan Island was largely ignored by the authorities, until their numbers were too large to control. A tense standoff between the city and the Swan Island Citizen's Committee ended after a few years, when the city government realized that containment was the most it could accomplish. As long as the islanders didn't expand their territory and kept to their place, self-rule was better than massive police action.

The enclave now had its own police and its own economic system, almost entirely reliant upon the underground economy. Bridge had been right—if the grapevine had any validity, these enclaves had become something quite more than homeless camps. They had become self-sufficient rebel communities in opposition to the ruling oligarchy. But that could actually describe a large portion of Portland, as the riot scene this morning had revealed.

A foot-worn path snaked down the slope in front of him, stopping at the perimeter fence, which was about two meters high and topped with razor wire. Just to the south of the trail was a gate. It would undoubtedly be locked, but the razor wire stopped on either side of the gate, leaving a possible vulnerable point where someone might climb over the gate unseen. He scrambled down the path and nearly reached the bottom when he noticed the greeting party moving up the hill toward him. *Fuck.* Four men arrived at the gate before he was half way down the hill. They were rough-looking men, likely ex-soldiers, and they held their guns like they meant business. He hesitated for only a second, then continued down the hill to meet them.

"What's your business here?" demanded an older, bearded man who carried an air of authority.

Joe hadn't really thought it all out, but he looked the man in the eye, unflinching. Might as well be truthful. "I'm looking for my daughter."

"You need to make your case at the main gate. You ain't coming through here."

"We don't know your daughter, pal," said another man. "Maybe you should piss off."

"Look," he said, "I attended a meeting. About Sweetland. Someone told me to check here at Swan Island. Please."

The first man furrowed his brow, appeared to be considering something. Then he motioned his compatriots closer, conferred with them, and after a moment, unlocked the gate. "Come on through." He pointed with his rifle.

They led Joe to a small Quonset hut. One of the militia produced a wand which he passed slowly down each side of Joe. "Just making sure you didn't bring any insects along," the man said. "The fence catches most of them, but some of them burrow down into your clothes. Bugs and arfids. Gotta use a little Black Flag on those guys." The man held up the wand before looking at its LED screen. "Seventeen arfids and two Beetles. You 're clean now."

"All those?"

"Arfids are everywhere. Average person on the outside's got a couple dozen of them at any given time. Mostly product trackers, but you can never be sure. The Beetles were most likely placed on you."

"Placed?"

"Shit, man, where have you been? Yeah, placed; these things are commonplace. Could be anyone—a lover keeping tabs on you, a stalker, or someone with political motives."

"Political motives."

"The biggest problems are the aerial drones. We call them wasps—they look like wasps. Those are government or corporate, and that's what the fence catches, mostly. It's more than a chain-link fence. It's an electronic wall 20 meters high, too high for most of the bugs to get over. The ones that do we got wasp killers to take care of them. Directional EMP's kill the high flyers and the drones."

The militia tucked the wand into his jacket and pulled a chair out from behind a table. He instructed Joe to sit.

"Name?" The tone returned from chit-chat to interrogatory.

Joe told him. He gave him Jessie's name. The man left. The other three stood over Joe, their guns menacing. It felt like most of an hour before a woman entered. She was a big woman, tall and blond, sharp, no-nonsense. Like the men, she looked street-tough. She held an iris scanner, which she pointed toward Joe's face. "Look into this, please."

He complied.

"So, Joe Larivee." She looked him over. "You work for county social services. You live at 1325 SE Belmont. Your ex, Jolene Larivee, works for DHS. Hmmm. Your fourteen-year-old daughter, Jessie, is… was a student at Benson High School. Your parents were Frank and Amy Larivee, deceased." She paused, looked straight at Joe, and continued. "Your parents carry a bit of a hero status to some people around here, particularly the older folks. Visionaries, they say. You must be proud of them." Her voice betrayed no interest.

"They gave up radical politics when I was born," Joe said.

"Maybe the hard-core organizing kind, but they continued to write, to stay in contact with activist friends.

They were real peoples intellectuals." She extended her hand to Joe. "I'm Margot Carlson, Commander of the Citizens' Defense Committee. A bit too young, myself, to remember any of that."

Joe shook her hand. So, Frank and Amy weren't so retired after all. But the knowledge gave him no comfort. It deepened his guilt in some way he didn't fully wish to understand. These people had surprising access to information. Too much, as far as Joe was concerned. Why were they trying to impress him with that fact?

"What I remember, Joe, is the terror and starvation. I remember the water rising to flood our home in Olympia. I remember my older brother — like Frank and Amy Larivee — taken off to a desert camp and shot. And the fascist spies," she said, her eyes penetrating Joe. He cringed.

"So, you see, I'm a little more cautious than the older folk. And a little less forgiving. Now," she said, "What is this about Sweetland? What is that?"

"My daughter left a message when she disappeared. She said she was going to Sweetland. At this meeting I attended last night, they were trying to convince us that Sweetland is a habitable planet somewhere, that they can teleport people there. I think that's bullshit. But that's all I know."

"What brought you to Swan Island?"

"I asked about my daughter at that meeting. A stranger approached me as I was about to leave. She said 'Swan Island.' That's it. I think Jessie's here."

"You know it's dangerous for strangers down here. Is it worth the risk, Joe?"

"My daughter is everything to me. You don't understand. They were saying bodies are left behind. People are going missing all over the city. People are disappearing everywhere. What could that mean? Are they disappearing poor people now?"

"Maybe they're telling the truth," said Margot. "Maybe there really is pie in the sky and you should just let your daughter go to a better life."

Joe's face grew hot with anger.

"Joe, let me be frank with you. You work for the state. You don't get a job with the government unless you've compromised your integrity. By definition, Joe. So, we really can't trust you, can we?" He cringed, thinking about Frank and Amy.

"I don't work for the state. I work for an independent agency."

"Oh, come on, Joe. You know there's no such thing. Corporate or government, it's all the same. Your agency takes federal money, and you all take their orders, and you go to work every day to keep the poor people in line. The only difference between you and a government drone is you get half the wages, and you still get Uncle Sam's dick up your ass."

"We have to eat. I just do what I have to do for Jessie and me to survive."

"Sure, Joe," said Margot. "I get it. I really do. And I don't blame you for that. People do what they can to get by." She paused and appeared to be considering his worth. "You must understand, we have to be careful. There are always bad guys trying to infiltrate the island. But I guess this is your lucky day. There are a couple of the older folk asked to meet you. Despite my better judgement. But Stu is on the Council—it's politics, you know. They knew Amy and Frank back in the day. Do you mind?"

Why the sudden change in Margot's attitude? Politics? What could he possibly have to say to his parents' old comrades? But if it was a way in, he would take it. He nodded stiffly.

☼

THEY LED HIM FROM THE QUONSET HUT, PAST A LARGE complex of industrial shops, down a street where the grass had thrust up through the asphalt, pushing aside massive chunks of pavement to reveal the compacted ground underneath. They came, at last, to what had once been a large office building, perhaps a bank or real estate firm, now residential. On a flagpole above the building flew the blue, green, and white flag of Free Cascadia. The landscaping around the entrance was overgrown with weeds, the original plantings long dead. On each side of the door grew a brown, stunted palm. In the lobby, an older couple — he guessed they were in their mid to late seventies — sat at a cafe table. The woman rose, a warm smile on her face.

"Joe Larivee," she said, putting her hand on his shoulder. "I haven't seen you since, oh, you were about six years old, I guess. I don't suppose you remember me? I'm Sandra Cole."

Joe shook his head.

"Your mama and me went way back, early eighties, socialist-feminist study groups, all that stuff. Stu and I here, we went underground before The Terror. We could see what was coming. I'm so sorry about Frank and Amy, Joe. I guess you never became involved in all the politics?"

"No, I was born after all of that. The end of history and all."

"That was a lie, Joe," said Stu, an edge of bitterness in

his voice. "That end-of-history shit. Look at what post-modern capitalist paradise has brought us. This, I'm afraid, is the real end of history. Why don't you sit down?"

Joe eased into a chair, eyeing Margot Carlson standing near the door, out of earshot, but watching. Outside, three armed men stood nearby. He had no doubt they were his guard.

"I remember sitting around with Frank and his girl-friend, what was her name? Cassie?" Sandra paused, drifting into reverie. "Amy and Susanne were there. Do you remember, Stu? We were smoking pot and playing Class Struggle."

"We were always smoking pot and playing board games. Or dancing. Or attending meetings that lasted three god damned endless days." Stu smiled at Sandra. "And then we went to sleep. We slept and the fucking fascists took it all."

Sandra leaned over the table. "Look, Joe, it's over. It's the end days, as the Christian loonies used to say."

"Except there ain't no Jesus fucking Christ," snarled Stu.

"But there's Sweetland, Joe," said Sandra. "We're too old, we would never make it. But Joe, you could go, help do things right this time. Carry on for Frank and Amy. You young people, Joe, you're the hope of the world. That's what Amy used to say."

"Yeah," said Joe, tasting the bitterness. "You don't know what it's like to have that burden on you."

"Don't you have a daughter, Joe?" asked Stu. "I remember Amy gushing about her granddaughter. Jessica?"

"Yes," said Joe. "That's why I'm here, Stu. Jessie… they say she's in Sweetland. But is Sweetland real?"

Stu nodded toward Margot Carlson, who was walking toward them. "Sorry, Joe, we can't talk about this anymore.

She only gave us five minutes. A little generation gap here on the island."

They all rose from their chairs as Margot arrived. Sandra gave Joe a hug. "Have faith, son," she whispered in his ear, "it's real."

The word *faith* echoed in his head as Margot led Joe away, back toward the Quonset hut. What did it mean that these people, too, wanted him to believe in Sweetland? It seemed as though he was the object of some conspiracy. *Have faith?* Was Sandra suggesting religion? They would play the religion card, wouldn't they? But why were they teasing him? Why not just send him off to Valhalla? It would be easy with the river right there. Who would find him? Who would look?

MARGOT AND HER GUARDS LED HIM AWAY TOWARD GOING Street. The early November sun now approached the horizon, and the pale light reflected off the downtown high rises. Only another hour until dark. Margot walked ahead down the disintegrating roadway. He quarreled with her, demanded she let him look for Jessie, but the woman was intransigent. Two armed men flanked them, the third followed, leaving Joe no room to make a break if he were brave enough to do such a thing. Off to his right, Joe noted another man, dark blue raincoat and neatly trimmed blond beard, watching with interest as they passed. Far off in the distance, near the river, a small procession moved along in the opposite direction, a half-dozen people silhouetted against the sky, walking beside a bicycle-powered trailer. In the twilight, the thing on the trailer looked like a coffin.

After a considerable walk, Joe and his guards came to a line of old concrete Jersey barriers, once used for highway construction. Beyond rose the chain-link fence, the razor wire. The main entrance to the island on Going Street. A half dozen young militia gathered around a burning barrel, their hands extended toward the flame. Several other armed men, women, and adolescents stood vigilant next to the barricade. Some appeared to Joe to be as young as twelve. He thought he recognized a familiar face among them. Melissa, Jessie's friend. Did that mean Jessie was here somewhere, not yet in transit to Sweetland?

"Melissa," he called out.

The soldier on his left prodded him with the butt of his carbine. He saw Melissa walking quickly toward him. "Jessie, Mel? Where's Jessie?"

"She's all right, Mr Larivee," Melissa called back. "She wants you to come to Sweetland. She's okay. And Bridge. Bridge says come, too." How could Melissa possibly know Bridge? Or was this all in his mind?

Before Melissa could reach him, the soldiers pushed him outside the encampment, their guns threatening.

"She's okay," Mel yelled one more time.

Joe made his way to the edge of the precipice where the ruins of the collapsed Going Street bridge spilled over the railroad tracks below. In the fading light he searched for a way across the abyss, saw what appeared to be a path and began his descent.

Behind him a single drum tentatively called out, beginning the nightly rhythm, and by the time he crossed the tracks several others had joined it. The darkness had long settled in by the time Joe reached home, and across the city the drumming now sounded from every direction.

"Trust me, Joe." Bridge's voice echoed in his head. And what had Sandra Cole said? "Have faith, son."

How can I have faith? How is that possible?

☼

JOLENE INSISTED ON AN AISLE SEAT. THE FLIGHT TO ST Louis would be unpleasant enough without being reminded that she was in a plastic box, made with a 3D printer, nine thousand meters above solid ground. She closed her eyes as the ascending jetliner hit turbulence, attempted to think of something pleasant. But all she could think of was the coming meeting with Miglia, and whatever the hell he was up to. He was playing her, but why? This would not be a vacation, and she resented that fact.

New America Corporation sent a black stretch limo to meet her at the airport, and Jolene's sense of prestige was not diminished by her certainty that it was their intention to impress her. They wanted her, and they were going to some considerable trouble to show it. The limo pulled up in front of the St Louis Hilton at 16:30, and she and her baggage were promptly escorted to her room, an executive suite. She had only tipped the attractive, flirtatious young man who deposited her suitcases beside the bed, when a voice whispered in her auds, "You have a call, Ms Cheng." It was Richard Miglia, himself. The CEO of New America Corporation would arrive at 18:00 to take her to dinner, a five-star restaurant, where they would discuss her new position. She noted he didn't say, "prospective position."

"I apologize profusely, Ms Cheng," he said, "for not meeting you personally at the airport. It couldn't be avoided, I'm afraid. I trust there were no unpleasant issues upon your arrival." She assured him that there had been none.

"Good," he said. "I look forward to getting to know you, Ms Cheng."

"And I, you, Mr Miglia."

Jolene reclined on the bed, luxuriating in its opulence. She was glad she went on this little excursion. The relaxation would do her good. She was finally forgetting the afternoon's unpleasantness as the residual anger faded. Whatever they had done to her in that sim, the lab boys hadn't prepared for it. She didn't like that. And she didn't enjoy leaving a case mid-way, but she really needed to step back and think this thing through. And consider her future.

First, though, she had to dress for the evening.

DICK MIGLIA ARRIVED AT 18:00 SHARP. JOLENE WAS surprised to see a man of about forty, not much older than she, dressed in the uniform of the business class, with a certain roguish, entrepreneurial look about him. She couldn't identify, precisely, what gave her that impression. A certain roughness in the haircut, or a rebellious sloppiness in the way his tie hung, unpinned, to his shirt. Maybe the suspenders, harkening back to the Turn. His smile was warm, but something familiar in his eyes left her with an uneasy feeling.

"I wasn't expecting I would be getting such a lovely Chief Security Officer," he said.

She returned the smile, examining his face. "I must remind you," she replied, "that I haven't accepted yet. But if you keep the charm on like this, I might find it difficult to resist."

"I assure you, the pleasure is mine." He smiled again and offered her an arm. "Shall we?"

They dined at a French restaurant on a pier overlooking

the Mississippi, and Miglia enchanted her with his smooth masculine voice and a bottle of vintage 2003 Beaujolais which would have cost Jolene several months of salary. She noted his wedding band and asked him about his family. He was married with two daughters, Carmen and Charlotta. Old-fashioned names, she noted. His wife, Deanna, was a corporate attorney. Jolene already knew all of this. Dick Miglia had been raised among wealth and power, and the conversation soon turned to tales of the rich and famous, a subject which never ceased to fascinate her. Yet as she listened, she was distracted. What was it about him that made her queasy?

"Well, enough about me," he said, at last. "Why don't you tell me about Jolene Cheng."

"There's probably not much you don't already know," said Jolene. She smiled. "I'm sure you've vetted me."

"Of course," he said, "but that tells me little about the person. Don't you agree?"

Her own investigation had turned up a paucity of useful information about Dick Miglia, and after all his talking, she *still* knew very little about him. And she wouldn't reveal anything she didn't need to, either. This was how the game was played, with your cards close to your chest. She told him what he must already know, that she grew up in what she termed a "struggling family," that her grandfather had been a third-generation Chinese-American, ostracized by his family for marrying a white woman. He left San Francisco for Portland after World War II. Her father died when she was 10 years old, and her mother remarried. She told him about Joe and Jessie so she could put to rest an issue Miglia was surely aware of: Frank and Amy Larivee, her former, notoriously radical in-laws.

"I see you are a virtual," noted Miglia, about half way through dinner. He pointed toward his ear.

"Very perceptive of you," said Jolene. "I hope it's not too gauche for the moneyed classes."

Miglia laughed. "Not at all, my dear. It tells me you are dedicated and serious." Miglia raised his wineglass, tipping it slightly toward her in a gesture of salute.

Jolene reached for her own glass, but seeing it empty, drew her hand back. The server was there instantly on her left. He reached across her to pour wine into her glass, momentarily blocking her view of her dinner companion. As the server stepped back, Jolene lifted her own glass, but Miglia appeared to have forgotten the moment. She brought the glass to her lips and felt herself loosen up. She told him about her work, that she had made her way up from a real world street grunt to a comfortable position as a cyber agent, not mentioning that the expensive hardware was paid for by Uncle Sam. She confessed boredom with her job, because it was no longer a challenge. Then she fell silent, feeling she had nothing more to say on the subject, and Miglia smoothly took over the conversation until the server presented their tab on an elegantly etched silver tray.

Miglia laid $500 on the tray. Jolene was certain it was a great deal more than the dinner actually cost. He was either showing off his wealth or intended to be spectacularly generous with the server. The server brought the change back mostly in 10s and 20s. A muscle twitched around Miglia's mouth as if he were about to smile. The server was a couple of steps from the table, when Miglia called him back. "Young man, this is not suitable."

"Sir?"

Miglia held the tray with the money toward the server

without turning to look at him. "Surely you have some larger denominations in your bank."

"Certainly, Sir. I will change it, if you wish."

As the server took the tray and reached out for the cash, Miglia turned with the quickness of a cat. "You don't imagine there is a gratuity for you after your miserable, inattentive service."

The server's face was pale. "Sir?"

"If you intend to make waiting your career, you will thank me for this. Never, ever pour wine from the left."

Now, Jolene understood that hard glitter in Miglia's eyes. She saw Dwight there, bullying a small child with ruthless determination. He was someone who needed to be King of the Hill in every human encounter, no matter how petty. She knew how to deal with the Dwights of the world. No bully would get the best of her. Ever.

By the end of the first week, Jolene wanted to run screaming from the New America Corporation management orientation. So far, the orientation had consisted only of presentations on New America corporate culture—the self-congratulatory crap she had to suffer through for every corporate and government step she had ever taken, from Walmart to Homeland Security. It was devoid of real information and offered superficial rewards only idiots would fall for. She had to remind herself that she was the only one tapped for the Chief of Security position. In fact, upper management had decided in advance who they wanted and weren't prepared to take no for an answer. It was an opportunity that would be hard to refuse. Still, she found herself only half-listening to the balding man at the head of the table.

"Resource acquisition and extraction account for 64% of our revenue streams," Tomas Diego, Chief Financial Officer, was explaining. "Developing these sources requires professional, independent teams dedicated to R and D, resource exploration, and security. Over the past twenty years, our streams have been slowly drying up, but now, a vast new opportunity has opened up to us. That's why you are here. You have been chosen because your profiles tell us you are the most qualified individuals for the job. You have the savvy, connections, and technical experience to put together the kind of teams we need—"

"Mr Diego," Jolene interrupted, "can we stop beating around the bush? Just tell us what we will be doing, how dangerous it is, and what we can expect to get out of it."

"Please have patience, Ms Cheng," said Diego. "I promise you, if you stick with us, we will answer your questions soon. But first, we must be sure of our relationship with one another. What we are going to tell you is very sensitive information. We must know that you will have unwavering loyalty to the company. I trust you, of all people, understand that."

Jolene understood. Secrets and confidentiality were the essence of her business. Yet she couldn't help feeling as though they were wasting her time with all this inconsequential bullshit.

"Now, having said that, I can partially answer your final two questions. The risk will be considerable, both in a physical sense and in a professional sense. And your compensation will be beyond your wildest fantasy. Imagine being one of perhaps three dozen of the wealthiest and most powerful individuals in the world, Ms Cheng. Can you fathom that?"

An audible gasp arose from the room, but Jolene held her enthusiasm in check. It sounded a bit like a no-money-down real estate scam. She wouldn't be buying into this until she knew exactly what Diego meant.

Jolene was relieved that Dick Miglia had not been a factor in the orientation beyond that first night welcoming dinner. She preferred little personal contact with most people, especially those in whom she perceived weakness.

She had made a habit of eating alone in her room, but tonight she was too stimulated for its confines, so she had a salad in the hotel restaurant and idly surveilled her fellow diners as she contemplated her day. But she soon became bored and decided it was time to return to her room and check in at the office. She had talked to Seven only a few days ago, but she could come up with two dozen reasons why the office couldn't get by without her. An actual vacation was an alien concept.

TWO STRANGE BIKES WERE LOCKED TO THE BIKE SHELTER in front of Joe's apartment building. Plain, black, expensive hardware, probably government issue, locks fabricated with spendy hardened alloy. Locks like that didn't belong in this neighborhood. He abruptly changed course toward François's Coffeeshop, hoping he might wait them out. He hadn't walked a dozen steps when Pedro stepped out of the shadows. "Hey, amigo. I'm really disappointed in you, man. You know, your friends come over to see you, and you don't even have the courtesy to come in and say hola. What's with that?"

"You're not my friend, Pedro, you little asshole," shot Joe.

"Now don't get all hostile on me, Joe. Dillon and me, we've just been trying to get to know you, buddy. Help you out with your little problem. So, I recommend we go upstairs and say hello to Matthew, and then we can all have a little chat about Sweetland. Okay, amigo?"

"Whatever," said Joe.

Pedro followed Joe up the stairs to his apartment. His front door was wide open, and Dillon sat on the couch with Joe's citspecs in his hands. "Hi there, Joe. Good to see you. I hope you don't mind, we stopped in for a visit. You know, the front door was open. You really should be more careful."

"I'm glad you're interested in my welfare, Dillon."

"Not yours so much, Joe. Just the taxpayer's," said Dillon.

"So, Dillon," said Joe, "what are you going to do when they privatize the F.B.I. next year?"

Dillon winked, "It'll be a whole different soccer match pal. We won't have to treat the shitheads with the respect they don't deserve."

Joe gave him a sardonic smile. He guessed they meant he should be grateful they weren't Free Market S.S. Goons. Yet. "Okay, what can I do for you, gentlemen?"

"For starters, Joe," said Pedro, "you can tell us about Anya."

"I told you, I don't know about Anya."

"Then, how about Gretel deVoid, Joe?" asked Dillon. "You gonna tell us you don't know Gretel?"

"Never heard of her," Joe said.

"We heard you been going to some Bol sims, amigo. And other unsavory places."

"New Life?" Joe was stunned. "You guys have been following me on the Grid?"

"The Eye has been on you, Joe," said Pedro. "And it sees

your little Gretel is in big trouble. We know about her ties to terrorists."

"Fuck you, Pedro."

Dillon pulled a photo out of his pocket and thrust it in front of Joe's face. He immediately recognized the scene of chaos at the Rose Quarter Apartments. Dozens of young people throwing rocks; in the foreground, a tall, thin woman in a green sweater and two girls slipping away from the crowd. One was Jessie, her profile unmistakable. The other girl was her friend, Mel.

"That was this morning," Dillon reported. "But of course you know that, don't you?"

His fists tightened. It was the wrong thing to react to them, but he was growing tired of this. "Bullshit," he snapped. Why were these fools interested in him and Jessie. And for that matter, Anya. It suddenly occurred to him that Jolene had something to do with this. Were these her goons?

"We know you're looking for her, amigo," said Pedro. "You been looking in places respectable people shouldn't go. We're looking for her too. So, Joe, this is how it's going to be. You find out something about Jessie or our little Anya..." Pedro winked and made a little pumping motion with his hand, "you make any contact, you will report it to Freedom Jones—he's got a jones for freedom, get it?" Snicker. Grin. "He's at the Ayn Rand building on Prosperity. In exchange, Joe, you don't disappear from the face of the fucking planet. That's the real life planet, Joe."

Joe shook involuntarily.

"All we need are a few answers, Joe," said Dillon.

"You people seem to have the answer to everything," he snarled. "Why don't you look up your ass for it?"

"You know," said Dillon, "there's really no call for that. You've been warned to not mess around with these people.

The ones you've been talking to. Now Pedro's getting pissed. You don't want to get Pedro here mad. He gets real nasty when he's angry, Joe."

"What do you want from me, Dillon?"

"He wants to know about the terrorists, shithead," said Pedro. "We're trying to protect the good, honest citizens of this country from the scum of the earth. And you, Joe, you are not cooperating with us. That makes you, maybe not a terrorist, Joe, but a shithead. And you know what we do with shitheads?"

Out of the side of his eye, Joe caught a light reflection as Pedro's right arm came up, something like a steel rod clasped in his hand. As it came down on the back of Joe's head, Pedro's left fist struck him in the solar plexus, and he bent over, retching. Then blackness.

BRIDGE WAITED NEARLY AN HOUR BEFORE SHE UNDERSTOOD in her bones. She had lost Joe. She had no one to blame but herself—she must have sounded insane to him in her unbridled enthusiasm. Her heart had overruled her mind, and she'd lost him.

She laid her head on the digital grass and closed her eyes. She dreamed about Sweetland and that forest which stretched forever to the horizon, the unknown wilderness, the chance to begin again, and maybe not screw it up this time. Was it possible to not screw it up this time? Or were humans just fated to mess up whatever they touched? She recalled the cool wind on her face, and the smells, the sweet exotic smells of a garden, a garden like no one has ever touched before. Pristine. Was that what it was like when her ancestors came over from Asia thousands of years ago to a beautiful land empty of people?

She wanted Joe to be there with her, to find his Jessie and be happy and walk with her into that wilderness. But she couldn't wait. She didn't know if Joe trusted her anymore, if he would ever speak to her again.

And the forest. The forest waited for her.

Part Six

Sweetland

"Matter itself is the starting-point, and the point of arrival is the soul."
> —Victor Hugo

"Not until we are lost do we begin to understand ourselves."
> —Henry David Thoreau

The drums beat their way through the thin apartment walls into Joe's throbbing skull. He opened his eyes; he was lying on his living room floor, his forehead in a small pool of sticky blood. He winced at a piercing stab of pain and touched the back of his head where Pedro's club came down. A big, tender lump, but no open wound. The blood issued from a gash above his right brow, probably caused by the fall. He touched the wound tentatively, flinching at the tenderness. Congealed blood caked in his hair. He sat up slowly, steadying himself on the coffee table. His citspecs were still there, where Dillon had left them.

The clock read seven hundred. It was morning already. He had missed Claire—Bridge, he reminded himself. He cursed silently, remembering her crazy words yesterday.

In the bathroom he threw back a handful of pain relievers, then stumbled into the kitchen, poured himself a glass of apple juice, took a sip, and promptly spat it into the sink. He dumped the glass, filled it with tap water, and attempted to rinse away the mold taste. Nothing more left in the fridge but dried out and furry remains.

He returned to the couch and considered the citspecs. *Bridge says come, too.* Melissa's odd words ate at him. How did this all fit together? He had to find Bridge. He handled the citspecs indecisively, finding himself thinking about the nanos, how they would suppress his hunger and his headache, not surprised to hear the voices still whispering to him, *the answers are here.* Where the hell was Claire? She was the only hope left of getting Jessie back, of solving this riddle.

And he had missed her.

"Good morning, Joe," chirped Kali.

"Put me in the street in front of Claire Deluna's building," he said, skipping the unnecessary social greetings.

Kali switched to a more somber look. "Dropping in public would be rude, Joe."

"I'm not asking you about etiquette. Just *do* it."

"Of course, Joe. As you wish." Kali wore a contrite smile with possibly a little sarcasm leaking around the edges. Her new attitude irritated him, but he had asked for it, after all. Before he could process what now looked like resentment on Kali's ever-morphing face, the fashionable street res'd before his eyes. Passersby glared at him and he glared back, defiant. "What the fuck are you gawking at?"

He looked frantically down the street for the bookstore he had seen earlier, the one with books about Sweetland. It should have been here, but he soon realized it was gone, a temporary flash, like so many small businesses. He noticed that the other businesses on this street also looked abandoned, and he felt suddenly foolish. He had been running around, driven by his emotions. But he was trained in conciliation, in mediation, in looking at the world with a clear eye. It was time to use reason; to think things through.

He recalled what the server in Old Paris had told him.… *it will all be meaningless in the next week when everyone moves to the enclaves.* The disappearances, the troop movements in the past few weeks, the drumming—something was coming. An uprising was coming, and he had been asleep.

But he still didn't know what Sweetland had to do with it all.

"You have new mail, Joe." Kali's voice intruded into his thoughts.

The note he pulled from the air with a swipe of his hand, read: "The presence of Joe Justjoe is cordially requested for a private meeting with Claire Deluna at Borealis Meadow."

Claire… Bridge wasn't gone after all.

JOE DROPPED INTO BOREALIS TO FIND THE FOREST SIM EMPTY of avatars, no trace of Claire, no message. He was about to resign himself to failure when, out of nowhere, Claire landed face-first on the ground beside him. She rolled over and looked up at him, giggling.

"Hi, Joe. Long time, no see."

"Bridge, are you stoned?"

"Not drunk. Not Bridge. Bridge has gone bye-bye, Joe. She said to give you… she said to give you… she said to tell you… she said Claire, tell Joe you are on the wrong side of the looking glass, Joe. Things are backwards there on that side of the looking glass and you should get over here on the right side."

"Bridge—"

She handed Joe a folder. "Not Bridge. Claire, not Bridge. Bridge said to give you this."

"Bridge—"

"Not Bridge, Joe. Claire. Bridge said come to her side. Bridge said come to her side of the looking glass. She said, tell Joe to send Joe over to this side of the looking glass so we can have a picnic, just me and Joe and Jessie, and tell him, no wine yet, but the sandwiches are really good over here."

"Bridge—"

"Not Bridge, Joe. Not Bridge. Must go dancing now. Bye-bye, Joe."

The avatar vanished.

. . .

Stunned, Joe stared at the folder in his hand. What had just happened? Claire's avatar seemed too autonomous, too erratic, to be pre-programmed. But it must be, somehow. What did it mean?

He opened the folder. It contained Bridge's notes on Futures, LLC, and its subsidiary firms. She believed that D-Brane Technologies and Mitologias were collaborating on a secret project called Sweetland. "What is Sweetland?" she had written. There were references to Brother Dave and the Temple of New Life. Scrawled at the bottom of the note: "DBT mods - ask Stan," and "DBT (D-Brane Tech????)." In the right margin: "Someone is trying to break into my file system. Who is the man in the blue raincoat? The Feds? The Mob? Mr Bigshot? Must find out who."

He recalled the mysterious man on Swan Island. The man in the blue raincoat. On the next page he found an image file of a man in a lab coat, around his neck a medallion, an astrolabe. He noticed for the first time that the starfield in its background was not the familiar milky way. The photo was labeled Carlos Seguda. In the margin a single word, "Brotherhood." On the back, another note, "Whitehall University—Dr Stephens."

When he arrived at the final page, a message popped up into his AR window:

"Dear Joe, I'm sorry I messed this up. They only gave me a short time to decide, but the thing is, I have made up my mind. I feel bad because I failed you. But I didn't really let you down, you see. I can't make this choice for you—you have to come to it yourself. Jessie is waiting on the other end for you. And I am too, if you care about me. There isn't much time, Joe. The Grid is going down permanently. You need to be prepared. There's going to be an uprising...."

He stopped reading. A stab of anguish tore at him. God damn it, Bridge, why did you do this?

Drumming invaded the wall of his citspecs, a nagging voice in the far distance, until joined by neighborhood pots and pans the drums rose like a crescendo, insisting that he listen. "Do you know what they are saying?" the young man at the mall had asked him. Anya, Allison, Jessie, Bridge, the mysterious strangers with the astrolabes, they were *all* trying to tell him something. Why was it so hard to hear?

He closed the folder, and it vanished as he filed it away. He removed his citspecs. The sound of the drumming now thundered in his ears. He still had time. He had to go to Seattle. Bridge was in trouble, but she was still here, still alive. As dark as this world had become, Bridge was a light, a tiny piece of hope, and how could he go on without her? Without Jessie? What would be the purpose?

The Eugene-Seattle shuttle was a twelve-year-old biodiesel coach that coughed and sputtered when it started. It ran seven days a week and, while technically breaking the rules, it was common for his colleagues to make use of it on days off to visit friends and family in Eugene or Seattle or stops between. He was required to produce his Essential Social Services ID to board. Administrators turned their heads at the practice in order to keep peace with an unhappy workforce.

He recognized none of the passengers on the early morning bus. He sat alone and pulled out the Libro from the seat in front of him. He dialed the news and found on the front page the usual celebrity crap. "Bread and circuses," Amy used to say. He had to click through to page five before coming to any actual news. *War in Central Asia may falter without infusion of cash,* the headline read. The Central Intelligence Security Corporation would pull out, the article said, if the government didn't come up with another five billion. CISC was the largest of the private armies, and without them the war effort couldn't be sustained.

Authorities puzzled by missing persons, read a small headline at the bottom of the page. *Investigators say problem world-wide,* noted the cut line. *Phenomenon most notable in the poorest neighborhoods.*

Scientific breakthrough in consciousness. He read on:

Scientists at Living Laboratories announced today a breakthrough in the decades long effort to transfer human consciousness to a storage device. The exabyte quantum device, made of nano-organics, is about the size of a common memchip and can hold the contents of the human mind, along with an artificial environment.

Scientists believe that by networking these devices, a sort of super-intelligent virtual universe may be created. Dr Paulson Gooding of Science Watch, however, was outraged. "Even if this were possible, and I highly doubt that it is, it would be morally reprehensible. They are talking here about enslaving a human mind inside a machine."

Dr Gooding's statements were roundly denounced by the scientific community as anti-progress.

Joe's head hurt. He had no desire to read any further. It was all too much, too fast. He turned off the Libro, pushed it back into the seat, and closed his eyes.

JOE DISEMBARKED ON BROADWAY. FROM HERE HE COULD walk the short distance to Yesler Way. Bridge said her window overlooked the Sound, she could see Smith Tower, and she could see a sliver of the water, as well. The tower could be seen from several locations on the west side of the hill. Or from one of the old multi-storied apartment buildings up on Yesler Terrace. But few of those apartments would be able to see the water.

The unfamiliar cityscape dismayed him, but as Joe neared Yesler Way, he noticed an old neon shop sign, no longer lit. It read, *Stan Davies, Computer Repair.* Underneath, a hand-written sign, *Citspecs Mods Available Here.* The window was dark, dusty, and cluttered with old computers and peripherals. He recalled Claire's note. *"DBT mods - ask Stan."*

An old-fashioned bell rang as he entered, and an old man, about seventy, emerged from a back room. "May I help you?" he asked, look at Joe suspiciously.

"I'm looking for a friend," Joe said. "She lives in this neighborhood. I'm just wondering if you might know her."

"Could be, but I'm not in the habit of giving out that kind of information to strangers."

"Her name is Bridge Whitedeer. She might have come in about some DBT mods."

The old man's eyes looked at the floor evasively. Joe was certain he knew Bridge.

"Like I said," the old man replied, now giving Joe a penetrating look, "I don't give information about customers to strangers. If you're a friend of this Whitedeer, then you should know how to reach her."

Anger and desperation overcame him. Joe leaned over the counter and grabbed the old man's collar. "Look, old man, I don't want to hurt you, but I have to find Bridge. She's in danger. My daughter's in danger. I have to find her. Please."

The old man's hand disappeared behind the counter, and when it came back up, Joe saw the handle of the gun. He panicked and pulled Stan hard toward the counter. He was surprised at how light and frail the old guy was. The gun fell to the floor with a clamor.

Clearly frightened, the old man gasped for air. *Shit, thought Joe. What if I've given him a heart attack?*

"I'm sorry," said Joe. "I'm really sorry."

"I don't know what Bridge has got herself into," Stan panted, "But like I told the two FBI goons who came in here Thursday, my customer records are none of your damned business without a warrant."

"Wait, the FBI is looking for Bridge?"

"They were looking into the bombing of the cybernetics lab up at the U."

"Cybernetics lab? I don't understand."

"Sorry, they warned me not to talk about it. Let me give Ms Whitedeer a call—"

"No way, old man, I don't want you calling the cops. Just stay the hell away from the phone."

"I have nothing to do with the police. Bridge is a sweet young woman. I wouldn't want anything bad to happen to her. Why don't we talk? Maybe you can convince me you're a good guy in this."

"You come around to this side of the counter and kick away that gun as you come."

"Sure." Stan did as Joe said. "Okay, now tell me what Bridge is mixed up in."

"Do you know what Sweetland is?"

"Not really. I know these DBT chips are connected to it. When the kids come in to get them installed, they're all talking Sweetland. I never really got that simulated world stuff. I'm strictly a web two point oh guy, myself. A Pitter, as they say."

"My daughter is mixed up with this Sweetland thing somehow. Bridge was helping me. She had these DBT mods installed, and now she's like a crazy woman. She talks crazy. You know about all those missing people? You listen to the news?"

The old man looked alarmed. "Yeah, I listen. It's pretty weird, alright."

"Well, you're going to think I'm nuts, but I bet if you tried to track down the people who bought those mods from you, you would find that many of those people have disappeared or are dead."

"That sounds nuts, alright. But…" The old man trailed off. He knew more than he was letting on.

"According to the files Bridge left me, D-Brane Technologies, and an outfit called Mitologias are behind this Sweetland business. Your customers believe they're about to be teleported to another planet."

Stan looked as though he were deep in thought. "Well, I took a look at those DBT chips, and I got to say, its technology way out of my league. Do you believe these people are actually going off to another world, somewhere? Is that what you're trying to say?"

"People are possibly being sent off to die. I don't know where their soul or mind or whatever goes, but I think this is mass murder like the world has never seen before. These mods are acting like some kind of drug. Shit, Stan, I want to believe my daughter, Jessie, is still alive. I want to believe that Bridge is okay. But it can't be true, can it?"

"I don't know," said Stan. "I read the science mags, and they have discovered some pretty amazing things. Tech has gone way beyond my understanding in the last couple of years. But nothing like what you're describing. I don't think they're anywhere near even testing this kind of stuff yet. I guess you don't ever really know, with secret government programs and all."

"So, do you think it's possible?"

"Who knows. They proved last century you could take a subatomic particle, a gluon, and manipulate an identical particle at the other end of a quantum string. They can teleport particles—even tiny objects—from one place to another. But a whole human being. I don't know. Can you imagine the complexity of that? I don't think they could be anywhere near that kind of breakthrough. It's all just theory. And highly dubious theory, I might add."

"But with the right breakthroughs, you think it's possible?"

"Son, I know you want some hope here, but why don't you think your daughter maybe just ran away? That makes more sense than either of these wild ideas."

"She left a message. She said she was going to Sweetland. Bridge left me the very same message. And they met somehow. The two of them live nearly two hundred miles apart. What can I make of that?"

"Look," said Stan, "I'll tell you something. Those files I looked over… I can't say for sure what this Sweetland is, but they are going to destroy the Grid. The Bols, the rebels, I don't know who. And something else… that code will not only take down the Grid, but it has a trojan in it. Someone is trying to subvert the original intent — not by sparing the Grid, but bypassing particular nodes. The nodes seem to center on the worldwide facilities of New America Corporation."

"New America?" Weren't they the ones strip-mining coal in Missouri with some kind of nanotech?

"That's them. It's what Bridge and I discovered, and that's why she received that death threat. And that may be why my friend at the University was killed in a bomb blast."

"Killed? Death threat?"

"Yeah. A couple of nights ago. Look, I'm not supposed to be telling anybody about this, right? But if we can keep Bridge safe… what if I dial her number for you? You take the phone. Can you trust me to do that?"

"Okay," said Joe. "Okay, do that."

Stan picked up what looked like an old-fashioned telephone, the kind Joe remembered as a kid, a popular imitation Ma Bell Classic. Stan flipped through a genuine antique Rolodex like Joe hadn't seen since forever. He stopped, punched a number, then handed the phone to Joe. Bridge's mobe rang several times before going into recording, "Hello, you have reached Claire Deluna, New Life Investigations. Please leave a message."

"Claire, this is Joe," he said. "If you get this, please leave me a message. I'm in Seattle. I need to know you're okay." Joe hung up.

"Stan, that just connects me to her New Life ID."

"Yeah, that's the way it's set up these days for most of the young people. You call them in real life, you call them in their virtual world. It's all the same."

"Shit, Stan…"

"Look, Joe… I shouldn't do this, but I don't want to be responsible if anything has happened to that girl." Stan walked over to a coat rack and grabbed a jacket, pulling it on over his frayed gray sweater. "Let's go." He indicated the door.

Stan shut off the lights and locked the door behind Joe. The old man walked at a brisk pace, much more agile than Joe had imagined he could be. When they arrived at an ancient 1930s brick building, Stan pressed the buzzer and waited. No response.

"Damn," said Joe.

"Hold on, young man." Stan pulled a key from his

pocket. "Bridge and I live in the same building. That's how I met her."

He led Joe to the elevator, put in a dollar coin, and pushed the button for the seventh floor. The elevator creaked and groaned, giving Joe the shivers. When it opened, Stan pointed to a door down the corridor. "Go on ahead," said Stan, gasping. He stopped to catch his breath. "Down on the end."

When Joe arrived at the door of Bridge's apartment, he found it open, just a crack. He held his hand up, signaling Stan, who was close behind, to stop. He rapped on the door and watched it swing fully open.

Bridge's studio apartment was completely trashed, papers and personal items scattered across the floor, a small dining table tipped over on its side. Someone had gone through the place. In the kitchen area, several days' worth of dishes were piled up on the counters. Bridge nowhere in sight.

JOE STARTED TO BACK OUT OF THE APARTMENT WHEN HE heard a soft moan. An arm emerged from the overturned sofa.

"Bridge?" A waifish young face, topped with short-cropped black hair, peered at him across the back of the sofa. She appeared intoxicated.

"Bridge?"

"Claire, not Bridge." She looked up at him with wide, innocent eyes. "Is that you, Joe? Because you sound like Joe, but you don't look like Joe."

"Bridge." Stan kneeled beside her. "It's Stan. Are you okay?"

"Not Bridge," she said. "I remember Stan, I think. Joe, do you know Stan?"

Stan gasped. "My god, what have they done to you?" His voice was barely a whisper.

"Joe," said Bridge, "you don't look like Joe."

"It's Joe Larivee, Bridge, not Joe Justjoe."

"Oh," she said. "Joe, Bridge said to come over to the other side. The other side of… of something. I don't remember, Joe. Did Joe tell you?"

"Yes," said Joe, "Joe told me."

"I don't feel so good. Gotta sleep now, Joe."

Bridge went limp. Joe noticed the two sockets implanted behind her ears and touched them. "What are these?"

"Mod implants." Stan frowned. "Bridge is a virtual."

He had heard that term before. The salesperson at SimWorld. "A virtual? What does it mean?"

"It means that her life is on the Grid. Her Citspecs are on her eyeballs, contacts called ocs, and tiny earpieces called auds. It means she doesn't take care of herself, because she doesn't really live here with us flesh-and-blood mortals. Hell, man, I don't know what it means, because I stay away from that shit."

"Does she think she's on the Grid? Is that why she thought I was Joe Justjoe?"

Stan looked at him, puzzlement on his old face. "Who's Joe Justjoe?"

"It's my avatar on New Life, or persona or whatever they call it these days."

"Does she think she's her persona? Hell, Joe, I don't know. Maybe you're right about all of this. The man who came on Thursday. He was FBI, but I think he was working with DHS or something."

"Tall black guy with a scar on his nose?" he said, certain

it would be Dillon. That would confirm his suspicions about Jolene.

"Yeah, that sounds about right. Oh god, Bridge. I'm so sorry. This is all my fault."

"What do you mean, old man? Why is it all your fault?"

"I just mean… I told her what was on that code, and—"

"And what, Stan? Did you tell someone else about that code?"

"I called the ATO. I was alarmed, but I swear, Joe, I didn't think they'd go after Bridge. I never would have—"

Joe grabbed Stan by his collar and drew him up close. "What else do you know?"

Stan shook violently, and Joe backed off. "Only that the Bols have discovered something huge," Stan gasped. "This New America outfit I told you about has pirated their technology—some inside job. These folks have recruited people in high levels of government and in the DHS. They have a big operation back in Missouri. That's their main node. They will do anything to keep the Bols from finding out. It's a war, and Bridge got caught in the middle."

"So, New America Corporation has an inside man planting trojans. Why do they want the Grid to go down?"

"They'll have tremendous power if they're the only guys who can effectively communicate. They might be able to control the government."

"Shit!" Joe let go of Stan. "I have to get Bridge somewhere safe."

"Where will you take her?" asked Stan.

"My ex lives around here. She's out of town, but she's got a house up near Lake Washington somewhere." She owes it to me, he thought. Damn Jolene.

"How do we get Bridge there, Joe? Hijack a laundry truck?"

"Maybe. But first I need to find her address. Can you find an address for Jolene Cheng?"

"I can try. I'm hooked up to some databases back at the office. County records, that sort of thing. If she owns the house, then… maybe."

"Let's go."

Stan leaned over Bridge, nudging her gently. "Wake up, Bridge, sweetheart. It's Stan."

Bridge opened her eyes. "Hi, Stan," she said weakly.

"Bridge, Joe is going to take you somewhere safe. Get on your feet, now."

Bridge was much too thin. And she was dehydrated. Joe found a reasonably clean cup and made her drink some water from the tap. Then he helped her to a standing position. "Can you walk, Bridge?"

She nodded. "Not Bridge. Claire can walk okay, but she is tired, Joe."

"Okay, Claire," he said, "We'll go where you can rest. Just lean on me if you need to."

"Okay, Joe. Let's go."

BRIDGE CLOSED HER EYES, AND HER HEAD FELL ON JOE'S shoulder. Joe gently shook her awake again and half-carried her to the street. Then, with Bridge between them, Joe and Stan shambled down Yesler to the corner of Broadway. Across the street, under a shop awning, a man huddled as though taking shelter from the rain. Except it wasn't raining. Was he watching them? Joe couldn't tell. He looked back every few steps as they maneuvered Bridge to Stan's shop.

She put her head on Joe's shoulder again, and he tightened his grip on her, propping her up while the old man unlocked the door.

They slipped inside, and Stan booted up one of his old work-horses. Joe peered through the slits in the venetian blinds. The man across the street was slowly making a line toward Stan's shop. Joe recognized him, the trim blond beard and the blue slicker. The man on Swan Island. The man in Bridge's note.

"Shit, Stan, we have company. You have that address, yet?"

"Got a house on Lake Washington owned by a government holding company. I know because I've dealt with these people years ago."

"That's probably it," he said, hoping it was true.

Stan handed Joe a slip of paper and a memchip, then shut down the computer. "It's the code. I've annotated the trojan, so it stands out. You can go out the back, into the alley."

"You better come with us, Stan."

A fist pounded on the shop door, and Stan picked up the gun he had dropped earlier.

"We're closed." Unmoving, he looked at Joe and said, "Get her the hell out of here."

The pounding on the door intensified.

Joe grabbed Bridge and dragged her into the back room. As he flipped the bolt to the alley door, he heard breaking glass, the front door slammed open, three muffled shots. Adrenalin-fueled, Joe dragged Bridge down the alley, attempting to keep her on her feet. Why hadn't they been followed? He hoped it meant Stan had prevailed, but he wouldn't count on that.

At the end of the alley, Joe turned back up toward Yesler

Way and the bus stop. There was still no sign of rain slicker. He put his arm around Bridge.

"Okay, Claire, you just lean on me and I'll help you walk. Is that alright?"

"I can walk, Joe, just a little tipsy is all."

"We are going down to Yesler Way, Claire, and we're going to catch a bus. Okay?"

"Okay," she said, "I like the bus, Joe. Funny people on the bus."

"Let's play a game. You want to play a game?"

"I like to play games, Joe. I like to dance, too. We could go dance. I know a great place to dance… at The Downbeat, Joe. You would like Jasper, he works at The Downbeat, but he's not a real avi, like us. He's just a bot."

"I've met Jasper, remember, Claire?"

"I forgot, Joe. But we never danced at The Downbeat."

"I know, Claire. I would like to dance with you, but now we need to play a game. Here's a game I would like to play. You pretend you're my girlfriend, and you've had too much to drink. Anybody on the bus asks us, that's what we tell them. Okay?"

"Okay, Joe. I like to pretend I'm your girlfriend. I like you, Joe." She leaned her head on his shoulder. Suddenly, Joe felt a huge weight pressing down on him. Another level of sadness settling in his bones, in the cells of his body, pushing at the surface of his membranes.

Bridge hanging onto him, they crossed Yesler to the bus stop. The bus route took them directly to Lake Washington. They would have to walk only a few blocks. When the bus arrived, he helped Bridge stumble up the steps. He found an empty seat near the back and sat her down. She clung to his arm for a while before she laid her head on his shoulder again and fell asleep.

He remembered the memchip, still gripped tightly in his palm. He opened his bag and dropped it in next to his citspecs. Stan said he had annotated the code so they could spot the trojan, but who was "they?" And how could he find them? He didn't know what he would do with it, and he couldn't think about it right now. All he could concentrate on was getting Bridge to safety.

☼

Bridge stumbled as they disembarked. Joe managed to catch her, but she was becoming increasingly unsteady. The sun slipped beneath the horizon, and they traversed three long blocks in the growing darkness until he found the address Stan had given him. He sat Bridge beneath a dying maple tree in what he hoped was Jolene's yard, its branches covered in fungus, gaping cankers in its bark.

"Stay here," he whispered, but he could see she was already sleeping.

Joe walked the circumference of the house, searching for a way in. The back yard was overgrown with weeds. He climbed the two steps up to a small deck and tried the back door. No luck. He scanned the deck, empty except for a small faux wood table next to a matching plastic chaise lounge. Jolene would keep a key here. He knew exactly where it would be. He'd lived with her long enough to know her meticulous behaviors. He found it taped to the underside of the chaise lounge. He hoped there was no alarm system. Jolene never liked alarms. She was one of the deadliest-calm people he knew, but certain things unnerved her. She'd set off the alarm at her office in Portland more than once because she couldn't remember the code, and Jolene had a phenomenal memory. She just froze, and her mind went blank. Maybe working for DHS she had learned some tricks to overcome that flaw.

He put the key in the door lock, ready to run if an alarm system was armed inside. When he had the door open, he quickly scanned the walls, noting an ancient key punch system, unpowered and harmless. The tacky kitchen decor told him it was undoubtedly Jolene's place. He let out a sigh, rushed through the house and out the front door, where he found Bridge slumped over on her side with her face in the wet humus, still sleeping. He picked her up and brushed the damp plant matter from the side of her face, then carried her inside the house, gently laying her on the sofa.

In the kitchen, he scrounged for food. They both desperately needed to eat. He found bread in the freezer and peanut butter in the cupboard, along with some vegetable soup in a carton. He thawed some bread in the toaster and spread on the peanut butter. Then he activated a soup package and scarfed down the sandwich while he waited for it to heat. When it was hot, he poured the warm liquid into a glass bowl for Bridge.

He shook her gently. "Bridge, I have some soup for you. You need to eat."

She moaned and turned over, rubbing her eyes. "Not Bridge, Joe," she said, "Bridge gone."

"I know, Claire. You need to eat something."

"Don't need to eat, Joe. Need to go dancing?"

"Only if you eat."

"Avies don't need to eat, Joe, you silly man." she giggled. "Want to talk to Jasper, Joe. Dance. Take me, Joe. Jasper has vodka crans and cashews. Not real. Funny, Joe. I always laugh. You think it's funny?"

"Yes, Claire," said Joe. "But you must eat first. Otherwise those vodka crans will make your head all woozy."

Bridge giggled again. "I like you, Joe. You make me laugh, silly man."

Joe held out a spoonful of soup, and Bridge ate it like an awkward child, the liquid dribbling down her chin. She took only a few bites, then laid her head back on the sofa cushion and fell fast asleep again. Joe put down the soup and sat in the chair across from her, watching her sleep. She was nothing like he imagined. She was very young, maybe early twenties. He had no clue she would be so young, and so unlike the sophisticated Claire Deluna. And yet, here she was, the real thing, not the mask. A bitterness ate at him. Maybe he deserved this world, but others did not. Bridge and Jessie and Anya.

The sun had gone down, and darkness enveloped the house. From the lake came the sound of a drum, and then another, speaking to one another, call and response, until others joined in, until a steady, insistent beat filled the night. It wasn't just some local Portland thing, he realized. The entire world was changing again. Forever.

Curled up in the chair, Joe's eye caught the letter on Jolene's coffee table, its elegant letterhead announcing, "New America Corporation, 12980 New World Dr, St Louis, MO." He read it with growing alarm. What the hell did Jolene have to do with these people? What did it mean? What did any of this mean? Was Jolene with them now, trying to decide the fate of the world? He tried to puzzle it out, but it was all too complex, too far beyond his frame of reference.

When Joe finally slept, he dreamed about his childhood,

in the yard of his parents' little bungalow near Mt. Tabor, Amy and Frank on the porch engaged in one of their endless conversations, a strange man stands in the yard, maybe the man who reads the meter. *"Are your parents terrorists, little boy?"* the man asks. *"No,"* he says. *"Then why are they making a bomb?"* Joe runs around to the front of the house, where his mother sits rocking on the porch swing. Instead of her usual knitting, in her lap rests a big black ball with a fuse coming from it. A cartoon bomb. Frank holds a lighter in his hand.

"Daddy," he screams, *"No. Don't do it."*

JOE WOKE IN A SWEAT. A DIM LIGHT FROM THE RISING SUN filtered through the curtains. He had spent most of the night in fitful half-sleep. Bridge was no longer on the sofa where he left her, and he panicked. Check the front door. Latched. Sigh of relief.

"Bridge? Claire?"

No response. She must have wandered into another room, perhaps fallen asleep there. He began a methodical search, going through each room on the bottom floor before moving upstairs. The first room at the top of the stairs appeared to be the master bedroom, its bed unmade. Very unlike Jolene, he thought. He finally found Bridge in a sunlit room on the east side of the house, bent over a desk. He touched her shoulder, gently, and her arm slid off the desk, fell limply to her side. A tiny trickle of blood had pooled on the corner of her lip; her eyes were wide open, staring. He knew before he touched the cold skin of her face she was gone.

Joe doubled over, retched. He howled in pain.

When he could stand again, he lifted her into his arms

and carried her to the guest bed next door. For a long time he watched her lying on the bed, her eyes now closed by the soft brush of his hand. He wanted to pull the blankets over her, keep her warm, take care of her. His eyes felt like sandpaper, his throat dry and raw. Carefully, he enshrouded her in the bedspread and lifted her seemingly weightless body into his arms. The basement was cold, but not damp. He laid her on a potting table there, in a bed of dust.

THE AFTERNOON SKY HAD GROWN DARK, AND RAIN WAS falling in heavy waves. A blast of wind shook the house so hard it felt as though the earth trembled beneath him. He curled up in the chair, closed his eyes, and fell asleep, exhausted.

He dreamed of Claire and the Boreal forest. Only Claire was Bridge; the avi had become the person. She had spread out a blanket and a picnic lunch, and she was saying, "Don't worry about Jessie. Jessie is happy now, Joe."

"Are you happy, Bridge?"

Smiling, she searched his eyes for an answer. She reached out to touch his cheek, but her fingers passed through his skin, and then she faded away. When he looked up again at the forest, the trees had all died, their blackened arms reaching into the sky, and he let out a terrible howl that shook the ground beneath him.

He awoke to a great gust of wind rattling the windows, bringing sheets of rain slamming against the side of the house. He had no appetite, but he stumbled his way to the kitchen, put on some tea, slipped a slice of cold bread into the toaster. At the sink, he splashed some water on his face, took his toast and tea into the living room, and settled back into the big chair, where he picked up his citspecs. He had some people to see and a decision to make.

FROM THE STAGE OF THE DOWNBEAT, A BILLIE HOLIDAY look-alike sang "Stormy Weather." Billie had been one of Frank's favorites, and to Joe's ear the performance was indistinguishable from the real thing. Maybe it was the real thing. Or maybe there is no real thing, anymore, he thought. Or maybe there never was.

Jasper moved smoothly down the bar toward him. "Hi, Joe. Claire came in the last couple of nights talking about you. All giggly, like she was in Sweetland or something, you know? She said, if Joe comes by, you give him a vodka cran on me."

Joe felt the weight press down, choking him up.

"So, Joe, you want that vodka cran? It's on Claire."

"Wouldn't miss it, Jasper."

"Funny thing, when she came in the first time, I had the distinct feeling she was saying goodbye. Goodbye for good. It's a shame, because I'm really going to miss that lady." Jasper handed him his drink.

"It's true, Jasper," he said, choking up. "She's gone."

"I'm sorry to hear that, Joe. She gave me something else to give to you." He handed Joe an envelope.

Joe opened the envelope and found a note inside. He unfolded it slowly, not sure he wanted to see the contents. It read, *"Dear Joe, My time is up and I have to go now. I'm sorry I couldn't persuade you. I guess I'm really inept at this relationship stuff. I want you with me, but you need to make up your own mind.*

"I love you. You once said, 'maybe we can find a way.' I will believe it as long as I'm alive. Bridge."

He closed his eyes. On stage, the singer crooned, "I'm weary all the time, I'm so weary all the time," punctuated by its lonely trumpet, muted and haunting. When Joe opened his eyes again, Jasper was drying imaginary glasses, performing his programmed bartender routines.

"You said Claire came in again?" Joe asked.

"Yeah, it's the funniest thing. The next night—she was going on about you, but to tell you the truth, Joe, most of it made little sense. Something about Joe and a bridge and a looking glass. Couldn't make heads nor tails of it."

"So, Jasper, may I ask you for some advice?"

"That's what I'm programmed for, Joe. Is this about Claire?"

"Yeah, Jasper. Claire told me she was leaving. She's going to a place… a place where we could start over. She says my daughter, Jessie, is there. But I don't know if this place really exists. I'm afraid Claire is gone forever, and so is Jessie, and I'll be too, if I try to follow them. On the other hand, Jasper, this world we live in is dying, people are dying, war is coming. I don't know if I can be of any help here any longer."

"That sounds like quite a dilemma, Joe. Have you weighed all the alternatives? Do you know your sources?"

"I don't know, Jasper. It's Claire, and I want to believe her. And all I have for evidence is her dead body. Her dead body and my missing daughter."

"Sounds like a question of faith to me," Jasper said. "Like I told you, Joe, I'm not religious. Maybe you should talk to a priest or something."

"I'm not religious, either, Jasper. I don't think a priest would be any help."

"Well, Joe, do you trust Claire?"

"I don't know. I want to, but I don't even trust myself."

"There you go. Trust yourself, Joe. That's the first rule in trusting someone else."

Dr Andy Stephens snored quietly, his head lost in a jungle of paper and books. Joe cleared his throat and the Professor woke with a start. He hastily straightened his tie and shuffled some papers on his desk. "Sorry, I was attending to necessities."

Joe smiled. "Quite an *Away Routine*, Professor."

"Thank you, Mr Larivee. I programmed it myself. A little humor is needed around this stodgy old place. I'm Andy." He offered his hand, and Joe shook it. "Claire said you might come around, but I'm afraid she gave me no details. How is Claire, by the way?"

Joe choked up. "Andy, she's dead. Bridge is dead."

"Oh, my God. What happened?" Stephens was clearly shocked.

"That's what I'm trying to find out. The Temple of New Life. Sweetland. She said she was crossing over. She raved about the forest. I just don't know." Joe produced the folder Claire had given him and opened it to the image of the astrolabe. "What is The Brotherhood?"

Stephens studied the image. "Sit down, Joe, please. I'll tell you what I've learned about the Temple of New Life since Claire came to me two weeks ago."

Joe sat in the only unoccupied chair in the office. "Go on Andy, please."

"The Temple is a labyrinthine organization, hierarchical, similar in ways to the Catholic Church, except that its beliefs are gnostic. Within the Temple are orders—again like the Church—of Sisters and Brothers. These orders seem to have various functions, some which appear at cross-purposes to one another."

"What do you mean?"

"According to my students' research, the main purpose of the Temple seems to be recruitment for Sweetland, but some orders appear to be about deliberate obfuscation, creating congregations—if you will—which are clearly crackpot cults. One order seems to undermine the more—say—credible ones. But we have no way of knowing if some group at the top is walking the puppets, or if there are clearly differences in the ranks."

"And this astrolabe."

"It's a symbol of the Brothers of Chaos. Who are they? I'm afraid we don't know—they are extremely secretive."

"Any theories?"

"A small minority of my students believe they are some ancient cult—you know, the Templars and Illuminati, all that crap. Others have postulated everything from extra-terrestrials to mad scientists led by some artificial uber-intelligence. I don't really buy into any of it, but it's clearly an extraordinary phenomenon."

"What do your students believe about Sweetland, Professor?"

"I would like to ease your fears, Joe, but we just don't know. I'm afraid that the most popular opinion among my students is that Sweetland is indeed an inhabitable planet, and that's why I had to shut down the program two days ago—too many of them were being recruited to this idea, it seemed. I couldn't face the responsibility for that. You see, when Claire came to me, she told me about bodies being found—bodies associated with the Temple. My students discovered that indeed it was true. A suicide cult? I don't know. Mass delusion? It's certainly happened before. An artificial cyber world? They say it's possible. But a real physical destination? I just don't know. Even if I believed it, I couldn't take that chance with my students."

"Did Claire know all of this, Andy?"

"I filled her in when she called a few days ago. She appeared nervous. She said a death threat had been left at her door and that she was being followed—that she was going to see Brother Dave again. My God, I can't believe she's gone. She was a sweet, young woman—very insecure, but genuine—you don't run into them like her, anymore. Sweetland, Joe—I hope there's a Sweetland."

"Yeah, me too."

"What are you going to do now, Joe?"

"I've got no choice. I'm going to see Brother Dave."

"Be careful."

"I've been cautious all of my life, Andy. The time for caution is over."

Brother Dave pushed back his black hood, revealing bushy red hair, and the large brass astrolabe around his neck. "Glad to meet you, Joe. So, what is your interest in Sweetland."

"I have to know, goddammit, what the fuck this is all about."

"You really should stop and take a deep breath and let's try again." He felt like exploding, but it was the same thing he would have told an angry client. Slow down, count to ten. He breathed down in his diaphragm, let the air out slowly.

"Better, Joe?" said Brother Dave after a few seconds. "Now, what do you have to know?"

"If it's real. If my daughter is safe. If Bridge is alive."

"I can assure you, Jessie is fine. Bridge Whitedeer is fine. But I feel my word won't be enough for you. You need to experience it for yourself."

How was it possible they knew so much about him, including his connection to Bridge. But somehow it didn't surprise him. Nothing much surprised him anymore. "I have to know. I have to see them."

"Well, it's possible. You come to us with good references."

"What do you mean?" Joe scanned the medieval cafe again, with its candle-lit stone bricks and low ceiling. A damned RPG. The idea surfaced again that this was some sort of role-playing game.

"Preceding immigrants spoke highly of you. And you've passed the preliminary screening."

"What preliminary screening? I don't understand any of this."

"The psychological screening, health screening, background check. All were performed at the last minute. It seems you're fit enough to cross over. A few tiny issues, but not something which should hold you back."

"Issues? What do you mean?"

"You will find out in the next step, if you decide to take it. Once you go through the door."

"What is this fucking game, anyway?"

"If you think it's a game, then what's the harm? You find your answers or you don't."

Joe wanted to punch the guy in the face. But it wasn't a real face, was it? It was a fucking avatar. He breathed, tried to calm himself. Brother Dave was right. Just pretend it's a game.

"Okay," he said, "I'll play along with you."

"Are there more questions I can answer before you walk through the door?"

Of course, he had a thousand questions. On the other hand, he really just wanted to get it over with. "Tell me what I need to know, the basics."

"First," said Brother Dave, "the process you are about to go through is different for everyone. Our minds put up unique defenses, based on our experiences in life. If your motivation and your conscience are relatively clear, then the going should be smooth. If you don't fight it, if you're honest with yourself, you will leap over any hurdles your imagination might erect—"

"Wait, wait, wait," said Joe. "How the hell do you know about my motivation and my conscience?"

"We don't. You *do*. We just suggest questions, a little subtle nudging. It's already there in your mind: the memories, the archetypes, the conscience. Think of our programming as your shrink, building a narrative, helping you reveal your truth."

Or brainwashing? Did he give a damn anymore?

"Okay, let's do this."

Brother Dave led him to a plain, unadorned door at the back of the café.

"Remember," Brother Dave said, "you can back out at any time until you pass through The Eye. When you return, you will still have four more days to think it all over."

Joe stepped through the door.

☼

"Looks like we got another one, Charlene," said a deep graveled voice. "Better take him back to the lobby, dear."

"Get your hands off of me, you old goat," replied a slurred, alcoholic voice. Joe lay in a mud-covered alley stinking of piss and shit and vomit. He looked up to see two street people, a man and a woman, standing against a grimy, graffitied brick wall. The man held a paper bag, from which peeked the neck of a liquor bottle. The woman was pushing him away in disgust.

"Excuse me," said Joe. They stared at him.

"Well, get your ass up," said the woman. "You better get some of that mud off you before you go into the interview. Don't make no good impression to go in there with mud and shit dripping from you."

The alley was filthy with trash and mud and feces. He felt nauseous. The man held out a hand to assist him to his feet. Joe ignored it, fearing he would pull the inebriated fool over. He stood and tried to brush away the mud clinging to his clothes.

"Where am I?"

"Sweetland Immigration and Naturalization Service. SINS," said Charlene with a bawdy laugh.

"Ain't that the fucking hoot?" said the man.

Joe wasn't about to laugh. "So, what next?"

"Well, you just follow me," said Charlene, and she led Joe down the alley to a blue, metal-clad door, "Eat the rich" spray painted across the surface in artful, graffiti lettering. "You just go in there and wait, young man. Somebody'll take care of you. Eventually. Provided they haven't cut the funding again." She laughed a deep gut-clenching guffaw.

Joe walked into a crate-filled room. Something ratlike scurried by his feet and out the door as it closed behind him with a bang. The dim light overhead had a slight green cast to it, and the boxes appeared to be vegetable crates. It was a restaurant storage room.

A man sat on one crate, black hair, elegantly graying at the temples, ruddy skin, slightly tanned. He wore a tailor-made suit with a silk tie. On the other side of the room, a woman sprawled on an overstuffed chair. She reminded Joe of Christi, the receptionist at The Agency, but she was dressed as though she were a street hooker in a bright green spaghetti-strap dress which barely contained her ample breasts. Her hair was fuchsia, and she wore hoop earrings large enough to fit over Joe's forearms.

"Over there, next to him," she barked. "We'll get to you when we get to you."

Joe sat next to the man in the suit, who was chewing at his non-existent fingernails. He doubted that the man's athletic physique had any relationship to reality.

"Trying to get into Sweetland, too?" the man asked.

"Yes," said Joe.

"I have little hope left, really." The man extended his hand. "I'm wondering how much it costs to get into this place. I'm Richard. Richard Allen."

"Joe Justjoe." Joe shook the man's hand.

"What do you do, Joe?"

"I'm a social worker."

Richard snorted. "Then maybe you can figure out the process here. I'm the chief financial officer for a sportswear firm in Minneapolis. Had to sell a second home in Aspen just to get in the door. I'm here to pick out a caseworker today. They said I could buy one for a couple hundred grand. No guarantee, but you know, a guy's got to try."

"My daughter's there, in Sweetland," Joe said. "She's only fourteen. She needs her father."

"Maybe they'll take that into consideration, Joe. Good luck."

A young man popped out of a door which turned up in the wall. Dressed in a blood-stained white apron, he looked like a prep cook. "Mr Allen. Please follow me."

J OE WAITED. AND WAITED. IT SEEMED LIKE HOURS. Richard Allen never came back out. At last, Joe's name was called and he looked up to see the spitting image of Connie Velásquez, right down to the McDonald's uniform.

"Mr Larivee. My name is Connie. I'm the Intake Specialist who will help you with your paperwork to get you into the system. Come this way, please."

"Connie, it's me, Joe Larivee." It couldn't be Connie Velásquez. Connie was dead. "Don't you know me?"

"Yeah, I know you, Larivee." Was that disdain in her voice? He had never heard that tone from her before.

He followed her through the crates, which were loosely arranged into a series of individual stations. At each, someone was being interviewed, someone interviewing, and the interviewers all looked to Joe like clients, home care workers, hamburger flippers, and former meth addicts with missing teeth.

They came at last to an empty station. "Please, pull up a crate, Mr Larivee. I just have a few forms we need to fill out."

Joe sat. Connie pulled a thick file folder from another crate turned on its side, a makeshift filing cabinet. "Sorry for the crude surroundings. We didn't get our full budget approved this year."

She opened the folder before her. "Okay. Your name is Joe Larivee." She started to spell it.

"Look, can't we cut the crap and just get down to what's important?"

"Certainly, as soon as we take care of the little… uhm… bureaucratic *details*. You know, Joe, you should consider yourself lucky just to get in to see me today. We have very limited resources. There are deserving families who fall through the cracks every day, who don't even make it to our front door due to hunger or drug addiction or illness. That should humble you, Joe."

"Okay, I'll play your little game. I get it. I'm supposed to feel guilty for trying to help you people."

"I really don't like your attitude, Joe. This is not a little game, and you certainly don't get it, or you wouldn't be here. Now, we have to separate the undeserving from the deserving. There's not enough room for everybody."

"You mean the deserving, like Richard Allen?"

She laughed derisively. "A little resentful of those who have more than we do, huh? Well, you know, things are not always what they seem. We are happy to let Mr Allen and his ilk unburden themselves of their earthly baggage. We can use the money for the guillotines." She grinned and made a sharp, chopping motion with her hand. "The problem with these rich guys is you strip them naked, and they're still too fat to pass." She winked at Joe. "Know what I mean? You, Joe, you're not so rich, but I think you still carry a lot of baggage. Look, just fill out these forms while I get a cup of java. When I get back, I'll see if we can't move you on to the next step, okay?"

Connie left him with a pile of forms. The questions were the standard kinds of questions The Agency asked of new clients: name, address, mobe number, social security, citizenship, income sources, family details, rental history, criminal record. He filled them out, fuming.

When Connie returned, she looked over the forms, smiled. "Okay, Joe, just a few more questions. You say you have no criminal record?"

"No. Nothing."

"Well, Joe, we have to do a criminal record check. Have you had any police contact at all in the past six years which might throw up a flag?"

Shit, he thought, here we go. "I've been questioned twice by the F.B.I. about a colleague who went missing."

"Yes, that would be Anya."

"Look, if you know this, then why are you asking me?"

"Just put it down, Joe, just put it down, and we'll cart it on out of here. Now is there anything else we should know about?"

"No," he said.

"You sure? Nothing,"

"No," he repeated.

"Okay, Joe. I'm going to refer you to an Assessment Specialist. That's all I can do for now, until we check out your record, and your rental history, credit history, all of that. You understand?"

"Yeah," he said. He understood too well.

JOE FOUND HIMSELF FACE DOWN, ONCE AGAIN, THIS TIME ON the hard sidewalk of a city street. Clumsily, he pulled himself upright. Before him stood what his colleagues referred to as a roach motel. A sign on the office door read,

Department of the Interior

Truth and Reconciliation Division

He entered a tiny lobby that smelled of tobacco and mold. In the center was a small desk with peeling veneer, and behind it a fat, oily-skinned man sucking on a cigar.

The man was reading an old, trashy paperback novel, rat-eared and yellowing. Joe cleared his throat. "Excuse me."

The man looked up and scowled. "May I help you?"

"I'm looking for… they said I was being referred to an Assessment Specialist."

"What room, pal?"

"I'm afraid I don't know where I'm supposed to go."

"The directory is over there." He pointed to a spot on the wall across the room.

The directory was huge, taking up much of the wall. Joe scanned the names of the various offices. "Office of Crushed Dreams. Office of Delusions. Office of Rationalization. Office of Mental Acrobatics."

He was dumbfounded. "I don't get it."

"Look, buddy, just pick one. You should go to the office which most closely fits the problem you're trying to reconcile."

He looked again at the directory, anger rising in him. To hell with them for playing with him like this. It was a freaking game. He continued down the list. "Office of Faulty Memory. Office of Stray Thoughts. Office of Guilty Conscience…." What the hell. He touched that one and found the door to Room 23 materializing before him, its blue paint curling where it had been patched; where some violent person had kicked in the lock. Except it wasn't a real door, he reminded himself.

He touched the door and it swung open. Inside, the walls were brown from cigarette smoke. In the center of the room stood a motel bed with a broken headboard and heavily stained covers. And lying on those covers with her head propped up on her hand was Celia Greene.

"Hi Joe," she said. "You remember me, don't you, Joe?"

"How do you people know the details of my life? Who are you?"

"I'm Celia Greene, Joe. I used to be your client. Funny how things turn out, ain't it, Joe?"

"Celia Greene is dead."

"Are you sure about that, Joe? Anyway, here's the thing. I'm the Assessment Specialist here. That means I get to decide if you go on to the Emigrant Placement Specialist. So I suggest you adjust your attitude, and let's get through this interview. You understand me, Joe?"

He swallowed. "Yeah, I get it."

"So, I see you believe you have a guilty conscience, is this correct?"

"I just picked a random destination."

"But you pushed that particular button, Joe. You see, all of those buttons bring you here to this office. But the one you pushed was The Office of Guilty Conscience," Celia pointed out.

"It was random," repeated Joe.

"Look, Joe, we can send you to the Office of Subconscious Choices to sort this out, but wouldn't you just end up right back here? Why don't we save that step?"

"Whatever." Joe was defeated.

Celia Greene picked up a clipboard and a pencil. "So, Joe, do you have something on your conscience? Something that might prevent you from going to Sweetland?"

"No, nothing I can think of."

"Maybe you didn't treat your clients so well, or something like that?"

"I always went an extra step with my clients. If you were really Celia Greene, you would know that."

"Well, I suppose you were better than most. A little patronizing, maybe."

He wanted to protest, but thought better of it.

"Any unresolved problems with folks you're leaving behind, Joe?" asked Celia.

"No one I can think of. They're all dead or gone to Sweetland or whatever."

"Do you have any medical problems which need to be addressed?"

"I'm healthy."

"Any mental health problems we should know about, Joe?"

"I said I'm healthy," he snapped.

"No use getting testy, Joe. You should know that. I'm just here to help you."

"You're here to screen out the undeserving. That's your job. You can call it 'help' all you want, but that's the truth of it."

"Interesting," said Celia Greene. "Very interesting. I think maybe we're getting to the root of something here, Joe. It must have been hard as a young man to rationalize going into social work. Frank and Amy put a real burden on you, didn't they?"

"Go to hell," he screamed. She was unflappable.

"Remember our goal here, Joe. It's Jessie. You need to know that Jessie's okay. Isn't that what's important?"

"I want you people to stop playing games with me."

"Ah, Joe. Your whole life has been playing games, don't you think? Playing games with yourself. And your clients. Didn't you make them play games?"

"They were The Agency's games, the government's, not

mine." He heard the false note in his words. He made the choice. It was the button he had pushed. "Okay. What do I need to do?"

"What do you do when you have a guilty conscience, Joe?"

Just then, a little head popped out of the bathroom. "Mr Larry!" The head bounced up to him, like a cheshire cat, snot dripping from its nose, growing the body of a child. The little girl put her arms around his leg.

"Gwendolyn," he said. "How are you, sweetheart?"

"I'm fine. I have a secret, Mr Larry." She motioned him down to her level, and she whispered in his ear. "Don't worry, Mr Larry. This isn't real. It's just a dream."

"Thank you, Gwendolyn. I'll try to remember that."

"Gwen, you run along now," said Celia Greene. "Leave Mr Larry alone. Joe, it's time for the next step now. The Office of Confessions."

HE STARED AT THE WALLS OF A TINY, GRAY BRICK ROOM. THE light was stark and glaring, stuttering like an irregular strobe pounding into his brain. From somewhere came the sound of water dripping. He was alone. He waited. It occurred to him only briefly, like a hazy memory, that he was Joe Larivee. That Joe Larivee was sitting in his ex-wife's living room in Seattle with a pair of citspecs over his eyes. That he could remove them. All he had to do was take them off. But he waited, and just when he thought they had forgotten him, the door opened and someone entered. Dillon.

"What the hell?"

"You surprised, Joe?" said Dillon. "Or do you prefer to be called Justjoe?"

"Call me whatever the hell you're gonna call me."

"Well, Joe. Our friend Pedro is bringing your confession. He's been a little delayed. I think maybe he's flirting with one of the ladies at the front desk." Dillon winked. "But he'll be here soon."

"So this is all about Anya. Is that it?"

"I don't know, Joe. Is that what it's all about? It's *your* confession."

Joe went silent. What did they want?

"Who the hell am I talking to? Who are you?" he demanded.

"Joe, you really shouldn't try to second-guess all of this. Trust me, pal. Things will be really simple if you just let it go."

Just then Pedro popped through the door. An avatar of Pedro, Joe reminded himself. Or was this illusion all in his head?

"Here it is, amigo," said Pedro. "Your confession. A bit of déjà vu, eh, buddy? Just sign there, at the bottom. Just like last time."

"Screw you. I'm not signing anything."

"It's for Jessie, Joe." said Dillon. "It's all for Jessie."

"Let me tell you a little story, Joe," said Pedro. "Once upon a time there was this couple. Oh, let's call them—what shall we call them, Dillon? Let's call them Frank and Amy. The bad guys put Frank and Amy in shackles and stuck them on a freight train to Lake County, Oregon, where they had built a concentration camp. Now, food is expensive and they needed a cost-effective way to deal with all of these detainees out there in Lake County, so they lined them up, along with a bunch of other people they had rounded up,

Joe. And they shot them. You been wondering about that these last several years, haven't you, amigo?"

Joe felt sick to his stomach.

"Now Frank and Amy had a kid, see," Pedro went on. "His name was Fuck Head. Now, all of their lives Frank and Amy tried to make their world a better place for little Fuck Head, but then the bad guys came to power, and little Fuck Head had to make a choice. You following the story, Joe?"

"Go to hell," said Joe. "You're the assholes who killed Frank and Amy, not me."

"You sure about that, Joe?"

"No. I don't know who in hell you are." He didn't. They were playing with his fucking head.

"We're the people who say whether you get to go to Sweetland, Joe. Or whether you get to stay here in hell. We're *you*, Joe."

"Here's the confession, Joe," said Dillon, pushing it in front of him. "You think about it."

Then Dillon and Pedro left.

Joe put his head in his hands, closed his eyes. Frank and Amy. The government had taken them away and killed them. He hadn't wanted to hear that, but he knew it in his heart. So, what the hell difference did it make? Why not give them what they wanted?

At first, Joe looked blankly at the confession in front of him. Then he read it. "I, Joe Larivee, do hereby confess to killing Frank and Amy." The sentence repeated down the page, over and over.

"Screw you," he screamed at the walls. "I didn't kill Frank and Amy. I just saved myself and Jessie. They would have taken them, anyway." He knew it was true—they would have murdered them, anyway.

He broke down crying and pulled off the citspecs.

Something deep in his subconscious mind shifted, so deep it was nameless and, instead of returning to Jolene's house, he still sat in the little brick interrogation room. Had he forgotten once again how to take off the citspecs?

Across the table from him now sat Anya, or something that looked like Anya. "It's no crime, Joe," she said, "saving yourself. Saving your daughter. We have to make those kinds of choices sometimes. For instance, we can only take a few hundred thousand to Sweetland. Mostly young, strong people with their lives ahead of them. You're young, Joe. No reason not to be with Jessie. You just need to let it go."

"I don't know what you people want from me." This wasn't Anya, just as it hadn't been Dillon and Pedro, or Celia Greene, or little Gwendolyn, or anyone else he knew.

"Joe, you shouldn't try to second-guess. That's not likely to be successful. What we're looking for is truth. You see, the way things are, we just can't trust you. You can't trust yourself, am I right? Admit the thing that's blocking you, and we'll let you go. It's that simple. Really."

What did they want from him? He felt utterly defeated. But it would do no good to wallow in his pity. The answers couldn't be there, could they? Then, suddenly he felt he understood. "Frank and Amy. It wasn't so much that they put us all in danger, you know. It was that they reminded me day after fucking day of the horrors going on everywhere. They kept insisting that we could *do* something about it. But we couldn't, and we can't. It's too late for all of that. It was their generation that failed us."

"But, Joe, it was their parents' generation that built the great war machines and promulgated the ethos of consumption, and it was generations before them that produced the robber barrens, and slavery, and the inquisition, and industrial capitalism. If you look at it that way, Joe, then every generation has failed the generation after. There's another way to look at it. Because it is every generation's responsibility to change things for the next."

"And I closed my eyes. I admit it. I'm guilty."

"Yes. You closed your eyes. And then they came for *you*, Joe."

ANOTHER SHIFT, A SLIGHT DISORIENTATION, THE ROOM fuzzed out and he sat in another small room, white walls and stainless steel, two men across from him in lab coats, one very tall and thin, the other a short, pudgy nerd with thick glasses.

"Hello, Joe," said the small one. "You may have felt a slight sensation just now. That means that the transfer process has begun. In the next few minutes, we will give you a brief description of what you will experience when you walk through the gate into Sweetland."

"You mean, that's it?" he asked.

"That's it, Joe. A bit of a rough go there, but you passed through the eye of the needle." The tall man chuckled. "Now you're in orientation. Please, we don't have much time. When you cross into Sweetland for the first time, you will not have completely made transference. You may stay for approximately four hours, Joe—it differs slightly for everyone—and then you will be jerked back before the damage occurs to your body here on Earth. This will be sudden and without warning. There is no way to prepare for that. You will then have only four days to return here for the final crossing. We call this the four-four rule. Don't forget it. Four hours, four days." The other man pushed a piece of paper in front of him. "Please sign here, acknowledging that you have received these instructions."

Joe looked at it and laughed, but he signed.

"Now," said the little scientist, "some people are frightened by what happens when you go through that gate, so we are going to try to describe it. First, everything will go dark except for some synaptic traces. Again, it's different for everyone, Joe, but the most common is the tunnel effect. You know about the tunnel effect—it's that thing people report who have come back from death. What you will be seeing are synaptic memory traces which linger before your brain shuts down. This darkness will last only a moment, but it may seem longer. Don't panic. When you arrive on the other side, the light will return, your senses will return, but you'll be in a different place. Any questions at this point, Joe?"

"You mean, I'll die here on Earth."

"If you decide to make the final crossover, yes. Basic motor functions will continue for some time. You will even have some consciousness, and mobility, and a child-like mental capacity for a couple of days. Then, four or five days after the transference begins, your involuntary motor functions will cease. Your body will die, and you will fully inhabit your new body on Sweetland."

"The same body?"

"Identical in nearly all respects. A sort of mirror image."

"Now, I will describe Sweetland." said the tall one. "It will be a shock, Joe, and you should brace yourself. You probably have in your mind a wilderness, like the wilderness of old. Tall firs and cedars, or oak forests, that sort of thing. You should remove that image from your mind. What you are going to see will be familiar in some ways, but in others it is nothing like you've ever seen before. It is another world. The light is more red, the sun a bit cooler. The smells, the sounds and colors will seem very alien at first. We have arranged to have your loved ones there for you, to help you adjust. Remember, you have only four hours."

"Now, we have to go," said the small one. "The quantum chain has been completed, and your new body is waiting."

They led Joe out the door and along a winding path to a high stone wall with a small arched gateway.

Joe hesitated.

The little man urged, "You must go now. Your four hours have begun."

Joe stepped through the doorway.

Swimming. He swam in a thick, mucus-like fluid that filled his lungs, but he had no sensation of drowning. Warm and calming. An almost imperceptible aching. Some sweet long- ago memory slipping away, like a dream from which he had no wish to awaken. Yet his eyes opened slowly, unbidden, to peer through the sticky liquid. A dim light, weak and diffuse, illuminated a featureless world filled with vague shadows, and far away he heard a woman's voice, low and sweet like Amy's.

"He's come through."

"Respirator ready?" said another woman's voice.

"Yes, doctor, we're all set to go."

"Okay, you can evacuate the Womb, now."

There was a slow flushing sound as the warm liquid drained away. He could now see the two women who stood over him, but he could no longer breathe. He was embarrassingly aware of his nakedness. He gasped and struggled to sit, but firm hands held him down. "Lie still, my dear," said the first woman. "Everything will be okay in just a moment."

Some sort of tube was being forced down his throat, into his air passages. He retched, but there was nowhere for anything to go. Then his lungs filled with air and he coughed violently and sat erect. This time the hands released him.

"Oh my god," he gasped. "I thought I would die."

"Yes. Leaving the Womb is unpleasant, but it is much better than coming into the world cold, I assure you. The first travelers will testify to that."

He scanned the room. There were four other wombs, open and drained. Behind the incubators, a dozen or so doors, like large lockers, lined one wall of the room.

The doctor said, "Those are the waiting rooms. When you return to Earth, your body here will be placed back in a Womb in suspension mode. You'll be there in room four, along with your fellow immigrants—until you come back permanently."

"Does that mean that I have to go through this whole process again?"

"Oh, no. No fluid this time, just some feeding tubes for the nutrients. And a controlled atmosphere to keep you healthy. I'm Dr Marta Ibanez, by the way, and this is Alita Collins, a certified mid-wife."

"Now, dear, you'll want to wash this yuck off and get some clothes on," said Alita Collins, the woman who sounded like his mother. "You're the final one to arrive. The others are outside waiting."

Alita led him to a shower room, where some fresh clothing lay, folded neatly on a bench beneath a full-length mirror. The face that looked back at him from that mirror wasn't his avatar. It was the face he saw in the mirror every morning—the face of Joe Larivee, the social worker, the pitter.

Joe hobbled to the cabin door on shaky feet, leaning on a walking stick the midwife had provided, feeling as though his legs might give out at any moment. This body felt all too real. But he wasn't ready to believe just yet. How could it be true.

At the doorway, he had no time to take in his surroundings, before Jessie was there, wrapping her arms around him.

"Oh, Dad. I was so afraid you wouldn't come."

Her arms pressed tightly, her heart beat against his chest. They were still playing with his mind, weren't they? It was the only possible explanation. He wanted to protest. He wanted to believe. He didn't know what he wanted.

"Jessie," he said, going with the illusion. "Jessie, I missed you, sweetheart. I didn't think I would ever see you again."

He touched his cheeks. He touched hers. Tears, wet, real.

"Dad, it's so exciting. We have a farm where everyone in the commune can raise food, and some people have learned to make musical instruments so we can have dances. I have so many new friends. It's hard work. We had to start work as soon as we arrived, but only part time, until our bodies gain strength. Everything is made from scratch. They've sent a few tools over, solar collectors, wind generators, that sort of thing mostly. I can't tell you all of it, because there's just too much to tell. I can show you. It's going to be a little freaky, though. Come on...."

She tugged at him. "Hold on, sweetheart. Just a little slower, please."

"Sorry, Dad. Take your time. I'm just so excited. They only told us a few hours ago that you were coming."

He took another tentative step. The sandy soil crunched beneath his feet. The air held a slight chill and a sweet, unfamiliar fragrance. The light gave an eerie alien cast. It all appeared so real, but, how could it be?

The sun was nearing the horizon. Late afternoon. The building he had emerged from stood on the edge of a large clearing. Several more cabins and other sorts of buildings were laid out in a small grid, some fashioned of rough-hewn logs, and others of more modern construction. Solar collectors adorned the roofs. Everywhere was activity; fields under cultivation, the deep, red earth in furrows sprouting strange crops, people working in the sun, tilling the soil, planting seeds. Children shouted and played in the open spaces between the cabins, looked after by a young, pregnant woman. The clearing sat amid a vast forest, as he imagined the huge boreal forest which once covered North America, disappearing into distant mountains. Breathtaking.

Jessie took his hand and led him along. His legs were slowly becoming more trustworthy. Half way across the clearing, they were met by a young Latina who appeared to be in her mid twenties.

"Dad, this is Cedar... I mean, Felicia. You met her mom, Marta."

They exchanged greetings, and Felicia smiled at him warmly. "Shall we go meet the Welcome Committee?"

"Just a moment." Joe bent and grabbed a handful of soil, bringing it to his nostrils. He smelled the pungent odor of organic things breaking down. It smelled like earth, and yet it didn't.

"I know it's hard to believe, Dad." Jessie put her arm around him. "But it's real—this is really me."

He smiled weakly.

"Not everybody speaks English here," Felicia explained as they walked. "But just about everybody understands it a little. It's the closest thing to a universal language, which is pretty unfortunate, because it's the language of the Empire and people don't much like it. It's very controversial. Some people think we should use Esperanto or make up a new language. Others think that language is intrinsic to how we see the world."

"Some languages," said Jessie, "actually show reverence and respect for nature, just in the way they're constructed."

THE WELCOME COMMITTEE COMPRISED TWO MEN AND A woman. He judged them to all be roughly his own age, somewhere in their forties. Jessie introduced them as Ahmad, Ricardo, and Angelique.

"Hello, Joe," said Ahmad. "Welcome to Sweetland."

Joe smiled. "I don't have words."

"It's all real, Joe," said the woman, Angelique, who had deep, brown skin and a strong island French accent. "Let us take you on a very short tour, and then there is someone else who is waiting for you."

His three guides took Joe around the commune and introduced him to several people, some working in the fields, others spinning cloth, weaving baskets, or making furniture. "Everyone may do the work for which they have skills and desire," said Ahmad, "but everyone must help with the agriculture and other chores. These plants are all native, and we are just getting to know them. Some talked of sending over seeds from Earth, but it was rejected. It is enough that we are introducing one alien species, and there are many suitable native plants for our needs."

"What sort of animals hang out in these woods?" asked Joe.

"There are bird-like creatures," said Ahmad. "And tree dwellers which have some characteristics of marsupials but haven't yet been studied. We have yet to meet anything larger than a dog. But who knows? Our settlements are all here, on this one continent, in a tiny area. We have a few small drone aircraft which run on solar power. These will be sent out once they are reprogrammed, but, right now, we don't even know how many continents. There are large rivers, and volcanic mountains with glaciers. We have just gone through our second winter, which was harsh. The length of the seasons is very Earth like. The year here is 354 days, and the days are a bit longer than Earth days. About 26 earth hours. So twenty Sweetland years are equal to about nineteen Earth years, more or less. It takes a bit of getting used to. The circadian rhythms must adjust."

"Do you really think you can make this work?" asked Joe. "How will you ensure you don't end up with the same old world all over again?"

"We have no way to control what happens a thousand years from now, Joe," said Ricardo. "We can only start with a foundation, and a dream. And then it will be up to each succeeding generation to renew that dream, build on it, or change it; or maybe scrap it all and start again. It is all an experiment and we can't guarantee anything will work. We just know that the old ways failed us."

"You see," said Angelique, "we live amid this primeval forest. A place where danger lurks and myths will be born. We are the creators of the new myths, Joe. Community, equality, respect for this land, these are the foundations which Ricardo has mentioned. And we have the story of Earth to remind us we must never let it happen again. We must keep that story alive, to say to future generations, this is what will happen if you let greed and exploitation rule you. The new world will only have the meaning which we give to it, yes?"

It's a dream, thought Joe. And even though he put his arm around Jessie, and felt her warmth and the soft flesh of her shoulder beneath his hand, he just couldn't shake it. The voice of little Gwen echoed in his head, "Don't worry, Mr Larry. It's not real." But that wasn't really Gwen, was it? It was an imaginary voice in his own head. One he himself had created.

"Now," said Angelique, "it is only about an hour until sundown, and the girls wish to take you to see someone. It was nice meeting you, Joe. Perhaps we'll see you later at the Community Hall."

Jessie took his hand and she led him down a pathway paved in flat, mossy stones to a small field at the edge of the forest, where a lone figure stood with a hoe; a small, thin, dark-skinned woman digging furrows in the rich soil. And even though she appeared tired and fragile, she had a look of determination on her face. Bridge.

"Bridge, you shouldn't be working so hard," said Jessie. "They said we need to give ourselves time to adjust."

Bridge stopped and looked at Joe, as though she were seeing him for the first time. Because, he thought, she *is* seeing me for the first time.

"Hi, Joe. You're nothing like Joe Justjoe." She hugged him. "A man of substance."

Her smile was warm, and her gaze lingered on his face for a long time. She said, "I have something for you," and she took his hand and led him to the edge of the field, where a blanket was laid out on the grass with two large baskets filled with bread and fruit. "I promised you a picnic. Sit."

Joe sat on the blanket and Bridge sat next to him. On the other end, Jessie, glowing in her joy, and her quiet, watchful friend Felicia. Jessie tore off a piece of flat bread and spread something on it. She handed it to him. "It's different, Dad, but you'll get to like it." He took the bread and tasted it tentatively. He could come to accept it.

"The thing is," said Bridge, "they've only discovered a small portion of possible food crops, so we have to make do with what we have for now." She looked at him and smiled, a weary sadness lingering behind it, yearning for a world lost. Saudade. But there was also a courage in Bridge's dark eyes, which looked straight ahead, unflinching. He put his hand out and touched her face. For the first time, Joe thought this might be real. It all felt so real. He wanted it to be real. He thought about her body in the basement of his ex-wife's house in Seattle. He turned to Jessie. Her body was somewhere, too. Yet, here they were, both of them, alive.

They ate, lingering over the strange food. He expected the orangish round vegetable to taste like carrot, but he couldn't figure out what it tasted like. Nothing he could identify. Jessie laughed. "You can't compare the food to earth food. It's just not the same. You keep trying to reach backward and you'll fall over."

"Is this forward?" Joe asked. "I don't even know for sure that I am here. That you are here, Bridge. I just spent two days with you. I just watched you die. Your body is cold, Bridge. Who are you?"

"I'm Bridge," she said. "That body is the Bridge that

was." She took his hand and placed it against her heart. "It beats, Joe. It's a heart. My lungs breathe. My breath." She put his hand to her lips. He felt the warm, soft breath, and yet…

Jessie and Felicia stood suddenly. "Felicia and I are going up to the Community Hall. There's going to be a dance tonight. Why don't you two stay here, and meet us up there later?"

"Okay, sweetheart," said Joe.

The girls waved goodbye as they strolled up the path to the village. The sun was nearly down. How long had he been here? How long left?

"I don't know what it was like for her before, Joe, but she's happy," said Bridge. "They told us that last winter was harsh, and many people died because there wasn't enough food. A lot of the new settlers are going north, toward the equator, looking for better weather, but I think we can make it here."

She looked out at the forest with such an intensity that Joe could only follow her gaze, taking in the setting sun, its last light filtering through the trees, casting a deep purple light on the dark earth. And then the stars appeared. There were no recognizable constellations in the night sky, but, like the sky he remembered on the High Desert, it reached into infinity. So starkly real. But maybe it didn't make a difference at this moment; maybe Bridge was all the reality that mattered.

"Joe," said Bridge, "I feel as though I've been dead for a long time. Now I'm alive and I'm feeling and seeing and hearing and everything is just so powerful and real."

She put her arms around him, and he kissed her. Her lips were warm and soft, and her smell was the smell of sweat and earth. His desire overwhelmed him, and he kissed her again, feverishly. She kissed back as though it were her final meal, her mouth an eager receptacle, her probing tongue drawing him into her. Then her hands were sliding along his body, inviting him down on top of her. His hand found her breasts under her tunic as he kissed her face and neck and behind her ear. She moaned and arched her back, thrusting her pelvis against his hardening cock, until they were scrambling to remove each other's clothing.

He lost himself in making love. For a while there was no Earth, no Grid, no doubt what was real and what was not. Afterward, as they lay beside each other, her head resting on his arm, she gazed into his eyes for a very long time, until the faint sound of music drifted across the cool night air, reminding them they were not alone. They lay for a while longer, staring up at the strange night sky.

"Look there's the Big Dipper," he said. They both laughed. There might be a thousand Big Dippers, but not one they could see.

"The dance is beginning." She stroked his hair, running her fingers through the thick strands. "We should go."

"Uh-huh. Just a few more minutes."

She ran her fingers lightly across his face and along his torso, examining him.

"Was it good?"

"Like a hungry man's meal after the famine."

She kissed him. "That's okay. We'll have plenty of time to do the slow-food thing later."

A little sadness tugged at Joe as he came back to ground, and he sighed. The sound of the dance grew louder. He felt just a little guilty—he should be with Jessie.

"I guess we had better get over to the dance," he said. "The kids will be waiting."

They put their clothes in order, and guided by the music,

walked hand in hand along the path to the Community Hall. Joe found his strength had improved, but he still walked slowly, carefully.

Inside the hall, it was warm and full of movement and life. It reminded Joe of an old-fashioned Grange Hall, like one where Frank and Amy had taken him when he was about ten, a building designed for evenings like this, evenings of dancing and social gatherings. He spotted Jessie on the sidelines, talking to a young man. Joe waved at her, and she came to him with the boy in tow. "Dad, this is Michel. He's from Quebec City."

Joe smiled uneasily. He looked too old for Jessie.

"Hello," he said, "bonjour, Michel."

"Glad to meet you, Mr Larivee," said Michel. The boy tried to smile, but Joe sensed a deep sadness in him. "What do you think of our little community?"

"It's lovely," said Joe. "Almost too good to be true."

"But maybe it only seems so because what we left behind was so horrible, you know. Do you think that this is possible?"

"Perhaps you're right. But people seem happy tonight. Maybe that's the best we can hope for. What we have right now."

Jessie wrapped her arm around him. "Will you dance with me, Dad?"

"I'll try," he said. "I'm still a little wobbly."

They left Bridge and Michel chatting while he swung his daughter around to a lilting two-step, feeling a sudden surge of energy. The band was definitely amateur, the instruments crude, but the players full of life and enthusiasm. Real music. Music like he hadn't heard since he was a kid and Frank and Amy would have friends over; Frank on his guitar and Amy singing harmony, and someone would have a fiddle or a banjo. They would sing old protest songs or silly songs invented on the spot.

"So," he said, "is Michel anyone special?"

She laughed. "No, Dad. He's just a boy, and don't you go getting all parental. Besides, I haven't decided if I like boys that way. I think I need to try a few of them out."

He scowled.

"Just kidding. But Dad, things are different now. You'll have to get used to that."

"I guess I will."

When the song ended, he made his way back to Bridge. She smiled as she watched him cross the floor. The musicians played a slow waltz, and Bridge protested as he pulled her out onto the dance floor. "I don't know how to dance, Joe."

"But you danced with me on New Life."

"That wasn't me, Joe." She looked sheepish. "That was Claire, with the help of some dance script."

"Okay, let me teach you. A waltz is easy. It's just one, two, three, step, step, glide, like this," and he showed her how to move her feet. Before long she was gliding in his arms with the music, and Joe felt lost in time, as though the universe stood still. This moment was all that had ever been, the music and this young woman who smelled like the soil beneath her fingernails, rich and wonderful.

Then, something grabbed him and suddenly he was back in darkness. And the voice of Gwendolyn whispered in his ear, *"It's not real, Mr Larry. It's all a dream."*

JOE RETURNED TO CONSCIOUSNESS, CURLED UP IN JOLENE'S chair. He tried to make sense of what had just happened to him, but he couldn't. How could he know it was real? Had he actually danced with Jessie, made love to Bridge? Everything in his being told him to believe, he wanted to believe, but how could he?

It was early afternoon and outside another storm wave shook the windows and seeped through the cracks. Thunder rumbled overhead. He went to the kitchen, thawed a slice of frozen bread, spread on the last of the peanut butter. He walked to a window, pulled back the curtain, and peered out. The sky was dark and ugly, and the wind slammed another sheet of rain against the pane. He saw something move through the shrubs across the street. A dog, perhaps. No one in their right mind would be out in this weather. Would they? It was the kind of weather that pulled down hillsides and toppled trees.

Joe put the citspecs in his bag. Solemnly, he descended into the basement, where the body of Bridge lay on the potting table. He kneeled beside her and touched the cold skin of her face as silent tears streamed down his cheeks. The putrid smell of death revealed its faint beginnings. In a few days it would begin to seep upstairs.

Joe cried until there were no more tears. What was left to hold him here? Yet Sweetland was so far away and insubstantial, like a dream or the memory of a dream.

It's not real, Mr Larry.

☼

Part Seven

The Drums of War

"The most persistent sound which reverberates through men's history is the beating of war drums"
      —Arthur Koestler

"If there must be trouble let it be in my day, that my child may have peace."
      —Thomas Paine

Joe sat near the front of the empty shuttle, eating Jolene's peanuts, absent-mindedly glancing at a zine on the Libro. Unlike the ride up, he had no desire to sleep or to escape into New Life—the nanos were silent. He felt oddly abandoned, yet he preferred to be in his head watching the lightning-lit afternoon pass, experiencing the roaring wind buffeting the bus.

North of Olympia, a large military convoy slowed the bus to a crawl. The procession comprised mostly blackwaters, but there were a few regulars, too, headed south, in the same direction as the bus. The driver prudently held back without attempting to pass. A series of mud slides slowed them further. The big trees which once stabilized the soil were gone, for miles only stumps remained and an occasional barren trunk, reaching up out of the dead earth. If it weren't for the need to keep at least one highway open between Portland and Seattle, the authorities probably would have just let it slide away years ago. In the distance, huge, eerie concrete maglev towers rose from volcanic ash every few hundred meters, beyond the reach of the mudflows, all the way into Portland. Abandoned by the engineers and the politicians for lack of funds, they had reached only halfway to Olympia on their way to Seattle. No rails, just odd-shaped spires pointing upward to the heavens, echoing the stumps of the dead trees. Closer to the highway, the old land tracks lay abandoned, undermined by the savage rains eating at the hillsides.

On the stretch into Vancouver, a loud explosion rocked the bus, followed by a *pop, pop,* like gunfire. The bus came to a sudden stop. The convoy waited for another several minutes before creeping ahead as it passed a burning military vehicle alongside the road, mangled from the blast. Medics were pulling a young blackwater from the wreckage.

Bright emergency lights glinted off the victim's blood-spattered body.

"They're getting bolder with their hit-and-run attacks," said the driver, a nervous waver in his voice. "Just hope they don't decide to target civilians. The countryside is full of guerillas. They move up the ravines under cover of the brush. Not like the 'ciders in the city, though. They ain't looking to kill themselves, just take out a few blackwaters. Dangerous shit."

"I had no idea."

"You drive this route like I do, you see plenty."

Joe turned back to the window, his mind on the turmoil. How could these rebels possibly believe they could win? And what were they hoping to gain? This dying earth? A few weeds reclaiming an unused parking lot? Some gnarled old beaten-down oak with a scattering of leaves? Was this enough to believe in? Nature would likely prefer we humans all went to Sweetland.

He put his hand in his jacket pocket, reassuring himself that the memchip was safely tucked away there. What he needed to do was clear to him—return to Swan Island, find Stu Garrison, give him the chip to pass on. Jessie's safety depended on it. He was still her father, and it was the one thing left he could do for her—the one thing that felt real, that was here and now. Then he could decide about Sweetland.

AT THE STEEL BRIDGE, JOE LINED UP BEHIND THE OTHER bicyclists waiting to pass through the downtown security checkpoint. Two guards on duty tonight, only one eye scanner, but the line moved swiftly, without incident. As he crossed the bridge, he examined the dark river below. On the north side, a grain barge docked at the silos; on the south, the remains of a floating walk, once part of the East-side Esplanade, clung to the shore, snagged beneath the Steel Bridge where it had been carried by the floods three years ago. It had become a fishing dock, used by the transient population to hook the few remaining fish in the river. It was a tossup between starving or eating the poisoned remnants of life in the Willamette. Tied to the makeshift dock was a tiny, battered boat.

He turned right off the bridge into the Halliburton Peace Plaza. He removed the memchip from his pack and pocketed it, then stashed his bike and bag between the shrubbery and the chain-link fence before slipping down to the waterfront. A few brave homeless men camped on the edge of the bridge, huddled quietly, unmoving, their ponchos wrapped around their shoulders. He couldn't tell if they were the same men he had talked to earlier. Did they have a claim to this boat?

The men watched without moving as Joe untied the craft and pushed it off into the river. "She leaks," one of the men shouted as the current grabbed it. "Won't get you a mile."

The river lapped quietly at the side of the boat. A light rain was falling and Joe pulled his jacket up tight around his neck. He rowed out far enough for the current to pull him along swiftly, but close-in enough to slip along the shadow of the shoreline. He waved at the men as the current ushered him by, his feet already in three inches of water. He passed swiftly under the Steel and alongside the grain barge, and he was a third of the way down the length of the barge before he saw the blackwater, half asleep, his semi-automatic pointed at the deck. Joe's heart raced, and a bead of sweat gathered on his brow as wind-driven waves pushed the boat toward the barge. He used his adrenalin-fueled body as a buffer, walking the fishing boat along the length of the barge until he reached the bow, and could push away into the current again. The blackwater continued to nod, fighting off sleep, unaware that Joe had passed.

Two more working silos and more cargo docks remained between him and Swan Island. He moved swiftly in the dark river, but never reached the first silos before he noticed his predicament; nearly a foot of water lapped at his shins. He attempted to steer toward shore, but the little boat was overwhelmed. Joe removed his shoes, tied the laces together, hung them over his neck, and slipped into the water. The river was icy and his feet and fingers already numb as he pushed the boat to shore. He crawled up the bank, shivering violently; stinging pain in his toes told him he still had circulation, but hypothermia could set in quickly in this weather. He would have to find warmth soon.

Above him, voices drifted through the fog. He wasn't alone here—hundreds of homeless camps dotted the riverfront. He followed a foot-worn trail up to the gravel railway bed and walked north toward the island.

He had been following the tracks for only a few minutes when he heard the crunch of foot steps behind him. Was someone following him? He quickly moved off of the gravel and instead of following the railroad bed, he veered back toward the river. The faint glow of a fire appeared ahead of him through the fog and he adjusted his course again, away from the campsite. Stopping at a thicket of tall brush, he crouched, listening, until he heard the unmistakable splash of a foot in a mud puddle. It hadn't been his imagination, someone was following him. He sat perfectly still, hearing his heart thump in his chest, mirroring the distant drums.

"He's passed now," whispered a voice after a few moments. Joe jumped, his heart racing. Through the fog, the unshaven face of a young man grinned at him. "Gonna be back, though. He's wearin' envees."

"Envees?"

"Night Vision," said the man. "I used them in the army in Africa. Not as effective in this thick fog, but they work good enough. When he realizes you're not out in front of him any longer, he's gonna come back and try to figure out where you left the trail."

"How the hell do you know he's wearing Night Vision goggles?"

"The wire. Come on down to the camp and warm up. I'll tell you about it."

Joe followed the man toward the glow he had seen through the fog, relieved to have company and a source of warmth. As they approached the camp, he made out two ghostlike figures sitting by the fire.

"I'm Shaun," said the young man, "and these here are my rads, Nathan and Kat."

Joe could see the faces now, a black man and a white woman, both about thirty. All three wore military fatigues. "I'm Joe," he said.

"Hi there, Joe," said Nathan. "I heard you come up from the river. You been out for a swim?"

Joe froze at the interrogation, suddenly unsure whether he was among friend or foe. "I had a little accident. I'm trying to make my way to Swan Island."

"We don't need to know where you're going," said Kat. "We just need to know what kind of threat that guy poses."

"I don't know," said Joe. Could it have something to do with the man in Seattle? That didn't seem likely. "I should really move on. I might be putting you in jeopardy."

Nathan laughed. "All of us are in danger all the time. Shit, man, you're not the only one down here who's hiding.

The guy's probably just a railroad blackwater. You should take those socks off. I might have a dry pair I could trade you."

"No better place to hide from envees than in a crowd," said Shaun.

"Shaun knows what he's talking about, Joe," said Kat. "Just sit down and take it easy for a while. We've got your back."

"Thanks," said Joe. "I guess I'll take you up on those dry socks, Nathan." Joe momentarily lost himself in the comfort of the fire, before he began removing his wet socks. Nathan left to find an extra pair.

"Shaun was telling me about the wire," said Joe. "How does that work?"

"Local, encrypted networks," said Kat. "We text each other up and down the entire length of the river."

"Local networks? Aren't those illegal?"

Shaun laughed again, from deep in his gut. "Man, what's all this 'illegal' shit? You're down here with us, where Big Daddy don't want you. Why aren't you up there on a respectable street where you belong?"

"Okay, point taken. But, why don't they bust you?"

"Fuck, man," said Nathan, returning with the socks, which he tossed to Joe. "They don't have enough loyal goons left to do it, that's why. Did you know that half the folks down here along the river are deserters? Where the hell you been?"

"I've been up there where the blackwaters shoot kids," said Joe.

"Those mercenaries are fucking fascist scum," said Kat.

"So, how does this wire work?" Joe pulled the dry socks over his somewhat warmed feet. They felt like heaven.

"We got trip cams up along the tracks," said Shaun.

"When somebody passes, it alerts us, and we send somebody to check it out. Then we send word down the wire. We get these kinds of visitors all the time. Blackwaters maybe. Maybe not. Some hired by the railroad, some by the City or who knows, really."

"How do you know I'm not a spy?"

This time, Shaun joined Nathan in laughter.

"Hell," said Kat, "we don't for sure. But the dude with the envees, he's not one of us, I can guaran-fucking-tee you that."

"Besides," said Nathan, "don't matter all that much. We probably got half a dozen spies down this stretch of the river alone. You see, it don't look like it, but we have a system down here. Only those that need to, know how everything works, so you'd be wasting your time to ask. Now don't turn around, but your guy's back. He's standin' up by the tracks looking down here on us. I can see him. Just a shadow, but I'm sure it's him."

Joe fought the urge to turn around. His muscles tensed, ready to bound up and away. He felt Shaun's hand on his shoulder. "Take it easy, Joe. Last thing you want to do is run from that guy. They leave us alone. They know we fight back."

"Okay," said Nathan, "he's moved on. Interest you in some beans? I'm about to heat up a couple cartons."

He was hungry, but he was anxious about moving on. He wondered if he would insult them by turning it down. His hesitancy must have been interpreted as a yes, because Nathan handed him a hot carton and a spoon. He took a few bites. The food felt so good going down. He dived back in, shoveling the beans into his mouth, before he remembered he was sharing. He handed the box back to Nathan.

"Looks like you were hungry," said Kat.

"I'm sorry. I didn't mean to eat most of your food."

"Don't worry about it," interjected Kat. "Supply train came in last night."

He decided not to ask. He stood up and said, "Thanks again. I think I better move on."

"No problem," said Nathan. "Maybe you'll do the same for someone else, sometime. We're all in this together, comrade."

"I don't know if that guy's hunting me or just watching me."

"Don't take no chances on that, man," said Nathan.

"Take care of yourself, Joe," added Kat.

Jolene's first instinct was to get the hell out of Dodge, but the devil on her other shoulder persuaded her to stay and find out all she could about New America Corporation. Miglia promised he would see her again before she left, and she counted on it. He would answer her questions, one way or another. She would play it cool, let him believe she was still open to his offer. And, in fact, she might be, once she had all the facts. Never close your options prematurely.

Miglia returned Thursday evening, a day before Jolene's orientation was due to end.

"I haven't decided yet," she told him. "It's not the compensation. Actually, it is partially that. What you are offering makes me wonder exactly what is expected of me."

"And that's why I'm here tonight," said Miglia as he sliced into the delicate New York cut steak. Real beef. She could see the grain of it and the fat layers, and she knew right away that it hadn't been grown in a tank in Alabama. Soft candlelight flickered across his face. "That, of course, and my desire to sit across the dinner table again from such a lovely woman as I answer her lingering doubts. There are lingering doubts?"

"Dick, I've learned some things in the past few days. Some things of which you should be aware." *Of which you are undoubtedly aware,* she thought, hesitating for just a moment.

"Go on, please, Jolene."

"I believe that there is going to be an attempt to disrupt the Grid."

"Let them. New America has its own private Grid."

"You don't understand, Dick. They are trying to destroy the Grid. The economy of the U.S.A. Poof. Gone overnight."

"No, my dear, it is you who don't understand. The economy of the U.S.A. imploded years ago. This planet is finished. Played out. Poisoned. The resources have been extracted. We can keep recycling shit with nanotech. But it's still just shit. These billions of addicted drones will just keep dying off, killing each other, spreading their misery everywhere. Those who survive will simply become poorer and poorer. We will be doing them a favor if we let the Grid come down. Maybe they'll be able to see their pathetic lives for what they are."

"You're right, Dick, I guess I don't get it. Assuming what you say is true, are you planning to just go down with the ship? Is that what you are saying? Or do you have a life boat somewhere?"

"Now, you're on to it, my dear. We have New America. A brand-new home, out there across the universe, waiting for our ingenuity and drive and destiny to tame her. And we have the technology to get there. And I want you as New

America's chief of security. Secretary of Defense, if you will."

She paused. Was this guy crazy or something?

"So Dick, who is it exactly we are defending against?"

"The same old enemy, Jolene. The Bolivarians. Socialists, anarchists, equalitarian goodie-two-shoes. People who want something for nothing. The same old enemies of freedom. Unfortunately, the Bolivarians beat us to their Sweetland. They developed the tech. Or stole it more likely. They have a three-year head start on us—at least—and they probably have a massive arsenal by now. But we have infiltrated their networks, and we are setting up base far away from their settlements. If we're careful, it will take some years before they catch on."

"And just how are we going to get these people to your New America if the Grid is down… that's how they're doing it, right? With the Grid?"

Miglia smiled. A little too smug, she thought. "We don't need the Grid, my dear. The question you should ask is, why are the Bols using the Grid to transfer people to Sweetland? The answer is secrecy and an intense psychological screening process, which is why NSA or DHS hasn't been able to break it. It's good. But, we have key players inside the Bol network—a certain brotherhood within the Temple of New Life."

"The Temple of New Life? You mean that crackpot religion?"

"The religion of science and progress—the new religion of New America."

"Fucking hell! A religion?" The blood rose in Jolene's face. "Fucking hell, you say."

"You aren't required to believe it, my dear. Look at this

strategically. We need a religion to control the proles, and what better than one with a stake in our success."

"But aren't these people tied to the Bols?"

"Lets just say that these particular brothers aren't enamored of the Bolivarian philosophy. And they've helped us reverse-engineer the transfer technology."

"So the Grid doesn't matter."

"In Latin America they are sending materials across using fixed d-gates. People require a little special something extra, which the Bols are providing with their citspecs mods. Nanotech. But it doesn't have to be done through the Grid. We lose a few more our way, but we have plenty of raw material. We have a few dozen d-gates operational, here in St Louis and elsewhere, and we're hiring workers through temp agencies. We already have several thousand people on the ground in New America."

"I still don't understand, Dick," said Jolene. "How can you keep an operation this big secret without government cooperation?"

"We own the government, my dear. Of course they're cooperating."

How true was this assertion? "Then why all the cloak-and-dagger?"

"The Bols think they've pulled one over on us. As I said, if we play our cards right, it will take them a while to catch on. But they'll discover us sooner or later. We want to be prepared."

"And that's why you need me? Why not hire military?"

"We're recruiting soldiers. But we need police and an army, Jolene. We need someone who knows covert operations."

"Okay, Dick. Speaking of covert ops, I'll let you in on something else I know."

"Please, do, my dear."

"I know you have a mole in my office. SUATO4, to name the little asshole. I know that you and your bitch had an old man in Seattle knocked off."

"Yes. That was number Four's doing, I assure you. And the… uhm… little asshole, as you call him, will soon get his just reward. Look, Jolene, you know and I know that international business is politics—it's a ruthless game. You do what you have to do, you monitor the bottom line. Period. I want you on my team. I'm willing to be very generous."

"So, assuming I take you up on your offer, just what are we going to do with these new resources, Dick? You are asking me to move to Planet Dumbfuck Nowhere with what? A few thousand soldiers and engineers? Why? To make a bunch of money and retire back here to an Earth you just told me is finished? Sorry, Dick, but I've lived in Dumbfuck Nowhere, and I don't plan on going back."

"No, not at all, my dear. I am asking you to move to an untapped, pristine land of potential, to help build an empire and live like a queen in New America. In whatever kind of castle you desire. Within a decade, we will have a million people or more, families, servants, shopkeepers. We'll have the best artisans, the best chefs and artists and musicians that this old hag, Mother Earth, doesn't need anymore. There will be a new Renaissance. And big, strong laborers to do the… uh… shall we say, the work of their station. We can have it all. Think about it, Jolene. Think about it."

Later that night, alone in her hotel room, Jolene thought about it. And the more she thought about it, the better it sounded. *Like a queen,* he said. Yes, she wouldn't mind living like a queen at all.

. . .

JOLENE ARRIVED BACK AT HER HOUSE IN SEATTLE ON Monday morning, finding the front door open, swinging wildly in the wind. She cursed under her breath and entered, holding her nose at the foul smell. She had been warned by Dillon that Joe had been here in the company of Bridge Whitedeer. So like a man. She was prepared to find a mess, but the disaster she discovered was a little more than she had bargained for. Especially the body in the basement. And the stink. My god, the stink was horrible.

But, it didn't matter, really, she told herself. She was here to pick up a few things to take back to St Louis. Yet the irritation persisted. Why did men always expect others to clean up after them? She opened the blinds and looked out her window at the gray Seattle sky, the dying tree in her front yard, a once-beautiful city crumbling before her eyes. Well, this was one mess Jolene wouldn't have to deal with.

Fuck them. They could clean it up themselves. She was going to be the Queen of New America. Fuck them all.

WITHOUT LOOKING BACK, JOE MOVED TOWARD THE THICK fog of the river, no longer feeling so much like stalked prey. He soon found the path that took him through the camps where people ate, or talked, or played music on battered old guitars and sang defiant songs. He heard a strain from "Palaces of Gold," and walked toward it in the fog. By the time he reached the camp, the song had changed, and a young woman with wild red hair wailed,

How sweet is life but we're crying

> How mellow the wine that was dry,
> How fragrant the rose when it's dying,
> How gentle the wind as it sighs.
> What good is in youth when it's aging,
> What joy is in eyes that can't see,
> When there's sorrow and sunshine and
>   flowers,
> And still only our rivers run free.

He recognized the old Irish folk song, it had been one of Amy's favorites, and they sang it often at those living room gatherings, sang it at the top of their off-key voices. *How fragrant the rose when it's dying.*

The campers invited him over. As much as he was tempted, he kept his eyes ahead on the Swan Island enclave. He waved back silently and kept moving. Where the path finally ended, the dark outlines of more warehouses and grain silos loomed in the fog, their shrouded wharves jutting into the river. A large ghostly gray ship docked there. Without warning, his paranoia resurfaced, and he considered turning around, camping out until morning, waiting for the fog to lift, but he couldn't—the window to Sweetland was closing.

Joe pressed forward until he had reached the silos and halted mid-step. Another footfall in the gravel? His imagination? The man in the blue raincoat? Could he have been located so quickly? He dismissed the idea. Much more likely it was the blackwater who had been tracking him earlier. Still, he couldn't erase the image of the Seattle killer from his head.

He quickly scanned his surroundings for something he could use as a weapon. He found only a broken willow branch about three inches in diameter, and two feet long.

Willow was strong, but this piece wasn't very heavy, probably old and rotting from the inside. He wondered if it could do him any good, but he kept it anyway, feeling secure in having something solid in his hand.

Through the fog, he made out the chain-link fence and razor wire that bordered the warehouse properties. Beyond lay the railroad switching yard, if his memory served him. He still had some distance to go, maybe a kilometer. Joe hefted the thick willow branch in his hand. Would it be enough if he ran into trouble? He doubted it.

He pressed forward, keeping close to the fence, until he had passed the warehouses and silos. In the fog ahead he could now make out the looming shadows of Swan Island, still some distance away. Ahead of him the broken pavement of an old road materialized in the mist. He must not be far from the enclave's perimeter fence.

Without warning, a powerful light hit him in the face, blinding him. As his eyes adjusted, he saw the yellow jacket of a rent-a-cop at the edge of the gravel. "You have business here?" the rent-a-cop asked.

"What the hell is it to you?" Joe lashed out. *It's a free country,* he nearly said. He heard it play over in his mind like a pre-programmed phrase. *It's a free country? Of course it's not. It never has been.*

"I can tell you what the hell it is to you, asshole. You're on private property." The security guard removed a gun from its holster. He was a big man with a bruised face, which looked as though it had recently gone through a meat grinder. Not someone Joe wanted to mess with. "Now, lay down on the ground, with your hands away from your body."

Joe was beyond fear. He had passed some threshold where his safety was no longer important. Did it really matter what happened to him? The void where the fear had been filled with a slow, boiling anger. Half way to the ground, he rose again to his feet in defiance, when two more figures emerged from the fog. One pushed a bicycle, Joe's bicycle, his bag hanging over the handlebars.

"Hold it right there." Yellow Jacket pointed his gun toward the newcomers.

"FBI," said the voice of Dillon. "We'll take custody of Mr. Larivee here."

"You Feds think you're hot shit, don't you?" said Yellow Jacket. "I heard that the FBI just got bought by the Pinkertons. You guys are rent-a-cops like the rest of us. So fuck you, FBI. This is our jurisdiction."

"Right now, we still work for the federal government, moron," said Dillon. "I suggest you put your little wiener away and let the big guys take over."

Joe noticed Pedro edging around slowly on his right. Then the gun flashed in Pedro's hand and Yellow Jacket crumbled on top of his bicycle.

"Motherfucker," said Pedro.

Dillon approached Joe, thrusting his bike toward him. Joe caught the pack, but let his bike fall to the ground.

"You really shouldn't leave your citspecs lying around like that, Joe," Dillon said. "Somebody's liable to steal them."

"Yeah," said Joe, "thanks for nothing, Dillon."

"No problem, Joe. How about we escort you to the Island?"

"I think I can make it on my own. What is with you guys, anyway? I thought you were trying to save us all from the rabble down there."

"Boss says change of plans, Joe. By the way, your ex

sends her regards. Says to tell you, no hard feelings. Says you should keep her little Jessie safe."

Fucking Jolene.

Pedro had disappeared in the fog, but now emerged again with two more bicycles in tow.

"I think I'll follow along, anyway, Joe," said Dillon. "Make sure you get there safe and all. Pedro can stay behind with the bikes."

Joe left his own bike laying on the ground and following Dillon into the fog. Pedro called after him, "Hey, Joe, you put in a good word for your amigos when you get to Sweetland, okay?"

"Not a fucking chance, Pedro," he said.

DILLON LEFT JOE AT THE SWAN ISLAND PERIMETER FENCE, where he followed it away from the river until he recognized the familiar Going Street entrance with its concrete Jersey barriers. A small knot of young militia lingered around a burn barrel. Some played hackeysack in the light rain, some warmed their hands on the fire. Behind them, the old pre-camp buildings spread across the sprawling industrial park, disappearing into the fog. Between the buildings lay a vast new city of makeshift shelters, everything from tents and broken-down trailers, to more substantial cob and straw-bale buildings, densely packed together. Screwing up his courage, he walked nonchalantly, hands in his pockets, slipping between a barrier and the fence. The kids on the barricade paid no attention to him, and he felt a momentary foolishness for all of his paranoia.

Yet Margot's people had not been so lax a few days ago. He figured they would be on to him soon enough.

The Island was a bee-hive, a constant motion of men and women moving between dwellings and larger community buildings; between tent and tent; between tent and who knew where. Head down, Joe set out across the tent city. His pants had ceased to drip, and with his stocking cap pulled low over his wet hair, he blended in and moved unnoticed through the shanty town until he saw a little girl peering from the flap of a tent. He was certain he knew her. "Gwendolyn," he called. But the child retreated into the tent, frightened. Not Gwendolyn.

Turning away, he nearly collided with a woman holding a lantern. She looked him up and down as he abruptly halted, his limbs still trembling from the cold.

"Don't you got a blanket?" she asked.

"I just arrived," he said. "I didn't bring anything with me."

"Hold on. I'll take you over to the community center. One thing we got is plenty of blankets. You got shelter yet?"

He nodded. "Over at the other end of the Island." He motioned vaguely to the south.

"You can warm yourself up at the center."

"Thanks for the offer, but I have to meet someone over on Basin Drive. That's over here, isn't it?" He pointed in the direction he had been traveling.

"Yeah, just up the other side of this camp. But the center is right over here. You got time to grab a blanket so you don't end up with hypothermia."

He didn't like the way she looked at him, a mixture of motherliness and suspicion.

"I guess you're right. I'm pretty damned cold."

"You're starting to turn blue. Follow me." She moved in

the direction of a large building on the other side of the lot. Joe could see lights inside and smoke pouring from a stovepipe chimney. "What's your name? I haven't seen you around here before."

"Joe."

She laughed. "Oh, yeah. Joe Blow, eh?"

Was he being interrogated? "Just Joe."

"Okay, I'm Jane." She gave him a wink. "Well, Joe, here we are."

Joe entered a building constructed of old pallets and plywood. Blankets hung from the walls, providing some insulation, and several people sat on old stuffed chairs and broken-down couches, engaged in energetic conversation. A few huddled near an old-fashioned cast-iron stove, turning brown with rust. Most of the men and women had blankets draped over their shoulders and condensation rose from their breath. Laughter drifted toward him. Her back to him, a woman with blonde, shoulder-length hair appeared oddly familiar. *Was that Anya?*

Just as he was about to call out her name, Jane said, "Anya, got a guy here needs a blanket."

Anya turned around.

"Oh my god," she said. "Joe. I can't believe it's you."

"Anya."

"So your name really is Joe," said Jane. "I'm Steph. I just thought you were... well, anyway, you vouch for this guy, Anya?"

"Absolutely." Anya hugged him. "Come over and warm up, Joe. You look miserable. What are you doing here?"

"I'm just as surprised to see you, Anya. I thought you'd vanished off the face of the Earth."

"I'm sorry I couldn't tell you, Joe. It was becoming too dangerous out there for me and Sam."

"Anya, what's going on? The FBI has been looking for you. They said you were part of a terrorist cell." Was that accusation in his voice?

"Joe, I'll try to explain. But first you need to get out of these wet clothes. I think I can find some dry ones that might fit."

Anya crossed the room to several large cardboard boxes lining one wall of the building. She returned with a wool army blanket and some dry khakis. "Put these on, and I'll get you a cup of coffee."

Anya left for coffee and Joe sheepishly pulled off his wet clothes, carefully transferring the memchip to his new, dry trousers. The chip was wet, but he wasn't worried; they were designed to resist moisture and cold. He put on the khakis and wrapped himself in the wool blanket. Anya soon returned with a steaming cup, and Joe took it greedily into his cold hands. He sipped. "My god, this is real coffee. How the hell did you get real coffee?"

"Bernard brings it up from South America." She looked around the room. "He was here a minute ago. He has some trade connections with the Bolivarians. We get a special deal."

"The Bolivarians?" asked Joe. "So this *is* connected to the Bols."

Anya looked at him with concern in her eyes. "You know it's coming, don't you?"

"What's coming?"

"Revolution, Joe. It's a matter of weeks, now."

"But Anya, it's suicide. There are huge convoys. I've seen them... the other day I saw one going south down 122nd. And this afternoon I saw... it looked like a thousand armored vehicles moving toward Portland from the Puget Sound area. Rebellion is impossible."

"Look, Joe, most of the army regulars are with us. At least, in this part of the country. Some of the blackwaters are ready to switch sides. The damned mercenaries have no loyalties, and they are bickering. We have people in the DHS and the police agencies and throughout the bureaucracy. We are going to win this. The revolutionaries elected a new Mexican government last week. The Bolivarian armies are moving up from the South. It's over for the greedy bastards."

"But what difference will it make, Anya? The Earth is going to cleanse us all from the planet, even if we could somehow change our behavior."

"Joe, that's far from certain. There's nothing we can do about the millions who've died, and the millions more who will probably die. But many of us can survive. Those who can cooperate can survive. And if not, well, we have Sweetland."

"I need to talk to you about Sweetland. Jessie—she's gone. I think I want to join her, but I don't know, Anya. First, I have to see this old guy who knew my parents, his name is Stu Garrison."

If he gave the memchip to Anya, he would have done his duty. But it was too dangerous for her—Stan's fate proved that. It wasn't fair to lay it on Anya. Stu was on the Citizens' Council.

"I know Stu. I can take you to him. Do you mind if we stop at my apartment first? Allison would love to say hi."

"Allison's here too?"

"Sure. Sam and Alli and I all live together over at the Swan Island Hilton." She laughed. "That's what we call the old insurance building on Basin Drive."

Pulling the blanket tight around his shoulders, Joe stepped out into the rain and found himself face-to-face with pale blue eyes and a blonde goatee. Joe's eyes lowered to the blue raincoat and fixed on the astrolabe around the man's neck. When Anya touched his shoulder, his heart felt as though it would burst.

"Joe, this is Bernard, the coffee man."

"Hello, Joe. Good to meet you." Bernard's voice was cold and aloof, giving no sign of recognition.

"Yeah, you too," was all he could muster as Bernard slipped away into the tent.

Joe exhaled slowly. Would Anya believe him if he told her about Seattle? Would that endanger her?

"Are you all right, Joe?" asked Anya.

Was it that obvious? "Yeah. I'm okay, just a little chilled."

Anya put her arm through Joe's and leaned into him. "I'm really happy to see you, Joe. I was so worried about you. I hate that I had to just abandon my friends, you know."

"I'm glad to know you're safe, Anya. I was afraid something terrible had happened."

"I had to get out. The feds discovered me, and I could have led them to Allison. There's nothing they can do now to change the course of things, but I couldn't put Alli at risk any longer. Or you."

"Look, Anya, there are some things I should tell you. The FBI has been harassing me. At first, they said that it was about you. Then it was about Jessie and someone she met in New Life — Felicia. They brought up this Bolivarian thing."

"Joe, that's their modus operandi. Once it was anarchists, then communists, then terrorists, and so on. Now every threat is a Bolivarian terrorist."

"Yes, but you know what you told me about the army—

about how many of them support revolution? Well, some Bolivarians also aren't what they seem. I met some people, Anya. Inworld. The corporations and the syndicates own a lot of influential politicians in Latin America, and they have infiltrated the Bolivarian network all the way up the west coast. I say this because I think I saw someone here. I saw him in Seattle yesterday. I think he killed someone, an old computer tech who knew something… who had some information they didn't want exposed, some code."

"Joe, what are you talking about? Do you need a paranoia check? You were in Seattle yesterday?"

"I know it sounds crazy, Anya, but trust me, I was there, I saw him, and I heard the shots, and I would have been dead too if I hadn't run. Before I left, the old man told me that some outfit called New America Corporation had stolen something really important, some technology, and they were doing everything they could to keep it quiet."

"So, what did this man look like?"

"He was blond, neatly trimmed goatee. Like your Bernard guy."

"Goatees are really popular here, you know."

"It was Bernard, Anya. I'm certain of it." He could see disbelief in her eyes. "Okay. Maybe this is all in my head. But I thought you should know."

Anya looked thoughtful. "Thanks, Joe. I'll get word up to Margot, but she'll be a tough one to convince."

Margot wouldn't be swayed without proof. He could give the memchip to Anya to pass on, but now he had another reason to resist: he didn't fully trust Margot. Stu had influence here, and he would take the evidence where it needed to go.

· · ·

ANYA'S APARTMENT WAS SPARSELY FURNISHED WITH AN overstuffed couch and an old rocking chair. A colorful braided rug and old maple coffee table were placed artfully on top of the ugly office carpet. Simple, found objets d'art on the wall gave the place a homey feel. The pleasant sound of quiet conversation and clinking dishes filtered in from an adjoining room. "Anya, is that you?" said a familiar voice.

"Sam, Alli, come see who I brought home."

Sam's dark face peered around the corner of the door frame. "Joe?"

"Joe?" Allison arrived at the door, let out a tiny squeal, and ran to him, hugging him tightly, kissing him on the cheek. "Oh, Joe, it's really you. I'm so relieved that you're here. I felt so guilty."

"It's true," said Sam. "She moped around forever. We all felt bad, but there was no way to let you know once the FBI started looking for Anya."

Joe was miffed, despite himself. Anya must have seen it on his face, because she said, "Sit down, Joe. We will try to explain."

"I'll get us some tea, and a bite to eat," said Sam. "We were just fixing a bit of evening repast." She disappeared back into the kitchen.

Joe sat on the couch, and Anya sat next to him. Allison took the rocking chair and picked up a basket from which she extracted knitting needles and what appeared to be the beginning of a sweater. For just a moment, Joe saw his mother, sitting for hours in her rocking chair, quilting or knitting, her hands always busy as she talked. A sudden feeling of warmth toward these women replaced his umbrage.

"Joe," said Allison, her hands working deftly, "we had

planned to bring you in with us. When Anya told me about her concern for you, we hatched the idea."

"So, the date—"

"So, the date was the first step." said Anya. "We were going to tell you, then—"

"—then the FBI came along," he finished. "So, I was your recruit." His pique briefly returned. He knew he was being unreasonable, but he wanted Anya's motive to have been something else.

"Joe, it's not like that. You're a dear friend and everything was so complicated."

Allison stopped her knitting and reached over to touch his arm. "You are a sweet guy, Joe, and a great kisser, by the way." She flashed a sexy smile at him. "I don't regret for a moment what we did. I only wish we could have followed through. I wish it could have been different."

Joe searched her face. She was being truthful, but it still hurt, and he felt ashamed of his self-absorbed reaction.

Sam arrived with tea and sandwiches. She poured tea around and Joe grabbed a veggie sandwich, attacking it with fervor. It all felt so normal, as though the world would just continue as it always had.

"Sweetland..." Joe paused to chew. "What was all of this about Sweetland, Allison? A marketing campaign, you said?"

"That's exactly what it was, Joe," said Allison. "It was carefully designed to lure potential young immigrants while obscuring its real nature. That's what marketing always does —it obscures. We just ramped up the obfuscation a notch or two. Underneath the glossy veneer and slogans, we ran a buzz campaign aimed at youth subcultures, using street lingo to entice smart young people. Then there was the Temple. The Temple was created by a group of scientists, former liberation theologists and political idealists to screen immigrants and baffle the authorities at the same time. It got way out of hand. No one thought it would become a cult. But it's worked beautifully for six months."

Joe felt anger rising again. "Well, that shit really screws up your head, Allison."

"I know that, Joe. I know that this world has been fucked up totally because of that shit. And yet it goes on every day, the layers of deception. That's why I can't do it any longer. That's why we have to make a total break and begin to dig out this cancer. Sweetland will begin fresh, inoculated by the truth."

"The truth, you say. I'm not sure that you or I or anyone knows the truth. I'm not even entirely convinced that this isn't all a cruel hoax. And Jessie… Jessie is gone."

"Go to her, Joe," said Anya. "She needs you."

Joe rose to his feet. "Look, I don't have time for this conversation now, I have to see Stu Garrison. But I'm glad you found me, Anya."

Allison and Anya walked him to the door.

"I'll point out the building," said Anya. "You should have no trouble finding it."

"Goodbye, Joe," said Sam.

Allison tenderly touched his face. "Jessie is going to be alright, Joe. You should go, but there's a place here for you, if that's what you decide."

He turned his head away, breaking her touch. He was thinking about Bridge, about lying with her under the Sweetland sky. How would he ever know if Jessie was going to be alright? If Bridge was alright? How could he ever know what was true and what was not?

He kissed Allison obliquely on the edge of her lips and said goodbye.

☼

THE RAIN HAD RECEDED TO A FINE MIST AS JOE STEPPED BACK into the darkness. A light fog had worked its way up from the river. The four story complex Anya had pointed out to him rose just beyond the sprawling tent village. The drums of the night washed over him like waves on the shore as he made his way along the lonely strand, his mind fighting with itself—run or dive into the ocean.

Somewhere in the city of tents, a dog howled, a baby bawled, an argument ensued. A group of young men crossed the road in front of him, their laughter holding an edge of nervous anticipation. Or was that his own uncertainty he heard? Was someone standing in the shadows somewhere ahead, waiting? He crossed Basin to the village side, looked back calmly to see a movement in the bushes. His instinct had been right. Someone followed him across the dark street, his face too indistinct in the night to identify. Joe didn't wait for a closer look. He darted into the bustling, anonymous crowd of the dispossessed, slipping between tents, away from his pursuer.

He realized with sudden clarity that he should have given the memchip to Anya. He couldn't risk losing it to Bernard. What was he going to do with it? Frantic, he surveyed the rain-soaked surroundings for a dry hiding place, somewhere he could stash the tiny object and recall it later, but to no avail. He would have to move on—only a matter of minutes before Bernard would look down this alley. He slipped back out into the crowd, hurrying through the throng. The tents here looked familiar. He had walked this way before, a few hours ago, when he first arrived. He could hear the windmill. The community center would be somewhere nearby. Could he hide it there? He mulled it over as he moved along, when he saw the little girl standing outside a tent. It was the child he had mistaken for Gwendolyn. She gripped a toy bear. Just like Gwendolyn's, he realized with a pang.

"Fuzzy Finnegan," said Joe, squatting in front of the child. "I know a little girl with one just like that."

"He's supposed to talk," said the girl, "but he doesn't work. My daddy found him."

"Maybe I can look at him," said Joe.

The girl thrust Finnegan at Joe. "Do you think you can fix him, Mister?"

"I'm Joe," he said. "What's your name?"

"I'm Lara. Can you fix him?"

"Let's see." Joe scanned the faces passing by as he popped open the tiny hidden compartment. He looked inside. No memchip. Quickly, he slipped the chip out of his pocket and into the memslot.

"Well, I don't think he can be fixed," Joe pronounced after examining the toy a little longer. "I'm afraid he has some parts missing."

"Oh. Well I love him anyway, even if he can't talk."

"You take good care of him, now. I have to run. Bye, now."

"Bye."

Joe ran, already regretting what he had just done in desperation. Now he needed to put as much distance between himself and Lara as possible. Beyond the tents he could see Stu Garrison's building, but he had no easy way to get there. He slowed again to blend with the crowd, then stopped beneath an awning to survey the passersby. A flash of blue three tents down. Bernard. He ducked his head and moved back into the flow, picking up his pace.

"Hey pal, watch where you're going." The voice came from somewhere behind him. He didn't have to turn around to know Bernard was closing in. Again, he ducked between tents, tripping on a concrete block, recovering, behind him the sound of Bernard's running feet. Joe burst back into the open, into the crowd. Would Bernard risk attacking him amid so many people?

Then he saw Margot, and two of her guards walking toward him. He released a sigh of relief.

"Margot," he called out, waving, as she gave a signal to her militia, who moved out to flank Joe. "Margot, I have something you need to know."

The guards moved in on Joe. "And what would that be, Larivee?" said Margot. Before he could speak, the guards slapped handcuffs over his wrists.

Out of nowhere, Bernard appeared beside him.

"You should have followed her, Larivee," said Bernard. "You should have gone to Sweetland when you had the chance. We did everything in our power to steer you and Ms Whitedeer on the right path. Too bad you're not as smart as she was."

"Let's get this loser out of circulation," snapped Margot.

Margot, followed by Bernard, and flanked by her guards, led Joe toward Basin Street, where a small three-wheeled electric vehicle waited. The guards jumped into the tiny truck bed as Margot climbed behind the wheel. Bernard, ushering Joe into the cab, became distracted for an instant by a group of arguing teenagers. When Joe saw the opening, he darted, without thinking, toward the camp. It was a foolish move. A guard easily overtook him, landing on him with the full force of his six-foot frame, throwing Joe's head against the pavement.

Adrenalin pumping through his body, Joe attempted to open his eyes, but dizziness overwhelmed him. They were dragging him, hoisting him into the cab. He faded out, and when he came back the truck was moving. He could hear Margot and the guard talking, their voices distant.

"We can't let him out of our sight." It was Bernard. "He knows too much. Three or four days and this will be all over."

"That soon?" asked Margot.

"The boys in St Louis say we're ready. It's the word we've been waiting for." *St Louis. New America Corporation.*

"I sure the hell hope you're right about those blackwaters, Bernard. You know what they'll do to us if you're not." There was weariness in Margot's voice.

"I'm right, Margot. They're mercenaries, they go where the money is, and that's New America. These amateurs will never know what hit them when those Securitech boys come off that train."

"What about the memchip?"

"Forget the memchip. He's ditched it somewhere, and it's come too late for them. It might help verify his story with the locals, but as long as we have him under our control…"

Joe strained to hear more, but found himself falling through a black tunnel, away from the light. When he awoke again, he was being dragged from the truck into a concrete block building. Margot walked along, silent. They were inside an office with several desks and old-fashioned computers like those at The Agency, and various other electronic devices lining both walls. A command center of some sort. They took him to the back, through a steel gate, to a small room with a bunk, toilet, basin, and small table. On the table were a few books, a writing pad and pencil.

"We'll be back for a little chat, Larivee," said Margot.

Then one of the guards closed the door and Joe lay alone in the dark.

Joe shivered in the morning chill. He pulled the thin blanket tightly around his shoulders. A light came on in the hall outside the cell door, followed by a bustle of activity, footfalls echoing through the concrete chamber, machines engaging, computers booting up. The morning shift.

Hunger opened its maw. Joe laid back on the bunk, pushing away the thought of food, allowing his mind drifting to places he didn't want to go, conjuring up images of war and starvation. He imagined Jessie and her future under a New America Corporate empire, possibly enslaved or hunted. He thought about his own life, light-years away from the ones he loved. Yet, despite all that, Sweetland remained an abstraction. He couldn't help but think Portland was where he belonged. Here in this place where he grew up; where all his history was written on the concrete sidewalks. He curled up on the bunk and pulled the blanket around himself, trying to escape his ugly rumination through sleep, which mercifully came.

Little Gwendolyn Greene peered out at him from a ragged tent, her eyes full of mucus and tears. Behind her stood Carolee, sniffling.

"Will you take care of us, Mr Larry?" Gwendolyn pleaded.

"I can't Gwendolyn. I have to go to Sweetland."

"But it's not real, Mr Larry."

"I'm afraid I don't know what's real anymore, Gwen."

"Me and Carolee are real. Aren't we, Mr Larry?"

Gwendolyn's voice echoed in his head, growing louder

until it startled him awake. He sat up in bed trembling, rattled by the lucidity of the dream. He remained like that, unmoving, for a long time, until he heard voices outside his door and the sound of a key in the lock, the bolt slide.

A guard, his neck thick, his face carefully blank, opened the door and peered in at Joe for a few seconds before stepping back.

A girl with a pretty, dark-skinned face entered. She carried a tray of food. He knew that face. It was Jessie's friend Mel.

"Melissa?" He whispered as she set the tray on the table

"Mr Larivee? What are you doing here?"

His mind was racing. "Do you know Stu Garrison?"

"Sure."

"Can you get a message to him? Without Margot finding out?"

"I have to leave, now. But I'll come back in a half hour to pick up the dishes."

"Everything okay in there?" The guard pushed the door further open.

Without giving him an answer, Melissa turned away and disappeared behind the door. The guard gave him a lingering look, frowning. Joe felt miserable. Had he caused trouble for Melissa? Would they hurt her? He quickly consumed his dinner of brown rice and vegetables in large, barely chewed bites, before reaching for the pad and pencil.

"Stu—Margot and Bernard working together for New America," he wrote. "Securitech *not* your friends. Not much time—Joe."

Joe waited, but Mel didn't return. His fear deepened as an hour crawled by. Had the guard overheard their whispered conversation? He tried not to think about what they might do to Melissa. Then, when he had just about given up hope, the door opened. It was Margot and one of the guards.

"I warned you, Larivee," Margot's face twisted in a snarl. Her eyes fixed on the note, which Joe had folded and placed on the bed stand. Crossing the room in two strides, she snatched it up, unfolded it, and stared at the words Joe had written. Joe glared at her defiantly. Then she nodded, and the big guard stepped toward Joe. Before he could react, the guard's right fist connected with his solar plexus. He went down hard. A steel-toed boot caught him in the jaw and his world careened to a swirling halt.

WHEN JOE PRIED OPEN HIS EYES, HE WAS MET WITH HARSH, autumn sunlight filtering in through venetian blinds. It was late afternoon. His bed was comfortable and smelled of fresh linen. He touched his head and felt bandages. It took a moment to realize that he was no longer in a cell. A scan of the room revealed medical supplies and equipment. A clinic.

Another realization hit him, this one disturbing: at least another day had passed, and, to make it all worse, he suddenly realized that he had been so pissed at Dillon and Pedro that he had left his bag on his bicycle, out there beyond the gate.

He tried to sit up, propelled by the urgency of his mission, but dizziness forced him to lie back down. Just as he attempted to sit a second time, a young woman in a blue smock walked in.

"Please lie down, Mr Larivee," she said.

"I have to talk to Stu Garrison. It's very important."

"Mr Garrison asked to be called as soon as you woke up. He should be down shortly. But you need to lie still and rest. You've had a nasty concussion."

The woman checked his pulse and left. Outside the door, he saw two militia standing sentry. Joe closed his eyes and waited. It seemed like only a minute or two when a warm hand touched his shoulder. It was the nurse again. "Mr Garrison is here to talk to you."

Garrison stood behind the nurse. Hanging back in the doorway was Melissa Monroe.

"I'm sorry they did this to you, Joe," said Stu. "It was totally out of line. The Council has locked up Margot Carlson and put her personal crew on suspension until we understand what happened. We're still looking for Bernard. Anya Kerenskaya came to me last night about him. Then when Melissa here came by this morning, we put two and two together."

Mel smiled. "Are you okay, Mr Larivee?"

"My head feels like hell. And I'm dizzy. But I guess I'll live."

"Mel said you had something to tell me," said Stu.

"Stu, Margot and Bernard are working together for New America Corporation."

"How do you know that, Joe?"

"Because I overheard her talking to her guard. She said within days she was going to have a trainload of blackwaters down here on the island."

"Oh my God. If she's working against us, then that train's a fucking Trojan horse."

"Yeah. That's pretty much what I understood. But it's not the only Trojan horse." Joe told Stu about the memchip. "There's a little girl named Lara, about five years old—she lives near the community center—the memstick is in Fuzzy Finnegan's memslot."

"Thanks, Joe. We'll find her."

"Maybe you could find someone to fix Finnegan while you're at it."

"Sure, Joe," Stu smiled tightly. "Now, I better go notify the Militia Command."

"One more thing, Stu. How long have I been out?"

"Since this morning. I'm sorry how this turned out, Joe."

"I still have plenty of time to retrieve my citspecs, Stu."

"Marley says you have a concussion, Joe, so take it easy for now. I'll come back this evening. Sandra would like to say hi, then Melissa can show you to the gate when you're ready. Or one of the guards. I'll let them know. Just don't rush it."

Melissa stepped into the room as Stu left and moved tentatively toward Joe's bed. "Do you mind if I stay, Mr Larivee? I'd like to talk about Jessie."

"I can't, Melissa. I have to get my citspecs." Joe struggled to stand, and the room spun around him as he passed out again.

JOE PICKED AT HIS FOOD, BUT HE REALLY WASN'T HUNGRY. The sun had gone down, and fog hung once more along the river. He looked at the clock, thinking about the citspecs in his bag, still hanging on the bicycle outside the perimeter fence. He had less than a day to get them. But uncertainty haunted him now. Would he be running away from the living, the ones he knew were living, the ones who really needed him?

He rose to his feet—carefully this time, his hand gripping the bedside table—and found that he could stand without dizziness. He was moving toward his clothes in small steps when the door opened and a nurse popped her head in. "You really shouldn't be up, you know. You have visitors."

Stu and Sandra walked in, and Sandra gave Joe a look of motherly concern. "Should you be out of bed, son?"

"I have to go, Sandra. My citspecs. If I go, I'll need them."

"Go, Joe," said Sandra. "Go to Sweetland and be with Jessie."

"I want to be with my daughter, Sandra. But I also want to do what's right. I just don't know what that is."

"There's not a fucking thing you can do here, Joe," said Stu. "In a few weeks, this whole damn country is going to erupt in bloody revolution. These young turks want heads to roll, and no one is going to be spared. And your clients, Joe, will have to pick up the pieces on their own."

"People are going to suffer on Sweetland, too, Joe," said Sandra. "Suffering is the human condition. Go, Joe. It's what Frank and Amy would have urged you to do."

"I know, Sandra," said Joe. "But there are still people here, too. I've spent my entire adult life helping those people." In his mind, he saw an image of Gwendolyn and her little sister, orphaned, lost in a bureaucratic nightmare. Sweetland was a dream and *this* was the real world he knew. Some unconscious part of him had already come to that conclusion, he realized. He had left his citspecs behind in the fog on his abandoned bicycle, hadn't he? Why had he done that?

"I can't argue with that, Joe," said Sandra. "As bleak as it looks, I believe there's hope. Stu and I, we don't see eye-to-eye on this."

"Before I decide, I'd like to see where Jessie is. Can you take me, Stu."

"You want to see the Departure Rooms, Joe?" asked Stu. "You want to see where their ashes are buried? Are you sure you're up to this?" Joe winced, feeling a sharp twist of anguish. He nodded. "Yes, I'll be fine," he said, although he wasn't sure if that was true.

"There's a monument where they put the names. You can see for yourself," said Stu.

"Yes." Joe swallowed. "I want to see for myself."

STU LED JOE TO A COMPLEX OF LOW-PROFILE INDUSTRIAL buildings that lay at the south end of the lagoon. The nurse had objected, but they promised to take their time and Joe agreed to let Stu know if he became dizzy or disoriented.

"If the corporate people have their hands on the gate technology, then the whole Sweetland project could be in danger," said Stu.

"It's possible they do," said Joe. "It's possible that the government knows about it, too. At least they know about the plan to disrupt the Grid."

"I'll pass it along, Joe. Maybe our fearless leaders are on top of this already, but we should play it safe."

"Yeah, that's what I thought." What else did he think? He realized he had no solid sense of what was real anymore. He just couldn't make the wrong choice again.

"If there's a chance, any chance at all, then I want Jessie to have it. And I want to be there for her if she's alive; if that wasn't some incredible virtual reality I experienced. But maybe it's not about me—maybe it's about what needs to be done. I know you understand that."

Stu sighed. "Sure, Joe. Hope, as Sandra says. All of us keep going on the dream, son."

Tall thickets of grass grew through the cracks in the asphalt, and Joe thought, it will only be a few more years before the Earth shakes off this skin and reclaims its supremacy over us. Is it too late for reconciliation with her? Or have we blown it?

"Hope," he said at last. "Where is the hope, Stu?"

"Hope, son, isn't some Kennedy or Martin Luther King. It's not Gandhi or Buddha or Jesus Christ, either. It's here." He clutched his hand to his chest. "It's inside us. It's that grass pushing up through the macadam. It's the struggle to go on, to become something better. That's what your mama meant, you know. She didn't mean to put a burden on you. She was trying to free you."

They continued to walk without speaking, yielding the space to the omnipresent drums. At what point had the drums become the backbeat to his life? By the time they reached their destination, the light rain had eased to a fine mist. Fog was rising from the river and settle into the island's depressions and crevices. There were no lights here but for the dim glow of organic LEDs escaping through gaps in the huge sliding doors of the concrete warehouses. Voices seeped through as they passed, people discussing, laughing, arguing, soothing, as though nothing in the world was wrong. The same as it has been since the beginning of time, he thought. Just people talking, spinning their stories, and somewhere in the spinning of the web lays the truth.

And somewhere waits the spider, said his cynical voice.

THE WOMAN WHO ANSWERED THE DOOR AT THE DEPARTURE Room might have been approaching sixty, but she was trim and muscular, dressed in fatigues and combat boots, one of those popular military caps over her curly, graying hair. She held a yellowing, old-fashioned paperback novel in her hand.

"Hello, Jeanine," said Stu. "I'm just orienting Joe here to the Sweetland operation. Mind if we pop in for a look?"

"Damn, Stu, this book is just getting exciting." She winked and shook Joe's hand. "Hi, Joe. I'm Jeanine Hargrove."

"Hi, Jeanine," said Joe.

"We take turns doing shifts here. Tonight is Jeanine's rotation. Joe is Frank and Amy Larivee's kid, Jeanine."

"Well, Larivee, that's a name that gets respect here, Joe."

"His daughter has made the crossing. He may be following her, but he needs to find closure here."

"I understand," said Jeanine. "My son Crossed last month, and he made it okay, but it was real difficult knowing his remains were being buried out there in the pit. You know, it's hard to comprehend that they can be dead, and still be alive somewhere. What's your daughter's name, Joe?"

"Jessie," he said. "Jessie Larivee."

Jeanine turned to a ledger. "Oh, yes, I remember her, a real young one. That must be particularly hard. Come in, Joe, and I'll show you what happens here. Have you made your first crossing yet?"

"Yes," said Joe, stepping into the room. He saw a small nook with a desk and chair. On the desk a cup of half-finished tea, and a bookmark, pad and pencil, a strip of OLEDs, just bright enough to read by. Behind the desk rose a partition, and Joe could see a line of bunks, four of them.

"This is where we care for their bodies while they are crossing," said Jeanine. Joe looked in and saw that the bunks all had occupants. Each of the young women wore a pair of citspecs. "The bodies on this side still carry some amount of consciousness, Joe. We've found the citspecs keep them in an anesthetized state so their minds can wander around on New Life and keep occupied."

"How do you know?" asked Joe. "How do you know this is all real, Stu? How do you know it's not a lie?"

"That's the problem with knowing too much, Joe. You see, the layers of deception and self-delusion we've created around us. You know that the world is not what it seems, and that you can never really understand what lies underneath the next layer. You're too skeptical to have blind faith in anything. Sandy says, 'Have faith,' but how the hell can you have that kind of faith when you don't even know what it is you are supposed to be having faith in? Oh, to be an ignorant fundamentalist."

"And what does Sandy have faith in, Stu?"

"The future, she says. How's that for faith, Joe? Like I said before, I'll take dreams and *possibilities*. Faith in the future, that's faith in some inevitability bullshit, it seems to me. Now me, I say this is your choice - you can die in the fucking holocaust, or you can die with a dream. Take the dream, Joe. Even if it's an illusion."

Stu turned to Jeanine. "Thanks, Jeanie. I'll take Joe to the memorial, now."

Stu took Joe back into the warehouse, through another door, into a fenced courtyard. The trunk of a huge oak tree stretched skyward in the center of the courtyard, its dead branches black and barren against the night sky. Every inch of the tree was covered with small wooden plaques as far up as Joe could see. Each had a name engraved on its surface. The strange leaves clacked in the breeze.

"My God," Joe said, "this many people? How many?"

"Over a thousand here."

"How many all together, Stu?"

"A few hundred thousand. From all over the planet. They're afraid of having too many people destroying the habitat of Sweetland. Some of us are already concerned that too many have emigrated."

"Jessie. Where's Jessie?"

"She'd be up near the top, Joe. There's a map over here." He pointed to the wall of the building where a huge list of names hung beside a graphic of the tree, which had been divided into numbered segments. Stu looked down the list and pointed. "There, Joe. It says 'Jessie Larivee, Crossed Over on November 1, 2037, L16.' That would be here." He pointed to a place high on the tree, but Joe was staring at Jessie's name on the list.

Joe stood motionless for a long moment, until the words in front of his eyes wavered and fuzz, leaving him disoriented.

"Oh shit," he said, "not again."

Suddenly lightheaded, he felt the world spinning around him, and he collapsed onto the hard earth.

JOE AWOKE IN HIS INFIRMARY BED AND A WANING GIBBOUS moon hung high over the young willows outside his window. It was just before dawn. Thick clouds of low-hanging fog had edged up from the water, and the moonlight outlined the trees with an unworldly glow. The sound of drums drifted in. He realized they had been the soundtrack to his dreams. Melissa was sleeping in an upright position on the chair across the room. It was sweet of her. Jessie had always made good choices with friends.

"Melissa," he called softly.

Mel stirred and opened her eyes lazily. "Hmmm?"

"Mel, it's time to go. Will you walk me to the barricade?"

"Sure, Mr Larivee." Mel stood and offered Joe her hand as he attempted to pull himself upright.

"Thank you, Mel. And call me Joe. We're comrades now, right?"

Mel grinned.

She stepped outside while Joe clumsily dressed. Then she led him out into the night fog, the two militia following close behind. Silent, they walked together toward the barricades on Going Street. Just before they reached the concrete barriers, Mel stopped.

"Will you give my love to Jessie? Tell her I love her and miss her."

"I will, Melissa, if I decide to go."

"You have to go, Mr Larivee."

"Why aren't you with her, Mel? Why are you here?"

"I couldn't do it. I gave my citspecs to this homeless guy Jessie knows. He was in so much pain and it was too sad to leave him like that. They told me they could get me another pair, but they took us to a room with these bunks and they wanted me to lie down with all these dying people. And even though I'd been there—to Sweetland—I just couldn't do it. I feel so guilty, Mr Larivee. I abandoned her."

Dying people. Jessie was one of them. He choked up, dabbed at the tears welling in his eyes.

"No, Mel," he said. "Jessie did what she had to do, and you did the same."

"It's not so bad, you know. I'm training to be a nurse's

aide, so when the fighting starts, I can help. Maybe it's ordinary people like us doing the everyday necessary tasks who will turn things around. Is Jessie safe, Mr Larivee? Do you know if she made it okay?"

"Yeah. She made it okay, Mel. Life is going to be difficult there, too. There are so many unknowns, but I think she's going to be fine. It's just New America that worries me."

"What's this New America thingie, anyhow? Are they the ones who've stolen the Sweetland technology? Everybody's been talking about it since the Council meeting."

"Yeah, Mel. And they're going to take the war with them to Sweetland if they aren't stopped. Maybe you're right. Maybe staying is the right thing. Maybe the best thing we can do for Jessie is to help stop this madness, help the Earth get back on its feet."

Joe looked at the ragged citizen's guard gathered around the barrels, talking and laughing, and beyond to a drum circle where young warriors pounded out their rage at the injustice of the world. Except for the context, they could have been young people anywhere, living their lives and sharing camaraderie. What would it be like in a few weeks when the fighting began? If he stayed, would he be able to carry a gun? Or would he be a dead weight?

He put his arm around Melissa, drawing her close. "Thank you, Mel. Jessie is lucky to have a friend like you." He kissed the top of her head.

"Goodbye, Mr Larivee."

Mel waved at him as he threaded his way through the barricades. Anya, Sam, Allison, Mel, the kids on the barricades, the ones staying to fight; it wouldn't be so bad struggling alongside these people. He didn't know if he could fight and kill, but he could heal. That was his gift to give.

Joe halted at the crossroads where Going Street met the

railroad. The drumming had grown louder now; it sounded as though the whole camp was beating on something, sending a message out to the sleeping city. We are waking, it said. We are waking, and you will notice us. On the horizon, a red sun rose through an opening in the clouds, rising against a city skyline that contained only the dead hulls of human structures pushing in vain toward the hostile sky. But his eyes fixed on a shimmer of green and gold alongside the road, the branches of a fast-growing young dogwood reaching upward, attempting to reassert itself. The leaves would soon be gone, the bare branches awaiting spring, when it would bud again and another cycle could begin.

He understood he had decided, then. He had said his goodbyes, but there would be more goodbyes now, the hard and countless goodbyes war always demanded. And if that was the planet's death song rumbling beneath the drums, a goodbye to everything. But the drums called him. They were now all around him and inside him, like his beating heart. *It's time to join the world.* His gaze fixed on the red sky, the clouds already moving in to close up the brief break in their gray solidarity.

It would be a hard winter.

–End–

Acknowledgments

I want to thank my wife, Patty McLean, who has been encouraging and patient as I've struggled with this manuscript over the past several years, and who has provided many insightful suggestions.

I would also like to thank editor Susan Grossman, who worked on an earlier version of this book and helped me gain the confidence I needed to carry it through. This book has taken about a dozen years, delayed and changed by the rapid evolution of the political and technological landscape, which had to be addressed to keep it relevant.

Others who have been immensely helpful include Diana Meraz, Paul Poncy (my scientist sibling), Kathleen Ellyn, Gabriele Hayden, the late Patricia Ann Poncy. I also want to thank Terry Freitag, Fufkin Vollmeyer, and the many other critique group members who gave valuable feedback on various portions of the still evolving Sweetland Quartet.

I'm sure I've left people out, and I sincerely apologize to anyone who feels they should be on this list. I thank you, sincerely, each and every one.

Did you enjoy this book? Please review!

If you read and enjoyed this book, your review is very appreciated. One of the most difficult things for a struggling author is to receive sufficient reviews on Amazon or other book sites. This is crucial for a book's success. Your review doesn't have to be a full essay. You need not write more than "I liked it," or "It was okay." But every one of those reviews will help.

About the Author

Duane Poncy is an author of eclectic literary works, including science fiction, mysteries and non-genre stories. He also co-writes with his spouse, Patricia J McLean. They live in small loft apartment in a Portland, Oregon arts community.

Duane is an enrolled citizen of The Cherokee Nation (Oklahoma) and a life-long organizer for social change. His books often include Native American characters and themes, and diverse individuals in struggle for a better world.

Also by Duane Poncy

With Patricia J McLean

Bartlett House: a Will Adelhardt/Lucy Hidalgo Mystery

Raising Our Voices: an Anthology of Poet Against the War, eds

Elohi Gadugi Journal: Narratives for a New World, eds

Forthcoming:

Searching for my Grandfather: A Saint-Pierre Ghost Story, (with Patricia J McLean) August 2022

Ghosts of Saint-Pierre: A Novel, (with Patricia J McLean) Fall 2022

Degrees of Freedom: Book Two of the Sweetland Quartet